Mixing wor .

Bey

Three exhilarating romances from three fabulous Mills & Boon authors!

FALLING FOR THE BOSS

BY
ELIZABETH HARBISON

My thanks to Andre Coutu and James Price,
who got me out of my old house. Thanks also
to Charles Clark of Waterworks Plumbing
in Snow Hill, MD — a true hero in times of need
(and leaky pipes and bathtubs) — who made my
new house so much nicer…and drier.

Beyond Business

ELIZABETH HARBISON

BRENDA HARLEN

ALLISON LEIGH

First published in Great Britain 2011
Harlequin Mills & Boon Limited,
Eton House, 18-24 Paradise Road, Richmond, Surrey TW9 1SR

Falling for the Boss, Her Best-Kept Secret and *Mergers & Matrimony* were first published in Great Britain by Harlequin Mills & Boon Limited.

Special thanks and acknowledgement are given to Elizabeth Harbison, Brenda Harlen and Allison Leigh for their contribution to the FAMILY BUSINESS series.

ISBN: 978 0 263 88340 4

05-0211

Printed and bound in Spain
by Litografia Rosés S.A., Barcelona

Prologue

The fact that he actually asked her if she was *really sure* she was ready to do it made her love him all the more.

What other eighteen-year-old guy with a normal libido would be that considerate? Meredith Waters knew—she absolutely *knew*—that if she'd told Evan she wasn't ready, that she was chickening out even though they'd planned this romantic evening together for the past five weeks, he would have backed right off.

He might have needed a cold shower. A really long cold shower. But he would have let her off the hook without the usual guy nonsense about everything from promises broken to the supposedly serious medical consequences of unsatisfied desire.

Guys were, by and large, idiots.

But not Evan Hanson. Evan proved there really were Prince Charmings out there, though they were few and far between. Evan was Meredith's soul mate. She was sure of it. Not that they were the same kind of people—far from it. He was wild and she was conservative. But they complemented each other. And they felt the same way about the most important things. They had the same standards and the same goals for their lives.

Most important, Evan was a guy she knew she could count on through thick and thin. The school and their parents might have thought he was sort of a wild kid, but Meredith knew he'd always be there for her.

Which made her all the more sure that she would never regret what they were about to do. She was a lucky, lucky girl to have her first time be with a guy like Evan.

"Are you sure?" he asked her again, running his hand down the length of her upper arm.

They were lying in her canopy bed, facing

each other. Her parents were out of town for four more days, so not only was the guy perfect but the setting was, too.

She smiled at him, taking in his dark good looks like a tall glass of cold water on a hot day.

And it was definitely hot in here.

"I'm sure," she said, then cocked her head playfully. "But I'm getting the impression *you're* not so sure."

"Oh, I'm sure." He pulled her over to him and kissed her deeply, rolling onto his back so she was on top of him. He wrapped his arms around her tightly, pulling her so close she almost couldn't tell where she stopped and he began.

She loved that feeling.

They kissed and kissed, just like they always did. They'd done it so much at this point that they practically had it down to a science. He moved his mouth this way, she moved her mouth that way, their tongues touched, and—*poof!* Magic.

"I love you, Mer," Evan whispered, slowly rolling her over so she was on her back on the soft mattress and laced-edged sheets she'd bought last month with this moment in mind.

"I love you, too," she said, her response automatic and completely without doubt. "More than you'll ever realize."

He gave that Cheshire-cat grin she adored and reached over to turn off the light on her bedside table.

It took a moment for her eyes to adjust to the light, but when they did she noticed a slash of moonlight cutting through the curtains and spilling onto her bed.

Perfect.

And it was. It was just…right.

Afterward, as she lay in the bed looking out the window while the moon slowly floated higher and crossed the sky like a big silver balloon, she felt more joy than she'd ever felt in her entire life.

Meredith smiled in the dark as Evan talked to her in hushed tones about how beautiful she was and how he wanted to spend the rest of his life with her and how if he didn't get over to the Silver Car Diner for some blueberry pancakes and vanilla cola fast he was going to die.

This, she realized, was perfect contentment.

What she *didn't* realize, in these last few moments of blissful ignorance, was that within two months Evan would be thousands of miles away, without so much as a goodbye, and that he wouldn't look back for more than a decade.

Chapter One

"And that concludes the reading of the will of George Arthur Hanson."

Evan Hanson sat still in the stiff leather chair, feeling like a caricature of the prodigal son, drawn in invisible ink.

He'd returned, as prodigal sons always did, against his better judgment. Instinct had warned him that this would be nothing but trouble—and probably painful to boot—but he'd ignored instinct.

That was a mistake.

His uncle, David Hanson, had been unusually

persuasive in convincing him to come back for the reading of the will. David knew Evan had suffered years of conflict with his father, and that George hadn't spoken to his son since he'd left. Still, David had pointed out to Evan that, while it might be too late to mend fences with his father, he could at least come and hear the patriarch's last message to him and perhaps gain some peace.

It had been peaceful, all right. In fact, his father's message was a resounding silence.

George Hanson had neglected to so much as mention Evan's name in his will, not even to say, "And to my second son, Evan, I leave absolutely nothing. Nada. Zip. Not even a stainless-steel spoon."

It was as if Evan didn't exist to his father.

No, it was worse than that. Evan knew his father well enough to know this lack of mention meant that, to George, Evan really *hadn't* existed anymore once he'd left the country twelve years ago. Since George had effectively run him out of town twelve years ago, that was, by holding the worst kind of emotional blackmail over his head.

Since then, his job presumably done, George had written Evan off, forgotten about him completely.

Everyone knows it's more of an insult to ignore someone than to tell them off. And George had ignored Evan like a champ. They hadn't spoken in twelve years. Sure, Evan could shoulder half the blame for that, but when he'd left he was only eighteen, and his father knew damn well he'd created a situation that made Evan feel as if he couldn't come back.

Surely George should have seen the crisis he'd sent his teenage son into and done something to fix it, or at least make it better. It wasn't in George's nature to extend an olive branch, but even pelting Evan with olives would have been better than the eerie silence.

George hadn't bothered to do anything. He probably hadn't even thought about his middle son more than once or twice in the time between Then and Now.

If only Evan had the same sort of control over his thoughts. He'd have liked to forget his father...and the difficulty of losing his mother when he was seventeen.

And one or two other heartaches—well, one in particular—that had shaped him into the man he was today. A man who wanted nothing to do with his family or with intimate relationships of any sort.

The lawyer closed his books, and Evan's relatives began to discuss the reading amongst themselves, expressing anger at what they had or had not received and at the fact that George had left his young wife full control of Hanson Media Group.

Evan didn't care. It wasn't his problem. None of this was his problem. So with full intentions of leaving it behind forever, he took a deep breath, got up out of his chair and walked purposefully out of the room, planning to keep going until he got to the airport and left American soil for good.

He must have actually convinced himself that no one was aware of his presence because when he heard someone calling his name behind him, at first it didn't register.

"Evan!" It was a woman's voice. One he didn't recognize, though there was nothing surprising about that. It had been more than a decade since he'd heard the voice of anyone in that boardroom.

"Please stop, Evan," she said again. "I'd like to talk to you for a moment."

He stopped and turned to see his father's wife coming toward him in the hallway, a worried expression knitting her flawless features. Her golden hair framed her face as if it had been painted by Vermeer, and her green eyes were bright and alive.

Helen Hanson couldn't have been more obviously a trophy wife if she had been gilded and nailed to a slab of marble.

He'd never met her before—his father had married shortly after he'd left—but, given the circumstances of their meeting now, it wasn't easy to feel any warmth toward her.

"I know you're probably angry about what just happened in there," she began.

"I'm not angry." His tone was cold like his father's, he realized with disgust. "What happened in there—" he gestured toward the room "—is no surprise. In fact, it's absolutely typical of your husband."

She gave a pained nod. "I see why you feel that way, but he was your father, Evan. Don't forget that. Though I know you must feel he rejected you."

He'd thought he'd reached his fill of pain but Helen's words managed to slice deeper still. "I don't *feel* he rejected me, I *know* he rejected me. But don't worry about it, it's not the first time. And knowing how spiteful the old son of a bitch could be, it's probably not the last time, either."

"Evan—"

"He could *always* find a way to express his displeasure with his family." Evan gave a dry laugh. "You might want to watch your own back. Not that you really have anything to worry about. I mean, you *did* get the company."

Helen winced slightly and hesitated before speaking. "Evan, the company belongs to the Hanson family. All of you, not me. It always will."

He gave a dry laugh and looked toward the conference room of the Hanson Media offices, where everyone was still arguing about the outcome of the will. "Try telling that to them."

"They'll find out in time," she answered. Her tone was dismissive of them, but she was looking at Evan intently. "But you—well, it looks like you're not going to stay in Chicago long enough to find out unless someone stops you."

He looked Helen Hanson up and down. She was beautiful—no surprise there—but she also had some nerve. "Is that what you think you're doing? Stopping me?"

She drew herself up and looked him in the eye. "That's what I'm hoping to do."

He shook his head. "Don't waste your effort. I've got no interest whatsoever in what happens to this damned company now."

"But you should," Helen urged. "Don't forget there's a stipulation that twenty percent of the company or company revenues will go to the grandchildren in twenty years."

Evan spread his arms and shrugged. "I realize my father probably didn't tell you much about me, so maybe it's news to you, but I don't have any kids."

Helen's expression softened. "I do know that. But you're only thirty, Evan. You don't know what's going to happen in the future. You might well change your mind."

It was on the tip of his tongue to contradict her, but he'd seen many foolish men make the mistake of banking on their single and childless status, only to be surprised by some turn of events later in life.

"Okay," he said. "I'll grant you that—I don't know what's going to happen. But if I should have kids in the future, they don't need the tainted fortunes of George Hanson, anyway."

She shook her head. "Don't let the sins of your father be visited upon your son." She smiled. Even though it was a small, sad smile, it was dazzling. "Or your daughter, as the case may eventually be."

Evan couldn't see that happening, and it

made him uncomfortable to hear Helen say it, but he didn't argue the case. There was no point. "I'll take my chances," he said, then added half-heartedly, "So will my unborn children."

"Evan, please. Reconsider. Take just a little time. This isn't *just* about the business. It's about your family. Not your father, but your brothers. The whole family is fractured, and they can't heal without you. You're part of them."

He knew he should just walk away, but the woman's desperation intrigued him. Why should she care so much whether a man she'd never met before stayed or went? Surely her husband had told her what a good-for-nothing his middle son was.

"What are you asking me to do?" he asked her.

"I'd like you to stay," Helen said, her voice ringing with sincerity. "I know it probably sounds strange to you, since we don't know each other, but I've got a good feeling about you. I'd like to have your help—actually, Evan, I *need* your help—in returning Hanson Media Group to its former glory."

He hadn't seen *that* one coming. If she hadn't looked so completely earnest, he would have laughed. Instead, he just asked the logical question. "Why me? You've got the whole team on your side." He gestured toward the conference room. "Every one of them has more experience with the company than I do."

Helen glanced behind her and took a step closer to Evan. Her light perfume surrounded her like a protective barrier of…flowers. "But I'm not sure they're going to stay onboard in light of your father's directives. George had a way of manipulating things, you know."

Oh, he knew.

"Anyway," she went on quickly, as if realizing she shouldn't have said that, "I don't know why, but, Evan, I have the feeling I can trust you."

He followed her gaze behind her. No one was there. He almost wished there was someone, though, because he wasn't at all sure he wanted Helen Hanson's confidence. "Look," he said uneasily. "I don't know what you've got in mind, but I can't promise I can do anything to help you."

She sized him up for a moment before saying, "I care about you and your brothers. I truly care about your entire family. Do you believe that?"

He shrugged. "I don't have any reason not to,

I suppose." After all, Helen held all the cards. With controlling interest in the company, she didn't *have* to deal with *any* of the Hansons now. If she was doing so, it was by choice.

Her smile was genuine. "Good. Then trust me when I say that the company *needs* you."

"The company has been doing just fine without me for a lot of years."

"Not really," Helen said. "In fact, the bottom line these past few years has been decidedly bleak."

Evan frowned. "How bleak?"

"Bleak enough that the porn scandal on the Web site was enough to push us firmly into the red."

Jack had e-mailed him—when was it? A month ago? Two?—indicating that the family should get more involved in the business, but Evan had assumed it was just a ploy to get him back into the fold. He'd never imagined that his father had actually dropped the ball and sent the business hurtling toward bankruptcy.

Still, what could Evan do? The only job he'd ever had was running a little beachfront bar in Majorca. And even that could hardly be considered work.

"Well, I'm sorry to hear that, honestly." Evan

shrugged. "But if you're looking to bring the business back to life, you're looking at the wrong guy. I'm not much of a corporate type. It's not just that I don't *want* to help, it's that I honestly don't have anything to offer."

"Maybe not, but you're a risk taker, from what your father told me. And I can tell you're an honest man. He told me that, too. Hanson Media needs that right now."

That stopped Evan. "My father told you that?" He gave a wry smile. "You do know my father was George Hanson, right?"

"He was more fond of you than you know," Helen said, and she sounded as though she really believed it. "He talked about you quite a lot. Said you'd left when you were young and that you'd been living overseas all this time."

"He told you that."

She nodded. "You know, he thought you'd be back. For years he thought you'd come crawling back asking for money, and when you didn't he was secretly impressed."

Evan was embarrassed at the small lump that formed in his throat. He wanted to believe this, even while he still loathed the man and what he'd done to Evan. He wanted, if only for his own peace of mind, to believe that his father hadn't been so detached that he'd just completely *forgotten* him. "Not so impressed that he ever tried to contact me."

"No." A distant look came into her eyes, and she shook her head. "But you know as well as I do that the fact that he didn't contact you had nothing to do with the amount of pride or lack of pride he felt in you. It was all about his *own* pride. *Everything* was about his pride," she added softly.

Evan looked at his father's wife with new eyes. Most women in her position would have been content to let the whole family dissolve so they could regain the money and power for themselves, but Helen was actually reaching out to them.

Now he was left with a choice. He'd already stood here for five minutes talking to her. Five minutes were chipped away from his intended release from the Hanson family. Now he was actually considering Helen's plea for him to stay, and he wasn't sure that was a good idea.

"Look, Helen, what's the upshot here? Give me the bottom line. What exactly are you asking me to do?"

She took a short, bracing breath. "Okay, direct and to the point. I can do that." She met his eyes. "The company is down but it's not out yet. For many reasons I want to fix that. My reasons don't matter that much to you, because you must surely have your own reasons for wanting to stay. It's your legacy. If you have children someday, it's *their* legacy. The time to fix it is now, and I've got a plan. If it doesn't work—" she shrugged "—at least you can't say you didn't try."

"And what do you propose a guy like me, a guy with no business experience whatsoever, should do within this corporation in order to up the revenues?"

"That's easy," Helen replied quickly. "You're smart. A guy with a social conscience and definitely a world view. And, not least, you are a Hanson."

He listened, unable to agree with her for fear of what he'd find himself committing to.

"So what I propose is that you take over the radio division of Hanson Media Group."

He gave a shout of laughter before he realized she was serious.

"The radio division," he repeated, visions of Rush Limbaugh and Howard Stern dancing in his head. "Me."

"Mmm-hmm." She nodded, her green gaze steady on him. "I think you'd be perfect."

"You do know I have no experience in that area whatsoever." He gave another laugh. He couldn't help it. "I wouldn't even know where to begin."

"Given the recent scandal, I think your lack of experience might, in fact, be a plus." She smiled, but there was pleading in her eyes. "I'm only asking you to stay on for three months or so. Just to give it a try. What do you say, Evan? Will you do it? Please."

He thought about it. Majorca would still be there in three months. So would St. Bart's, Fiji or anywhere else he wanted to go. When he'd sold the beachfront bar, he'd made quite a tidy profit. His father would have been surprised to learn that his "beach bum" son was smart enough to invest his earnings.

In any event, he could afford—at least in the monetary sense—to stick around for a little while and see what happened.

The question was, could he afford the mental toll it would undoubtedly take on him to stay?

Suddenly the words of his uncle, David Hanson, came back to him. David had been trying to convince Evan to come back and mend fences with his father several months ago, before it was too late.

Think about it, Evan, David had said. *You don't need to do this for George. You need to do it for yourself.*

Those were the words that had brought Evan back, even though he'd arrived too late. They were the words that had rung in his mind when he'd contemplated seeing his siblings again. Who knew where life would take them eventually? Right now they were all here, working together toward a common goal, and he had the opportunity to help with that.

Granted, failure was possible. All he could do was his own personal best. If someone couldn't accept him or forgive him, he didn't have to carry it.

"Okay," he heard himself saying to Helen, despite the fact that it went against every instinct he felt in his gut. Instinct that told him to run like hell and never look back. "I'll do it."

Chapter Two

"What I'm looking for is someone to work in advertising and public relations under my brother-in-law," Helen Hanson was saying to the young brunette woman before her.

Meredith Waters sat uncomfortably in the plush chair opposite Helen's sleek, modern desk, wondering if it was appropriate or wildly *in*appropriate to mention her history with the Hanson family before this job interview with Hanson Media went any further.

She *never* thought she'd set foot in the company George Hanson had built. Not after what he'd done to her family.

"I think you'll agree, the benefits are generous," Helen went on, handing a folder across the desk to Meredith. Her hand was delicate and smooth, her manicure perfect. Helen Hanson was perfectly turned out.

Meredith glanced at the folder, so it at least looked as if she was interested. Medical, dental, two weeks' vacation time, two weeks' personal time...yes, the terms were extremely generous. A person would have to be a fool to turn this down.

Of course, Meredith would have taken the job no matter what, even if it had paid minimum wage and offered the single benefit of a half hour's lunch once a week. Pretending to hesitate was just that—pretending.

It was all a game.

She just hoped she could play it without anyone finding out.

"I'd like to think about it," Meredith lied. She didn't need to think about it. She was ready to start now. "Could I take a day or two and get back to you?"

Helen looked uncertain. "I'd really like to fill the position as soon as possible. As you're undoubtedly aware, I've only just come back myself." She gestured at some of the packed boxes that were piled in the corner. "Plus, we have a major scandal we're still trying to clean up, and there's a lot of work to do. If you're unsure of your interest, that's fine, but please understand I'll have to keep interviewing."

Clearly, Helen was a master at this game.

Meredith tipped her head slightly. "You sure know how to make an offer a person can't refuse."

"Does that mean you accept my offer?"

"Yes." Meredith smiled and held her hand out. "You've got yourself a deal, Mrs. Hanson."

"Helen, please." Helen shook her hand, looking delighted. "I'm so glad to have you on board, Meredith. Now, you'll be working under my brother-in-law, David Hanson, in the PR department, but I'd like you to focus special attention on the radio division that's now being run by my late husband's son, Evan Hanson."

Whoa! This was *not* the plan.

"I'm sorry, did you say *Evan* Hanson?" Meredith asked, feeling as though Helen had just punched her in the stomach.

Helen nodded absently, taking a narrow silver pen out of her drawer. "Mmm-hmm. My middle stepson, Evan."

Meredith cleared her throat. "Forgive my saying so—perhaps the newspapers were wrong—but it was my understanding that Evan Hanson had shunned the family business and moved away. A long time ago." Twelve years, if memory served correctly.

Helen jotted a note on a pad next to her and returned her attention to Meredith. "Yes, he was. But he's back now, working with all of us to make Hanson Media the most successful business it can be." She raised an eyebrow at Meredith. "That's not a problem, is it?"

"N-no. I'm just not sure I understand." Meredith had to back off. She didn't want to look as if a person in the company could be her Achilles' heel. "You want me to concentrate my efforts entirely on *one* division rather than the whole company?" This wasn't what she'd had in mind when she took this job.

But now she was already committed.

"It should be an exciting challenge," Helen said, hopefully unaware of the tension that was building in Meredith. "I think you'll enjoy it. Yes, there will be some initial difficulties, perhaps, but once you and Evan start working together, everything should work out just fine. I have a feeling about it."

What was she, psychic? Did she know something more than she'd revealed in the interview?

"I have to say, I'm not used to dealing with radio," Meredith hedged, feeling a little frantic and trying to keep it out of her voice. "You might do better to have me learn the ropes there part-time while I'm also working other areas."

"Don't worry," Helen said lightly. "Evan's not used to doing anything with radio. I think, in this case, it will serve you well. Bob Smith had years of experience, but he couldn't make a viable go of that division. So now it's a blank canvas for you and the rest of the team to paint whatever future you want."

Normally that would be a very appealing offer. Not this time, though. "Still, it's hard to get by without *any* experience. I might be more of a detriment than an asset to a division I know nothing about."

Helen was clearly unconcerned. "You and Evan will both have a very strong support staff under you, but I think this inexperience you're concerned about is *exactly* the thing that's going to help you think outside the box. Both of you."

Meredith swallowed, but the lump in her throat wouldn't go away. Nerves. She'd always had trouble with them. "Okay, Mrs.— Helen.

Okay, Helen." She didn't want to do it, but she had no way out. "I'll give it my best shot."

Helen smiled broadly, revealing even white teeth and the kind of looks usually reserved for the covers of magazines. "Great, Meredith! I'm *so* glad to have you with us. I just know you're going to do a terrific job."

"Thanks very much. I'm thrilled to take it on." In truth, Meredith wished she shared even half of Helen Hanson's enthusiasm.

Unfortunately, all she felt now was a lot of insecurity about her job performance...and that was something she was definitely *not* used to struggling with.

It wasn't just the job parameters: she knew how to do her work, regardless of the details. All of that had been laid out quite clearly for her, and she was comfortable in the knowledge that she could do it, and do it well.

What worried her was doing her job well when she had to do it so close to the man who'd dumped her without a backward glance.

Helen told Evan she'd hired someone new for the PR department, someone who would concentrate their efforts on promoting the new face of Hanson Broadcasting. He was glad of that, because, with the support of the previously existing staff, he'd managed to contact three notorious on-air talents, two of whom had already signed on, but he was at a complete loss about what to do to promote them.

That was where the PR department came in. They were, after all, the professionals. Radio should be easy for them. A contest here, a print ad there, that should do it. Radio was free; it sold itself. Evan's meeting with David's underling should only be informative, involving the plans they already had for promotion of the radio division.

At least, that was what Evan thought. Until David's underling actually appeared at his office for their one o'clock appointment.

Meredith Waters.

Gleaming chestnut hair, with tinges of red that shone like copper in the sunlight; pale Irish skin that she'd inherited from her mother; green eyes; and a wide, generous mouth. Evan had never seen a smile so bright that could turn, in an instant, to a heart-aching sensuous curve that would drive any man to distraction.

He would have recognized her anywhere, anytime, even though he hadn't seen her in... well, twelve and a half years. It was marked indelibly in his mind since it was the night he'd left the United States.

The night of their senior prom.

He hadn't actually made it *to* the prom, of course, which was one of the reasons this meeting now was so…awkward.

The last time he'd seen Meredith Waters, it had been through her bedroom window as she'd sat in front of her vanity mirror, putting the final touches on her makeup and hair for a prom date that wasn't going to show up.

Evan.

The image had haunted him ever since. Meredith, in a thin-strapped deep-blue dress, her pale shoulders creamy and tempting. He could feel the curve of them in his empty hands.

Even then, but certainly now, he recognized what a sweet, innocent beauty she was. Hers had been a difficult life, with a lot of hard knocks, despite her best efforts. Her parents, too, had suffered at the hands of fate, and, unfortunately, at the hands of George Hanson, even though they were good people who deserved better.

Evan thought she'd do better without him around.

Apparently, it hadn't turned out that way. And

by the time he knew what had happened, it was far too late for him to come back and make things better.

He wished he'd had the advantage of wisdom then that he had now.

Instead of rising to the occasion, he'd left. It was soon after his mother had died, and the rawness of that loss probably contributed to his confusion. No one to run interference for him. No one to offer even an iota of warmth to the house that had never entirely felt like home.

Evan knew if he'd stayed he would have gotten as bitter and mean as the old man—they were so much alike in other ways it was practically a shoo-in—so rather than doing that to Meredith and himself, he'd just moved on.

Until this moment he hadn't stopped to regret his decision.

"Hello, Evan," she said, her voice smooth and modulated. It was familiar but, at the same time, unfamiliar. "It's been a long time."

He was as paralyzed with surprise—no, *shock*—as he would be if he'd been looking at a ghost. In a way, in fact, he felt like he was. He felt like he should say something profound, but only one word came to mind.

"Meredith?"

She nodded, but no smile touched that beautiful mouth. "You recognize me."

"Of course I recognize you. You look..." *Beautiful. Stunning.*

Haunting.

"You look the same as you always did." But she didn't. She didn't look the same at all. She looked like a sleek, sophisticated version of her old self.

This was awkward. Really awkward.

But Evan still didn't know what to say. Unfortunately the momentary uncomfortable pauses weren't buying him enough time to come up with something pithy.

She smiled. And for just a moment, he could see the high-school girl inside the woman.

"Clearly you weren't expecting to see me." There wasn't a trace of self-consciousness in her voice. "I was hoping Ms. Hanson would have let you know I was coming."

This wasn't making any sense. "Ms. Hanson?"

"Yes, Helen Hanson." Meredith nodded. "She just hired me in PR and has asked me to assist you in promoting this division."

A pause dropped between them like a tennis ball and bounced awkwardly into several silent seconds.

"Are you serious?" he asked after a moment. How was this possible? Of all the people Helen could have hired, and all the places within the company she could have placed a new employee, how on earth had it happened that she'd hired Meredith and wanted her to work with Evan?

Meredith's smile froze a little. "Yes. Will that be a problem for you?"

Damn right it was a problem. It was hard enough to be back in Chicago and working in the Hanson offices. He was running up against memories—including lots of unpleasant ones—at virtually every turn.

But this? This was too much.

"No, it's not a problem at all," he lied. Then he forced what he hoped looked like a casual smile, though it felt more like he was grimacing. "I'm sorry, I must seem rude. It's just that it's been more than twelve years since I've been in Chicago, and I'm still trying to orient myself. Needless to say, I've been seeing a lot of people I haven't seen in a long time and it's disconcerting each time I get one of these blasts from the past."

"I understand," Meredith said, her tone cool, professional. Clearly she'd grown far, far beyond the awkward kid he'd once known. She was detached in her interaction with Evan now. It was very clear that this wasn't personal for her.

Hell, maybe she didn't even remember what they'd once been to each other.

For that matter, maybe he'd imagined it. Maybe this thumping in his chest at the sight of her was just the remembrance of a dream he'd once had. His life had taken so many surreal turns at this point that he wasn't sure of anything at the moment.

"I do hope we'll be able to get past any awkwardness and work effectively together," Meredith went on, but for the first time her voice betrayed the merest trace of a waver.

"Absolutely."

"Good. So let's get to work on our plan to raise the profile of Hanson Broadcasting." She glanced at her watch. "Do you have time to talk about it now? I'd like to get up to speed on your plans so I can start my work as soon as possible."

There was no way Evan could just leap into this now. He needed a little time to collect his thoughts.

He'd begun outlining a mission already, of course, but it would have taken some time to prepare to discuss it even if it *wasn't* Meredith waiting for it, but the fact that it was... Well, he just needed a little time to get used to the idea.

"I'm about to have a meeting," Evan said, trying to sound regretful rather than unprepared. "Are you free later this afternoon?"

Meredith shook her head. "I told David I'd be available to talk to him this afternoon."

Another pause spread between them.

"So maybe tomorrow—" Evan began.

"I *am* available at lunch," Meredith suggested at the same time.

They looked at each other for a second before Evan said, "Lunch is fine."

"Okay, great."

"How about the Silver Car Diner around noon?"

The Silver Car Diner. As soon as the words were out of his mouth he regretted them. That was a place they'd been to together quite a few times in high school. In fact, it was his former familiarity with the place that made it the first thing out of his mouth, yet he couldn't have picked a more pointedly sentimental place unless he'd suggested the backseat of his ancient Chevy Monte Carlo.

Before he could retract the offer and suggest

something less personal, Meredith, with what could have been a look of surprise in her eyes, nodded and said, "Okay. Sounds fine."

"Great." Evan reached for some papers to straighten. "See you there at noon."

She gave a small smile and nod and turned to leave. Evan continued to straighten his pile of papers, half watching her go, until she was finally down the hall and out of sight.

Working with her wasn't going to be easy.

Meredith had felt Evan's eyes on her as she'd walked away. For a moment or two she'd actually worried that she might trip or stumble, betraying her nervousness.

How in the world was she going to work with Evan Hanson? It was preposterous! If she wasn't already so committed, she would have walked away from the job the moment she knew he was involved. But a lot of people were counting on her. This went far deeper than mere PR for Hanson Media Group.

Before she'd agreed to this job, she'd done some investigating and learned that Evan was hopping all over Europe and the Caribbean. She'd actually taken the care to make *sure* he wasn't going to be around if she had to get involved in his family business. It never even occurred to her that he might end up coming back to Hanson Media Group—which she knew he'd always disliked—the moment she was hired.

If someone had offered her a bet, she would have bet everything she had that he wasn't going to be there.

"Everything all right?" David Hanson asked her when she got back to their promotions.

"What? Oh, fine. Fine. I was just thinking about something."

David looked skeptical. She'd already learned he wasn't an easy one to fool. "You sure?" he asked. "There's nothing I can do to help?"

She smiled at him. "Actually, I could use some information on how the television stations have been doing over the past year or so."

He looked puzzled. "I thought you were working with Evan on the broadcasting division."

"I am," she said quickly. "But I think it will be helpful to know how Hanson Media is doing in other arenas. Maybe we can learn from other divisions' successes and mistakes."

David gave a dry laugh. "Hanson Media Group isn't doing all that great in any area, but the fact is, the television division is doing nicely. We've produced an original medical drama that's done really well, and also the reality show *Run for Your Life* will be back this fall."

"Ah." Meredith nodded and made a mental note. "That's in its third or fourth season now, isn't it?"

"Fifth."

Five seasons. That was pretty solid. Her employer would be pleased to hear it. "And are the advertising revenues for those shows on par with some of the other popular mainstream network shows?"

"Absolutely. In fact, last year *Run for Your Life* aired after the Super Bowl, and the advertising went really well. You might want to talk to Bart Walker about that if you want the details. I'm not sure it really correlates to the radio division but it might give you some ideas."

She smiled and nodded. "I'm very interested in getting details about the whole company," she said. "The more information I can get, the better I can do my job."

David studied her keenly and nodded. "That sounds good. We have an administrative assistant named Marla who's ace at doing just about any research you can think of. You might ask her to gather some facts for you."

Meredith fully intended to do all of her own research, but she didn't want to stand out in any negative way to David, and she especially didn't want to look like a know-it-all. Particularly since she knew more than she should about the workings of the company already.

"Thanks for the tip," she said, smiling and heading for her office. "I will definitely make a point of contacting her this afternoon."

"That reminds me," David said, apparently unsuspicious. "I'm going to be out this afternoon, so if you have any questions, you can get me on my cell phone."

Meredith took a sharp breath and glanced behind her, half afraid that Evan might be there and catch her in a lie about meeting with David in the afternoon.

But of course he wasn't there. No one was.

"Don't worry about a thing," she assured David, hoping her duplicity didn't show on her face. "I can feel my way around or find someone to help if I need to. It won't be a problem." She tried to project absolute confidence, though she was feeling anything but. "No problem at all."

Chapter Three

Why had he picked the diner, of all places?

He probably just wasn't thinking about it, Meredith decided. Perhaps it didn't have the same ring of melancholy for him that it did for her. Not that it was a *huge* deal or anything. After all, it had been years since they were together, and the fact that he had been her first lover probably gave the relationship far more weight in her memory than in his. Twelve years had passed, yet some memories felt like yesterday.

* * *

"I love you, you know," eighteen-year-old Evan had said to seventeen-year-old Meredith as they walked into the Silver Car Diner at 3:00 a.m. for a late-night snack.

"I thought you did." She smiled, still languishing in the afterglow and warmth of his touch, despite the cold outside. "Otherwise I never would have...you know. Done what we just did."

"Neither would I."

"Liar."

He smiled, that gorgeous devil smile that made her heart flip every time. "Maybe I would have," he conceded.

"You would." She smiled, privately secure in the wholehearted belief that he *did* love her, and nothing else mattered.

He echoed her thoughts. "Okay, but it doesn't matter because I *do* love you."

"I love you, too, and you know it," she said, thrilling at the feel of the words tripping off her tongue. She'd been with Evan for over a year now, but she still felt the tickle of infatuation. That, she decided, was how she knew this was real love.

Evan squeezed her hand, and a tired-looking waitress led them to their favorite booth in the corner and took their orders for blueberry pancakes and colas.

When she had gone, Evan put money in the jukebox. Their eyes met and, as was their custom, he pushed a random letter and she pushed a random number and they listened to see what would play.

This time it was Jerry Lee Lewis singing "Breathless."

Perfect.

"So you know what I'm thinking?" Evan asked.

"Probably the same thing you're always thinking," Meredith answered with a giggle. "But can we take a break to eat first? I'm starving. And it wasn't a half hour ago that you told me you were going to die if you didn't come here and eat some blueberry pancakes." She gave a mock sigh of exasperation. "Even Don Juan took a break *sometimes*."

He rolled his eyes. "That wasn't what I was going to say. I mean, I'm all for that, but I was going to say I think maybe we should get married after we graduate."

Her breath caught in her throat. Thrills filled her like bubbling champagne. "College, you mean."

He shook his head. "High school. Why not? If we know that's what we're going to do anyway, why wait?"

A voice somewhere in her warned that this

might not be a good idea, but at the moment she couldn't think why not. "Graduation is in two months!"

"Great." He reached across the formica tabletop and took her hands in his. "The sooner, the better. Let's make your prom dress a wedding dress instead."

"Come on."

"Fine, we'll go to the prom and you can wear something else for our wedding. What do you say?"

Meredith would have run off with him right this minute but someone had to be the voice of reason here, didn't they? "What would we do about jobs? A home?"

He shrugged. "Whatever we'd do anyway. We could stay and work here, of course, but what about that trip to Greece? Why not just go and stay a year? We could work in a bar at night and just lie in the sun all day long, doing whatever we want. *Whenever* we want," he added meaningfully.

She sighed. It sounded like heaven.

"Seriously, Mer, I would talk to your parents right now if they were in town."

She gave a laugh. "If they were in town, we wouldn't be here. And we wouldn't have been able to—" she hesitated "—do what we did tonight."

He twined his fingers in hers, and looked deep into her eyes. "And we wouldn't be able to go back to your house and spend the whole night together."

Spend the whole night together. She turned the idea over in her mind. She could sleep in Evan's arms and wake up with him, seeing his eyes and his smile before anything else in the morning.

God, she loved him.

"I wish it could be like this every night."

"It can," he insisted. "It will. You'll see."

But Meredith was always skeptical of things that seemed too good to be true. There was always something deep inside her warning her that she might be disappointed. "I hope so," she had said wistfully.

Instead of answering, Evan had kissed her.

At the time, she had taken that kiss as reassurance. A promise that would be kept.

Now she knew better.

As Evan and Meredith entered the restaurant together to discuss the mundane details of Hanson Media, the familiar smell of cheeseburgers and waffles drifted into Meredith's senses, and she had to remind herself to be as professional and as aloof as she could be.

It was hard to forget the past they shared here, but if Evan could be cavalier about it, she would, too. Since they had no choice but to work together, she needed to be very careful not to add undue discomfort to the situation.

"Man, this smell takes me back," Evan said, inhaling deeply as they followed a pink-uniformed hostess to a booth along the back wall. "This is one thing I really missed when I was overseas." He gave a laugh. "It's hard to find blueberry pancakes and wet fries in Europe."

Meredith thought he'd lost a lot more than diner food when he'd left, but she didn't say so. "I'll bet," she said, sitting down opposite him on the cold vinyl seat. She felt like a poorly cast actress in a play about her own life. "But I'm sure Europe had its perks."

"Yeah, chief among them being that it wasn't here." He looked at the small jukebox on the wall of the booth and shook his head. "Good Lord, they've still got Jerry Lee Lewis on here. You'd think they'd have updated that."

"The jukebox only runs 45s," Meredith pointed

out, sounding didactic and snooty even to her own ears. "It's not like you can just stick CDs in it."

He looked at her with amusement in his eyes. "I left the country, Meredith, I didn't leave the planet. I know how a jukebox works." He smiled. "Though they do make CD ones now." He reached into his pocket and produced a handful of change, which he dropped on the table with a clatter. "Still a quarter?"

She glanced at the box and felt for a minute as if she was watching a movie of her own life. How many times had they been here together? She'd probably studied the jukebox in this very booth before. Multiple times. It was a quarter. It was always a quarter here.

If only the rest of life were so consistent.

"You okay?"

His question startled her back into the moment.

"Yes, fine," she said. "I was just thinking about work."

"This ought to change that." He put the quarter in and hesitated for just a fraction of a second before pressing C and 7 at the same time. "Get you thinking about math homework instead," he added with a small laugh.

The sound of an old Platters song drifted

out of the small, tinny speakers. Meredith knew it because it had been one of her grandfather's favorites.

Evan had known that once. Was it too presumptuous to think that was why he'd chosen it this time?

"You're not the only one with a memory," he said, as if in answer to her unspoken question.

"What do you mean?" she asked. Where Evan was concerned, her rule was going to be Assume Nothing.

He gestured toward the jukebox. "You picked this song about a million times."

She repositioned herself, hoping her straightened posture would pass for a lack of sentimentality. "That's funny, I don't really remember that."

"Yes, you do."

"What?"

He cocked his head and said, "We have a past, Meredith. There's no getting around it, no matter how much you might want to. We can't pretend we don't know each other."

"We don't," she said, too quickly. She sounded defensive. She *was* defensive.

She was going to have to get some perspective.

He shrugged and fiddled with a sugar pack

from the little container on the table. "We did once."

"What did we have, Evan?" She looked him squarely in the eye, even though it made her feel weak inside. "Obviously, it wasn't that close, or that special, because you up and left it without so much as an *adiós*."

"That wasn't because of you, Meredith."

If she'd been successful at pretending nonchalance at all, she lost it then. "I didn't know *what* it was about."

"It was just…me. My own stuff. I'm sorry if it hurt you."

That was it? After all these years, that was what she got in the way of retribution? *I'm sorry if it hurt you.*

Like there was some possibility that it hadn't.

Like maybe she hadn't even noticed, at seventeen, that the boy she adored more than anything on earth—the guy she was sure she was going to spend the rest of her life with—had just disappeared into the night. Lord, she'd been so sure—so wrong, but so darn sure—about his feelings for her that for the first six months she had continued to insist that something must have happened to Evan.

Imagined him wounded somewhere, needing

help.... Thoughts had plagued her, night and day. She couldn't eat, couldn't sleep, couldn't focus.

And now he was sorry *if* he'd hurt her?

"It wasn't just about you," she said quietly, holding her outrage and disbelief deep inside.

"What do you mean?"

If he didn't know, she didn't want to have to explain it to him. It was all such old news now, anyway—how could she talk about it without sounding like a desperate loser who had been stuck in the past for all this time?

How could she explain what it was like for her—the girl who had trusted, and given of herself, and who thought if there was one thing in the world she could count on it was Evan Hanson—to find out that everything she'd thought was real for two and a half years was just an illusion? And even that revelation had come only after she'd gone through the undue stress of fearing the worst.

It sounded small to the disinterested audience, yet to Meredith it had been a life-shaping experience.

"What I mean is, we need to keep this about business," she clarified. "Whatever we had was over a long time ago. And opening old wounds isn't going to achieve anything positive or productive for either one of us."

"Right."

She went on, "Like I said, we don't know each other anymore, and if we move forward acting like we do, based on ancient information, it's just counterproductive."

He hesitated, studying her, then said, "Okay, then. Business, not personal. Got it." He pushed the menu aside. "I already know what I want, how about you?"

She knew she wanted to get out of there as quickly as possible, so she pushed her menu to the end of the booth with his. "I'll just get a cheeseburger."

"Medium well, cheddar cheese, no raw onions, right?" Evan didn't smile, but he may as well have. His eyes clearly showed that he had won a point.

And her heart conceded that point privately. Though she wouldn't have wanted to admit it to Evan—or anyone else, for that matter—she hadn't changed so much since she was a teenager. Basically Meredith Waters had always been the same person—she had simple tastes, a good work ethic and she could be counted upon to take the slow-but-steady route.

The only real difference, and it had come courtesy of Evan himself, was that now she had a very cautious heart.

Meredith Waters was determined to never fall in love again.

Chapter Four

"You're consistent," Evan said to her, having predicted her order. "That's a good thing."

"You're right." She looked at him evenly. "It's a quality I've really grown to appreciate in people."

He paused, then said, "But you don't mean that personally, right?"

"Right. It was just a general comment." She didn't sound convincing, even to her own ears, so when the waitress appeared to take their orders, she was glad for the interruption.

As soon as the woman turned away, Meredith

tried to put the conversation back on track, or at least get it off the track it was on. "So let's talk about your plans for Hanson Broadcasting. I understand you're planning to change the format to all talk?"

There was a moment's hesitation before he followed her into that line of conversation. "It's hard to do anything unique in music radio these days, but with talk we can corner the market if we get or develop popular talents."

"But there's a lot of danger in that, too," Meredith pointed out, comfortable to be back on less intimate turf. *This* she could talk to him about. This she could talk to *anyone* about. "As soon as I heard you wanted to switch to talk, I did some research. Almost every radio network that's succeeded with talk has done so with shock jocks." She hesitated, waiting for him to interject, but he just nodded, so she continued, "And though there's reward potential, the risks tend to be high. Too high." Especially given her current job description, though she didn't add that. It would be awfully hard for her to do a good job if she was trying to put out obscenity fires all the time instead of gathering pertinent information about Hanson Media Group.

"What risks are you referring to?" Evan asked.

She chose her words carefully. "A lot of these DJs have trouble toeing the line. They want to be outrageous so people talk about them and listen to them."

Evan shrugged. "If we want ratings we need people who are willing to push the envelope."

Meredith frowned. It sounded as if things she thought were dangers were assets to him. "Which envelope are you planning on pushing and exactly who do you have in mind for the job?"

He tapped his fingertips on the gray-and-white tabletop. "Envelopes, any. I don't care. Who do I have in mind? Several people. I already secured the Sports Addicts, Bill Brandywine and Zulo Gillette. But the biggest coup is that I've already talked to Lenny Doss about coming here for the morning-drive hours. I think I can get him onboard."

Suddenly it felt like the air-conditioning had gotten very cold. "Lenny Doss," Meredith repeated. His name had come up quite a few times in her research. So had the Sports Addicts, and though they weren't her cup of tea, they were essentially harmless. "You've got to be kidding."

"Nope." He looked quite pleased with himself. "All it took was the right offer."

Alarm bells were going off in her head and he was oblivious. "Evan, you can't hire Lenny Doss."

That got his attention. "Why not?"

Did she really need to spell this out? "The guy is a major liability. The last company that hired him ended up paying the FCC more than half a million bucks in fines."

Evan nodded with apparent understanding. "You're referring to him dropping the F-bomb on the air."

"No—well, yes, but not *just* that." She couldn't even imagine trying to clean up after Lenny Doss. "He also had his listeners go to the Washington Monument and—"

Evan put his hand up. "I know all about that. You're right, it's inexcusable, but it's not going to happen again."

She couldn't believe he knew this stuff and still wanted to hire the guy. "Evan, if you hire Lenny Doss, you are in danger of putting the final nail in the coffin of Hanson Media Group."

He looked at her and she noticed his jaw was tensing the way it always had when he was frustrated.

Evan Hanson didn't like being told he couldn't do something. Never had.

"I'm aware of the dangers," he said. "This

business may be new to me, but as soon as Helen put me on the job, I did my research, and I surrounded myself with some pretty knowledgeable people."

"I'm not saying you can't do your job," she said. "I'm saying..." What was she saying? How could she finish that sentence without coming off more adversarial than she already had? "That if you do this, you're going to make it hard for *me* to do *my* job."

Evan looked at her evenly, then smiled and said, "Tactful recovery."

Fortunately, they were interrupted by the arrival of their food.

"That was fast," Meredith commented gratefully as the young redheaded busboy set a plate down with a clatter in front of her. A French fry fell off and landed next to the plate, leaving a small splatter of gravy on the formica.

"I'm sorry," the kid said quickly, reaching to clean it up and nearly knocking her glass of ice water into her lap.

"It's okay, don't worry about it," she said quickly, noticing Evan pushing her plate a little to the side before the kid accidentally knocked into it, too.

Funny how they could be a good team in such

a small way, or at least work in harmony to save a plate, and yet they disagreed about virtually everything of any importance.

"We'll take it from here," Evan said in a way that was distinctly dismissive.

"Thanks," Meredith added to the kid.

The busboy left and Evan turned his attention back to Meredith. "I could almost swear that same kid worked here when we used to come." He smiled, and Meredith's heart did a stupid flip. "He looks like he hasn't aged a day."

She couldn't help smiling back. "There's always a kid like that working in places like this. I think they hire them from central casting."

They laughed and for just a moment the tension was lifted from the conversation. It was back a moment later, though, when Evan said, "Now, where were we?"

Meredith picked at her French fries. "I believe I was trying to get you to see how crazy it would be to hire Lenny Doss and you were being bullheaded about it."

"Ah, yes." He smiled again. The tension in the air between them lessened a bit. "You don't mince words."

"Not when I'm this serious about something."

He let out a long breath. "Look, Meredith,

there's also the chance that it will work, and it will raise the profile of Hanson Media Group in a really positive way. The business world needs to take us seriously and this could do it."

"I agree with your theory, but I'm not so sure about your methods," she said. "Are you willing to do this and take the chance of it blowing up in your face?" The air conditioner kicked off half-way through her sentence, and Meredith realized she was practically yelling to be heard. "Do you really want to be the one to blow this for your whole family?" she finished in a lower voice.

Evan tapped his fingers on the table again, louder, faster. His whole face—a face she'd once known so well, but which, at this moment, seemed like a stranger—pulled into a frown. Even his eyes appeared to darken. "Yes, Meredith, I guess I am willing to take that chance. And, with all due respect, I don't think it's your job to worry about it."

"But that's *exactly* what my job is. My department already has its hands full trying to salvage the image of Hanson Media Group from the whole porn scandal. Adding Lenny Doss to the mix is like trying to put a fire out with gasoline."

Evan shook his head and took a big bite of his hamburger, looking unperturbed.

Understanding began to dawn in Meredith's mind. "Oh, my God. You don't care, do you?"

He raised an eyebrow in question.

But it wasn't really in question. She'd seen this gesture before. It was an invitation for her to tell what she knew so he could either confirm or deny.

"You don't care if the whole company goes under," she went on, half to herself and half to him. "If you succeed, you're all right with that, but if you fail..." She studied his face. "My God, Evan, if you fail, you don't care about that, either, do you?"

The moment of silence that passed between them seemed so long that she felt as if she'd sat staring at him for five minutes, listening to the clanking of utensils and plates and the shouts and laughter around them. It was a standoff and he wasn't backing down.

Well, neither was she.

"You always were afraid to take a chance, weren't you?" Evan said finally.

"What?"

"You're saying I shouldn't do this because it's risky. I think that's coming from a personal bias on your part. You've always been afraid to take a risk."

She thought of the risks she'd taken with him. The ultimate risks she'd taken in giving him her virginity and entering the kind of intimacy she could never erase. "I've taken a few."

It didn't appear that he took her meaning. "As I recall, you were as straitlaced as they come, always playing by the rules. Even in science class, instead of switching the chemicals up a little bit to see if we could make flubber or something, you insisted on following the program." He made it sound like an insult.

But she was proud of having played by the rules in high school. It was easy to cheat, to lie and to deceive—she'd found that out later on. "Yes, I preferred to use the method that worked, that was tried and true. It's just good sense."

"Good thing Thomas Edison didn't feel that way." He took another bite of his burger.

How could he eat at a time like this? Meredith couldn't even think about her food. "Oh, for heaven's sake, you're not trying to invent the lightbulb, you're just trying to hire a proven jerk to put on the air so you can have the sublime pleasure of watching your family business explode like a firecracker."

"That's not true," he protested, gesturing at her with his burger. "I am not *trying* to make the company go under. Despite what you think, I *do* care. I'm trying to help. But you're right—if it doesn't work out, it's not going to be the end of my world."

"So you're willing to put everyone's future on the line." She felt the tug of an anger she hadn't felt in a long time. "And if things don't go the way you want them to, you'd rather bail on everyone who cares about you—no matter how much it hurts them—than do a little hard work to try and get along."

He winced. She was almost sure of it. "That's an easy explanation, isn't it? Blame me instead of the reality that some people and situations are not a good fit."

That stung. Meredith took a bracing breath and put her palms down on the cool tabletop. "Let's get back on the subject before we start getting personal, shall we?" *Shall* we? Did she really say that? Suddenly she was a Victorian spinster.

"Fine by me."

"But I want to go on record as saying I don't think you should hire Lenny Doss."

He shrugged. "Then put me on record as saying I still disagree with you on that one."

Big surprise. "Evan, please think about this seriously. The guy is a huge millstone. Obviously Megachannel Network didn't think he was worth the risk, because they let him go."

"I know that," he conceded.

"If you put him on the schedule, and he screws up—as he's *bound* to—it's not just Hanson, it's you, too. You're going to look like a fool. Your reputation will be shot."

He gave a single spike of a laugh. "You can do better than that, Mer. You know I don't care about my reputation."

His use of the old nickname disconcerted her. "Maybe you should."

"Listen," he went on, leaning slightly toward her. "I hear what you're saying, and I promise I took it into consideration before I ever approached Doss. But I really do believe he's learned his lesson. If I thought, as you do, that he was going to be a problem, I wouldn't be trying to hire him. Honestly. Besides, we have a six-second delay in place, too. If he says anything objectionable, it won't make it on air."

"You hope."

"I *know.*" He was always good at persuading her away from her better judgment. "Trust me."

Luckily for Meredith, her spine had gotten a

lot stronger in the years since she'd last seen him. "You haven't signed him yet?"

He shook his head. "It's just a matter of time. I'll have an answer in a few days. A week at the most."

"And are you looking into other options in the meantime?'

"Of course."

She nodded, thinking that bought her a little bit of time at least. Now she just needed to get away from this conversation—she needed to get away from *Evan*—so she could pull herself together and figure out a way to solve this problem she found herself swimming in. "Then let's revisit this when you have a better idea of who you're bringing into the company. Once you've hired the talent and set up the schedule, we'll come up with a plan to give you the best possible visibility."

He narrowed his brown eyes slightly and looked at her. "It isn't like you to drop something like this so quickly," he said, his voice tinged with suspicion.

"Maybe it's not like the girl you once knew," she corrected, though he was right. "But you don't know me anymore, Evan."

"So you keep saying."

She sighed. "Look, there's no point in spending the afternoon arguing with you when it's obvious neither one of us is going to back down."

He nodded his agreement.

"And I've got more important things to think about than whether or not you're foolish enough to hire Lenny Doss." She opened her purse, took her wallet out and dropped a bill on the table. "If you'll excuse me now, I'm going back to work." She started to slide out of the booth, not an easy thing to do gracefully, especially when she'd just taken that parting shot.

He looked at the money, then back at her. "I'll pay for lunch, Meredith."

She shook her head. "No need." She stood up and straightened her suit, hoping the gesture would magically bring back the objectivity she seemed to have lost. "Listen, I'm really sorry to have to cut this short, but, like I said, we'll revisit this later." She hoped to God she wouldn't really have to discuss this, or anything else, with him again. "Once you know more about who you're hiring."

"I know who I'm hiring."

"We'll see."

He nodded. "I guess I'll see you around the water cooler."

The old joke, "Not if I see you first," occurred to her, but it wasn't true. The thing that was going to be most difficult about working with Evan was going to be the irresistible urge to be around him.

That was why she had to keep as much distance as she possibly could, starting *now.*

Chapter Five

Meredith stepped out into the hot July sun. Chicago's streets and sidewalks were baking and so was she, but it had less to do with the weather and more to do with being so close to Evan Hanson again.

She'd only stopped a moment to catch her breath when the door opened and he came out behind her. "Oh, good, you're still here," he said.

She whirled to face him. "Evan! Yes, I was just heading back to the office."

He looked her over for a moment then said, simply, "Meredith."

She swallowed. “Yes?”

“Things are a little tense between us.”

No sense in being coy about it. “Yes, they are.”

“Are you sure you can do this?”

She didn’t have to ask what he meant. “Of course. Are you sure *you* can?”

He shrugged. “No problem.”

“Good. Why should a little ancient history get in the way of business?” She took a long, deep breath and let it out. “I wasn’t expecting to see you today—or any other time, to be perfectly honest with you—and it threw me for a loop.” He would never know just how much. “That’s all.”

“It was a shock for me, too,” Evan said. His eyes held a myriad of emotions. “But a good one.”

Was he suddenly going sentimental on her? Impossible. She gave a half shrug and nodded. “Then let’s have an understanding that from this point on, this is strictly business. Our past, such as it is, has nothing to do with the way we conduct our business. Deal?” She held out her hand.

He took it, sending a surprising tingle up her arm. “Deal.” His voice was smooth and low, a man’s voice now, yet still horribly familiar. She wondered if she would be able to keep her thoughts of him on a business level.

They held hands for just a fraction of a second longer than they both knew was appropriate. When Evan let go, Meredith's hand felt suddenly cold.

He looked as if he was about to say something but just then his cell phone rang. He took it out of his pocket and glanced at the caller ID. "Damn." He looked at her apologetically. "I've got to take this. Can I get you a cab?"

"No, no. I'm fine. Go back in and take your call."

He flipped his phone open and said to the caller, "Hang on, I'll be right with you," then looked at Meredith. "You're sure? About...everything."

"You bet."

"Okay, I'll be talking to you soon."

"Absolutely."

"Great." He looked at her for a moment. "This will work out just fine." Evan turned to leave. Watching his faded jean-clad form walking away from her, noticing the way his loose-fitting cotton shirt lay across his muscular back and shoulders, Meredith could have sworn she heard him add, "I hope."

The usually short walk back to the office seemed to take forever. With every step the heat got more intense, along with her conflicted feelings.

When she finally got to the building, the air-conditioning hit her like a slap in the face, and she told herself she had to regroup for a moment then make some tough decisions.

She went back to her office. Fortunately David wasn't there—he and his wife, Nina, were taking the kids to the Whistle Stop Circus—so she was alone. Completely alone. She sat down at her desk, a blanket of silence enveloping her like a warm fleece throw.

For a few minutes she couldn't move, couldn't think. All she could do was breathe deeply and try to still her pounding heart. Her eyes burned, but no tears would come, no release.

Just an empty silence.

How had a love that had once been so strong and so comfortable turned into the awkward exchange that had just taken place? It was as if she and Evan were two completely different people now. Strangers.

But they always had been, hadn't they? As it turned out, Evan had never been the person she'd thought he was.

But, darn it, he still looked so much the same. When she'd first laid eyes on him today, her heart had tripped with excitement. Not anger, not sadness, but excitement. Her first impulse was to reach out to him. Then, only after those first split seconds, she remembered why she shouldn't.

Fragmented thoughts of Evan's disappearance, George Hanson's sabotage of her own father's business and her father's subsequent heart attack and death ran through her head. And through it all, Evan had *never* contacted her. He hadn't even sent a card to say he was sorry to hear about her father, and she knew he must have known since it was his father who had had such a strong hand in discrediting her own father's small local newspaper so Hanson's knockoff could take over.

George Hanson had systematically dismantled her father's life. It was child's play for him—just a way to get what he wanted. If Terence Waters wouldn't sell the *Lakeside Gazette* to Hanson—at a greatly undervalued price—then it was the easiest thing in the world for the great George Hanson to force him out of business by creating his own competition.

The *Lake Michigan Gazette.*

The whole business had left her shell-shocked. If Evan had contacted her, said something—*anything*—compassionate, it would have gone a long way toward soothing her shattered nerves.

But he hadn't.

And she'd eventually gotten over him, comfortable in the knowledge that she'd never see him again.

So now that she had, she was paralyzed with a strange combination of resentment and longing.

Gradually the ticking of the wall clock cut into her consciousness, and she managed to stand up and walk to the water cooler. The icy water chilled a path down her throat, returning her senses.

She had to talk to Helen.

She had to tell Helen the truth before this went any further.

Meredith was running on high when she got to Helen's office. She stopped at the desk of Sonia Townsley, Helen's assistant. Sonia was tall, thin, midforties, with striking gray hair cut in a fashionable style that stopped just short of being geometric. But the thing that struck Meredith most about Sonia was that she was always—*always*—calm and cool as a cucumber.

"Is Helen available?" Meredith asked.

"Yes, she is," Sonia said, lowering her perfectly shaped eyebrows. "Are you okay, Meredith?"

Meredith nodded. "I'm fine, really. I just need to talk to Helen for a moment."

"What's going on?" Helen asked from the doorway to her office. She walked out and exchanged concerned looks with Sonia.

"It's just… I…" Meredith stumbled. This was *not* the professional image she sought to project.

"I'll go get some ice water for you," Sonia said, tactfully removing herself from what was clearly an awkward moment.

"I'm sorry," Meredith said to Helen when Sonia had gone. "I didn't mean to drive her away."

"Not at all. Come on in. Tell me what's on your mind." Helen gestured for Meredith to follow her. She sat behind her desk. "Is everything okay?"

Meredith perched uncomfortably on the chair opposite Helen's. "I'm not sure. There's something I think you should know about me. I should have told you before, but I just didn't want to be the sort of person who couldn't separate their personal life from business."

Helen frowned. "But now you find you are?"

"Sort of." Meredith nodded. "I find I could be."

Helen leaned forward. "What is it, Meredith? Tell me what's concerning you and we'll work it out."

"Evan and I have...a past together," Meredith began. She could feel her palms growing clammy and cold.

Helen raised her eyebrows. "Evan?"

"Yes, we knew each other in high school." Understatement. "We knew each other pretty well in high school."

Helen looked over at Meredith with a curious eye. "You're saying you dated?"

Meredith swallowed a lump in her throat. *Dated.* That sounded so impersonal. So milk-shakes-and-a-movie. So innocent. "It was actually a pretty serious relationship. At least it was to me."

"Ah." Helen nodded slowly and leaned back in her chair. "And this is the first time you've seen him since that time?"

"The last time I saw him it was the afternoon of our senior prom. He said he'd see me in a few hours." She gave a dry laugh. "It's been *quite* a few hours."

"I'm sorry, Meredith. It must have been a shock to learn you'd be working with him."

"It was a surprise," Meredith agreed. But, mindful that she didn't want to sound like a whiner who couldn't get over her past, she said, "I'm not saying I can't do what you need me to here—far from it. But my experience with Evan today made me think that, in the interest of full disclosure, I ought to let you know. If you're uncomfortable with me continuing under the circumstances, I'll understand."

Helen smiled. "The circumstances sound like they might lend themselves quite well to your success here. If you already know Evan, already have something of a rapport with him, that might make things easier, don't you think?"

There wasn't going to be anything *easy* about working with Evan, but Meredith nodded. "It could. But it could also make him uncomfortable. If he's reluctant to work with me, I'm not going to be of much use to you."

Helen glanced out the window for a moment with a faraway look in her eyes. Then she turned her attention back to Meredith. "*Is* he reluctant to work with you?"

"I honestly don't know." Meredith gave a self-effacing smile. It would have been too weak for her to admit that she didn't want to work with him. That she was afraid to even be around him. "He didn't seem as rattled by our interaction as I was."

"Are you able to work with him, despite feeling rattled by it?"

This was a moment of truth. Meredith prided herself on her reliability, and this was a turning point in which she could either give in to her weakness and do something she'd probably be ashamed of for the rest of her life or stand tall and work through her discomfort, knowing eventually she'd come out on the other side of it.

Intellectually, it was an easy choice.

"Yes," she said, more comfortable following her intellect than her heart.

"Then let's leave things as they are," Helen said, locking eyes with Meredith. "You came highly recommended, and with everything the company has been through recently we need the best people we can get so that Hanson Media Group recovers its once stellar reputation."

"I'll do my best." Meredith stood to go. She was feeling a little bit better now and was embarrassed about the alarmist manner in which she'd come to Helen at first. "I'm just glad you know the truth now."

"I am, too," Helen said. "Thank you."

Meredith left the office, then stopped outside the closed door and took a deep breath. She couldn't tell Helen *everything,* of course, but she'd at least told her what she needed to know about Meredith's past. Hopefully now that wouldn't come back to bite her.

Meredith set off down the hall, looking for David, when she ran straight into Evan.

He looked at her, then looked behind her at Helen's office door.

"Meeting with the boss?"

She swallowed. "One of them."

"Anything I should know about?"

She took a short breath. "No. Nothing important."

He looked at her for one long, hard moment. Then, without a word, he turned and walked away.

Chapter Six

Helen arrived at Shabu Hachi two minutes early for her 8:00 p.m. meeting with Ichiro Kobayashi, of the media conglomerate TAKA Corporation.

The restaurant hostess led Helen to the table where Ichiro Kobayashi and another man waited for her.

She smiled and bowed slightly, holding out a business card bearing her information in both English and Japanese to Kobayashi. He handed her one in return, likewise in English and Japanese, and though his manner was nothing short of courteous, she had the distinct sense that he was unhappy at having to deal with a woman instead of a man.

She repeated the process with the other man and felt the same sense of disconcertion from him.

His card said he was Chion Kinjo and he worked in acquisitions for TAKA, along with Kobayashi. His card listed offices in Tokyo, Kyoto and Shizuoka.

TAKA was a huge corporation.

It was distinctly possible that Helen was in over her head. She just needed to make sure she didn't let on that she felt that way.

She put the cards in her pocket, then took out a small ornament she'd purchased from a Chicago artisan and gave it to Kobayashi as a souvenir of Chicago. It was customary, but she also hoped he would keep it and be reminded that this was a town he liked and wanted to return to.

"This is for you," she said. "It's a token of thanks and, I hope, a happy reminder of our beautiful city."

He turned it in his hand and gave a nod of approval. "Very lovely. The detail is magnificent."

Helen breathed one small sigh of relief. So far, so good, given the fact that they would rather have been dealing with her late husband than with her.

Kobayashi indicated she should sit next to him,

which she took as a good sign. The moment they were seated, a waitress brought water to the table and, after a brief exchange with Kinjo in Japanese, filled their glasses, bowed and left the table.

"I've taken the liberty of suggesting a variety of foods from the eastern region of our country," Kobayashi said to Helen. "I hope that's agreeable to you?"

"Indeed." Helen nodded. "It's not often one gets to take a culinary tour like this with a native. I look forward to trying your selections."

This seemed to please Kobayashi. He gave a polite smile then leaped right into business. "I'm sorry to hear of your husband's death," he said. "I would have liked to have met him."

Had George been alive, there was no way he would have considered talking to these men about a merger. He would sooner have driven the company into bankruptcy.

In fact, he all but had.

"He was a good man," she said, swallowing the lie as smoothly as a tall glass of lemonade.

"As far as his company is concerned, my associate and I have grave concerns about the recent performance of Hanson Media."

Helen nodded. "I understand. However, a

comparative study would show that American media companies are all undergoing growing pains right now."

"Growing pains?" he repeated.

Shoot, she'd meant to avoid idioms. "Difficulty in a changing market," she explained. "Culturally speaking, things are changing rapidly in the United States, and a lot of news outfits have been hit hard trying to strike a balance between news, information and entertainment."

"Does that not make this a risky investment?"

"No, that makes this a savvy investment." Helen steeled her nerve. It was going to take a lot of confidence for her to pull this one off. "The reason for the growing pains in the media industry is that the growth is so rapid. Any investment made today will be multiplied tenfold within just a few years."

"Then why are you selling interest in the company?" Kinjo asked shrewdly.

She leveled her gaze on him. "Because I want Hanson Media Group to be heard around the world—" she cocked her head "—and I believe you want the same for TAKA. Together, Hanson and TAKA would be a very, *very* powerful force in world media."

The two men maintained masks of impassive

consideration. Not one readable emotion so much as flickered across either one of their faces.

"You wish to maintain some control over Hanson Media Group?" Kobayashi asked.

Helen turned her gaze to him and leveled it. "I'm looking for a merger, Mr. Kobayashi, not a takeover."

The men exchanged glances.

"We are not in need of saving," Helen added, although it was as preposterous as a drowning victim trying to negotiate with a lifeguard before accepting help. "We are in *want* of power. We believe that with TAKA we can achieve that. For both our companies."

"TAKA is already powerful," Kobayashi said in a clipped voice. "It is my impression that that is why you approached us with this offer."

She wanted to point out that it was a *proposal* more than an *offer.* Characterizing it as an offer made it sound as if she were willing to sacrifice Hanson Media Group completely, and she wasn't.

But Helen knew it didn't make sense to argue with the man, particularly since Kobayashi wasn't the person ultimately making the decision. Better to play nice and try and work up their interest. "TAKA could be *more* powerful," she said, smiling confidently.

Kobayashi didn't answer that directly, but the short breath he took before speaking again gave him away. He wasn't willing to walk away.

He was at least interested.

"There is one concern we have, which you have not addressed," he said to her.

"What's that?" Apprehension nibbled at Helen's nerves. Were they going to throw a curve ball her way?

"Hanson Media Group appears to have a growing liability in the radio division. We believe this is endangering any investment advantages."

The radio division was turning out to be more trouble than Helen had anticipated. But after all the time she had spent longing for more contact with George's children, she wasn't about to offer one of them the opportunity to help the company then snatch it away.

Besides, she had faith in Evan. He didn't have a lot of nine-to-five business experience, but he was smart as a whip. And he had a good sense of what people in their company's most desirable demographic wanted.

"I've just hired new staff to head the radio division, including my late husband's son, Evan."

She smiled, hoping her confidence in Evan shone through, rather than the occasional uncertainty she felt as George Hanson's widow.

"It is our understanding that he is intending to change your programming to what you call 'shock jock' programs, specifically that of a Len Doss, who has already cost other broadcasting companies hundreds of thousands of dollars in Federal Communications Commission fines."

Helen was surprised that Kobayashi had this information, which should've been classified. But she trusted Evan and Meredith to do what was best for the company.

"Hanson Broadcasting hasn't made any commitments to Mr. Doss. It is Evan's full intention to investigate the possibility thoroughly and make an educated decision based on the balance of risks and gains." She gave her brightest smile. "And if Evan Hanson decides that hiring Mr. Doss is in the company's best interest, I have absolute faith in him."

"Is that so?"

She nodded, and she meant it. Evan knew what appealed to young men his age more than she or Kobayashi did, that she was certain of. "Believe me, the division is in excellent hands."

Kobayashi looked dubious. "Are you able to prove that?"

"Our numbers for the next quarter should bear it out." She took a steadying breath. "Believe me, Mr. Kobayashi, *nothing* is standing in the way of Hanson Media and nationwide success."

Spying was such an ugly word.

Meredith preferred to think of herself as brokering information that would benefit all parties involved.

She was an *investigator,* not a corporate spy.

Still, as she crept around the offices of Hanson Media Group by the fluorescent semi-light of 2:30 a.m., jumping at every tiny noise, she felt like a spy. A sneak.

A liar.

Yes, she was doing what her employer had hired her to do. This was, in reality, her job. And she'd do it well; she always did. But this time it was personal, and that made all the difference. Instead of gathering sensitive corporate information from one company and handing it over to another, she was gathering sensitive information about Hanson Media—a name that had invoked various strong and conflicted feelings in her for over a decade—and providing it to a company that potentially wanted to take over and push the Hansons out entirely.

Meredith didn't know what her employer's ultimate goal for the company was: it wasn't her job to know.

It was her job to collect pertinent information and pass it along to her boss.

The ignorance of what would then happen because of it should have been bliss.

She wouldn't let her trepidation stop her, though. It was just raw emotion, and this job had no room for emotion. Emotion was a liar. It made a person believe things that might not be true. Whatever she felt, she needed to soldier on and get the job done.

Just as she'd always done.

So she proceeded. Her heart pounded with the fear that someone—some weary soul who wanted to get his work done before taking his family to Disney World, or some ambitious soul who wanted to impress his boss with work done early—would show up around one of the quiet corners.

But the only sound was the hum of the building air conditioner, whooshing cold air through miles of air ducts.

Meredith went to David Hanson's office first.

With any luck she'd find everything she needed there and she wouldn't have to dig around in anyone else's files.

With a quick glance to make sure no one was standing in the shadows watching her, she turned on his computer to look for the files he'd told her about earlier in the week.

"You can see our recent performance history broken down by day, week, month and year," he'd said, proud of a former administrative assistant's elaborate spreadsheets. "It's like forensic science. I can tell you how many newspapers were sold in lower Manhattan by 1:00 p.m. on Tuesday, January 13. I can tell you how many people listened to Garrett Pinchon's Gospel Hour every Sunday morning from 1998 to last November."

This was just the kind of information her boss wanted to look at.

When the operating system on David's computer came up, she typed in the password she'd watched him enter earlier.

Bubby.

Whatever that meant.

The system beeped and rattled through the rest of its processes and produced a desktop background photo of David's wife, Nina, and his kids—Zach and Izzy, he'd told her proudly—smiling at the camera and giving Meredith a twinge of guilt.

Pushing the negative thoughts away, Meredith quickly maneuvered her way through the system, finding the files David had alluded to earlier. She zipped them into a single file, then saved them to a thumb drive she'd put into a USB port. Once upon a time this had been the stuff of CIA espionage. Nowadays, every college student in North America could carry the equivalent of every paper they'd written since elementary school on a device no bigger than a child's thumb.

It worked for Meredith, who was currently saving spreadsheets that would have sucked up all the memory and then some on an older computer. Even now it wasn't an instantaneous process. She tapped her fingers impatiently on the desktop while the large files took their time being converted and transferred.

At one point Meredith thought she heard a sound like a cough in the distance. Immediately her hand flew to the monitor button, and she turned it off, waiting breathlessly in the dark to see if a security guard or, worse, another employee would come to investigate the quiet hum of David's hard drive as it did her bidding.

She waited a good five minutes in the dark, holding her breath nearly the entire time. Finally, thinking it must have been her imagination, she crept to the door and peered around the corner, down the hall. She braced herself for a shock.

Nothing.

With a sigh of profound relief, she went back to David's office. The computer had finished saving. She pocketed the thumb drive, erased her virtual footsteps on the system and shut the computer down.

Still cautious, she listened with the paranoid awareness of a lone wolf at night as she made her way through the maze of halls.

She saw no one. Heard no one. But she had the most disquieting feeling that someone else was there. Maybe it was surveillance cameras. Or building security out in the main hall. Or the constant hum of countless computers hibernating or showing *Star Wars* screensavers to no one.

For one crazy instant Meredith thought about going to Evan's office. Something about the still of the night and some long-dormant knot of emotions called her there. As if she could go and breathe him in...and breathe him out. And maybe get rid of the memories that haunted her still, once and for all.

But there was no time for that. She'd done what she needed to do and now she needed to get the heck out of the building before anyone figured her out.

She opened the main door and, after a surreptitious glance out into the hallway, she stepped away, letting the door to Hanson Media Group close harder than she'd intended.

It was a careless mistake, but it didn't matter. She'd proven to herself time and again that there was no one there.

No one but the ghosts of a man who once meant the world to her and whose name now meant only a biweekly paycheck, excellent health and dental insurance and a dull ache in her heart that she almost couldn't bear.

Chapter Seven

Evan Hanson woke to a bang.

He sat bolt upright in the converted sofa bed before he had even a moment to think, his body tensed and ready for fight or flight. For one crazy, disconcerting moment he couldn't remember where he was, then it came back to him. He was sleeping in his office. Unable to commit to staying in Chicago—or even admit to himself that he'd come back—he'd been camping out in the office, using the executive washroom for bathing and either eating out or ordering food in.

What point would there be in getting an

apartment to keep a job that he knew wasn't going to last long? He was no ace executive but he could see the writing on the wall—Hanson Media Group was going down. If he could do anything to help stop it, he was willing to give it a hundred percent, but at the same time he wasn't going to bet his life that it would work out. Not that he wanted to come out and say that to anyone still working there.

Either way, there was no way he was going to be in Chicago for the rest of his life.

He missed the sun of Majorca. The fresh regional produce he'd come to enjoy picking up at sunny outdoor markets across Europe. Already he felt like one more quickie takeout meal would kill him.

Helen's hopes for the company were admirable. Noble, even. But impossible. Anyone could see that. Offices that used to be filled with enthusiastic employees, reflecting the prosperity of what was once one of the most powerful media groups in the United States, were now half empty. There was little laughter, less water cooler talk, and almost no optimism on the faces of the employees he saw every day.

Most of Hanson's best employees had left a while back, knowing their résumés would look better if they reflected tenure at a successful company than if they showed a tenacious grip on a ship that was going down faster than the *Titanic*. It might not stay down—he was fairly sure some other company would snatch it up at a bargain price—but it was going to go down long enough for those onboard to suffer. Unless they were brave enough to hold on to their stock options until the price went up.

But from what he was hearing around the office, most people weren't. The general consensus was "get out while you can."

So what the heck was Meredith Waters doing here?

The Meredith he'd known was far too savvy to align herself with a losing cause.

And honestly, it would have suited him a whole lot better not to have her around. She was a distraction.

A *major* distraction.

Hell, Meredith's ghost had haunted him for years, her memory floating around the outskirts of his consciousness more frequently than he liked to admit. He didn't always see it, but often, late at night, when it was just him and his thoughts alone in a room, it was Meredith's voice that spoke to him.

Which was nuts, because he knew she had to hate him by then. He knew that she wasn't lying in another bed across the ocean, thinking the same thoughts. And he was fairly certain that she had moved on to a much better and more reliable prospect.

Someone he could never live up to.

He'd spent a lifetime feeling as though he couldn't live up to his loved ones' expectations. For a long time it was his failure in his father's eyes that had disturbed him the most. One would have thought after the snub in the reading of the will that his feeling of failure toward his father would have grown even deeper, but something in him had snapped. Somehow—by some miracle—he had stopped caring what his father thought.

And for a brief but glorious time he'd enjoyed the feeling of not caring what *anyone* thought.

Then Meredith had appeared. And suddenly who he was as a man, and what she thought of him, mattered more than ever.

And *that* was what was distracting him the most. It was going to be hard to get her out of his mind: he knew that the moment he first saw her.

He had spent his life since Meredith dating a series of women who were ill-suited for him. He preferred it that way. A fling was one thing, but he'd felt love before and he didn't ever want to feel it again. And he'd definitely avoided anyone who reminded him at all of Meredith. It was too painful.

At first it was a conscious effort, but soon it had become a habit. He dated blondes. He dated redheads. Deep black hair was fine.

But he never dated girls with that rich, chestnut-colored hair, or pale Irish skin, or laughing green eyes.

He thought of her, and how she had always applied herself completely to every task, whether it was studying for a history exam or helping a friend fill out a college application, or simply making that amazing sour-cream bread she used to make.

He doubted any of the women he had dated in the past decade could make their own breakfast, much less their own bread.

But he couldn't afford to make those comparisons now, or think of the things he had once loved about Meredith. Particularly now, when they were laboring through this frigid situation they had found themselves in.

Yet even while part of him resisted their new business relationship, he knew she would do the job well. He knew if anyone could help him succeed, it would be Meredith.

And they'd agreed that that was what they were going to do. They were going to work together and make the business succeed. Regardless of what had happened or not happened between them in the past.

The past was dead.

The future was short, at least here at Hanson Media.

All he needed to do was whatever he could to bring about the success of the radio division, then he could get the hell out of Chicago.

His thoughts returned to Lenny Doss. Sure, the guy was a bit of a renegade. He was definitely notorious. But Evan had faith that Lenny could keep his nose clean as far as the FCC regulations went. Lenny was brash, Lenny was bold, Lenny was crude, but Lenny was not stupid.

And he was popular.

Unable to sleep, Evan went to his desk and booted up his computer to check his e-mail. That seemed to be Lenny's preferred method of communication, so Evan decided he'd write to the guy and ask if he'd made a decision about the contract Evan had offered him.

Amidst what looked like a hundred spam messages offering everything from investment opportunities to physical enhancement, Evan found an e-mail from Lenny himself.

To: ehanson@hansonmediagroup.com
From: ossmanhimself@lennydoss.com
Subject: You've got competition, Bud!

Yo man! DigiDog Satellite Radio has given me a pretty sweet offer. You willing to up yours by 10% with a three-year guarantee? That's the only way you'll get the Doss Man.
LD

Evan muttered an oath.

He quickly typed DigiDog into a search engine. It turned out they were an up-and-coming satellite company and they were paying big bucks to acquire high-profile talent—which could certainly define Lenny Doss—as well as high-end music catalogs. A quick scan of the projected programming showed that DigiDog had expended a lot of money already on what was really an uncertain venture.

Lenny Doss's name, however, did not come up in a search of DigiDog. Not even in tangentially related articles in which programming directors talked about their dream lineups. So the question of whether anyone had actually approached Lenny Doss with a deal wasn't necessarily answered. They *might* have, but then again, it could have been a ploy on Lenny's part to work up Hanson Media's enthusiasm for him.

The problem was that Evan couldn't be sure which it was. And Evan was convinced that Lenny Doss was the first and most important step toward success for Hanson Broadcasting. He was sure of it.

After just several minutes' consideration, he came up with a plan.

"I'm taking Lenny Doss out for drinks tonight and you need to come with us and convince him to sign on with Hanson," Evan said to Meredith later that morning.

What he didn't say was *please,* though the word repeated itself in his mind.

"*What?* You're joking, right?"

"Nope. Dominick's on Navy Pier. Seven-thirty or so." He could already picture her there, in the soft light of Dominick's, wearing something—anything—other than her conservative work clothes.

"And you want me to come with you," she said incredulously, watching his brown eyes for signs that he was just pulling her leg. Especially given the heated conversation they'd already had about the wisdom of hiring Lenny Doss.

"Yes, I do," Evan said, straight-faced. She could always tell when he was joking, because even though he could keep his mouth still he always got a hint of a dimple on the left side. She used to think it was adorable.

There was no dimple now.

He wasn't kidding.

"Why would I do that, Evan?" she asked. "Why would I go out and actively try to hire a guy like that?"

"Because you know I want to bring him on board."

"And you know I'm adamantly against it."

"And you know you're wrong about that."

"I do not!"

"Well, I do." He took her by the arm and led her to his office, saying, "Technically, I'm your boss and you need to do what I ask you to."

She wrenched free of his grasp and said, "Yeah, well, technically, I'm not working for your department, so you have to clear this kind of thing with your stepmother, and I think if she reviewed both sides of this issue, she'd be inclined to agree with me."

"Not if she looked at the facts."

"What facts could possibly condone what he's done?" Meredith wanted to know.

Evan stopped walking and looked at her. "Nothing can *condone* what he's done, but his statistics are impressive and that makes him worth considering, even if you don't like his past."

"It's his future I'm concerned with."

They rounded the corner into Evan's office and he said, "That's why you need to consider *all* the facts, not just the Internet gossip you've looked up."

She shot him a look of disagreement, but he was right. She'd known as soon as he'd mentioned Lenny Doss's name that the guy was a ticking time bomb, so she'd gone online looking for evidence that proved her right, not evidence that proved her wrong.

Apparently Evan had done the opposite.

As usual.

"You've got to look at the statistics here." He sat her down in his chair and leaned across her to type an Internet address into his computer. "Check out the numbers on WRFK," he said, pointing at a chart on the computer screen. "This is about the time they moved from a regular news format to talk radio with Lenny Doss."

Meredith leaned forward and looked, taking the mouse in hand and moving around the chart a bit to get a more detailed picture. "What month did they hire him?" she asked, concentrating on the demographics and the charted increase in listeners.

"February." He pointed. "Right there."

"Mmm-hmm." She clicked on the date and checked for the entire programming schedule, to see if there was another reason that could account for all or some of the increase. "They also had religious programming on Sundays at that time," she pointed out half-heartedly. Religious programming virtually never pulled in big ratings.

"Check the ratings," Evan said, his voice ringing with smug confidence at what she'd find.

She checked. The religious programming had abysmal ratings. Worse than most. "Oh."

"Exactly."

Meredith frowned, looking for any evidence there might be that Evan was assigning too much credit to this one man. "When did they fire him?"

"They didn't."

"No?" Darn it, she should have armed herself with more specific information before meeting with Evan about this.

"He left for Gemini Broadcasting here." He pointed at the computer screen again, leaning so close across Meredith that she could smell not only his cologne but the achingly familiar scent of his skin. "In November of the following year."

"And the ratings went down," Meredith observed, so distracted by the close proximity of Evan that she almost couldn't concentrate on the matter at hand.

Evan, on the other hand, didn't appear to be having any such problem being close to Meredith. He gave a chipper nod, his face devoid of anything other than triumph that Meredith appeared to be seeing the light, now that he was shining it directly in her eyes. "The ratings went way down."

She went back to the search engine and typed in Gemini Broadcasting, just as Evan had a week earlier, and typed in the pertinent dates.

He waited a moment while she studied the higher ratings before saying, "See what I mean?"

She clicked off and rolled back in the chair to face him. "Yes, I do."

"But you're conflicted because, while you like what he could potentially do for the company, you don't like what he stands for," Evan said, trying to read the unaccustomed sternness in her eyes and her posture. Every time he got anywhere near her she tensed up and resisted whatever he was saying.

If she'd shown any form of emotion at all—which she hadn't—he'd have thought her reaction to him was personal.

As it was, he could only conclude that she hated Lenny Doss, or what he stood for, so much that she felt angry at Evan for even wanting to hire him and for pointing out that there were good things to be considered in the process.

"Right," she admitted, taking a short breath and moving slightly away from where Evan stood. The chair she was sitting in knocked against the desk behind her. "But as I've said before, I'm also hesitant about his potential as a liability. That's really important," she added.

"Fine. Check the e-mails he's written to me about that," Evan said, switching to another program and pulling up a folder in which he'd stored his correspondence with Lenny Doss. He kept a little more distance this time, not so much because he was afraid to get near her because of her reaction, but because he didn't want to see her react by recoiling again.

If she did, he'd know it was on purpose and not just some small coincidence, and he didn't want to know that. "Read them all, if it will make you feel better," he said, stepping back and going to the small refrigerator under the picture window to take out a bottle of spring water and give himself something to do other than just stand there gazing at Meredith and trying to figure out how the years had only made her prettier instead of older.

"Okay." She looked back at the screen. "Just give me a couple of minutes."

He hadn't thought she'd really do that, but it was nice to be away from her scrutiny for a moment, even though it seemed like forever that he stood there waiting for her to read through the e-mails.

One by one, date by date, she clicked through, stopping every once in a while to make a note on the small pad on his desk.

He noticed that her handwriting was still the same messy scrawl it had been in high school. Something about that small fact made him feel a little warmer inside.

A little more at home.

But that was all she gave in terms of comforting vibes. The rest of her was completely cool and impersonal. He tried to read the expression on her face, but though the face itself was undeniably familiar, some of the expressions she wore now were completely new to him. He had only his experience with people to go by, and he got the distinct and uncomfortable feeling that, for Meredith, this was all just standard business.

Finally she finished scrolling through the notes and turned the chair around to face Evan. Her green eyes were bright, probably from the sudden light change of looking from the computer monitor to Evan, and she said, "Okay, I will admit I *kind of* see your point."

He couldn't believe his ears. "You *agree* with me?"

"Wait a minute." She held up a slender hand. The left one, actually.

The one he'd once thought would wear his wedding and engagement rings.

"I didn't say I *agree* with you," she went on, blissfully ignorant of his disconcerting thoughts about their past. "There's still plenty we disagree about."

That hadn't always been the case.

"But I am saying," she continued, "that I see your point about his ratings and I understand why his contrition has given you confidence in potentially hiring him."

This was good. She was agreeing with him. Wasn't she? "So you'll come with me and meet him?"

She frowned, hesitating. Her delicate brow lowered toward those bright green eyes in a way that he hadn't seen in so long it made him ache to think about it.

"I'm not sure there's anything *I* could do to help you attain your goal."

"Come on, Mer," he said, catching the familiarity only afterward, when it was too late to stop himself. "You can charm the pants off him, that's what you can do. You're damn good at that."

She glanced at him sharply and said, "I don't think any of us wants that."

He had to be careful of this thinking about her personally, because obviously some part of his subconscious was having trouble distinguishing between the way he used to feel about her, back when they were just kids, versus what he felt for her now that they were nothing more than casual work associates.

What he needed to concentrate on was the success of his plan. Securing Lenny Doss and saving the company. The idea had taken hold and was mattering more and more to him. He couldn't say for sure if his desire was more a compulsion to help future generations who were innocent of his father's poison, or if he just wanted to "show up" the old man by saving the company that George had nearly destroyed.

He wanted both, but the balance tended to swing a little more toward the latter than the former.

Not that it mattered. Everyone involved had a common goal, and it didn't matter how they got there, did it?

"Okay, I'm sorry," he said. "But you know what I mean. There's a lot you can do to help persuade him, because you are a smart, beautiful wo—person. And you can present the case in a truthful and persuasive manner."

She faced him, looking surprised for a moment, then gave one conciliatory nod. "Your faith in me might be a little unfounded. But, fine, I'll do it."

"You'll go?" He couldn't believe it.

It was almost a date.

At least, the prospect of it made him feel as nervous as he would have if it was a first date. And he was seventeen.

"I'll go." She nodded again, that rich brown hair gleaming in the light. "But only to meet the guy and feel the situation out. I'm not promising I'm going to be buying a ticket for the Lenny Doss love train."

"Honey, that train doesn't even stop at this station," Evan said with a smile. He could have pulled her into his arms and kissed her at that moment, but he didn't.

This was business, he reminded himself. And everything that happened would remain just business, even if the look in her eyes or the curve of her mouth made him think of things that were distinctly unbusinesslike.

So he would take on the manner of the gregarious boss, enthusiastic about his work. "All we need to be concerned with is the Lenny Doss ratings train. And that—" he opened his arms "—is about to call Hanson Broadcasting its home station."

Chapter Eight

This was, of course, *not* a date. And they both knew it. So Meredith hated the impulse she had to make herself up for the evening.

More than that, she hated that she wasn't able to stop feeling the impulse.

Her mother had moved back to Tampa almost a year ago now, and Meredith was back in the suburban Chicago home she'd grown up in. It had made sense for her to move in, since her mother wasn't emotionally ready to let go of the house, yet wasn't physically able to maintain it any longer.

Meredith was back in Chicago for her work and, since she needed a place to live, the old house had fit the bill perfectly, though it was sometimes disconcerting to find herself having her Cheerios in the same old kitchen.

That was changing. Meredith wasn't the sort of person who could actually live in that kind of time warp. But renovation was going slowly, thanks in part to slow contractors and in part to Meredith's limited funds, so the house still looked very much as it had ten or twenty years ago.

This hadn't bothered her at all until now, when she was looking into a bathroom mirror that had reflected her image when it was that of a fresh-faced high-school girl getting ready for a date with the somewhat wild, but deep-down sweet, bad boy Evan Hanson himself.

"You shouldn't be going out with that kid," her father had told her one night as she was getting ready to go see the new Hal Burkett movie with Evan. "He comes from a bad family."

"Oh, Daddy, he doesn't come from a bad family. His father's just a bully, that's all."

Her father had snorted and it was only now that she understood the pain that had tightened his expression for a moment. "If the boy is anything like his father, you would do best to stay as far away from him as possible."

"He's really great, Daddy. Honest. You trust my judgment, don't you?"

"I don't trust anything where George Hanson's family is concerned."

She'd gone to him and hugged him tight, her arms closing too easily around a frame that used to have a lot more bulk to it. He wasn't healthy. He worked all the time. She worried about that.

"Evan must have had a wonderful mother, because he's one of the best guys I ever met. Besides you, of course. I know she's gone now, but he had her up until last year. That's a lot of time for him to learn to be something other than his father."

"You always see the best in people," her father had said with something like amazement. "But you have to believe me when I tell you that sometimes people are not what they seem. Trust, but always be at least a little cautious. Take care of yourself when I'm not there to do it for you."

She'd kissed his cheek. "I'll be fine, Daddy, I promise you."

Her own words had echoed tauntingly in her memory for some time after that.

Now look at her.

Life had changed a lot since those days, yet here Meredith was, still looking at the same old face—though somewhat older—in the same old mirror, trying to accent the same old green eyes and too-full lips to make the same old boy think she was pretty.

She had to be crazy.

Why did this matter so much to her?

It didn't, she told herself as she carefully brushed a mossy green shadow in a thin line along her lashes. Not too much, just enough to make her eyes stand out.

It made sense that she should look her best for a meeting with talent the company was trying to hire, didn't it?

So this wasn't really to impress Evan, she reminded herself as she struggled to bring her long, wavy, chestnut-colored hair under control with a ceramic flat iron. She merely wanted to look her best so that these men would take her seriously *professionally.* It would have been foolish for her to face them with the distraction of sleep-deprived pale skin and wild, unruly hair.

She had to make herself look like the sleek professional she was.

The clock ticked slowly forward as she

prepared for the evening. The truth was, the time seemed to be going extra slowly. It didn't take that long to do her makeup and hair, but she was so agitated about spending the evening out with Evan that she wanted to keep busy until it was time to leave.

Instead, she found herself dressed up with nowhere to go and nothing to think about other than Evan for an hour before she needed to leave for Navy Pier.

Meredith purposely waited in her car an extra few minutes before meeting Evan and Lenny Doss.

Evan had volunteered to pick her up and give her a ride, but she had declined, and though she couldn't say exactly why, it probably had a lot to do with the fact that it was weird enough seeing Evan again—she couldn't quite bring herself to look at him under the front porch light of her parents' house right now. It would be just too…eerie.

Besides, she wanted to maintain as much control over the situation as she could. And as she sat in the car watching the minutes tick away on the digital readout in the dash, she reminded herself that was exactly what she was doing.

Maintaining control.

Ten minutes past the time that her stomach began twisting and telling her to hurry up you can't be late she got out of her car, pushed the lock button on her key chain and walked at a measured pace to the restaurant.

Her biggest dread was being the first one there, sitting like an idiot alone at the table waiting for a man she had once known and loved.

Fortunately, both men in question were already there, sitting at a mercifully large round table with half-filled glasses of beer in front of them.

Evan looked amazing in a light-blue band collar cotton shirt and khakis that emphasized his physique without being so tight they looked like he was about to hit the dance floor for a disco contest.

Lenny, on the other hand, was wearing exactly that kind of pants: tight dark-blue jeans with a loud Hawaiian-print shirt that looked about two sizes too small and should have had at least three more buttons fastened in order to look acceptable, if not great.

"Meredith," Evan called when he saw her. He stood up and beckoned her over to the chair next to him.

Was it her imagination or did he looked relieved?

Meredith gave a smile of thanks to the hostess, took a short, bracing breath and smiled at the two men. "Hi there. I'm sorry if I'm late."

"Not at all," Evan said. "Please, sit down. This is Lenny Doss. Lenny, this is Meredith Waters. She works in the publicity department. She'll be helping us come up with some promotional ideas for your return to network broadcasting."

"Oh?" She shot Evan a questioning glance. "Did the two of you come to terms on a contract?"

"Not yet," Lenny said. "But now that I get a gander at the talent they got back at the office, I gotta say, I'm a little more inclined to sign."

Evan's ire was immediately up. "Hey—"

Meredith put a hand up to stop him. She could handle this herself, without ugliness. "It's the on-air talent that we're concerned with at the moment, Mr. Doss. Do you think you can really live up to our expectations?"

Lenny started posturing, exactly as she'd thought he would. "Just you watch," he said, sliding a hand through his slicked-back, thinning hair.

The waitress stopped by and discreetly took Meredith's order for a glass of Chardonnay.

"And can you keep yourself in line?" Meredith went on to Lenny. "It's my understanding that you've had a little trouble with that in the past. Hanson Media won't put up with you incurring FCC fines, you know."

"It's in the contract," Evan said to her quietly.

She was impressed. For a guy who'd never really worked in the business world, he was pretty good. She turned and gave him a quick wink.

"So what about it, Mr. Doss?" she asked, then took a sip of her wine. It was bitter. She hated wine, actually, but not as much as she hated beer or any of the other alternatives. And ordering a soda would have looked so prim and proper that a guy like this would probably have held it against her. "Should we give you a chance? And if so, why?"

He wasn't that easy, unfortunately. "The question is, should *I* give *you* a chance." He took a long swig of his beer then belched hideously. The look in his eyes was one of sheer pride. "And I'm not so sure about that yet."

Evan moved in his chair, effectively putting himself fractionally closer to Meredith. He didn't do it consciously, she could tell, but it was a protective move nevertheless.

And she found it comforting.

She sank, ever so slightly, against his presence and, bolstered by that, said to Lenny, "You're going to have to make up your mind, because we're in talks with Howard Stern, as well."

Lenny's eyes shot up to hers. "You are?" Then he frowned and said, "No way. No, you aren't."

"He costs more than you do," she said casually, taking a roll out of the basket in the center of the table. "But, as you know, he's got better ratings."

"Only because he's been in more markets."

She shrugged and pulled the roll apart, buttering half of it with deliberate slowness. "I don't know. We're just looking at the bottom line. Right, Evan?"

His brown eyes were bright with amusement. It looked as if he'd been planning to simply sit back and watch the conversation between Lenny and Meredith unfold, so when she mentioned his name it took a second for him to say, "Right. Bottom line. It's all about the bottom line."

Lenny's small dark eyes shot from Meredith to Evan and back again. She could practically see his mind working. "I hear that," he said, with much forced casualness. "Uh-huh." His cell phone rang—an aggressive measure from a Green Day song—and he pulled it out of his pocket and flipped it open. "Yo," he said into the phone. "Speak."

After a moment, he said, "Heeyyyy, Roberts." Meredith guessed by "Roberts" he was talking about Karl Roberts, his agent. "I'm just meeting here with Hanson and a chick from the publicity department. They're trying to talk me into signing but I don't know, man. What you got for me? Is Clear Channel Radio still nipping at us, too?" He flashed a self-satisfied glance at Evan and Meredith.

It disappeared quickly, though. "What's that?" Lenny asked. It may have been Meredith's imagination, but she thought she saw panic flicker in Lenny's eyes. "They're not?" He glanced in Evan's direction again and quickly turned away, saying, "So what's their offer?"

Another pause during which Lenny looked distinctly uncomfortable. "Interesting. But I want to wait and see what Hanson can come up with. It's not just about the money. I like these guys." He winked at Evan and Meredith. "You tell Clear Channel they're just going to have wait and see what I do with Hanson. I think they may pull through with the winning bid." He smiled, but his face had definitely paled a shade or two.

Meredith took the opportunity to turn to Evan and when she did she saw by the telltale dimple that he was holding back a smile. So he was clearly hearing everything she was, and they both knew they had Lenny Doss in their sights if they wanted him.

"All right, man," Lenny said, paling another shade. "There's more to a deal than just money. You let me finish talking to Hanson here and I'll give you a call back. In the meantime, you can tell Clear Channel to just cool their jets. We'll answer them when we're ready." He flipped the phone shut and put it back in his pocket, shaking his head and muttering, "Agents. Can't live with them, can't kill them."

Meredith smiled. "Was that your agent?" She knew it was, of course, and she was almost positive from all of Lenny's blustering and body language that Hanson was his only offer. She almost felt sorry for him.

Nevertheless, she had to play hardball.

Lenny nodded in answer to her question. He was clearly trying to appear ultracasual. "Yeah, he's going on about some other offer. But, as you may have heard, I'm interested in what Hanson's putting out there."

"You know what Hanson's putting out there," Evan said, then made a point of looking at his watch. "But listen, Len, I've got time constraints tonight, and I know Meredith is on her way someplace else, so I think we're going to have to wrap this up."

Meredith nodded, picking up Evan's cue. "That's right." She glanced at Evan. "Don't you have an appointment tomorrow to speak with…?" She mumbled a name that she hoped sounded like Artie Petro, one of Lenny's biggest competitors.

Evan picked right up on it. "Yes, I do."

They both turned to Lenny, who now looked like a raccoon caught going through the trash in the middle of the night.

"Then let's sign, man," he said loudly. "Let's get this show on the road."

"Okay, then." Evan smiled. "We'll get the contracts to your agent tomorrow."

"Great. Got another appointment," Lenny said. "This one's personal, if you know what I mean." He gave Evan a lascivious wink.

"I know *exactly* what you mean," Evan told him evenly, his voice hard but tinged with humor.

Meredith had to suppress a giggle.

Lenny nodded, oblivious. “Monday morning, 6:00 a.m. shift?”

“You’ve got it,” Evan said.

Meredith was amazed at how soon Evan had him slated to start, but she said nothing.

“Great.” Lenny gave a bobbing nod. “So, it was cool meeting you,” he said to Meredith. “Evan, man, I look forward to working with you.”

“Same here,” Evan said. “You just make sure you keep yourself in line. Don’t forget paragraph eleven.”

Lenny looked blank. “Paragraph eleven?”

Evan nodded. “The contract you’re about to sign. Paragraph eleven says you pay all FCC fines you incur and that incurring such a fine makes our side of the contract null and void.”

“Oh, that.” Lenny waved a hand, but there was a nervousness in his eyes that he couldn’t hide. “Don’t worry about a thing,” he assured them. “I’ll be walking the straight and narrow. No problem.”

“You’re sure?” Meredith interjected worriedly. She’d never, ever been able to keep her straight-and-narrow self in check for long and now she followed her compulsion to make sure

Lenny would be inoffensive, even though she knew—she *knew,* darn it—that she was supposed to be playing it cool.

Lenny looked at her and—she could have sworn—looked empowered by the fear he'd heard in her voice. "Oh, sure," he said, with a confidence he hadn't displayed for the past fifteen minutes or so. "The Doss Man can do whatever he wants."

"Then I hope you want to succeed with Hanson," Evan said, his voice free of any signs of tension or worry. "Because that's what we have in mind."

Meredith sat and watched, ashamed of her momentary exhibition of insecurity and grateful for the fact that Evan seemed to have recovered the situation.

"So I'll be seein' ya, man," Lenny said. "And hopefully you, too," he said to Meredith, making a grand gesture of reaching for her hand and giving it a gallant medieval kiss. "Here's to our future."

She nodded and gave her most winning smile because she couldn't think of one clever or appropriate thing to say. "Welcome to Hanson," she said lamely. "I look forward to your success."

"Aw, honey, you can count on it." Lenny

tipped an imaginary cap and hauled his behind out of the bar, presumably hoping to leave his audience in awe.

Little did he know their thoughts would soon have far less to do with business than with pleasure.

Chapter Nine

Once Lenny Doss was gone, Evan and Meredith looked at each other and smiled with triumph.

"That was brilliant," Evan said, reaching for what had to be a warm beer by now. He took a gulp and set it down on the table with a bang. "Acting like at the last minute you were uncertain of the wisdom of hiring him?" He smiled, and his smile melted her heart. Or her libido. Or *something* deep inside her. "That, Ms. Waters, was genius. Pure genius."

She took just a fraction of a moment to bask in his praise before saying, "I didn't mean to do that."

Why was she confessing? Evan was impressed with her performance. She'd made a Hanson executive feel she was doing a good job. Why blow it by admitting it had almost ruined everything by a misstep? "But I'm glad it worked out."

"We make a good team," Evan said, still smiling at her. His eyes met hers and his smile faded slightly at the corners. "We always did," he added earnestly.

It would have been easy for her to come up with a smart-aleck retort but they'd fought about the past enough already. It was foolish of her to keep holding on to that when it was so long ago. She'd lived through it, grown up, finished her education, gotten a life. It wasn't the end of her life and she shouldn't act as if it was.

"That is assuming Lenny Doss is a good acquisition," she pointed out. "We may have just put a nail in Hanson Media Group's coffin."

Evan shook his head. "No way. Your instincts told you the same thing mine told me—this guy's a blowhard, but he's a blowhard with an audience. And he wants to keep his job this time." He finished his beer and put the bottle down with a hollow clatter. "Do you want anything else?" he asked, gesturing at her half-consumed wine.

"No, thanks."

It was clear he was wrapping the meeting up, and that gave Meredith a strange feeling of disappointment. She watched him gesture toward the waitress and indicate he wanted the bill.

Meredith sat back in her chair, a little unsure what to do with herself. Part of her wanted to stay with him for just a few more minutes, looking at that handsome face by the flattering light in the restaurant, but logic finally prevailed. "I'd better get going," she said, standing up and picking up her purse.

"Got a date?" Evan asked uneasily.

She smiled, without committing. "I just need to get some sleep, Evan."

"Alone?" That half smile was on his face, making her wonder if he actually cared a little or not at all.

"That's none of your business."

"I'll take that as a no."

"Take it however you want," she said, trying to sound flip but failing miserably.

"Then how about I at least walk you to your car?" he suggested.

By then they were both standing, and he put his hand on her elbow to guide her out of the restaurant.

It would have been difficult for her to deny

him that, since all he was asking was to take her to the car. It wasn't as if she could claim that an escort would slow her down so much she'd miss out on her imaginary date.

"Fine," she said. "Thanks."

"Look," Evan said, as they walked outside into the muggy summer air. Navy Pier was alive with activity, and high above them the clear night sky shone with diamondlike stars. "I know this isn't the ideal situation for you, working with me. And, truthfully, I never thought I'd be back here at all, much less asking you to help me save the company. Nevertheless, I think we did a good job together tonight. Maybe Helen was on to something when she asked you to work with me."

Meredith took a short breath inward. "Do you think she knew about our history? Did you tell her anything?"

Evan scoffed. "I hadn't talked to my father since—" he hesitated "—well, since I left, all those years ago. And probably not for a couple of weeks before that. I definitely didn't talk to Helen. Hell, she didn't show up until after I was gone."

That was true. All of Meredith's research confirmed that. Evan was merely a family member, called in at the last moment to try to salvage a company that wasn't entirely salvageable.

At least, not under its current administration.

"Do you think it was to her advantage or her disadvantage that you and I were...previously acquainted?" she couldn't resist asking. But she shouldn't have asked. She knew that from years ago: never ask a question you're not willing to hear the honest answer to.

Evan looked at her, considering. His brown eyes were warm, like melted chocolate, and Meredith figured it was the result of the beer he'd had rather than his proximity to her. "I think it was to her advantage," he said at last. "*Our* advantage, the entire company," he clarified. "You and I have a certain shorthand between us, I think. It helps in a situation like tonight's."

"Shorthand?" she repeated dumbly, though she thought she knew what he meant.

"We understand each other." He must have seen something in her that resisted that idea because he added, "Just a little bit. A little better than strangers would, anyway."

Meredith wasn't ready to agree with any of this, so instead she just let out a long sigh and said, "Maybe. I guess whatever works, we shouldn't justify it one way or the other."

Evan appeared taken aback by this, but after just a fraction of a moment, he nodded. "Yup, whatever works."

They were outside the restaurant now, close enough to hear the raucous music inside, yet far enough to feel distance from the merriment it brought most of the patrons.

Meredith turned her most confident smile on Evan. "I can get to my car myself," she said. "But thanks for thinking to walk me out, I really appre—"

She wasn't able to finish her sentence before a small, thin man—maybe a teenager—rushed past her like a cartoon villain, grabbing her purse and yanking it off her arm with such force that she actually fell to the ground.

"Meredith!" Evan was at her side in a moment. "Are you all right?"

"Yes, but—" she panted "—he took my bag. My license, credit cards…" The realization hit her like a ton of bricks. "He has my address."

"Wait here," Evan instructed, immediately on guard. "Or go back in the restaurant. I'll come back and find you."

"No, Evan, don't try to catch him," Meredith objected. "He might have friends, accomplices—"

"I don't care if he's got Tony Soprano himself waiting in the wings, he's not getting away with this."

Before she could object—and she was ready to—he had taken off, running like a thoroughbred into the night, so fast that she only saw him for a moment before he literally disappeared into the darkness.

Evan Hanson had failed her before, back when it really mattered, but now—at a time when she was at war with her memories—suddenly he was a knight in shining armor.

As soon as he was back safely and she could stop worrying that he was going to get hurt, she'd have to figure out what to think about that.

And whether she wanted to do anything about it.

It was a cheap shot.

Evan almost had him, his hand was just *inches* away from at least grabbing Meredith's purse back, if not actually clobbering the guy who took it, but apparently the mugger had an accomplice waiting for him. As he approached an alleyway he shouted something that sounded like "Yo, Carmen!" and another guy—much bigger than the first—stepped out of the shadows and sank his fist into Evan's cheekbone.

The impact stunned Evan, and he was pretty sure that for a few minutes he looked like a cartoon character, wobbling around, disoriented.

Then the guy grabbed him by the shirt—Evan heard a loud rip—and head-butted him just for good measure.

By the time he righted himself, the two assailants were long gone.

His pride might as well have been in Meredith's stolen purse as he went back to where she still stood, wringing her hands and waiting for him.

"I'm sorry," he said, holding his arms out to the side as he approached her. "They got away."

"They?"

Evan nodded as he approached. "Our pal had a friend waiting for him back by some trash dumpsters behind Melville's."

She looked at him in horror. "Oh, Evan—"

"The guy got me when I wasn't looking," he said, shaking his head. "Turns out I'm not as young or as fast as I used to be." In truth the shock on her face made him feel that much more ashamed. He *should* have been able to overtake one guy and get her bag back. "I'm sorry, Meredith."

Her eyes were still wide. "We've got to get you cleaned up, quick."

"Nah." He waved her off. "Don't worry about it. It's just a ripped shirt." He looked down, expecting to see his shirt torn open to the navel, but instead he saw his light-blue shirt had a large dark stain down the front.

Blood.

Reflexively he lifted his hand to his cheek. As soon as he did, he felt the wide gash and the slick, warm, sticky blood running from it.

That was when it *really* started to hurt.

He swore under his breath.

"You can say that again," Meredith said, moving toward him and hooking her arm through his. "My car's just in the lot over there. Do you think you can make it?"

Her touch felt nice on him, and part of him really wanted to go with her, but it wasn't necessary. "My car's just a couple of blocks away," he said. "I can get to it, don't worry."

"You are *not* driving yourself," Meredith said firmly.

"Well, I'm not bleeding all over your car."

"I've got tissues in my glove box."

Evan laughed. "That ought to take care of it."

Meredith gave him a stern look. "It will until we get you to the hospital."

"Oh, no. No way. I'm *not* going to the hospital. This is just—" he touched his cheek again and winced at the pain "—it's just a flesh wound. By tomorrow it will be invisible."

Meredith snorted and pushed him along toward her car. "Yeah, because it will probably be under more bandages than Boris Karloff had in *The Mummy*."

"That was Brendan Fraser," Evan joked.

"No, I mean the original, and anyway, Brendan Fraser wasn't the mummy in that movie, he was—" She stopped, seeing the look on his face. "Okay, you got me."

"You're so easy."

She halted in front of a small green Japanese economy car. "Yeah, well, you'll be sorry when I clean that gaping wound up with hydrogen peroxide. I may need to go over it a couple of times, just to be sure, you understand."

He groaned and got into the passenger seat where she'd pretty much pushed him. "I understand."

She shut the door and hurried over to the driver's side, her quick steps betraying her nervousness at the whole situation. Blood. Wounds. It was horrible.

"Evan, I really think we should go to the emergency room. That looks like it might need stitches."

He shook his aching head. "No, Meredith. I'm not going to wait in some overcrowded waiting room all night for treatment I could give myself."

She started the car and drove to the intersection with the main road. "Where do you live?"

It was a question he wasn't prepared to answer.

"Evan?" she prompted, when several seconds had passed and he hadn't answered yet.

How could he tell her he was sleeping in his office without sounding like a pitiful loser? Even though it made perfect sense to him because he wasn't sure he'd be sticking around long and he didn't want to commit to a year-long lease of an apartment or condo when he might be gone in a month, saying the truth right out loud to Meredith was embarrassing at best.

But there was no way around it without sounding as if he didn't want her to know where he lived.

Which, of course, he didn't.

"If you drop me on the next corner I can just take the El."

Meredith slowed the car and turned to look at him, her left eyebrow raised. "You want me to drop you off so you, looking like that—" she made a point of looking him over "—can simply get on public transportation, frightening old ladies and small children and possibly passing out and spending the night riding aimlessly from station to station until you finally bleed to death."

He gave a half smile. "You make that sound like it's a bad idea."

She rolled her eyes. "Come on, Evan, pony up. What's the address?"

He hesitated a moment, then gave it.

She started to drive, then stopped, pulled the car over and put the transmission in park. "That's the office."

He nodded. "That's true."

"Are you trying to avoid telling me where you live, for some reason?"

He shook his head. "No, I *was* trying to avoid telling you where I live, for the simple reason that I know it sounds odd, but now you've forced it out of me."

"You live at the office."

"At the moment, yes."

"Are you serious?"

"Don't I look serious?"

"You look frightening."

He gave a concessionary nod. "That's serious."

She gripped the wheel and looked straight ahead without moving. Finally she said, "I'm going to have to take you to my house."

Evan gave a laugh. "You are taking this way, *way* too seriously. Look, just take me back to the office. I'll go clean up, slap a bandage on and be fine. Honestly, Mer, I've been in worse condition than this before. I know what I'm talking about."

Something passed between them. Whether it was surprise at his use of the old nickname, Mer, or horror at having to deal with such an indelicate situation, or simply irritation at realizing how many calls she was going to have to make to cancel credit cards, checks and so on, Evan wasn't sure.

But it sure felt…familiar.

"Evan," she said. "I think I can actually see your cheekbone through that cut."

"Oh, come on."

"God knows what I'll see in good light." She took a short breath, put the car back in gear and merged into the traffic on Lake Shore Drive. "We can clean you up at my place," she said. "If it still looks as awful as I think it's going to, I'm going to make you go to the hospital."

He knew it wouldn't, so it was an easy thing to agree to. "Fair enough."

"Okay." She drove on, and he watched her from his convenient vantage point beside her. She had to keep her eyes on the road, so he could study her profile as closely as he wanted, for as long as he wanted.

So he did.

"What are you looking at?" she asked almost immediately, glancing sideways at him.

"You," he answered softly.

"I know that. Why?"

He shifted his weight in the seat, trying to get more comfortable. "Why do you think? Because I used to know your face better than I knew my own and seeing it again after all these years is fascinating."

She shook her head. "The aging process in action."

"You're not aging, you're maturing—"

She scoffed.

"Now, wait a minute, you didn't let me finish. You've matured from a cute girl into a really beautiful woman," he said, meaning every single word of it.

In fact, he meant it more than he could say. And the realization of what he'd missed the past twelve years hit him fully, like a blow to the gut. He should have been with her through all the changes. He should have been the shoulder she cried on when her father died; he should have seen her blow out the candles on her twenty-first birthday cake; he should have been the one to put those first faint smile lines around her eyes.

There was so much he should have done for her. And with her.

So much that could never be regained.

"You're a really, seriously beautiful woman, Meredith," he found himself saying. "In every way."

Even in the dark of the car, he could tell her pale Irish skin had pinkened several shades. She tipped her head down—a gesture he'd seen her make a thousand times—so her veil of chestnut hair hid her face, at least from where he was sitting now.

"I don't know what to say, Evan."

"It's a pretty standard compliment," he said.

"'Thanks' would do. Or nothing. Nothing would do, too."

She gave a half laugh. "Thanks."

He smiled to himself. A few weeks ago, he'd had no idea he'd ever see Meredith Waters again. Then, when he first did, their interaction had filled him with dread and residual adolescent awkwardness.

But tonight something had changed.

Or maybe something had clicked into place.

Because until he'd gotten punched in the face, he'd thought he and Meredith were going to be these strange semiacquainted former lovers—until he left and she would thank the good Lord he was finally gone.

Now…it was hard to describe. But now he felt like something inside him was complete again.

Evan stayed lost in his thoughts as they drove through the familiar-yet-unfamiliar streets of his childhood. It was odd, but he still knew the timing exactly. Left on Travilia Road, left again onto Denton, bear right onto Farm Ridge, then turn left onto…

Village Crest Avenue.

Was he hallucinating?

"Meredith, where are you going?" he asked, feeling the beginnings of alarm in his chest.

"My house."

Well, yeah. Her house. Sure. He'd been there hundreds of times. He'd known the answer even before he asked the question. But the thing was, he knew it wasn't her house anymore. She'd grown up, graduated from high school, graduated from college, moved on with her life.

So clearly, either she meant something else or he was dreaming.

For a crazy second he actually wondered what year it was. The song on the radio was an old one, so that didn't help. The houses, well, they all looked the same. So that didn't help, either.

"Who's the president?" he asked stupidly.

"The president of what?"

"The United States?"

"What?"

He swallowed. It was a dumb question. He wasn't time traveling. She was just driving to her parents' house for some reason that would make sense in a few minutes.

Maybe she was driving him there because she didn't want him to know where she really lived. Or maybe she felt as if she needed help. Hell, she might have just been afraid to be alone with him. The way he probably looked, he couldn't blame her.

But now she was looking at him with something more than concern. "Okay, that's it, we need to go to the hospital *now.* I think you have a concussion."

"I don't," he said immediately, though of course he couldn't be sure.

"Then you're crazy and in need of psychiatric help. Evan, you're asking me who the *president* is!"

"I know, I was kidding. Sort of. It's just that I could swear you're driving me to…" He didn't finish his sentence. He didn't have to. She'd pulled up right in front of it.

Her parents' house.

Looking exactly as it had the last time he'd seen it, twelve and a half years ago.

Prom night.

The night he'd left Chicago and the girl of his heart, and thought it was for good.

Chapter Ten

When seeing Evan in the office, Meredith had managed to somehow separate her memories of him from the reality they were living today.

But pulling up outside the house she'd lived in when she'd dated him in high school—a house she'd only been back in for a short time now—she felt as if she were time traveling.

From the look on Evan's pale face, he was clearly feeling the same thing.

"I bought the place from my mother when she moved to Florida last year," she explained.

He looked relieved. "For a minute there, I thought I was going nuts."

She took the keys out of the ignition and said, "For a minute there, I thought you were going nuts, too."

"Thanks."

She loved his dry humor. "I should have put a Pixies CD on and asked how you did on your term paper," she continued. "As long as we didn't pass a Hummer or something, I probably could have had you going."

"You're cute," he said, getting out of the car. "Real cute."

"Uh-oh, I've been demoted." She singled out her house key as they stepped onto the front porch. "A few minutes ago you said I was beautiful."

He pointed at his head. "I was injured. I didn't know what I was saying."

"Ah." She put the key in the lock and clicked it open. "Good excuse."

They stepped into the cool, air-conditioned foyer.

Evan looked around as if he was in a time warp.

"I know," she said. "I have to redecorate. I just haven't had time. You remember where the kitchen is?"

He nodded. "Sure."

"Go on in and have a seat. I'll run and get the first-aid kit, then meet you there."

She rushed upstairs on legs that were shaking. Evan looked bad. He looked really bad. And it was all her fault, she thought, scrambling into the bathroom and throwing the cabinet doors open. Her father had always told her she had to be *way* more careful walking around downtown Chicago. He'd warned her over and over again that she was too lax about things like personal safety.

She, in turn, had told him he was paranoid, that she'd be *fine* and he just had to stop worrying so much.

She pushed around in the cabinet, moving cleaning supplies, curlers, half-used bottles of shampoo, until she finally found the white plastic box with the red cross on the front. It was about a thousand years old, but she doubted anything in it had ever been opened.

She grabbed a washcloth to clean Evan's face, thought about the amount of blood, and put the washcloth down in favor of a full-size bath towel.

Thus armed, she hurried back downstairs to the kitchen, where Evan was sitting on a stool by the counter, shirtless, still looking around in a bemused way.

He'd already cleaned the blood off his cheek and while the wound was a bit less dramatic than she'd thought, it was still more dramatic than he'd indicated. He had folded a square of paper towels that he was using to alternately apply and release pressure.

"I threw my shirt away," he said, in answer to her unasked question. "I figured it was less rude of me to sit here half-naked than to sit here in a disgusting bloody shirt."

"Good call," she said, but her mouth was suddenly dry.

His upper body was far more muscular and developed than it used to be, cut and contoured with sinewy muscle. His skin was bronzed from the sun of wherever it was he'd been this past decade, and he looked like he'd just stepped out of the pages of a *Sports Illustrated* sun-and-surf edition.

"Does it hurt?" she asked, pouring antiseptic onto a cotton pad.

"It doesn't tickle," he said, eyeing the pad dubiously.

"Neither will this," she said, gently pressing the antiseptic to the wound.

Evan cussed and drew back.

"I'm sorry!" Meredith stepped back. "It's a necessary evil. You don't want to get an infection."

He gave a rueful smile. "I'm not sure about that. It might hurt less than this."

"Yeah, until your face turns green and falls off. Come on." She put her hand on his head, her fingers touching his dark hair for the first time in ages. She swallowed, took a quick, steadying breath and said, "On the count of three."

"Don't you want to say 'this is going to hurt you a lot more than it's going to hurt me'?"

She smiled. "Sort of, but I'll refrain."

"Thank you." He winced as she put the antiseptic to his face again.

Once it was cleaned up some, a closer examination of the wound revealed that it actually wasn't quite as bad as Meredith had feared. It probably didn't need stitches. "I think one of these sealing bandages will be good enough," she said to Evan.

"I told you it wasn't so fatal."

She shrugged and took a bandage out of the first-aid kit and unwrapped it. "If it were me, I'd still go to the E.R. and make sure I don't need stitches. You might end up with a scar."

"My face isn't as pretty as yours to begin

with." He grinned. "Besides, a scar would make me look more rugged, don't you think? I'll have to make up a story that's a lot cooler than being outrun and sucker punched by a couple of punks, though. Maybe I could say I killed a guy defending a nun and a group of orphans. *Ouch!*"

"Sorry." Meredith grimaced. "It wasn't on smoothly."

"Jeez, did any skin come up with that bandage?"

"Don't worry, I've got another one." She smiled and put a new bandage on neatly. "There. Good as new. Almost."

He reached a hand up to touch the spot and grazed her hand instead. For a moment they lingered, fingertip to fingertip, and something coursed through Meredith's chest with the power of a freight train.

She drew her hand back and tried to look as if she hadn't noticed the accidental contact or felt the intense reaction.

Evan touched the spot on his cheek. "Perfect." He looked into her eyes. "You could have a future in nursing."

"I hope not," she said absently, still thinking about his touch. "I'm already working two jobs." As soon as the words left her lips, Meredith clapped her mouth shut. How could she be so stupid? She was *never* that unprofessional. It was *absolutely imperative* that she keep her secrets under wraps. And Evan Hanson was the last person in the world she should let her guard down in front of.

There was so much he must never know.

"Two jobs?" he asked, of course.

She thought fast. "Yes, working for Hanson Media and working with you." The explanation wasn't hard to come up with, but trying to make her voice sound light and casual was almost impossible.

He laughed. "I see. I'm a whole additional problem, huh?"

She let out a tense breath. He'd bought it. Thank God. "I can't believe it's the first time you've heard something like that."

"Hell, Meredith, it's not even the first time I've heard something like that from *you*."

Thank goodness he was good-humored about it, but she really hadn't wanted to insult him. "I was only joking, Evan. You're not *that* bad."

"You're not so bad yourself." His brown eyes caught hers again and held.

Meredith's breath caught in her chest and lodged there like an iron fist. She couldn't breathe, couldn't even move, for fear of stopping something that she knew in her mind should never happen.

He was going to kiss her.

She *wanted* him to kiss her.

His gaze lingered one, two, three beats longer than she expected. Inside, she squirmed under it, hoping like a schoolgirl that he wanted her as much as she wanted him.

Finally, without saying a word, he scooped her into his arms and put his mouth over hers.

A small voice inside of her resisted, almost begging her to pull back before it was too late. Meredith knew herself well enough to know that she had never been able to resist Evan, no matter how hard she'd tried. Though years had passed and granted her more self-control where Twinkies and pizza were concerned, it seemed she still had an irresistible weakness for Evan Hanson.

She sank against him and deepened the kiss, momentarily heedless of good sense. Lots of time had passed since they'd last met like this, and part of Meredith still held the energy of waiting for him. It was as if she was righting some long-standing wrong—even though she knew in reality she couldn't do that.

Still, she could have kissed Evan for a week. A month. A year.

Twelve years.

Evan held a piece of her that had been missing all that time.

His mouth moved gently across hers, tentatively feeling for her reactions, clearly reaching the end of his ability to stop.

She didn't want him to.

His tongue touched hers, and every nerve in her body tightened like strings on a dulcimer. She ran her hands up his back, languishing in the feel of his muscled back beneath her touch, until she reached his upper back and pulled him closer to her.

Closer, something in her cried to him. *Come closer. Don't let go. This time, never let go.*

He ran strong hands down to the small of her back, holding her firmly against him. She felt safe in his embrace. It felt right. When his fingertips slipped under her shirt and pressed against her lower back, the feel of his skin touching hers in such an intimate way made her wild with desire.

As if reading her thoughts, he dipped his hand lower, sending shivers of pleasure through her core.

As Evan's mouth moved against hers and his hands played against her skin and held her close to him, Meredith felt the ache that had sat hollow in her stomach for so long finally beginning to ease.

The voice within her still tried to insist that this was wrong, that Evan had betrayed her heartlessly before and he might well do it again, but it didn't matter what she thought was wrong.

It only mattered what she felt was right.

Whoa, what was she *thinking?* Since when did Meredith Waters allow herself to do something she knew was wrong?

She pulled back abruptly. "I forgot to ask if you wanted some ibuprofen or something."

Evan looked surprised. "I'm good, thanks." He reached for her again, but she stepped back.

"Shot of whiskey?" she tried halfheartedly. "You must need something for the pain."

"No, really, Meredith, I'm fine." He eyed her, and hesitated before adding with finality, "In fact, I should call a cab or something and get out of your hair."

"No," she said quickly. Too quickly. "Evan, there's no way I'm letting you go back to sleep in the *office,* for crying out loud. You need to stay here."

He did a slight double take. “Stay here? Where here?”

“Here. Up in the guest room. In fact, you can have your pick of three guest rooms.”

He raised an eyebrow. “Any of them?” he asked with a lascivious grin.

She smiled lightly. “As long as it’s not already occupied.”

He snapped his fingers in mock disappointment. “I hate to sleep alone.”

“Yeah, and I’m guessing you haven’t had to do it that often, either.” She was joking, but something about the words stuck in her craw a little bit.

“More than you’d think, Meredith,” he answered, his voice serious.

Their eyes met, and a frisson of energy zapped between them.

She could have thrown herself right back into his arms and kissed him until she forgot about every other thing in her life and in the outside world, but she knew better.

She had to keep *reminding* herself, of course, but she definitely knew better.

“Anyway,” she said pointedly. “The fact is that tonight you’ll be sleeping alone and you’ll be doing it here.”

"That's really not necessary."

"What kind of person would let someone risk life and limb to get a stupid purse back and then just send him on his way?" She shook her head. "Not me. Now get upstairs, mister. You need to rest."

He stood up and faltered, losing his balance ever so slightly, but enough for her to say, "See? That proves my point."

"Yes, ma'am."

"I have some big old T-shirts," she went on. "I'll get you one and you can sleep in that."

"I sleep naked," he said, a sly grin playing on his lips. "Have you forgotten?"

She sucked in a breath. No, she hadn't forgotten. When she was sleeping with him, *she* slept nude as well.

It saved time.

But she wasn't going to think about that and she wasn't going to give Evan any indication that she'd thought about it, so she simply said, "I thought the circumstances might make you more modest."

"The circumstances are making me more…" He shook his head. "Well, anyway, I get the point."

"Good. Keep it covered. There's a bathrobe on the door of the bathroom. You can put that on and toss me your jeans and…everything. I'll wash them."

"You really don't have to do that."

"Stop saying that. Just give me the clothes, would you?"

"You've sure gotten bossy over the years."

"Evan."

He put his hands up in surrender. "Okay, okay, I hear you. I'll strip for you. No problem."

She sighed. "You know all that stuff I said about being able to work with you?"

"Uh-huh."

"I'm starting to think I should ask for a raise." She smiled. "They're not paying me enough for this."

He laughed. "I'll talk to the boss on your behalf."

"Good." She led him to the bottom of the staircase. "Now go. Toss your stuff down to me when you've got it off."

"Fine." He made his way up the stairs and she leaned against the wall and waited for him.

About two minutes later he tossed his things down and said, "No starch!"

It was going to be a long night.

Chapter Eleven

It was a strange feeling having Evan Hanson sleeping in her house.

A very strange feeling.

As Meredith sat by the washer and dryer, waiting for them to complete their cycles so she could take Evan's clothes to his room and go to sleep, she had to keep reminding herself that this was all really happening.

There was once a time when she would never have imagined herself forgiving him and facing him again, but that was fading now. It wasn't Evan's fault that her father's business had been ruined, it was George Hanson's. The more she dug around Hanson Media Group, and the more people she spoke with, the more obvious it was that he had been a completely ruthless businessman for whom nothing was personal and everything had been war.

Now, instead of blaming Evan for his father's misdeeds, she pitied him for having had that sort of man for a father. As rough as it was to compete with him in business, it had to be almost as rough to live up to his standards as a son.

As a matter of fact, she remembered some of Evan's struggle with George Hanson. Not that Evan had talked about it much, but he'd gone through periods of quiet introspection that had worried her sometimes, and it wasn't until she'd drawn him out that she knew it was because of his father's heavy hand.

For her, it was just one more thing to hate about George Hanson.

When she'd taken this job, she'd thought it would be easy because of the unpleasant connotations she had with the Hanson family name. She thought she'd feel no hint of conscience or betrayal because any personal warm feelings she'd had for anyone in the family had long since died and been replaced by the opposite.

In a way it had seemed like the perfect opportunity to get back at them, even though they'd never know it was her.

Now...well. Now things were getting a little more complicated. She'd still do her job; she was nothing if not professional.

But she was going to have to get some perspective where Evan was concerned. And that she would get by reminding herself how, even though he didn't have anything to do with the greatest tragedy of her life—her father's ruin and death—he was *directly* responsible for the greatest heartbreak of her life.

There was no way around that one.

The dryer stopped and she took the warm jeans out. Size 32 waist. He'd filled out.

But of course she knew that.

She started up the stairs and remembered a conversation she'd had with him once. The memory hit her with crystal clarity and hit her so hard she had to stop and sit down.

They'd snuck out in the night once because it had seemed so romantic. It had been her idea, as she recalled, but Evan had indulged her. He'd come to her window at 2:00 a.m. and she'd climbed down the trellis, just like a cliché in a movie.

It was summer, and hot. Even the nights were hot, and the air was damp with humidity. They'd gone to a small private cove he knew of on Lake Michigan and they'd sat on the beach and talked for hours.

She couldn't remember most of what they'd said. It was a lot of talk about their pasts, their dreams and the other typical things that kids that age could expound upon.

She remembered the night specifically because a quick but wild thunderstorm had come out of the blue, interrupting the clear starry night with about ten minutes of drama.

Kissing in that thunderstorm had been one of the most romantic moments of her life.

It was amazing that she could remember anything else, but she did. Evan had asked her if her father had ever thought about selling his newspaper business.

"I don't know. Why?"

Evan had shrugged. But now, when she saw it again in her memory, she realized he had looked tense.

"Just seems like a really competitive business. I've heard sometimes it gets ugly, one paper accusing another of publishing lies and whatnot. It's hard for a newspaper to come back after that kind of accusation."

She'd laughed—laughed!—seeing no significance in what he was saying at all.

"Oh, come on, Evan, no one takes that stuff that seriously. Look at all the tabloids at the grocery store that say aliens are walking among us. Everyone knows they're full of lies, but they're still in business."

"It's different, Meredith. I wouldn't want to be in the news business for anything. I'd hate to see a nice guy like your dad get into trouble in business."

"As long as he keeps the aliens off the front page, he'll be fine." She could remember saying that, because then she'd looked up and seen a shooting star.

She'd wished for a long, happy future with Evan.

Maybe the star had been an alien.

She started up the stairs with his warm clothes now, playing and replaying his words in her head. How on earth had she forgotten that hugely significant conversation until now?

Or, on the other hand, how had she remembered it at all? Given how little thought she'd put into it at the time, and how many other things had happened that night that were a lot more interesting to the mind of a teenage girl, she was amazed that it was still in her head at all.

She wondered if Evan remembered.

She stopped at the door to the guest room she'd directed him to and knocked softly.

No answer.

Slowly she opened the door and peeked in. Light from the bathroom spilled in and she could see he was on his side, breathing softly and rhythmically.

She set his clothes down on the dresser and started to leave but then she turned back.

As if watching someone else, and completely incapable of stopping them, she walked back over to the side of the bed and looked down at him. She told herself she just wanted to make sure he seemed all right, in case he had a concussion, but the truth was she wanted to be closer to him, to see him without his knowing it.

It might have been ten minutes that she stood there, looking at that handsome face half hidden by the shadows of the night. It was a face she'd thought about many times over the years. At first with love, then later with pain and confusion, then finally with anger.

Now she wasn't sure how she felt.

And that scared her more than anything.

She turned to leave and stepped on a creaky floorboard that protested loudly.

She froze, listening for the even breath of his sleep.

Instead she heard his voice. "Meredith?"

She turned back to him. "I just brought your clothes back. They're on the dresser."

He looked through sleepy eyes at the dresser across the room, then back at her by the bed and clearly not anywhere near the clothes.

"Then I came to check on you and make sure you were breathing normally," she explained in answer to his unasked question. "You know, all the typical concussion checks. Steady breathing, ability to wake up. Congratulations, you passed."

He sat up in bed and the sheets fell away from him, revealing a bare torso.

So much for the T-shirts she'd offered him.

And so much for her resolve to keep a professional distance from him. This was a sight that would easily fuel the romantic fantasies of any red-blooded American woman, and it was right here in her own house.

"Thanks," he said. "Am I okay?"

"I think you'll live."

"Can't ask for more than that, I guess."

This was hard, all this small talk in a room filled with such big tension.

"If there's nothing you need, I'll be going to sleep now," she said to him. She swallowed. "Do you need anything?"

Three heartbeats passed.

"There is one thing…."

"What is it?"

"I—" He stopped. "Never mind. It's nothing."

"Oh. Okay. If you're sure…"

He nodded.

"Good night, then."

"Good night."

She started to go, then stopped and turned back. She had to ask him this. If she didn't, it would drive her crazy. "Evan?"

"Hmm?" He sat up again.

"Can we talk for a minute?"

"Sure." He scooted back in the bed. "Have a seat."

She went over and sat on the edge of the bed, facing him. "I want you to be absolutely honest, okay?"

He frowned. "Okay."

"Did you know what your father was planning to do to my father's business?"

He blew air into his cheeks, then let it out in a long, tense stream. "I guess we were going to get to this someday."

"So you did."

"I had an idea, yeah."

"An idea? Or you *knew?*" The possibilities mounted in her mind. "Did he tell you?"

He raked his hand through his hair and looked at her. "You sure you want to do this?"

Her stomach began to feel shaky and upset. It was like getting a phone call and knowing it was bad news before even picking up the receiver. "Tell me," she said.

"I knew my father wanted to buy your father's paper. Everyone knew that. He even made an offer, but your dad refused."

"He loved his work."

"I know," Evan said softly. "It wasn't his fault."

"Obviously not," she said, a tad too defensively. "So your father told you he was going to plant lies about my father's paper to cast doubt on the credibility?"

"No, he didn't tell me." He was choosing his words carefully, talking slowly.

Meredith wanted answers now. "Then how did you know?"

"I heard him talking to someone on the

phone one night. It wasn't hard to put two and two together and figure out what he was planning to do." He shook his head. "I tried to warn you one night—"

"At the beach?"

"That's right." He nodded. "You remember that?"

"It only just occurred to me." She shifted her weight, and the mattress squeaked. "But if you knew, why didn't you tell me directly? You were so vague…. I had *no idea* you were trying to make me aware of something so important." Her eyes burned but she wouldn't cry. "Why didn't you just *tell* me?"

There was a long moment where Evan said nothing. Then at last he said, "Because I was a kid, Meredith. I didn't have firsthand information about the plan, and even if I did, we're talking about betraying my father." He shook his head again, the slow movement showing his regret. "I thought I needed to be loyal to my family. To my father."

A terrible thought occurred to her. "Did our relationship…did it have anything to do with helping your father take over my father's company?"

"Of course not," Evan said, clearly offended at the suggestion.

Relief coursed through Meredith, calming her tight stomach.

But it was short-lived.

"I would never have dated you in order to help my father get access to the newspaper," Evan went on. "In fact, when he suggested our relationship could be of use to him, I ended it."

She felt like she'd been punched in the stomach. Had she heard that correctly? "Wait a minute. You're saying you left because your father wanted to use us to gain access to my father's business?"

Evan nodded slowly. "That's exactly what I'm saying."

Chapter Twelve

It was the first time in her life Meredith had ever even *thought* about quitting a job halfway through. Her job description of corporate researcher had a lot of mutations, and while she wasn't usually a corporate spy—or, as some put it, *competitive intelligence agent*—it wasn't unheard of for her.

As long as she felt comfortable with the reasons for her research and believed she wasn't breaching her own personal morals and standards she was able to do a good job.

This time, though, things were getting foggy.

She'd told her employer she might have a

conflict of interest, and her employer had guessed right off that it might have something to do with her relationship with Evan.

It was hard for Meredith to explain that it did because of something that had happened a long, long time ago. How could she say that she'd just learned he'd once had the chance to do almost the same thing to her that she was doing to him and he'd opted not to?

It sounded so…unprofessional.

So she'd had to settle for explaining that she'd never before taken this kind of job with a company she had any personal relationship with—even a relationship as tangential and outdated as the one she had with the Hansons—and that she was finding it more difficult than she'd anticipated to completely fulfill her obligations to everyone involved.

Especially when the end result would be the hostile takeover of Evan's company.

To Meredith's surprise her employer had assured her that there was *no* hostile takeover in the works. That they were seeking a merger—a way to take two strong companies and put them together to make them both even more powerful.

Hanson Media Group wasn't going to lose

in this deal, Meredith was told—they were going to win.

That was believable, Meredith supposed. Hanson could accept an offer to share partnership instead of being subject to a hostile takeover and thereby having no choice.

"So are you prepared to stay on and finish the job you began?" her employer had asked.

The sixty-four-thousand—only in this case it was more like million—dollar question.

Meredith thought about it for a moment. Her instincts told her she could believe what she was being told, and in the past few years her instincts had become pretty good.

"Yes," she said at last. "I am. You can depend on me."

Evan was starting to have a hard time getting his thoughts straight.

Being at Meredith's parents' house the other night was just too strange. How many hours had he spent there in his lifetime, enjoying the company of the girl he had once been absolutely sure he'd marry?

It was weird to come back, now that she was a grown woman—a woman who had spent more than a decade growing away from him—and see her in that same environment.

It gave him a strange feeling, a combination of unease and melancholy.

Not to mention the all-new desire he felt for Meredith as she fit right into his life and his mind now. The way she'd handled Lenny Doss was amazing. More to the point, the way she handled everything at work was amazing. She was a perfect professional, always conservative but always right.

It was ironic that the very quality that had driven him crazy when they were dating—her unwillingness to take a risk—was the very thing he appreciated in her now.

After he'd spent the night in her guest room, he'd gotten up early, written a note of thanks and called a cab to take him back to his car at Navy Pier. It was better that way, he figured: no awkward morning talk, no uncomfortable silences.

He'd been at work for three and a half hours, with no sign of Meredith, when he finally decided to take a casual look around for her.

But she wasn't in the PR offices, and David said he hadn't seen her all day. So when Evan found her at a lone computer at the far end of the accounting department, he was puzzled.

He watched her for a few minutes from a distance, clicking on the computer keyboard, squinting and looking closer, then jotting notes down on a pad in front of her.

Now what was *that* all about?

He moved closer, hoping to catch a better glimpse of her work without making his presence so obvious that, if caught, he couldn't say he'd just wandered in.

So very carefully he walked up behind her and tried to see what was on the computer screen.

Revenues. Debt. Balances.

Meredith was studying the entire financial profile of the company.

Why?

He backed off again, unnoticed, to contemplate his next move in the hallway.

Was Meredith a corporate spy of some sort?

No, that was too absurd. What had made him even think such a thing? Meredith was far too principled to be dishonest in any capacity, much less lie to someone's face, as she would have to with Evan, David, Helen and everyone else she came into contact with at the office.

Come on.

It was far more likely that ever-responsible-and-forward-thinking Meredith was checking out the company's vital statistics because she was interested in some personal investing, rather than reporting back to some supersecret source.

If anyone was bold enough to take a chance on investing in a company at rock bottom, it was Meredith. She'd see, as he did, that Hanson Media would rebound one way or another.

That was definitely more in keeping with Meredith's personality, yet...Evan wasn't quite sure. Something about this didn't sit right with him. An investor would have plenty of ways to monitor the debt-to-income ratio and the viability of the company as a potential investment. There were books, Web sites, portfolios and, hell, *people* who dedicated their entire existence to providing that kind of information.

Still, the idea of Meredith checking the company information for some sort of nefarious intention was unlikely in the extreme.

He'd have to keep an eye on the situation. He'd keep Meredith close and see if he could figure out what she was up to without his ever having to ask.

* * *

Several days passed since Evan had stayed at Meredith's house, and they never really talked about it again. His cut healed fairly quickly, she was glad to see. He'd probably been right: she was too paranoid in suggesting he needed to go to the hospital right away for stitches.

The strange thing was, he was barely talking to her.

Despite the great strides he'd made in the company—after getting Lenny Doss, he'd managed to secure contracts with three other famous names, including the Alleyway Guys, who had a popular, irreverent car talk show—his conversations with Meredith were brief and to the point.

She couldn't argue with his professional decisions, so it wasn't as if he had that to worry about. The Alleyway Guys, at least, wouldn't be as great a liability as Lenny Doss could be, and the radio psychologist he'd hired had a reputation for being aggressively conservative, but that always ended up making for good listening, both because of the callers who disagreed with her *and* the callers who agreed.

So the radio division was shaping up. Despite the risks involved—and they were many—the acquisition of Lenny Doss would probably be a profitable one. Evan was smart to create an interesting but reliable mix of talent. All of them were proven talents with good, solid numbers behind them.

That would undoubtedly help with her employers' plans for a merger.

"So how's everything going over at the Web site?" she asked David, late in the afternoon. It was almost time to go, and she hoped it would sound like a casual question that he could answer and then leave without thinking too much.

"Actually, things are great," David said. "All squared away. Hanson Media Group is on its way back."

"Really? What do you attribute that to?"

David hesitated. "I guess it's everything combined. The family has come in and worked really hard to save the company, and I think it's showing in every department. We're not in the clear yet, of course, but things are really looking up."

Meredith smiled. "So you think the company can survive on its own?"

David looked at her sharply. "As opposed to what?"

She'd spoken too fast. "I mean you won't need to file for chapter eleven or get a loan?"

David narrowed his eyes and looked at her. "Are you worried about keeping your job?"

She was relieved that that was his only question. She opened her arms into a wide shrug and said, "I'm a single woman working to pay for a house and make my way in this world." She smiled. "It ain't easy. Any reassurance you could give me about job security would be greatly appreciated." She hated to lie to him that way—job security was the least of her worries—but she needed his input on how the company was doing. David Hanson's word was gold within the industry, and she needed a little of that rich, shiny news to take back to her employer.

"I can't assure you of anything," David said, to her disappointment. "This is a wildly uncertain business struggling in wildly uncertain times. However, I can tell you that the public interest in Evan's programming is high. The kid has good instincts, just like Helen figured he would."

"He's a little reckless," Meredith interjected, with a ping of conscience at saying something potentially negative about Evan.

"*Ambitious* might be a better way of putting that," David said gently. "He's been working against the odds, and against the opposition of many within the company, but he's still arranged for a lineup he feels good about, and the industry buzz is on his side." David shrugged broadly. "How do we argue with that?"

"Hopefully, we don't," Meredith agreed. It was a good recommendation of Evan and his work, and she knew David Hanson was far too meticulous a professional to say anything he didn't mean, just to flatter his nephew.

"So the company's in good shape?" She was careful to sound interested but not too eager. "It's not about to go down the tubes or anything?"

"It's all good," David said shortly, but with what sounded like confidence. "No worries."

"Well, good," Meredith said with a smile. "I'm glad to know I'll be safely employed in the immediate future."

"You can count on it," David said, looking her in the eye.

And she already knew it. She *was* safely employed. The question was, how many people at Hanson Media Group could say the same thing?

Not too many.

* * *

She was asking a lot of questions, Evan noticed. Questions that *could* be normal, in the line of business, but which seemed just a little bit…outside the bounds of her job.

It wasn't as if he could take a lot of time to follow her around, though, to see what she was up to. Evan still had his own job to do, and after a decade of killing time all day until his bartending shift at night, he wasn't too keen on the idea of figuring out why anyone should want to the know the Arbitron ratings for the last three years when it was his primary concern to make sure the *next* three years were more successful.

And somehow he had to do that with Meredith Waters by his side, driving him to distraction with almost every breath she took.

He'd never forgotten her, of course. He didn't even try to fool himself about that one. But what was really striking him was how interested in her he was getting *again.* It wasn't just the shadow she cast in his past—she had grown into a fascinating and exciting woman. A strange blend of professional savvy and goofy good humor.

There were more facets to her than he could count. And he wanted to learn about them all.

Was it just because of what they'd shared

once? Was all of the heat he felt between them simply a matter of a once-sizzling love affair? Or was it possible that what he'd seen in her once was something that he needed still, something that complemented his soul in a way that was to be profound all his life?

He turned the thought over in his mind and tried to imagine how they could possibly be together now, even theoretically. He wasn't going to be here long. Chicago held nothing for him. God alone knew where he'd go next, but it was a fairly safe bet that Meredith wouldn't want to join him. She had her life here. Her career was here. And one thing about Meredith that didn't seem to have changed was her inclination to be a homebody.

So there was probably nothing more to say about it than that. The past was the past, and Evan was going to have to get a grip on himself and stop fantasizing about the girl who got away. He'd let her go and there was no getting her back now.

Both he and Meredith needed to look toward the future. Of Hanson Media Group, that is.

Nothing more.

Why couldn't she get her mind off him?

Meredith sat in her office, trying to do the advertising analysis that David had asked her to do. But all she could concentrate on was Evan.

And he wasn't even around.

Well, he was *around,* somewhere in the office, but she'd barely seen him, except for running into him occasionally when she was alone in the copy room and again when she was returning from an early lunch. Both times Evan had been cordial, polite, but basically he'd acted as if they were strangers.

Was he *mad* at her?

The last time they'd really spoken he'd admitted that he'd known his father's intention had been to sabotage her father's business. Or at least he'd *suspected* it, and that was enough for Meredith. He'd had an inkling of what was to come, but he'd barely alluded to it in conversation, much less actually come out and *warned* her.

She *should* be mad at him.

But she wasn't. That was ancient history now, and whatever his culpability for not revealing what he suspected, he had been part of George Hanson's campaign to steal her father's newspaper and, in fact, after warning her in his far-too-subtle way, he'd left the country. So even the greatest cynic couldn't say he was actually *part of* the conspiracy.

So, no, she wasn't mad. Not at Evan. Not for that. Not anymore.

Instead she found herself watching for him every time she heard footsteps in the hall. When someone entered the room, she looked up quickly, hoping it was him. And when it wasn't, as it inevitably wasn't, she was disappointed.

What was going on here?

Finally, at almost five o'clock in the afternoon, when she was about to seek him out and ask if and why he was avoiding her, Evan knocked on her door and poked his head in. "Got a minute?"

She should have been cool and professional but she was so glad to see him that she couldn't help the excited smile she felt on her face. "Sure."

He came in. "I was hoping you might go out with me and grab a bite to eat. There's something—" he hesitated "—there's something I want to talk to you about."

She frowned. "Sounds serious."

"It's not that big a deal. I just thought it would be nice to get out of the office. I'm not used to being trapped under fluorescent lighting all the time."

"I guess it doesn't compare to the Mediterranean sun." There was a tiny sharp edge to her voice, and she hoped he wouldn't notice it.

However, the quick glance he gave her said he had. "You should try it sometime."

"Maybe I will."

He raised an eyebrow. "Really?"

"Why do you sound so surprised?"

"I'm not, I just… You never expressed much interest in travel before."

She shrugged. "I've never in my life had the time to travel. First it was school, then it was work, now it's like some pathological habit. I think it's time I broke it."

He smiled, the smile that had always made her heart flip. "Starting tonight, then. We'll go to a little Greek restaurant I know on the outskirts of town."

She was ready to go farther than that. At this moment, she could have gotten on a plane and taken off for Greece itself, with nothing more than a bathing suit and some sunscreen.

Of course, the image was so unlike her it was almost funny, but suddenly she found herself—unexpectedly and uncharacteristically—hungry for something new, and Chicago just wasn't offering it to her.

Maybe tonight it would at least give her a little taste.

"Should I change my clothes?" she asked, feeling unexpectedly girlish at his offer.

Evan looked her over, and her skin prickled in response, as if he'd touched her. "No, you're fine."

Fine. It wasn't high praise, but it would do. Especially given the way he'd looked at her.

"Okay, then." She shut her computer down and picked up her purse. "I'm ready if you are."

They took the elevator down to the parking garage and went to Evan's car. He went to open the door for her and she mused, "It's been a long time since someone opened a door for me."

"Chivalry's dead, huh?"

"That or it's been asleep." She got into the car and leaned back against the buttery soft leather seats. "Sound asleep."

"So." Evan started the car. "Do you date a lot?"

She was taken by surprise at his question. "Do I *date* a lot?"

He nodded, his eyes on the road in front of him. "Or is that an inappropriate question."

"I don't know if it is or not." She thought for a minute. "Do *you* date a lot?"

He gave a laugh and glanced at her sideways. "Never mind, that *is* a hard question to answer."

"Because there have been so many?" She was unable to stop herself from asking.

"Hardly."

But she wasn't sure she believed him.

"Let me try this one," he said after a couple of moments had passed. "Have you been married? Engaged?"

This was so weird to be talking to Evan about this. "I was engaged once," she said, though part of her didn't want to confess it to him for some reason. "But it didn't work out."

"Why not?"

She looked out the window and gave a dry laugh. "He wasn't ambitious. Didn't have solid plans for the future. I was afraid he might not be…reliable."

The single moment that passed before Evan spoke was so rife with tension that she had no doubt he understood the irony of her failed relationship.

"Maybe you just expected too much of him."

"Certain expectations are so basic that to call them 'too much' is ludicrous." She kept her gaze fastened on the road, watching the yellow lines on the black street disappear under the car. But inside she was thinking, *Please give me a good explanation for what you did, please make me understand.*

"Sometimes people can't fulfill basic expectations for really good reasons," Evan said. "Sometimes things are different from what you think."

"All I know is what I see," she countered, wishing it was enough to believe him but knowing she needed something more. Something concrete. "It's hard to speculate about 'theoretically' when the facts are slapping you in the face."

He took a deep breath. "If they're really the facts. In our case, I just…" He lost the words and shook his head. "It doesn't matter. We're not talking about us."

Meredith stiffened in her seat. She felt her face flush hotly. She was far too ready to talk about them. It just wasn't healthy. He'd moved on. And she'd thought she had, as well.

She just needed to remind herself of that now and then. "Of course not. That was a long time ago. It has nothing to do with now."

"Right."

She couldn't help goosing him a little. "Despite how defensive you seem to be about the past sometimes."

A mile passed.

"Look," Evan said. "I'm sorry. We were talking about your fiancé, and I turned it into my own postmortem defense. It really wasn't appropriate and I apologize for that. I was…just remembering."

"I remember sometimes, too, Evan." *Please make me understand, please make it believable.*

He swung the car in past the Sophie's sign at the entry to a dingy parking lot and slowed to a halt. Then he turned in his seat and said, "Do you?"

She gave a half smile. "I'm not senile."

"Do you ever have any regrets?"

"No," she answered firmly.

They eyes locked, then slowly Evan moved toward her. Meredith sat still, not drawing back, even though her mind screamed for her to run.

Okay, don't make me believe. Just kiss me and make me forget.

His lips grazed lightly across hers, suggesting the satiation of a desire that had gone unanswered for much too long.

A moment rested in stillness, then Evan's mouth descended on hers again, but this time it was more fervent. He moved his mouth across hers in a hungry, almost urgent, way, drawing her in by the sheer force of his passion.

His tongue touched hers, and the taste of him sent a shock of remembrance through her core.

She trailed her hands across his upper back and curled them around his neck, resting her arms on his broad shoulders. He pulled her closer, moving his hands across her body and hungrily exploring her mouth with his own.

The sound of their mingled breaths increased as their ardor grew.

Evan ran a strong hand down to the small of Meredith's back, and she arched toward him, hitting the hard console between them. She didn't care. The pleasure outweighed the pain by a hundredfold. His fingertips dipped lightly inside her panties, and an explosion of excitement arched Meredith's back and she gasped against his mouth.

"I want you," he whispered to her.

"I want you, too," she said, ignoring the tiny voice of conscience that insisted this was a mistake.

Evan's kisses deepened and a pulse throbbed in the pit of Meredith's stomach, extending to her core. It was an ache that only he could reach and she was half ready to let him do it right here and right now.

Evan slipped his hands under Meredith's shirt and swept them across the bare skin of her back and down again. Her breath caught in her throat. She wanted him.

Oh, how she wanted him.

And she'd *told* him so.

She realized with sudden horror what she was doing and how crazy it was. She drew back, nearly slamming her head into the window behind her.

"We can't do this," she gasped.

"Yes, we can." He reached for her again and kissed her.

She gave in to it for one languorous moment, then pushed back again. "No, we can't. I don't want to."

"I don't believe you."

She took a short breath that betrayed her truth. "You have to."

"I have to respect the word *no,*" he said. "I don't have to believe you mean it. Even if I didn't know you before, Meredith, what we just had spoke volumes. Your body told me everything you're not willing to admit."

"*That—*" she gestured lamely "—what just

happened was…it was meaningless. Curiosity, nothing more." She swallowed, then continued. "Now that we've gotten it out of our systems, it must never happen again."

"It sure as hell isn't out of my system," Evan said. "In fact, ever since I saw you again, you've been slowly working your way right back into my system. It's almost like—"

"Don't say it." She raised a hand. She didn't want to hear it was like old times or that it was as if nothing had changed or, worse, it was like they were meeting for the first time. "Don't say it. There's no way you can finish that sentence without sounding like a line from every melodramatic movie ever made."

Evan gave a sharp laugh. "Thanks."

Warmth washed over her face. "You know what I mean. Don't you?"

"Maybe. What I don't know is why you're so damn eager to ignore what your heart is telling you."

"Who said my heart was involved in this transaction?"

"Okay, your body." He gave a rakish grin. "I'll take that."

No you won't. I'm not giving it again. "No

way. There's nothing to gain by getting involved in something that we both know can never work."

"You don't know that."

"I do. Look, Evan, you left once without saying a word. I wasn't enough for you then, and there's no reason to think things would be different now. "

He straightened his back and looked out the window in front of him. "I didn't leave because you weren't enough for me. It was nothing like that."

"Then what was it?"

He looked at her, his face shadowed by the twilight. "It was complicated."

"Too complicated to explain?"

"What's the point?"

"I don't know." She couldn't admit that she wanted the peace of mind of knowing. It sounded too pathetic. "Maybe there isn't one."

There passed a moment of eye contact between the two of them that sent shivers rushing up and down Meredith's spine. He looked as if he was going to kiss her again.

More to the point, she wanted him to kiss her again; she wanted to feel herself in his arms again; she wanted to feel that rough beard against her cheek. Heat pulsed between the two of them.

He moved toward her and she leaned in ever so slightly until he was just the merest breath away.

Then her phone rang.

She started in surprise. Who would be calling her at this hour?

Her first thought was that it might be an emergency, something to do with her mother.

"I'm sorry," she said to Evan, fumbling through her purse. "I have to get this. It could be my mom."

She answered the phone.

"I'm sorry to call so late," the voice on the other end of the line said. "But I'm getting ready to leave for Japan and I need to know if you finished assembling the data you were working on about Hanson Media Group."

Chapter Thirteen

Meredith moved the phone to her other ear and subtly turned the volume on the earpiece down. "I don't have that information with me right now. I can go home and get it, though, if you need me to."

"You're not alone?"

"Um…no."

"I need to talk to you about this. Can you call me back soon, in private?"

She didn't want to, but Meredith knew she really had no choice. "All of those records are at home, Mother." She hated having to stoop so low as to pretend it was her mother. "Can it wait until morning?"

"Sorry, you have to do this now."

"Okay, let me just call you back in—" she glanced at her watch "—about forty-five minutes. Is that okay?"

"That's fine. But sooner is better. Try and hurry, Meredith, okay?"

"You got it." She gave Evan an exasperated look as she flipped the phone shut and put it back into her purse. "I'm sorry, I've got to get back home and get some documentation together for my mother. Something to do with her new housing situation and needing to prove she sold her assets out here."

Evan nodded. "I'll take you home right away."

That just seemed wrong. With everything she was doing she couldn't bear to make him feel like he had to accommodate her. "No, no, I know you were looking forward to eating here. It's not a big deal for me to take a cab back to the office and drive home. Heck, I'd walk if I had the time."

"Meredith, I'm not letting you take a cab back to the office so I can go get myself some souvlaki. I'll drive you."

"You don't—"

"Don't be ridiculous," he interrupted. He started the car and put it in gear. "This isn't a big deal."

"Well, thanks."

He pulled out of the parking lot. "Is everything okay with your mom?"

"What? Oh. Yes. Fine. It's just—" She had to tell herself this really was about her mother, that it was routine personal business and not something that could affect Evan or his family. "She's constantly needing one document or another from the house. She left a ton of stuff behind." That much, at least, was true.

"Your mom is lucky to have you," Evan said as he drove. "After she lost your dad, she must have been really lost."

"She was," Meredith agreed.

"I remember how close they were," Evan continued, smiling more to himself than Meredith. "They'd be worse than teenagers at the dinner table, laughing and finishing each other's sentences."

Meredith smiled, remembering. "I always thought that was the definition—"

"—of true love, yeah," Evan agreed, apparently unaware that he had just finished Meredith's sentence himself.

But she was aware of it.

"When you know each other so well, *and* agree with each other so completely, that you can finish each other's sentences," he went on, "that really shows a certain comfort level. It's enviable, really."

"Yes," she agreed, looking at him through the darkness, illuminated only occasionally by the streetlights they passed. "I think you're right."

"It probably had a lot to do with how you turned out."

"Meaning…?"

"You have always been secure in yourself, Meredith. Some might even say a little bull-headed—" he gave a quick smile "—but definitely secure with who you are and what you think. I think that comes from growing up in a house where everyone was loved and accepted for who they were."

"As opposed to how you grew up?" she asked, before she could think better of it.

He didn't even hesitate to answer. "Definitely. I knew before I could talk that I had to watch what I said around my father. The strain of keeping us all quiet and agreeable for him probably had a lot to do with my mother's eventual illness."

And death, Meredith thought, but she didn't say it. She didn't have to. She knew they were both thinking it. "You must have had some good times with your family," she ventured. "It's not like you were a miserable kid."

"Not when I was with you." He kept his eyes on the road and his hands on the wheel. "Maybe whatever you had in your upbringing spilled over to me when we were together. The only time I really felt comfortable back then was when I was with you."

The thought warmed her heart, even while it rang every warning bell within her. "It obviously didn't mean *that* much to you," she said. "You didn't have too hard a time leaving it."

He drew to a halt at a stoplight and looked at her, the red hue illuminating his left cheek, casting shadows that made him look older. *"That,"* he said, "is not true."

Once again she found herself wishing he'd explain. Yet even while she wished, she didn't want him to. "No? Then how did you do it? Evan, you never looked back. No call, no letter, no message in a bottle."

"It was best for you that you didn't hear from me."

She scoffed. "*Best* for me? Who do you think you're kidding?"

"It was," he insisted. The car behind them honked its horn and Evan looked up to see the light had changed. He drove forward and went on, saying to Meredith, "You'll just have to trust me on this."

"Evan, we're grown people now. This happened more than a decade ago. I'd like to know what happened. This cryptic 'it was best for you' business just doesn't cut it. Either tell me the truth or don't talk about the past at all."

"You're right. We shouldn't talk about it at all."

She sighed. "Just *tell me the truth.*"

He laughed lightly. "Fine, Meredith. It's simple. My father wanted to use our relationship, yours and mine, to his advantage over your father. He wanted me to get information on your father's writers, the stories they were coming up with, how best to get in there and switch the facts around and cast doubt on your father's credibility."

Meredith felt the blood leave her face. "He wanted you to *spy* for him?"

"Essentially, yes. Though that's a pretty dramatic label." He blew a long breath out. "Either way, what it would have come down to was me using you, or appearing to." The next light turned yellow, and Evan slowed the car again.

"Why didn't you tell me?"

He looked at her. "Because I was eighteen and I didn't know how to betray my father like that."

"But you could betray me."

"I *didn't* betray you. I left the country. I cut out of the whole deal so I wasn't part of hurting *anyone*."

Which felt to her like a betrayal of the highest order. He *had* hurt her, and he still didn't seem to realize it. "It was pretty damn easy for you," she said, hating the bitter edge to her voice, even though she couldn't soften it.

He shook his head. "It was the hardest thing I ever had to do!"

"But…?"

His gaze landed evenly on her. "But I did it. It was the best I could do for everyone."

This wasn't going anyplace good. Meredith *knew* she shouldn't have indulged her impulse to talk to him about this. It made her regress to an angry, confused teenager, and she had gotten so far away from that until Evan had reappeared.

She didn't want to be this person.

"Okay, okay. *Uncle,*" she said, glad to see they were approaching the entrance to the office building's garage. "We're not getting anywhere with this conversation."

"Agreed."

"So let's drop it."

He gave a single nod. "Consider it dropped."

The entered the grungy grey garage in silence, the dim fluorescent lighting acting as the perfect punctuation to Meredith's dissatisfaction.

"Okay." She pointed to her little blue sports car. "That's it right there."

"I remember." He pulled the car up behind hers and turned to her. "Here you go."

"Thanks." She started to get out of the car, then stopped and turned back to him. "I'm sorry I had to cut dinner off. I hope you're not starving."

"I'll survive." He smiled. "I'll just drive through and get a burger somewhere."

She nodded. "Good night, Evan."

He looked at her evenly, his gaze inscrutable. "Good night."

She got out of the car and felt him watching her as she unlocked the doors, got in and started the ignition. He pulled his car away, and she backed up and followed him out of the garage. He turned right and drove off in the opposite direction of where she was going.

She was struck by the thought that soon he'd be back in the building, staying in his office overnight. It was a nice office, of course. Luxury accommodations by almost any standards. But what made her sad about it was the fact that he was staying at the office because he wasn't going to be in Chicago long.

He was leaving. Again.

As soon as Evan's car's taillights were out of sight, Meredith put hers in Park and put her head in her hands. This was so much harder than she'd thought it would be. Her nerves were not as strong as they usually were.

Neither was her willpower, come to think of it.

What a fool she was to keep having these romantic leanings toward Evan Hanson. For heaven's sake, he'd left her, abandoned her. Made promises he'd clearly had no intention of keeping, and when faced with the challenge of standing up and being a man against his father, or running away, he'd chosen to run.

Okay, that was then and this was now. The fact remained that Evan had always been a wild kid. It was as if he was incapable of following the rules. She'd seen it in school, then she'd seen it again when he ran away from his promise of commitment.

Guys like that didn't change. People like that didn't change, she amended.

And if being with Evan now was going to create this rush of longing in her, then she was just going to have to avoid him. As hard as that might be.

She drove home in silence, not daring to turn on the radio for fear of hearing some old love song that would make her feel even more melancholy. What was wrong with her? Why was she suddenly feeling so hung up on Evan Hanson again?

It wasn't the Evan Hanson of the past that she was wanting, either, it was Evan today. Past Evan was the main obstacle, that was for sure. She couldn't trust the today Evan because of what he'd done before, and it didn't look as if she was ever going to get a satisfactory resolution to that.

And frankly, she felt like an idiot for even trying.

She got home and went inside, hating the emptiness of the house and the way her footsteps echoed on the hardwood floors. Once upon a time she'd crept across these floors on tiptoe in the middle of the night, trying to avoid the creakiest boards so she didn't wake her parents up.

Now she could jump and yell and sing "The

Star Spangled Banner" if she wanted to and no one would come.

It was lonely.

And it hadn't struck her that way until Evan had returned. She hated how much she loved being with him, and more than that she hated how alone she felt every time he left.

She couldn't wait until this job was over so she could move on. That he was staying temporarily in his office with the intention of leaving himself should only make her feel better.

She took out a key and went to the back room, where she'd locked her confidential work files. She found them, carried the folders into the kitchen and spread the information out on the counter.

Then she picked up the phone and dialed.

"Okay, I'm home," she said when the line was answered. "And I've got the information you need. Are you ready?"

Chapter Fourteen

Evan knew he shouldn't go back to Meredith's house.

He knew, even as he turned the car onto Lake Shore Drive and headed across town, that it was a mistake.

What they had was in the past and, considering the fact that they couldn't even talk about it at all without arguing, it was going to have to stay there.

But he was drawn to her. Not as the boy was drawn to the spunky cheerleader, but as the man was drawn to the woman. She was the realization of everything he'd ever wanted in a woman and hadn't been able to find.

The only problem was that they had a past.

And that was precisely why it was so foolish of him to be retracing his steps down that path right now, parking outside the house she'd lived in with her parents, walking up the same walk, over the same cracks that had been there for years, going to the same door that would open to reveal the girl of his dreams.

Somehow he had to convince her of that.

He wasn't quite at the door yet when he caught sight of her through the window. She was sitting on a bar stool in the kitchen, the phone to her ear, poring over what looked like maps spread out on the counter.

Evan stepped back and watched her for a moment. He remembered the way she'd pushed that chestnut-colored hair back off her face, and the way the front of her hair bent from being constantly pushed back or tucked behind her ear.

He smiled when she laughed into the phone and tossed her head back.

She was so pretty.

He didn't know how long he stood there, or what he hoped to achieve. Maybe to talk himself out of going to the front door. But the more he watched her, the closer he wanted to get to her.

She ran a pen down the paper and spoke into the phone, looking very serious. At one point she stopped, frowned and looked through another pile before triumphantly producing whatever it was she was looking for.

He'd seen her like this in the library of Showell High School and in the offices of Hanson Media Group. Meredith was a woman who took great pleasure in a job well done, whether the job was a term paper, a report or finding a telephone number someone had asked for.

He found that brand of concentration particularly endearing on her.

When she hung up the phone and started to collect her papers, he didn't even take the time to think things through. He just strode to the door and knocked.

For several moments he stood there, wondering if she'd heard and if he should still turn and leave as if he'd never been there.

He'd almost convinced himself to do just that when she opened the door.

"Evan!"

A thousand things ran through his mind. A

million explanations, a billion apologies. But it all boiled down to one salient point.

"I was a fool."

She looked puzzled. "What?"

He stepped toward her, and she opened the door and stepped back, allowing him in. "I had no idea what I was giving up when I left here."

"Evan, have you been drinking?"

He laughed. "Not a drop. In fact, I'm more sober than I've been in years."

She closed the door and stood her ground, even when he took another step toward her.

He looked down into her beautiful face and wished he could erase every stress line he or his family had put there. But then again, he liked the gentle lines on her face. He liked the new maturity there. He liked everything about the way she looked.

"I didn't know how to betray my father, and the only way I could think of to avoid betraying you was to leave. To remove myself from the equation altogether. I thought you'd be better off. And I honestly thought—" he sighed "—I thought you'd forget all about me in no time and that it wouldn't matter."

She swallowed. "I never forgot."

He shook his head. "Neither did I. And that

was the worst error in judgment I made. Because I also thought that someday *I'd* forget, too. Everything everyone says about young love—that it's fleeting, that you remember it later with a smile and a little embarrassment but no heartache, that it never lasts. All of that was untrue."

Her eyes were shining with unshed tears. "We shouldn't be talking about this."

"I know, but *not* talking about it isn't working, either."

"I know." She sniffed.

"Look, you can tell me to go to hell." He gave a dry laugh and shook his head. "I wouldn't blame you one bit for that. But I at least want you to understand that, whatever my stupid and misguided reasons for leaving, I never *ever* stopped loving you."

He heard her breath catch in her throat. "Then why did you *stay* away? Why, when you realized how you felt, didn't you come back? Or contact me somehow?"

"Because all I knew was how I felt and that I'd let you down. I couldn't imagine that you would be willing to talk to me."

She shook her head.

"And honestly, Meredith," he went on, "I

could imagine, all too easily, that you'd moved on and forgotten us."

"You didn't have much faith in me."

"No," he said firmly. "I didn't have much faith in *me*. And, hell, I didn't deserve it."

They stood looking at each other in silence for a long, shuddering moment.

"No," she said at last. "You didn't."

He accepted that.

He had to.

"You're right," he agreed. "I just wanted you to know the truth." He started to leave.

"Why?" she asked behind him.

He stopped and turned back to face her. "What?"

"*Why* did you want me to know the truth? Why now, after all this time? In fact, why now after the nonconversation we had about this earlier tonight?"

"Because even though we'd like to be mature people who don't sweat this kind of thing, it's been the elephant in the room ever since we started working together. It was starting to spill over into everything I did, everything I thought about."

"So you needed to get it off your chest," she challenged. "To relieve your conscience."

"Mer, it would take a noble explanation for

leaving to relieve my conscience," he said earnestly. "That's not gonna happen. The reason I wanted to tell you this is because you deserved to know it because it's the truth. I love you, Meredith. I always have. And, God help me, I guess I always will." He gave a small smile. "That's the last I'll say about it, though, don't worry. Good night, Meredith."

He turned to leave and had taken two steps toward the door when she said, "Evan, wait. Don't go."

She should have let him go, but she couldn't.

She ran to him, and it all happened as if in slow motion. He turned to her, she threw herself into his arms, and they kissed. Long and deeply, and expressing all of the unanswered passion they had felt for all this time but had been unable to share.

Wordlessly she took his hand and led him up the stairs to her bedroom. He didn't ask questions. He didn't need to.

They stopped in the doorway of her bedroom and kissed again.

"Not the same room you used to have," Evan murmured.

"That would be just too weird, wouldn't it?" She smiled at him, and they kissed again.

He moved his hands up her back in tantalizing slow motion, moving his fingertips across her back so lightly she arched against him when it tickled. When she did, he unhooked her bra with one quick flick of his fingers.

She remembered that move.

The fabric fell loose and he pressed his palms against her back, drawing her closer to him still. She went willingly, eagerly. If she could have, she would have gone right into his soul.

They kissed for long minutes, maybe ten or fifteen of them, unhurried but both certain where this was going.

Just as Meredith began to feel as if her core was melting into a puddle at her feet, he whispered, “Let’s move to the bed.”

She didn’t argue.

They crossed the room and fell to the bed together, resuming their kiss and increasing the urgency. Evan yanked at Meredith’s shirt and it flew open, the buttons popping off and clattering to the floor like pennies. She didn’t care. The sooner he touched her, the *more* he touched her, the better.

His hand skidded across her rib cage to her breast, his touch hot against her skin. He moved his hand to her nipple, playing her like an instrument, until her breath came in short, shallow bursts, her heart pounding urgently, begging for satisfaction.

She cupped her hands to his face and kissed him deeply, then moved her hands down the length of his chest and the flat of his stomach, until she got to the buckle of his jeans.

She hadn't forgotten her own moves, either, and she dipped her hand inside his pants, and snapped them open as Evan groaned against her mouth.

"If you're going to stop this, you'd better do it, like, five minutes ago," he said against her mouth.

"I'm not sure…." She smiled and kissed him again, enjoying the game.

Apparently, he was, too. He slid his hand inside her pants and cupped her, dipping one finger into her womanhood for just a moment. "No?"

She gasped. "I guess we could keep going." She moved her own hand to hold him. She was awed by the power of his desire and it made her crazy with her own, but she tried to sound controlled. "Unless you want to stop…?"

"You play dirty."

"You don't seem to mind." She moved her hand, looking into his eyes. "Do you?"

Evan finally lost the control he'd been holding on to. He rolled her over onto her back and slid her pants down, his breath traveling hotly across her thighs as he did so. She reminded herself that this was Evan, that this was the love of her life, and finally—*finally*—she was going to feel him within her again.

She'd waited a long time for this, even while she'd told herself she didn't want it.

All of her thoughts disappeared when Evan took her to new heights of pleasure.

"You're amazing," she breathed.

"You ain't seen nothin' yet," he said, with a pirate's smile.

He moved over her, and she couldn't wait any longer. She pushed his jeans down over his slender hips with her feet and pulled him on top of her. She wanted him.

She *needed* him.

She ran her hands across his tightly muscled backside, then around to the front, where she found him more than ready for her.

Their tongues moved against each other, echoing the drumbeat that was pounding within them. They were like a well-oiled machine whose sole purpose was to join their bodies and move them toward ecstasy.

She started to move, and he stopped her. "Wait," he said. "Let me. Relax."

So she did. She lay back against the cool, soft sheets and let herself sink into the magic that was making love with Evan.

His hand moved across her stomach and her muscles tightened in anticipation. He took his sweet time to move his hand lower, and lower, grazing her pelvis and slowing tantalizingly before finally cupping over the part of her that wanted him so desperately.

He paused for only a second, looking into her eyes, a moment that said more than words could, before slipping his fingers in and plunging her depths.

Meredith's hands clutched at the sheets beneath her as Evan brought her to heights she'd never even imagined before. She closed her eyes and let it happen, feeling waves of warm and cold wash over her while she writhed under his careful ministrations. She could barely breathe. Every time she reached the brink, he backed off, until finally he allowed her release.

With perfect timing, Evan lowered his weight onto her, and she finally felt the satisfaction of being completely one with him.

She'd dreamed of this moment.

Breathlessly she opened her mouth, deepening their kisses. The sensation was exquisite: the weight of Evan on her, the feel of him inside her, the touch of his hands on her hair as he looked down into her eyes.

Everything felt right.

They both moaned in pleasure as her body accepted his again and again, and they moved together, slowly at first and then faster, until she heard him hold his breath for a moment, then give one final thrust as she felt herself float into ecstasy once again.

Chapter Fifteen

Evan just lay there, watching her sleep.

He had waited a long time for this. Now that he and Meredith had finally made love again, it was clear to him that all the other women he'd met along the way had paled in comparison to Meredith.

He didn't know how long he watched her—it may have been an hour or more—but finally he decided to take a break and get a drink of water. It had been a long, exhausting night and he was thirsty.

He crept down the stairs and went into the

kitchen. Everything was still in the same place. Glasses in the cabinet to the right of the stove, cold water in a pitcher in the fridge. He poured a glass, drank it fast, then poured another one and sat down at the counter to drink it.

That was when his own name caught his eye.

The papers Meredith had been looking at earlier were still on the counter. He hadn't meant to pry—if he hadn't seen the words "Evan Hanson—wild card" from the corner of his eye, he might not have noticed them at all. Despite the fact that they had Hanson Media Group and the names of many of his family members and coworkers scrawled all over them.

Jack Hanson—definite keep. Major asset, works well with Samantha.

Parker Lemming—fishy accounting; look closer. Not sure if incompetent or dishonest.

Lily Harper—keep for merger, very good worker, being headhunted by competition.

David Hanson—good worker, trustworthy. Invested in own family but not to the detriment of HMG.

Marla Cooper—very promising, on the fast track to success. Keep her!
Andrew Hanson—on the right track, keep an eye on him. Looks like he'll be okay.
Stephen ?? in mail room—real possibilities. Keep and promote.
Evan Hanson—wild card.

Stephen in the mail room hadn't even needed a last name, and she thought he had "real possibilities," but she had gone on to list pros and cons about Evan.

Pros:
- Has Hanson name to protect.
- Capable when he puts his mind to it.
- Determined to succeed if only to prove everyone wrong about him.
- Is respected around the office and in the business, despite glaring inexperience.

Cons:
- Doesn't always seem to care if his father's company goes down in flames.
- Could possibly be sabotaging efforts as "revenge."
- No experience to see things through;

might do some good things in starting up the broadcast enterprises but might not have the gumption to finish.

- A little immature, impulsive. Maybe not capable of being a professional?
- Tends to run away when the going gets tough.

He read the lists a couple of times, shaking his head in disbelief. If this was what she thought of him, why on earth had she just slept with him?

More to the point, why was she documenting everyone's performance at Hanson Media Group? Why would she even care? She was a new hire, working in the PR department, for Pete's sake. What that had to do with Jack or David or Samantha or Richard Warren or *anyone* else, he couldn't imagine.

Except…he looked at more of the papers. Numbers, flow charts, strengths, weaknesses, *Wall Street Journal* references, the assets of the competition and their interest in acquiring.

It all became very clear, very fast.

Meredith was a corporate spy.

The revelation was stunning. A spy. Meredith, who had always prided herself on being so honest. Meredith, who held honesty in others to be the most important quality. Meredith, who had just melted in his arms and made him feel like the luckiest man on earth.

Everything about her was a lie.

For a few minutes, Evan couldn't move. If he stood up, he wasn't sure which direction he'd take: out the door or upstairs to wake her and demand answers. He didn't want to do either one of those things without thinking it through first.

Why would she do this? The first reason that came to mind was revenge. She couldn't have planned on Evan coming back to work here, so her initial motivation might have been to get back at the company that had ruined her father's.

In truth, Evan could sort of understand that. He didn't particularly *admire* it, but he understood why she might have felt that way.

What he didn't understand was how she could make love to him, all the while knowing she was assisting *someone's* efforts to steal his family's company. Hell, she was even listing his own bad qualities—or what she perceived to be his bad qualities—for the same purpose.

The Meredith he knew would never have been able to have sex with someone as a way of using them to her own advantage. Or, worse, to the advantage of her employer, whoever that was.

Yet that was exactly what the woman upstairs had done.

And he wanted no part of it.

He stood up and took his glass to the sink, opening the dishwasher in what felt like slow motion. The small gesture felt ironic when balanced against the enormous amount of feeling he was battling with. He'd risked his own heart—love was always a risk—he'd take his lumps for that. Maybe he even deserved it, after what he'd done to Meredith all those years ago.

He'd think about that later.

The immediate dilemma was what to do about the deception. He'd faced this same issue once before, when his father had sabotaged her father's business, and he had done the wrong thing. A weak warning to Meredith and a mad dash out of town hadn't amounted to anything good.

This time he'd have to take definitive action. He could tell Meredith he knew what she was up to and demand answers, but she might not give them to him. And, once she was caught, someone else might be sent in her stead, and he wouldn't be so lucky as to catch the next person.

So maybe he should talk to Helen instead.

That was probably the answer. It was probably the mature and responsible thing to do. Of course, it went against everything inside him to do that, but Evan Hanson had to learn to be *mature,* as Meredith herself had noted.

He had to be *professional.*

And more than anything, at the moment he had to get out of this house.

Meredith woke as the dawn sliced through her window, feeling uncharacteristically happy. It took her a full minute or two of thinking through her groggy state to remember why.

When she did, she smiled.

"Evan?"

She wished he was in bed next to her, but he must have gotten up first. Maybe he was in the shower or downstairs making bad coffee like he used to.

She got out of bed and walked toward the bathroom. "Evan?" she called again.

The silence that answered was noticeable.

No one was here.

But that was impossible. Evan wouldn't just cut out on her after something like last night. She walked around the house looking for him, and calling his name every once in a while, finally arriving in the kitchen. Maybe he'd gone to pick up some breakfast and had left her a note.

But there was no note.

Meredith paused in the middle of the kitchen, wondering for a moment if she'd imagined the whole night. If she had, she'd done so in great and frightening detail.

But she hadn't; she knew she hadn't.

She sat down at the counter, miffed, trying to figure out where he would have gone and why he wouldn't have left a note or something.

The realization came all too quickly:

"Hanson. Hanson. Hanson Media Group. Evan Hanson. Pros. Cons."

The writing was on the wall, or at least all over the counter. All of her notes, all of her reports, all of her unflattering doodles about Evan himself, all lying right there on the counter for him to see when he got up.

Oh, God.

He'd seen it all. She didn't even have to think about it or speculate about other possible explanations for his absence. He'd seen her life laid out on the counter, figured out what she was up to, and he'd left.

What was she going to do now?

Meredith had never been good at wringing her hands and clutching her pearls in an emergency—and this was definitely an emergency—so what she decided to do was take the bull by the horns and let her employer know exactly what had happened.

There was no point in sitting around the house, hoping Evan had somehow missed the glaring evidence before him and had gone out for doughnuts.

Meredith took the quickest shower of her life, dried her hair in no time flat, skipped the make-up and got dressed for work. During that time, Evan did *not* show up again with a bag of bagels and a goofy grin, so it was pretty obvious that he was gone and not coming back.

Within forty-five minutes of realizing that Evan was gone, Meredith was in her car on the way to admit her carelessness and risk the wrath of her employer.

Evan was still struggling with the question of what to do about Meredith's spying when he got back to work.

It wasn't so easy to simply go to Helen's office and let her know. If he'd had the power to fire Meredith, he might have done so, just to spare himself and her the agony of retribution from Hanson Media Group and Helen.

He could have kicked himself for being suckered in by Meredith. Why had he believed that she felt the same way he did after all these years? After all, it was always easier for the one who stays in place—she was able to work through the grief and the loneliness. She'd moved on with her life, formed other relationships, developed her career.

Evan, on the other hand, had taken an extended vacation, working odd jobs in various places far away, and he'd never quite gotten to the point where he was able to forget her.

Certainly when he got back to Chicago, Meredith was primary in his mind. And if being back and thinking about her wasn't enough, Helen had to go and *hire* her, for Pete's sake, and have her work closely with Evan.

It was the worst kind of bad luck.

And the best kind of good luck.

It was every conflicted feeling, good and bad, rolled up into one.

The morning passed at the slowest pace of any day Evan could remember. Every time he decided it was best to let Helen know what was going on, he'd get no further than one step from his desk before he changed his mind and sat down again to reconsider the problem.

Yet when he resolved to tell Meredith what he knew, he hesitated there, too, and for much more complicated reasons: one, he didn't want another corporate spy—potentially someone he wouldn't have the luck to spot—come in her place; and two, he didn't want her to leave.

It was the latter that really tortured him. What a fool he was to want to keep Meredith around, even though he knew she was betraying both him and his family in the biggest possible way. And yet, he could almost understand why. She had a legitimate gripe against George Hanson.

And, arguably, against Evan himself.

But in mulling the situation over, again and again, he finally decided that even if she believed she had sufficient motivation for getting back at the Hansons, it was primarily because of him.

And he couldn't just sit by and let future generations of Hansons—his siblings' sons and daughters—be ruined because of what boiled down to his own mistake.

Whatever Meredith was doing, it was because of him and because of the way he and his father had treated her and her father, more than a decade back.

It was time he made things right.

Unfortunately, he wasn't going to be able to make things right for Meredith if he made things right for the company.

He was just going to have to be *mature* and *professional* about this.

Contrary to Meredith's stated opinion.

But by 4:30 p.m. he still hadn't made a move toward Helen's office to reveal what he knew about Meredith. It was one thing to intend to handle it, but actually going forward and telling was a whole different thing.

He didn't want to do it.

But when Helen summoned him to her office just before five o'clock, he realized he couldn't put it off anymore.

He was going to have to do *something.*

Chapter Sixteen

Approaching Helen's office, Evan decided that he would talk to Meredith about this privately.

Yes, his loyalty should have been with the company—especially under the circumstances—but he just couldn't turn Meredith over to the wolves like that, no matter what she'd done. It could ruin her professionally, and he just didn't want to do that.

His decision was solidified when he ran into her outside Helen's office.

"Evan," she said, startled when she looked up and saw him.

She looked as if she was leaving Helen's office. And she looked upset.

"You left so early," she went on.

Had that only been this morning? He'd spent so much time waffling back and forth on what to do about Meredith that it seemed as though it had been days instead of hours. "I had to get to work," he said.

She raised an eyebrow. "Is that all it was?"

"What else *would* it be?" he asked pointedly.

She swallowed but held his gaze without flinching. "I thought perhaps you had changed your mind about me for some reason."

"I'm not the one who's changed, Meredith."

She took a short breath, looked as if she was going to say something, then stopped.

Standing there before him, she almost looked vulnerable. And she definitely looked alluring, with her rich, shining hair hanging loose, framing her still-youthful face. Was it his imagination or did her cheeks still have some of the glow he'd seen in them after they'd made love last night?

It didn't matter. That was a mistake. One he wasn't likely to make again.

"So you're here to see Helen?" Meredith asked awkwardly.

"Yes." He nodded. "Where are you going?"

Home? Had Helen already figured her out and fired her?

"Just back to my office. David's got a lot of work piled up for me, and of course you and I have to finish the new promotional campaign."

It was crazy, but some part of him was glad to hear that she'd still be in the office. She would probably quit once he'd talked to her, but in the meantime she'd still be here.

"I'll call you when my meeting with Helen is finished," he said. "Are you still going to be around for a while?"

"I'll wait as long as I need to. I can work all night, if necessary." Her cheeks went pink and she looked down.

It was on the tip of his tongue to make a flip joke about working all night with her, and he had to remind himself that things had changed. Despite last night, he and Meredith couldn't have an easy rapport.

Tension stretched between them.

"I'd better get in there," Evan said at last, gesturing vaguely in the direction of Helen's office.

Meredith nodded and stepped back, allowing him room to pass. "I'll see you afterward," she said. Then he could have sworn she added quietly, "I hope."

He went into Helen's quiet office and closed the door behind him, settling uneasily into the seat before her.

"I'll get right to the point," Helen said to him from across her desk. "Not everything here at Hanson Media Group is what it seems."

That was for sure. But he sat back and said nothing, waiting for Helen to continue, which she did.

"Not every*one* here is as they seem."

He nodded noncommittally. "People seldom are."

"I think you know what I'm talking about, Evan."

He met her eyes. "Why don't you tell me?"

"I'm talking about Meredith Waters. She's been doing some corporate work for another company. Digging up information on Hanson Media Group to determine its viability for a merger."

"What company?"

"TAKA Corporation."

"The Japanese conglomerate?" He'd done some homework on his industry. Enough to know that TAKA was enormous.

Helen nodded. "That's right."

"And you're not upset about this?"

She folded her hands on the desk in front of

her and looked her stepson straight in the eye. "No, Evan. I sought TAKA out and proposed a merger to them."

It took a long moment of silence for that to sink in, and even then he couldn't quite believe he'd heard her correctly.

"I'm sorry," he said. "I don't think I understand."

She took a short breath and hesitated a moment before explaining. "I don't like the idea of sharing Hanson's power with anyone. I don't want to change the structure this company has had for so many years. Your father worked hard to build this empire, and I wish it could just go on without him, exactly as he'd envisioned."

Evan was surprised by her vehemence and her support for George. "You really loved him, didn't you?"

"Yes. And I respect what he built. But times have changed since Hanson first gained power. There are too many media outlets today, it's hard to monopolize, and if a company can't monopolize, it runs the risk of going under completely."

"Which is what you were afraid of when we first talked about me staying on and trying to help you keep in business."

"Exactly." She nodded. "And it's what I'm still afraid of. If Hanson doesn't get a boost of some sort, it's *going* to fold. And TAKA's interest might be just the boost we need." She leaned back in her chair and sighed. "The truth is, no other company has expressed even the slightest interest in a merger."

"So TAKA is our only hope."

She nodded again. "It looks like it."

"They're getting pretty specific information, from what I could tell. Lots of financial-risk stuff. What if they want a takeover instead of a merger? Then Hanson is lost just as much as if it had gone bankrupt. Maybe even more."

"I won't allow a takeover of this company," Helen said firmly. "I assure you of that. In fact, you can see for yourself. I would like you to go to Japan with me right away for a meeting with Ichiro Kobayashi. He needs reassurance on your latest hire, Lenny Doss, and I'd feel better if you gave it to him in person. Now that everything's out in the open."

Now he was going to Japan? What the heck—it wasn't much weirder than anything else that had happened lately. "Fine."

"I'm leaving tomorrow. Can I have Sonia make a reservation for you to join me?"

He nodded and spread his arms. "I'm at your disposal."

She buzzed Sonia and asked her to make plane and hotel reservations for Evan. He waited, trying to process all this new information.

When she hung up the phone, she smiled at him. "Thank you, Evan. I know this is all sudden and surprising, but I think it's for the best. Perhaps after you've met with TAKA yourself, you'll be able to help me persuade everyone else that this is the right move."

"We'll see." He considered his next question before asking it. "So TAKA comes along and expresses an interest in merging with Hanson. You decide you're not completely averse to the idea. What I want to know is, where does Meredith fit in? Did you uncover her double dealings and get the truth out of her?"

"No." Helen gave a small chuckle and shook her head. "No, it was nothing like that. Meredith is here digging up all the relevant information for TAKA because I hired her."

Evan went back to his office more confused than he'd been when he left it. Two months ago he'd been as far away from this company and this lifestyle as he could get, and now suddenly he was right smack in the middle of it all: black ink, red ink, mergers, takeovers and corporate espionage.

He could really use a shot of tequila right about now.

Instead it was just more of the same. He got to the office he was beginning to resent, sat down at the desk he was beginning to hate and called the woman he was beginning to love.

Meredith appeared within five minutes, looking pale and drawn. "Did Helen tell you… what's going on?"

"That you're a spy for TAKA?" Evan asked casually. "Yes, she mentioned that."

"But you knew that."

He gave a concessionary shrug. "I knew you were spying for someone."

Her eyes grew bright. "Evan, I'm really sorry I couldn't tell you. But it's my job to be discreet. If I'd let on what I was doing, it could have compromised all of Helen's plans."

"Assuming I couldn't be trusted."

She winced. "I didn't know. I still don't know. I understand that you're mad that I lied to you, and I don't blame you for that, but I don't know where you stand on the truth."

He gave a half shrug. "Well, that makes two of us."

"You see, don't you?" She moved toward him and leaned on the desk, next to where he sat. "You see why I couldn't let on."

"In theory, I suppose. But in practice…I'm not so sure. Was last night part of your work or was it extracurricular?"

It took her a moment to realize what he was asking, and he could see when it registered. Her eyes grew wide and flashing mad. "Are you asking me if I *slept* with you to get information about the company?"

Man, it sounded harsh when put that way. "I'm wondering what last night was for you, Meredith, and how it fit into your plans to assist in a takeover of my family's company."

Her eyes burned with anger. "If Helen told you what was going on, then she told you that this merger is the only way to save the company. If anything, my efforts will *help* your family, not hurt it."

"So this was altruistic of you."

"No, this was a job for me." She raised her chin defiantly. "It didn't matter to me what Helen wanted the information for. She asked me to get it and I did."

"So—"

"But," she interrupted, "as soon as I did, she made me aware of her intentions and the fact that she was doing this for the good of your company and your family. So by the time last night came along, I was well aware that I was not hurting you or your father's company, though he may have richly deserved it once."

She was right. He knew she was right. Her rationale was completely legitimate. How could he argue with it?

He stood up, standing over her, but she didn't move, didn't flinch. "Did last night have anything to do with your work on this potential merger?"

"No," she answered evenly. "Did we even *talk* about business last night? As a matter of fact, did I ask you to come over last night or did you just show up on your own?"

Good point. "Maybe you planned it."

"Not unless I'm psychic."

"Maybe you took a chance on getting it right."

"Then I wouldn't have been stupid enough to leave the evidence out for you to find, would I? Or I wouldn't have been stupid enough to fall asleep and let you wander the house and find my supposedly secret evidence."

Hard to argue with that one. "Then why did you do it, knowing that you were plotting against the company?"

She looked exasperated. "Number one, I wasn't plotting *against* anyone, and number two, it had nothing to do with work. At least for me it didn't." She shifted her weight, changing to a more combative posture. "What about you? What was *your* motivation, Evan?"

"Mine... My motivation was—" He pulled her closer and lowered his lips onto hers. The heat of the desire that washed over him was a surprise, even though he'd been feeling it in every interaction with her since she'd joined the company.

This was bad.

"It doesn't matter," he finished lamely. "Look, I've got to go. I'm flying to Japan tomorrow with Helen to meet with your bosses. I need to get some rest."

"They're not my bosses," Meredith objected. "Helen is. Same as you."

His head was spinning. The only thing he knew for sure was that he couldn't continue this conversation right now.

"They might be all of our bosses pretty soon," Evan said. "Now I have to go and make sure that's in the best interest of the family."

"And the company."

"The company *is* the family," he said, feeling it for the first time in his life. "Now, is there anything you can tell me that would help me in my conversations with TAKA?"

She nodded. "That the broadcasting division is already up, thanks to the announcements of Lenny Doss's addition. You made a good decision there. That will snag a good portion of the eighteen to thirty-four demographic. Dr. Ebony Lyle, airing in the afternoons, will pick up women in the same age group. And the Sports Addicts have a primarily male audience from eighteen to sixty-three. You've done really well," she concluded.

So had she. He hated to admit it, but he was really impressed with the facts she had at the ready.

In fact, he was impressed with just about everything Meredith did. But that wasn't a surprise to him. She'd always been capable and smart and creative.

The thing she hadn't always been was part of his daily life. For twelve years, though he remembered her frequently, he'd managed to live without her from day to day.

Now he wasn't so sure he could do that. He

found he wanted her around more and more, that he'd look for her even when he knew she wasn't there, and he'd listen for her voice on the wind.

He needed her around him.

He was a better man with her around.

Worse, he felt incomplete without her. And that scared him to death.

Chapter Seventeen

There was a silence in the TAKA offices that was unlike anything Evan had ever experienced. It gave him the creeps. Back home the Hanson offices were bustling, even though there were empty offices these days. But TAKA ran like a smooth engine, no bangs or dings, just a quiet hum.

Evan and Helen sat in the executive office with Richard Warren, Helen's attorney, discussing details of the merger.

When Evan was called upon to address the issues surrounding the broadcasting division, he answered all of the questions easily. Evan wouldn't have imagined he'd be so comfortable with corporate parlance but he was.

After the meeting was over, Richard and Evan stood in the hallway talking.

"I'm concerned that they mentioned the word *takeover,*" Evan said. "Is that a language idiosyncrasy or are they thinking takeover instead of merger?"

Richard took a short breath. "I don't know. I'm concerned about the same thing."

That didn't make Evan feel any better. "I wonder what Helen's take on this is." He saw her from the corner of his eye. "Helen—"

The woman who stopped and looked at him wasn't Helen. She had copper-colored hair, for one thing, and was a couple of decades younger than Helen. Evan did a double take, then said, "Sorry, I thought you were someone else."

Finally Helen did appear, and when she did Evan was glad to see her. "Is TAKA looking for a takeover instead of a merger?" he asked her.

"*I'm* looking for a merger," she said firmly. "And your coming and telling them about Hanson's assets has really helped in that pursuit. Thank you."

"I hope it helped," Evan said uncertainly.

"It did." Helen was completely confident. "Believe me. Things are definitely going the way I want them to."

They got back to the office late at night. Because Evan had stopped to get something to eat on the way home, Helen had gotten back to Hanson Media Group some time before he did.

When he arrived, she seemed to be the only one in the office.

Helen stopped him on his way to his office. "You've got to talk to Meredith."

"What?"

"She's here and she's trying to resign," Helen said.

"Resign?" he repeated, numb. "Why?"

"Because she sees herself as an impediment to your comfort here. She talked about how well you're doing and how she doesn't want to get in the way of that."

"But she's got so much to do with how well I'm doing."

Helen nodded. "She's been an asset for sure."

Something about the way she said it gave Evan pause. "You knew, didn't you?"

She assumed a blank expression. Too blank. "Knew what?"

"About Meredith and me. You knew about our past. That's why you threw us together."

"Meredith and you are both good workers, and you worked well together," she said, but her momentary glance at the floor told him everything he needed to know.

"You can't make up for everything my father did to all of us," Evan said quietly.

She gave a shrug and a small smile. "But I can help make up for some of it."

He shook his head and gave her a hug. "You're too much. I wish I'd met you years ago."

She looked pleased. "I do, too. Now get back into Meredith's office and stop her from leaving. I've got to go now, and the cleaning crew has already been here, so that will leave you two alone." She said it pointedly. "So remember to lock up when and if you leave." She didn't wait for an answer, just gave him a coy smile and a wink before leaving.

He hurried to Meredith's office. He stopped at the door and watched her putting things from her desk into a box in sad, slow motion.

"What do you think you're doing?" he asked her.

"I've got a new job."

"No, you don't. You just want to get away from this one."

"That's not true."

"Helen told me." He walked toward her. "She told me a lot, in fact. Did you know she knew about us before hiring either one of us?"

Meredith's face registered such genuine surprise that he knew immediately that she'd had no idea. "She set us up?"

He took her hands in his. "I'm afraid so. What's worse, she predicted what would happen exactly."

"What happened?" she asked, looking into his eyes.

"We fell in love again."

"You…? Are you saying you *love* me?"

"Baby, I've *always* loved you. I'm saying I've finally realized it."

Meredith's breath caught in her throat. "So you really don't want me to leave?"

"If you do, I'm leaving, too." He smiled. "And you know how hard it is to pull me out of corporate America."

She gave a laugh. "So what do we do?"

"Glad you asked," he said, and lowered his mouth to hers.

The moment their lips touched he felt as if an

electric shock jolted through him from her. He tightened his fingers on her shoulders and pulled her closer, willing her to stay with him, in this moment, and not to pull back and call it a mistake.

Evan hovered, just for a moment, with his lips almost touching hers. Their breath mingled and Meredith found herself trembling. He asked, "How do you like my plan so far?"

"So far it works for me."

Never in his life had Evan felt such a tsunami of desire. The kiss went from hungry to gentle, then back to hungry again. For long moments they backed off, lips barely touching, teasing, inviting more.

Her scent was heady up close—sweet and floral with just a hint of the familiar.

Meredith lifted a hand to his five-o'clock-shadow-roughened cheek and ran her fingertips across the contours of his face, her small hand soft against him.

Neither of them could find the words: all they had was the motion.

Evan ran his hands down her back, and she arched toward him, her pelvis pressed against his increasing arousal.

He wanted her.

In one fast motion, he pushed everything off her desk, the hell with the mess. Then he slowly lowered her to the desktop and positioned himself over her.

She let herself mold beneath him, allowing his body to dictate the direction they'd take. She countered his every movement with a complementary movement of her own.

Evan's arms tightened around her waist, and he kissed her more, trailing kisses along her jaw and down to her shoulder.

"So does this mean you forgive me for lying?" she asked, breathless against his neck.

"Only if you forgive me for every stupid thing I ever did."

"That could take a while," she responded with a giggle. "I hope you've got time."

"All the time in the world." He pulled closer.

She lifted her arms to rest on his shoulders, and tangled her fingers in his hair. "Promise me we'll never part again."

"I promise." He moved his hands across her body and kissed her sweetly. Her lips opened under his and he deepened the kiss, aroused by the semifamiliar taste of her. It had been a long time and she'd certainly gained experience since he'd last been with her, yet there was something about her that felt not only familiar but also right.

He ran his hands slowly down her sides, then drew them around her waist, pulling her closer still, pressing her against his own desire for her.

Meredith slid her hands down his shoulders and sides, slowly, as if she knew that every small fraction of an inch raised his desire. Indeed, he felt as if he came alive under her touch. These were feelings she hadn't enjoyed in years.

She wasn't even sure she'd *ever* felt them before.

All she knew was that the moment she'd first laid eyes on Evan again, despite the fact that twelve bitter years had passed, she'd felt something drawing her to him.

Now she suspected he felt the same.

Meredith trailed her hands across his stomach then flattened her palms against his chest, his skin warm against hers, making what almost felt like fire.

Evan eased his hands down to the small of her back. She felt beautiful. Her body molded softly against his and he felt warm, despite the fact that the office air-conditioning was on full blast.

When he finally eased himself into her and

satiated her longing, she felt as if she'd been given water after four days of dying from thirst. This was no longer about the personal pleasure—it was about survival. And, with Evan—at least for the moment—she had found a way to survive this crazy life she was living.

With Evan she knew she could survive anything.

* * * * *

HER BEST-KEPT SECRET

BY
BRENDA HARLEN

This project came together with a lot of help
from various people and I'd like to thank:
Susan Litman, for inviting me to be part of the
FAMILY BUSINESS continuity;
the other fabulous authors of this series,
for answering all my questions and making
this project so much fun;
Jeff Mahoney, for information and insights
about working in a newspaper business;
Dave Ferguson, for stories and pictures
from his trip to Tokyo;
Bruce and Peggy Wallace, for sharing
their cottage so I can escape to my writing;
my mom, who watched the kids while I escape;
and especially my husband Neill,
who loves me even when I'm under the pressure
of deadlines (because I know that isn't easy!)

Chapter One

Richard Warren waited outside the fourth floor boardroom hoping like hell that the difficulties of the past twenty-four hours weren't an indication of things to come. He helped himself to a desperately needed cup of coffee and stood back, on the fringes of the crowd, searching for Morito Taka. It was by invitation of the CEO of TAKA Corporation that Richard was attending this meeting today.

As legal counsel for Hanson Media Group, his sole purpose was to observe and report back to his boss, Helen Hanson. Only after the proposed merger was approved by the majority of shareholders would Richard take an active role in negotiating the terms with TAKA's executive and its legal team. If all went according to schedule, everything would be finalized within the next few weeks and he could go back to his life in Chicago.

He hoped all went according to schedule. This merger was too important for anything to go wrong. In the six months since the death of George Hanson, his widow had done everything possible, if not more, to save the company from bankruptcy. And with almost no help from her husband's three children, who were too busy resenting Helen's position in the company to appreciate the sacrifices she'd made and the work she'd done.

But Richard forgot about his boss and everything else when he spotted the goddess across the room, all rational thought obliterated by three simple letters: W-O-W.

His gaze skimmed over her sling-back shoes, up endlessly long legs to the short, slim-fitting skirt and neatly tailored pin-striped shirt that hugged feminine curves, to the elegant knot of copper-colored hair at the back of her neck. She turned, giving him a glimpse of glossy peach lips, high cheekbones, and deep green eyes, and he felt as if all of the oxygen had been sucked out of the room.

It was attraction, immediate and intense. But it was also recognition, and that shook him more than the desire stirring in his blood. He was sure that he'd seen her before. And yet, he was equally certain she was a stranger.

Maybe jet lag was scrambling his brain—it was the only explanation for such an incongruous thought.

She poured herself a cup of coffee, glancing up as she brought the cup to her lips. Their eyes met across the room, just for a second, before her gaze slid away again.

Richard felt a stirring of desire and realized it had been quite some time since he'd wanted a woman. Somewhere over the past year, he'd simply lost interest in the pretenses and deceptions that were an integral part of the mating ritual.

But he was definitely interested now.

He turned toward her just as a voice spoke behind him.

"Mr. Warren?"

Mentally cursing the interruption, Richard nevertheless put a smile on his face and turned. "Yes, I'm Richard Warren."

"I'm Yasushi Nishikawa." The young Japanese man bowed, offering a business card that he held in both of his hands.

Richard set his cup aside to accept the card, carefully reading the inscription before sliding it into the pocket of his jacket. Yet another helpful TAKA employee; yet another name to remember. He retrieved one of his own cards and presented it in the same manner.

"I have been given the honor of sitting with you to interpret the proceedings," Yasushi told him.

Richard nodded. *"Arigato."* Thank you.

The translator grinned. "You are learning our language."

"It's one of the few words I know," Richard admitted. He'd added good morning, excuse me and I don't understand—which he imagined he would be using frequently over the next few weeks—to his repertoire by studying his Japanese phrase book over his first cup of coffee that morning.

"It's a good start," Yasushi said. "I've also been asked to tell you that the commencement of negotiations has been delayed."

So much for keeping things on schedule.

"Mr. Tetsugoro was called out of town this morning on personal business. A death in the family," Yasushi explained. "He sends his apologies along with a promise to return by Monday morning."

While the man could hardly be blamed for a family emergency, Richard knew that would be little consolation to Helen with the future of Hanson Media at stake. He considered trying to call his boss now to advise her of this delay, but the meeting was scheduled to begin at eight o'clock and the sea of suits was already starting to flow toward the open doors of the conference room. The copper-haired goddess merged with the crowd that walked past.

Richard picked up his briefcase and followed Yasushi inside. Helen would have to wait.

He wasn't sure if it was lucky or not that his assigned companion selected a pair of chairs directly across the table from the woman who'd caught and held his attention.

"Jenny Anderson," Yasushi said softly, following the direction of his gaze. "She moved to Tokyo from New York about six months ago and is a society reporter for the Tokyo *Tribune,* TAKA's English language newspaper."

"Is it common for reporters to attend shareholder meetings?" he asked.

"No," Yasushi said. "But her parents are shareholders. She sometimes attends meetings on their behalf when they are out of the country."

A beautiful young reporter with jet-setting parents. The scant information didn't begin to answer all of the questions that came to mind.

He watched her riffle through a sheaf of papers she'd set on the table, and noted the absence of rings on her hands. He knew that wasn't conclusive evidence of anything, just as he knew that her marital status shouldn't be any of his concern. There was too much riding on this merger to allow his attention to be diverted, and the last thing he needed right now was the distraction of a woman.

Still, he found himself asking, "Is she married?"

Yasushi smiled. "No, but determinedly unavailable, much to the disappointment of every single man in this room."

Jenny hated these meetings, but she'd been unable to avoid this one as both of her parents were out of town and had left her with their proxies. When the final votes were taken and the meeting adjourned after a long and tedious three hours, she quickly slipped out of the room.

Unfortunately, she wasn't quick enough to avoid Kogetsu.

Cornered by the coffee pot, Jenny decided to pour herself another cup as she listened to his speech. Kogetsu was always trying to persuade or cajole or even bribe Jenny to visit his sister's art gallery in the hope that she would write it up for the society pages of the paper. She didn't object to giving some free publicity to a struggling entrepreneur, but she'd already written two articles about the gallery in the past four weeks. Lucky for Kogetsu, Jenny liked his sister, the gallery and usually the art she showcased.

She nodded her head in response to his enthusiastic call to support local up-and-coming artisans and glanced at her watch, hoping he would take the hint that she needed to be somewhere else soon. Of course, he did not, and she was forced to stand and listen another few minutes before she could interject to remind him that she wrote feature pieces, not advertising copy.

Somehow Kogetsu managed to look wounded by her remark, forcing Jenny to admit she'd already planned to cover the event—because it was an event and not because he'd asked her. Kogetsu didn't care about her reasons, of course, and she bit back a sigh as she turned away.

She'd taken only three steps toward the door when *he* stepped into her path.

He being a man she'd never seen before. At least, not before she'd caught him staring at her before the meeting. And several times during the endlessly long ordeal.

He was American—she'd known that immediately. It was more than just his impressive height and Western style of dress, it was the aura of success and self-confidence he wore as easily as the tailored suit jacket that stretched across his broad shoulders. She knew the type—she'd already fallen in love with and had had her heart broken by other men who fit the same mold. New York would be her first guess. Maybe Boston or Philadelphia. But definitely American and definitely trouble.

She spoke to him in Japanese, knowing he wouldn't understand the words and hoping he'd take the hint that she didn't want to talk to him.

His lips curved in an easy smile, but she wasn't in a mood to be charmed.

"I have no idea what you just said," he responded in English, "but the words sure sounded good rolling off your tongue."

"She said, 'Please, excuse me,'" Yasushi translated for him.

Jenny couldn't help but be amused by the deliberately loose interpretation of her words. "Actually what I said was, 'You're in my way.'"

The American's smile never wavered. "It sounded so much prettier in Japanese."

"The language is irrelevant," she said coolly. "The point is that you're blocking the door."

"I'm Richard Warren." He offered his hand.

After a brief hesitation, she accepted it, her initial reluctance bolstered by the unwelcome tingle that reverberated through her system. "Jenny Anderson."

"A pleasure to meet you, Jenny Anderson." He lowered his voice conspiratorially. "Is it safe to assume we won't need a translator for the next few minutes?"

"I don't have a few minutes." She realized he was still holding her hand and quickly tugged it from his grasp.

"Two minutes," he said, nodding to Yasushi, who discreetly stepped away.

She glanced at her watch, not bothering to hide her impatience. She had no inclination or interest in making conversation with any man whose simplest touch could affect her in such a way. Not any more. "Two minutes," she agreed.

He smiled again, clearly a man accustomed to getting his own way. "Have we met before?"

"No." Her tone was as succinct as the single word response.

"Are you sure?" he pressed. "Because you really look familiar to me."

"I'm sure, and if that's all—"

"It's not," he said.

She shifted the leather folio she carried from one hand to the other.

"It turns out I have the next few days free," he continued. "And I was hoping you might be willing to show a fellow American around."

"You might have the next few days free, Mr. Warren, but I don't."

"How about the nights?"

"Excuse me?" She shook her head, convinced she couldn't possibly have heard him correctly.

"It wasn't an indecent proposal," he said, then gave her another one of those heart-stopping smiles. "I was suggesting that you could show me the sights after you finish work."

"I don't think—"

Her refusal was interrupted by arrival of Shiguro Taka, making her wonder if she would ever get out of the building and back to her own job.

"Miss Anderson." He gave a slight bow before turning his attention to the American, bowing more deeply. "Mr. Warren. I wanted to apologize personally for the mix-up at the airport yesterday."

"Not a problem," Richard said.

"It was a poor reflection of Japanese hospitality. You must let us somehow make up to you the inconvenience."

Jenny managed a small step closer to the door before Richard shifted, again blocking her path.

"That really isn't necessary," he responded to Mr. Taka's offer.

"It is," Shiguro insisted. "Perhaps tickets to the Kabuki theater or sumo tournament."

"Well, I was hoping that someone might be able to show me around the city."

The other man nodded. "We have any number of employees who would be eager to take you on a tour of the sights."

"Actually," Richard said, "I was hoping that Ms. Anderson might be persuaded to fill that role."

"Of course," Shiguro said. "I can understand that you would enjoy the company of a fellow American, and an especially beautiful one at that."

He smiled in her direction, and Jenny got a sinking feeling in the pit of her stomach.

"I'm sorry, sir, but as much as I'd like to help—" it was

a lie, but one she had no compunction about uttering "—I don't have any time to spare over the next few days. I'm in the middle of an assignment for Lincoln Kelly and—"

"Mr. Kelly can reassign it," Shiguro said easily, already pulling his cell phone out of his pocket.

And he had the power to see that it was done, Jenny acknowledged bleakly. She might not work directly for Shiguro, but he was one of the key executives at TAKA and TAKA owned the newspaper.

Frustration churned inside her. She'd spent weeks on research-interviewing witnesses and corroborating facts—because she knew that this story would prove her skills as a journalist and open up new opportunities for her. If she lost this story, it could be months, maybe even longer, before another opportunity came along. More importantly, if she lost this story, she'd renege on a promise she'd made.

"It's an important story, sir—"

"Nothing is more important than showing our visitor proper Japanese hospitality," Shiguro countered.

Of course not—Japanese hospitality was legendary. And though she had no idea who Richard Warren was or why he was in Tokyo, it was obviously important to Mr. Taka to make a good impression on him.

As he started to dial the phone, the opportunity Jenny had waited too long for already slipped from her grasp.

She was furious.

Not that Richard could blame her, considering the way she'd been manipulated by Shiguro Taka and himself. The TAKA executive had steamrolled over her objections and coerced her into being his tour guide for the next couple of days, and Richard hadn't protested.

As he followed her hurried strides across the parking lot to the newspaper building next door, he was thinking he should regret his part in the whole arrangement. Should, but didn't. He was too intrigued by this woman and already looking forward to the opportunity to know her better.

She stormed past the reception desk and into what he guessed was the newsroom. She dropped her folio onto a desk and dropped into the chair behind it.

Richard stayed on the other side of the desk, a safe distance away. "You're angry."

"You're incredibly insightful." She picked up a pile of message slips and began sorting through them.

"Would it help if I said I was sorry?

She glanced up through narrowed eyes. "Are you?"

"Not really," he admitted.

"Then, no, it doesn't help." She crumpled up one of the messages and tossed it toward the garbage.

It missed.

Richard bent over to pick up the discarded scrap of paper and drop it into the metal can. "I've had a hellish two days," he told her. "My head is swimming with names I can't possibly remember, and when I saw you, I thought we might have something in common—two Americans in Tokyo."

"It sounds like the title of a bad movie."

Despite the derisive response, he noticed that she sounded more resigned than angry now.

"Is it really so horrible—a couple of days off to play tour guide?"

"Yes," she said through clenched teeth. "I don't want to play tour guide, I want to play reporter. That is, after all, why I went to college and got that little piece of paper they call a degree."

Despite the scathing tone, she really did fascinate him. "Where did you go to school?" he asked.

She crumpled another message and tossed it. "I think you missed my point."

He retrieved it from the floor, fighting against the smile that tugged at his lips. "No, I'm just trying to move beyond the fact that you're obviously annoyed with me for something that wasn't my fault."

"You told Mr. Taka that you wanted me to be your tour guide."

"Yes, but I didn't know he could make it happen. Now that he has, I can't regret it since this may be my only chance to spend time with you."

"You're right about that," she grumbled.

He lowered himself into one of the chairs across from her desk. "Where did you go to journalism school?" he asked again.

"Stanford."

"Impressive."

She shrugged and started shuffling through a pile of faxes from her in-box.

"Where'd you learn to speak Japanese?" he asked.

"Here."

He glanced around the tiny cubicle, raised an eyebrow in silent question.

Finally she smiled. "In Japan. My family moved to Tokyo when I was nine."

"From where?"

"Zurich. Before that we lived in Athens. Before that it was Venice." She frowned. "Or maybe it was Paris and then

Venice. With periodic trips back to the States—New York or Dallas or San Francisco."

"Bet that really racked up the frequent flyer points."

She shrugged again. "My parents like to travel, and their business demands it."

"What's their business?"

"Hotels."

He felt as though a light bulb had clicked on inside his head. "You're *that* Anderson? Of Anderson Hotels?"

"It's the name on my driver's license," she said lightly. "And no, I'm not going to get you a discount on your room."

"I should have guessed. A woman who wears Cartier isn't working as a reporter for the money."

She tugged the sleeve of her blouse over her wrist, tucking the gold watch out of sight. "You are observant."

"That's part of my job," he said.

"And your job is?" she prompted, showing the first sign of interest in his reasons for being there.

"I'm a corporate attorney with Hanson Media Group."

"A lawyer," she said. "Figures."

He frowned. "You have a problem with lawyers?"

"Not lawyers in particular," she said. "Just pushy people in general."

"Pushy?" he tried to sound indignant.

"I'm sure I'm not the first person to bring that particular attribute to your attention," she said dryly.

"No," he admitted. "That would have been my mother when I was about three. Of course, I learned it from her."

She smiled, but it was the hint of sadness in her eyes that intrigued him more than the curve of her lips. There was a story there, he was sure, and damned if he wasn't determined to find out what it was.

"It was my mother's idea for me to become a lawyer," he continued.

"She must be pleased that you did."

There was a time he thought she would have been, too, before his father's death. Since that fateful event, Richard had given up hope that his mother would ever accept the choices he'd made that conflicted with her own agenda.

Although he was glad Jenny was finally participating in the conversation, he wasn't so pleased that she was steering it in a direction he didn't want to follow, reminding him of things he didn't want to remember. "Why don't we get to know each other over coffee?"

"Because I've had enough coffee today and I have work to do if you want me to be available tomorrow."

"Are you?" He smiled again. "Available, that is?"

"I'm not interested, Mr. Warren. That's an entirely different scenario."

"Is it just me—or are you always this prickly?"

"Only when I've had a hard-earned assignment taken away."

"I really didn't intend for that to happen."

She sighed. "Unfortunately that doesn't change the facts."

"Maybe you'll end up with a bigger and better story."

"Maybe." She didn't sound convinced, but then she leaned back in her chair and looked at him. "So you're here to work on the merger."

It wasn't a question, but he nodded anyway.

"How long have you worked for Hanson Media?"

"A little more than a year."

"What happened?"

"What do you mean?" He asked the question warily, but he'd already sensed her agile mind switching gears. She was in investigative mode now, full of questions and searching for answers.

"How did a publishing giant end up on the verge of bankruptcy?" she asked.

"That's a long and complicated story."

"I might be interested in hearing about it over dinner."

As tempted as he was to take the bait she'd dangled, it wasn't an option. "Unfortunately, it's not my story to tell."

"That is unfortunate," she agreed.

"How about dinner, anyway?"

"I don't think so."

He was disappointed though not really surprised by her response. "You're brushing me off because I won't divulge privileged information?"

"I'm merely keeping my schedule open to explore other investigative opportunities," she countered.

"I thought you were a society reporter."

"A temporary assignment," she assured him. "I have bigger ambitions than that."

He'd already concluded as much. "Why don't we talk about those ambitions over dinner?"

She shook her head. "Nice try, though."

"I'm trying to show that I can be persistent as opposed to merely pushy."

"I'll see you tomorrow," she said.

It wasn't quite the response he was hoping for, but he knew it was the most he could expect at this point. He sighed. "What time tomorrow?"

Samara's low whistle of appreciation drew Jenny's focus from Richard's undeniably appealing backside as he walked away.

Her oldest and best friend, and her roommate since she'd returned to Tokyo, perched on the edge of the desk. "Who's the hunk?"

She had to admit it was an apt description for Richard Warren. The dark brown hair, deep blue eyes and quick, easy smile were a combination any woman could appreciate. Add to the equation six feet of height, broad shoulders and narrow hips, and even Jenny was tempted to sigh. But she'd made the mistake of being taken in by good looks and magnetic charm before—it was a mistake she wouldn't make again. "Your so-called hunk is my current nightmare."

Samara's dark eyes sparkled with interest, her lips curved. "Tell me everything."

"Richard Warren, lawyer for Hanson Media Group. He's in town to negotiate terms for a proposed merger with TAKA. And he cost me my byline on the Kakubishi story."

Samara's smile faded. "What? How?"

"By suggesting to Shiguro Taka that he wanted me to show him around town."

"You were pulled off of a front-page assignment for that?"

"Apparently there was some kind of mix-up at the airport and Shiguro Taka is bending over backward to make up for it."

Her friend winced sympathetically. "Who's taking over your story?"

Jenny shrugged. "I don't know, but it makes me furious that I did all the legwork, I sold Lincoln on the story, and now I don't even get to write it."

"I'm sorry, Jenny."

"Not as sorry as I am."

"We could make a trade," Samara suggested. "I'll give you my camera for your hunk."

"As tempted as I am to take you up on that generous offer, I'm not sure Kazuo would appreciate it," she responded dryly.

Samara waved her left hand. "Until he puts a ring on my finger, I'm a cheap agent."

Jenny laughed. "The expression is free agent."

"Whatever." She shrugged. "So what are your plans for Richard Warren?"

She couldn't prevent the smile that tugged at the corner of her lips. "I'm considering a couple of possibilities."

"Uh-oh."

"What?"

"I know that look," Samara said.

"What look?"

"Devious innocence." Her friend's gaze narrowed. "What are you planning?"

Jenny laughed again. "I'm planning to get free of Mr. Warren."

"How?"

"By ensuring that he's so bored after our first day together he won't want to spend any more time with me." She could picture it already—Richard Warren's eyes as glazed as the *chawan* he'd be holding awkwardly in his hands, wishing he'd never approached her outside the shareholders' meeting.

"How?" Samara asked again.

She smiled. "Two words—*tea ceremony.*"

Chapter Two

Tea ceremony?

"A lot of Westerners have the mistaken impression that tea in Japan is simply a pleasant pastime," Jenny told Richard as they exited the subway station. "But *cha-no-yu* is really a spiritual ceremony—a religion of the art of life."

She'd said nothing about their plans for the day until they'd disembarked from the train, promising only that it was an experience Richard wouldn't forget. The way she said it, he wasn't sure it was a good thing. She'd been pleasant and scrupulously polite since meeting him in the lobby of his hotel, but he sensed some residual resentment about the way she'd been coerced into spending time with him.

"There are various forms of the ceremony," she told him. "Even some of the local hotels offer an abbreviated version, but I thought you would enjoy participating in a more authentic celebration."

He tried to hide his skepticism as he listened to her explanation. While a traditional Japanese tea wouldn't have been his first choice of how to spend the day, he was happy to be with her—and only her. Since his arrival in Japan, he'd been shadowed by one or more of TAKA's people and while they were incredibly polite and hospitable, he was tired of constantly being on his best behavior. He wanted to relax for a little while and share unstilted conversation with a pretty woman.

Except that he was getting the impression they wouldn't have much time for casual conversation. Even now, on the way to the teahouse, she was providing a steady flow of information as if she were a professional tour guide. If he'd been seeking company knowledgeable about the culture and history of Japan, he couldn't have chosen anyone better. But what he really wanted was a glimpse into the woman behind the mask of polite reserve.

So far, he'd seen that mask slip only once—yesterday afternoon when Shiguro Taka had appointed her to be his personal tour guide. Since then, she'd seemed to accept her unwelcome fate with stoicism.

"It was a Zen priest who first brought tea to Japan," she informed him. "And the simplicity and purity of the religion was a strong influence on the form of the tea ceremony. But Zen focuses on the enlightenment of the individual through isolation and mediation, and *cha-no-yu* involves the communication of people through spirit and mind."

He watched the subtle sway of her hips as she walked ahead of him, his mind more focused on the urge of his body to communicate with hers than any spiritual matters.

It was a desire he knew would go unsatisfied. Jenny had made it clear that being with him today was nothing more than a command performance, the fulfillment of a professional obligation.

Disappointed though he was, he knew it was for the best. He couldn't afford to have his attention diverted from the task that had brought him to Japan. So he tore his gaze from the enticing curve of her backside as he followed her up the stone path toward a small building made of wooden logs that seemed to be held together with mud.

"Japanese tearooms and gardens are designed to blend harmoniously with their natural surroundings," she explained. "Because the ceremony is linked closely to nature, parts of the ceremony vary according to the season. The flowers displayed, the utensils used, the cakes served."

He watched as she removed her shoes and set them neatly at the entrance. He did the same, then followed her into the building. She set her purse in a woven basket on the porch before turning to him. "Do you have a cell phone?"

He nodded. It wasn't actually his but one that had been loaned to him for his personal use while he was in Japan. He might be frustrated with the delay in negotiations, but he couldn't fault the TAKA people for their gracious hospitality.

"You leave it here—" she gestured to the basket "—in the *yoritsuki,* the entry."

"Leave my cell phone?"

She lifted one perfectly arched brow. "Is that a problem?"

"Of course not. But..." he faltered, wondering how to convey his objection, wondering why he wanted to object. Because he was here on business and he needed to be accessible to Helen. Because he was a lawyer and his cell phone was like a natural appendage.

"You could just turn it off," Jenny said. "But it's more respectful to leave such obvious symbols of the outside world outside of the teahouse."

Despite the nonchalant tone, he sensed a hint of disapproval in her words. He unclipped the phone from his belt even as he wondered why her censure bothered him.

Still, he couldn't resist teasing her. "Do you think I could have coffee instead of tea?"

She turned back, her expression no longer neutral, and he took a perverse sort of pleasure in the sparks in her deep green eyes. "This isn't Starbucks," she said frostily.

"I've just never been much of a tea drinker," he explained.

"Tea is only part of the ceremony," she told him. "It's more about achieving harmony with your host and spiritual satisfaction through silent meditation." She glanced at the cell still clutched in his hand. "If you can't part with your phone for a little while, you're welcome to wait outside."

Although a part of him still balked at being unavailable if Helen needed to get in touch with him, he couldn't refuse her challenge. He turned the phone off and tossed it into the *yoritsuki* with Jenny's purse.

"I wouldn't miss it for the world," he told her.

They were words Richard would regret as soon as he realized there were no other guests for the tea ceremony.

Maybe he should have been flattered that Jenny had arranged a private demonstration, instead he felt as if he were a foreign specimen being examined through a microscope. An apt description as he was foreign to the setting and completely out of his element. Unlike Jenny who was obviously familiar with the customs and rituals.

He tried to follow her lead, bowing when she bowed, kneeling when she knelt. But he remained silent while she made conversation, complimenting their host on the ink painted scroll and the beautiful arrangement of flowers. At least that's what Jenny told him she was saying—as the entire dialogue was in Japanese, he couldn't be sure.

The woman hosting the ceremony was introduced as Izumi. She wore a silk kimono of deep blue patterned with silver fish jumping over it. She was obviously elderly, her hair more gray than black and fashioned into a knot at the back of her neck. Her face was deeply lined, her posture slightly bent, but there was a quiet strength evident in the grace of her movements and a sparkle in her dark eyes befitting a woman half her age.

"*Kaiseki,*" Jenny said, offering no further explanation for the selection of dishes that was set in front of him.

He was both impressed and confused by the elaborate presentation of the food, each item or a small selection of items—most of which he'd never seen before and couldn't have guessed at the names—served on individual dishes. Small glazed bowls, shallow square plates, crescent-shaped dishes, miniature cups for sauces and garnishes. Growing up, Richard could only remember eating salad from a separate dish if there was company at the dinner table. Otherwise, his mother insisted the greens went on the same plate as the rest of the meal.

He wondered if that was still true. It had been so long since he'd had a meal in her home, he was no longer certain. With the thought came a sharp but now familiar pang of regret. He'd lost his father almost ten years ago and his mother had distanced herself shortly after that, more concerned with putting her husband's killer behind bars than maintaining a relationship with her sons.

Izumi spoke softly to him, interrupting the painful memories of his past and returning his attention to the present. Unfortunately, his Japanese vocabulary was too limited to even attempt a translation.

"She asked if you're enjoying your *sunomono,*" Jenny told him.

He assumed she meant the grated vegetables he'd just sampled. *"Oishii,"* he responded. Delicious.

Izumi smiled and placed yet another series of dishes in front of him.

Jenny, he noticed, seemed annoyed rather than pleased by his reply. And he was starting to suspect that she hadn't brought him here to enjoy the ceremony but because she expected that he'd be bored by it. Rather than be offended by the realization, he was only more intrigued. As interesting as the rituals of the tea ceremony were, he found his reluctant companion even more so.

In his thirty-four years, he'd indulged in several casual affairs and a few more serious relationships. He'd even been married once. But he couldn't ever remember feeling the kind of basic pull toward a woman that tugged at him now.

Unfortunately, he was in Tokyo for the merger and she worked—however indirectly—for TAKA. While a personal relationship might not result in a direct conflict of interest, it would complicate the situation for both of them.

Besides, she didn't strike him as the type of woman to indulge in brief affairs and he wasn't going to be in Tokyo long enough to offer her anything else.

So resolved, he decided to use this time of contemplation to refocus his thoughts, mentally organize his questions and concerns about the merger. He was annoyed to find that his thoughts refused to focus.

In the past his attention had always strayed to work and work-related issues, but this time he found his attention straying to the woman beside him. While he allowed himself the occasional distraction of a woman—of his choosing and on his timetable—he'd never allowed himself to be distracted *by* a woman. And the women he'd chosen had always been those more interested in blowing off a little steam than a relationship, and that had always suited him fine.

Since his divorce, shallow and temporarily satisfying interludes were all he'd wanted or needed. Until a few months ago when he'd crawled out from between the silk sheets of a district court judge with whom he'd spent the night and suddenly wondered if that was all he could hope for in his life.

Izumi's gentle voice interrupted his thoughts.

"She noticed that you're frowning," Jenny told him.

"Sorry," he apologized automatically. *"Sumimasen."*

"Don't be sorry," Jenny translated as their hostess measured some kind of green powder into a bowl. "Be at peace. Clear your mind of disturbing thoughts. Relax."

Easy to say but impossible to do when the source of the disturbance was so close—and his thoughts about her were anything but relaxing.

Jenny felt Richard's gaze on her. She was conscious of his attention, of everything about him, though she wished she wasn't. And she was annoyed with herself that she'd so obviously underestimated him.

She really hadn't expected that he would still be here.

In her experience, career-driven men didn't appreciate the opportunity to sit down and relax for five minutes, never mind five hours. She knew for certain that her ex wouldn't have lasted this long—Brad was too restless and edgy to ever completely unwind. Maybe that was one of the reasons they were so fundamentally wrong for each other. Or maybe she was only looking for reasons now that they'd gone their separate ways.

It had been her choice to end their relationship, and as she hadn't seen or heard from him in the six months that had since passed, she found it strange that she was thinking of him now. Or maybe the thought was a warning from her subconscious. Because while there was no more than a surface resemblance between Brad and Richard, she couldn't help but feel they were alike on the inside. Brad's only thought had been the next story; Richard was—even now, she imagined—preoccupied by the merger between Hanson Media and TAKA.

She needed to remember that single-minded drive and forget about the tingles that danced through her veins whenever he looked at her. No matter how strong the attraction between them, she wasn't going to play second fiddle to any man's career again. She had her own hopes and dreams and she wasn't going to be sidetracked.

On the other hand, she wasn't going to let her ambitions dictate the course of her life, either. She believed in balance and harmony—it was one of the reasons she loved the tea ceremony. The serenity and history were as important to her as the ritual preparation and sharing of food and drink.

She'd needed that serenity today. As annoyed as she'd been about losing her assignment, she relished the time for silent meditation, the opportunity to purge the negative emotions from her soul. The fact that the very same rituals were likely boring Richard Warren to tears was merely an added bonus. He might be graciously enduring the ceremony, but she would bet that after it was over, he'd be not just willing but eager to undertake the rest of his sightseeing alone. Or at least without her.

She felt a brief prick of guilt, released it with a long slow breath. She had no reason to feel guilty. If the American lawyer was too uptight to relax and enjoy one of the cornerstones of Japanese culture, she could hardly be held responsible.

"It didn't work, you know."

They were the first words Richard spoke to Jenny upon exiting the teahouse.

"What didn't work?" she asked, feigning innocence.

"Using the tea ceremony to convince me to find another tour guide."

"I'd hoped you would enjoy it," she lied. "*Cha-no-yu* is a fascinating part of Japanese culture."

His smile was quick, easy and completely disarming. "Then you weren't hoping to bore me to death?"

She felt her own lips start to curve, fought to keep her expression neutral as she turned down the path leading away from the tea house. "Mr. Taka would never forgive me if I was responsible for the demise of an honored guest."

"And if you could do away with me without risk of any professional repercussions?" he asked, falling into step beside her.

"They'd never find your body."

He laughed. "That's what I thought."

This time she let the smile come. "You're a good sport, Mr. Warren."

"Richard," he corrected. "And I had a good time."

"I'm glad," she said, surprised to realize it was true. Although her original intention had been thwarted, she found she wasn't disappointed. She didn't know many men—and none who weren't Japanese—who could relax and enjoy the traditional ceremony that she loved. It made her wonder if she might have been too quick in her judgment of him.

Or maybe not.

As he clipped his cell phone back onto his belt, she reminded herself that he was a lawyer in town on temporary business. Definitely not a man her fickle heart should be weaving any romantic fantasies about. She knew only too well that the charm and attentiveness would dissipate in an instant when the demands of the job called.

"You seemed to know Izumi quite well," he said.

Obviously he'd been paying more attention than she'd given him credit for. "She's my roommate's great-grandmother."

"You have a roommate?"

She smiled at the surprise evident in his question. "You apparently have no idea how expensive rent is in Tokyo."

"But your parents are Anderson Hotels."

"They are," she agreed. "I'm not."

"Why not? Surely there must be numerous career opportunities for you within the family organization."

"I wanted to be a reporter."

"And that was okay with them?" he asked.

"They weren't thrilled with my choice at first, but they've always supported me."

"You're lucky."

She nodded. It was what she reminded herself every day—she *was* incredibly fortunate to have parents who loved and stood by her. Unfortunately that knowledge couldn't silence the questions or lessen the pain that came from not having been wanted by the woman who'd given her away only a few hours after giving birth to her.

"You were telling me about Izumi," he reminded her.

"Why are you so interested?"

"She seemed like an interesting woman," he said. "Someone who's lived a satisfying life, with a sparkle in her eyes that suggests she's not nearly finished living it yet."

Again, he'd surprised her. And because he'd so clearly understood the woman who was dear to her own heart, Jenny couldn't help softening toward him.

"She would love that description," she admitted.

"You're close to her," he guessed.

She nodded. "I don't have any grandparents of my own, but I spent enough time at Samara's when we were kids that Izumi became like a grandmother to me.

"But long before she was a grandmother, she was a geisha," she told him. "It was while working as a geisha that she met and fell in love with Samara's great-grandfather. They got married three weeks after their first meeting and had four children together before he went off to war. He never came back."

Jenny had cried the first time she heard the story and almost every time since. Especially when Izumi told it—the emotion in her voice reflecting her love and grief as clearly as if it had been a recent loss, not something that had happened many years ago.

"She said that when she learned of his death, she felt as though a part of her had died, too. Then her baby—Samara's grandfather—cried to be fed, and she realized she hadn't lost him completely. So long as she had her children, she would always have part of him."

It had made Jenny realize that she wanted the same thing—to love and be loved, deeply and forever, to have a family of her own and children who were part of herself as no one else was.

"It's a beautiful story," he said. "Almost enough to make the most cynical person believe in true love."

"Almost?"

He shrugged.

"I'm guessing you would be that most cynical person."

"Let's just say that my experience has been different."

"Every experience is, as Izumi would agree." She turned to Richard and smiled. "She married three more times."

"So much for true love."

She shook her head. "You are a cynic."

"Four marriages is a lot by any standards."

"What's your standard? How many did it take to destroy your faith in love?"

"Just one marriage and one divorce."

"And you have no intention of trying again," she guessed.

"I like to think I'm smart enough to have learned my lesson the first time."

"Izumi's situation is different. She didn't divorce her husbands, she buried them. And I think her willingness to still believe in love is admirable. Of course, being widowed three times might explain why she's currently married to a man almost twenty years her junior." She smiled again. "It might also explain the sparkle in her eye."

The glimpse of humor caught him off guard and completely captivated him. She was relaxed now, her defenses seemingly forgotten as she stopped trying to keep him at a distance and really talked to him.

When he'd first seen her across the room at TAKA yesterday, he'd been struck by her looks—both the uncanny sense of recognition and the cool, poised beauty. Now, with her eyes soft and her lips curved, the sun shining down on her, she was warm and real and infinitely more appealing.

The attraction he'd felt from the first stirred again, more insistently this time. Richard reminded himself that he had a lot of valid reasons for keeping things casual and only one for making a move—he wanted her. But that want was starting to prove a more powerful force than logic.

"What would it take," he wondered aloud, "to put that kind of sparkle in your eye?"

Her smile didn't fade, but there was no doubt it cooled. "More than you'd be willing to give," she said in a level tone.

"Now that sounds like a challenge."

"It's not—just a fact."

"You're determined not to like me, aren't you?"

"I don't dislike you, Mr. Warren. I just have no interest in being a diversion for a guy like you."

"A guy like me?" He felt his irritation mounting. "What does that mean?"

"You're good-looking, charming and successful."

How, he wondered, did she manage to make the statement so that it flattered and insulted at the same time?

"And because you have time on your hands," she continued, "you assume any woman you want should be willing to help you fill it."

He scowled, not just because of the accusation but because he realized there was some truth in what she'd said. He'd seen her, wanted her and gone after her.

"I'm a novelty for you—a woman who isn't falling at your feet."

"I've never actually had to step over the bodies," he said dryly. "But I've also never met a woman so obviously opposed to my company."

She met his gaze evenly. "I have no intention of being your plaything for the few weeks that you're going to be in town."

"Well, that's certainly blunt."

"I just want to make sure there are no misunderstandings."

"For your information, I'm not in the habit of pursuing a woman who's made it clear that she's not interested."

"Then there shouldn't be a problem."

She started to walk away.

He grabbed her arm and turned her back to face him. "Except I'm not convinced you're not interested."

Chapter Three

Jenny wanted to be annoyed by his arrogance, except she knew that he was right. His fingers slid down her arm to her wrist, his slow smile confirming that he'd registered the skip and race of her pulse. She could find all kinds of words to deny the attraction between them, but she couldn't deny her physical response to him.

"Tell me that you don't want me to kiss you," he said, his lips hovering mere inches above hers.

Right now, with his body so close to hers she could feel his heat and hear his heart pound, she wanted his kiss more than she wanted to take her next breath. And that was precisely why she couldn't let it happen. Wanting anything from a man like Richard Warren could only lead to heartache. So she opened her mouth to voice the denial—even if it was a lie.

Before she could speak a single word, he kissed her.

At the first touch of his lips, desire swept over her in an unexpected and overpowering wave. Recognizing the futility of struggling against it, she let herself flow with it—the deep, almost desperate need.

His arm banded around her waist, holding her tight against him so she couldn't pull away. Heat seared her body everywhere it touched his. Her breasts, her hips, her thighs. Too much heat. It was impossible to even think of pulling away when she was melting against him.

She laid her palms on his chest, felt the quick, steady beat of his heart. Her own was pumping to the same rhythm, her blood pulsing heavily in her veins. Her hands slid over the hard contour of muscle to link behind his neck, holding on, as any protests she might have uttered turned into desires and her subconscious denials became needs.

His hand stroked up her back, the bold touch shooting arrows of pleasure through her. Then he cupped her neck to tilt her head back, his fingers sifting through her hair.

Again, he surprised her. Instead of deepening the kiss, the pressure of his mouth gentled. His lips moved away from hers to trail soft kisses along the line of her jaw. He nibbled gently on her ear, cruised slowly down her throat. Featherlight caresses that whispered over her skin.

He was no longer taking but giving, and Jenny couldn't refuse what he was offering. She didn't know how to fight against such tender passion. She didn't want to. She trembled against him, her body quivering with desire.

"Richard."

When she spoke his name, it was a sigh, a plea.

His mouth moved back to hers. Slowly, patiently, he took

her deeper. It was like a dream—soft and warm and misty, with just the hint of danger hovering around the edges.

His tongue slid between her parted lips, skimmed over hers. She welcomed him, felt rather than heard the soft whimper deep in her own throat.

She tried to tell herself that she didn't want this. She knew she *shouldn't* want this. But reason and logic had abandoned her, and she only wanted him.

Richard had intended to make a point—to force Jenny to acknowledge the attraction between them. He hadn't expected that he'd end up wanting so much more. He eased his mouth from hers with unexpected reluctance and drew in a desperate lungful of air and willed his mind to clear, his thoughts to focus. Then he made the mistake of looking at her again.

Her lips were still swollen from his kiss, her eyes still cloudy with desire, her body still soft and warm against his. He felt an almost overwhelming urge to kiss her again, to take everything she didn't seem to realize she was offering.

It was the obvious vulnerability and the almost imperceptible hint of fear in her eyes that held his passion in check. He didn't know what she was afraid of, but he knew she was smart to be afraid. Whatever was happening between them was too much too fast—they both needed to take a step back.

"It seems as though you were right about my interest," he murmured. "And wrong about your own."

She opened her mouth, probably to argue the point, then closed it again. They both knew it was absurd to protest when she was still in his arms.

"It doesn't change anything," she said. "I'm not going to sleep with you."

He wondered if she was aware of the tremor in her own voice, or how incredibly arousing it was to know he'd been the one to shake her cool poise. So arousing that he was tempted to interpret her words as another challenge and set upon changing her mind. But he'd been as shaken as she by the kiss they'd shared, and he decided it might be wise to accept the boundaries she was setting—at least for now.

"All right," he agreed. "No sleeping together on the first date."

She narrowed her eyes. "This isn't a date."

"Does that mean we can sleep together?"

"No." Her response was firm, but he saw the smile tugging at the corner of her lips in response to his teasing.

It had been his intent to lessen the tension, but the hint of a smile had drawn his attention back to her mouth, tempting him to kiss her again.

He tore his gaze away. "Okay, then. What's next on the agenda?"

She hesitated, as if she didn't trust the easy compliance his question suggested. "How about the theater?"

"That sounds great," he said.

A theater would at least be filled with people and the action on the stage might keep his attention focused—and away from the temptation of his tour guide.

The theater had seemed like a good idea when she'd first decided upon it. Jenny had been certain that a few more hours of inactivity after the lengthy tea ceremony would be more than enough to drive Richard to abandon her company completely. Of course, that was *before* the kiss.

The kiss she should never have allowed to happen. But now that it had, there was no way to pretend it away, and no denying her response to him. And as she sat beside him in the dark, every nerve ending in her body was painfully attuned to his nearness.

She tried to remain immobile, her gaze focused on the stage. She didn't remember the seats seeming so close. Or maybe it was that Richard was so tall. But every time he shifted in his seat, which he did frequently, his shoulder brushed hers or his thigh pressed against hers. The disproportionate response of her own body to these casual touches reminded her that it had been a long time since she'd had sex.

Not that she intended to sleep with Richard Warren. Certainly not after spending only one day with him. *No way.* She was definitely through with single-minded men and dead-end relationships.

The thought faded away as his knee bumped against her leg again.

She'd often thought it was more of a curse than a blessing that she enjoyed sex. Her relationship with Brad had lacked a lot of things, but she had no complaints about the physical aspects of it. Maybe that was why she'd waited so long to end a relationship she'd recognized was at an impasse months earlier. Or maybe it was because she'd really wanted him to be the one.

She'd made excuses for his frequent disappearances and hasty departures. He was an investigative reporter and traveling was part of his job. She'd known that when they'd first started dating and could hardly expect him to change his career for her.

She had hoped he would want to make *some* changes, though. To talk to her before making his travel plans rather than calling from a plane that was already in the air.

But Brad had become accustomed to flying solo long before she'd ever moved in with him, and she'd been too afraid to sound like a nagging wife to make an issue of it. She'd gratefully accepted the part of his life he was willing to share with her because she'd believed it was preferable to being alone.

Two and a half years later, she'd realized that she was alone even when she was sleeping beside him. She'd finally accepted that he would always want the next big headline more than he wanted her.

Always being second best hurt more than she wanted to admit—even more so because he wasn't the first man in her life to put his career ahead of her. With James it had been his research; Kevin his music. Richard, for all his current attentiveness, wouldn't be any different. He was looking for a temporary diversion, and she had no intention of being one.

Or maybe she was looking at the situation from the wrong perspective. Maybe spending time with him was the most effective way to prove he was the same as the other men she'd dated. That would certainly kill any attraction she felt.

His thigh brushed against hers again and her hormones exploded like a Fourth of July fireworks display. She definitely needed to get past this physical pull, learn more about him, find his faults. Because if she ever gave in to the traitorous desire pumping through her veins, she would end up with her heart broken all over again.

Richard wasn't answering his phone.

Helen Hanson paced the confines of her office, gnawing on her bottom lip as the long-distance ring sounded again before finally connecting to his voice mail.

She hung up without leaving a message. She'd left three already.

She pushed away from her desk and stared out at the array of lights blinking below her. It was four o'clock in the afternoon in Tokyo and she'd been trying to reach him for hours. Where could he be?

He'd given her a cell phone number so that she could keep in touch, but that wasn't happening.

She knew he wasn't in a meeting. He'd called yesterday to tell her the start of negotiations had been delayed. One of TAKA's key executives had been called out of town because of a death in the family.

She knew only too well how the loss of a loved one could send a person's entire world into turmoil. Six months after burying her husband, she still felt as though she was swirling in a vortex of confusion.

She'd loved George dearly, but if by some miracle he could be standing before her now, she'd cheerfully throttle him for making such a mess of the company that should have been a legacy for his children. Instead it had been—to varying degrees—a curse.

Of course, if the company had been the financial success he'd led them all to believe, none of his sons would be where they were right now.

Jack had put his legal career and his own ambitions on hold to help out at Hanson. In the process, he'd been reacquainted and fallen in love with Samantha Edwards, whom he'd first met years ago when they were in business school together. Helen smiled, thinking that she deserved at least a little bit of credit for that match, as she'd been the one to suggest Samantha to Jack as a viable candidate to lead the Internet division.

Andrew, a typical rich playboy before his father's death, had reluctantly returned to Chicago to assume some responsibility at Hanson Media Group. In doing so, he'd come face-to-face with a former one-night stand who was pregnant with his child. Now he and Delia McCray were happily married and looking forward to parenthood together.

Evan's journey had, perhaps, been the most difficult. Cut out of his father's will, he'd almost turned away from the family business completely. Fortunately, Helen had managed to convince him to stay—at least for a while—and he'd reunited with Meredith Waters. Although the former high school sweethearts were still working out some of the kinks in their new relationship, Helen knew they were committed to one another.

Yes, she thought with satisfaction, George's sons all had reason to be grateful rather than angry with their father.

But what about me? She couldn't help but wonder.

What had George left her except controlling interest in an almost bankrupt company and the resentment of his children who were now working for her?

She hated knowing that the boys thought of her as nothing more than a trophy wife. She resented that George had let them believe it, and she was disappointed with herself for letting him make her into one.

She hadn't minded so much when he was alive. She'd loved George and being his wife had given her life both purpose and pleasure. His death had taken those away—along with her illusions.

Sometimes she wondered why she was even still here, trying so desperately to hold together the business that he'd let fall apart. But she knew it was what she needed to do—it was the only way she could prove to herself that the last ten years of her life had served any purpose. That was why she was so desperate for this merger to work.

She picked up the phone to try Richard again, then hung it up without dialing. While she had every confidence that he could handle the negotiations, she felt anxious being so far removed from the action. Maybe she should go to Tokyo herself. If nothing else, a change of scenery might help her put everything into perspective.

Richard should have guessed Jenny would pick a sushi restaurant for dinner when his mouth was watering for a thick juicy steak.

When in Rome, he reminded himself. Except that in Rome he'd be more likely looking at a bowl of noodles with a chunky marinara sauce than cold fish wrapped in seaweed, and he loved pasta.

Not that he disliked sushi so much as he disliked the idea of sushi. His ex-wife had, on several occasions, tried to entice Richard to try it. It had never appealed to him. Then again, Marilyn had indulged in a lot of things he never had—and while he could accept her liking of unusual foods, he couldn't overlook her infidelity.

Jenny stopped in front of an illuminated window display that showcased the restaurant's menu. Richard stared at the assortment of plastic food searching for anything that looked the least bit appealing. Each dish had a label—in Japanese, of course—and a number.

"What do you think?" she asked.

"I think I'd like meat—preferably cooked."

She smiled. "Have you ever tried sushi?"

He shook his head. "The thought of eating anything raw, other than vegetables, does not appeal to me."

"Today is a day for experiencing new things," she reminded him. "The tea ceremony, *Noh* theater."

"That seems like enough new experiences for awhile."

"And just when I thought you had an adventurous side."

"Do I really have to eat sushi to prove I'm not a straight-laced conservative?"

"You don't have to prove anything to me," she told him.

Of course, he ordered the sushi. Rather, he told Jenny what he wanted and let her order for him.

Tekka-maki, she explained, was cold, vinegary rice wrapped with tuna in a sheet of toasted seaweed. The description was innocuous if not exactly appealing.

She ordered something called *kappa-maki* and, when their meals were delivered, she demonstrated the proper way to pick up the roll with the chopsticks and dip it into the sauce.

He followed her example and was both surprised and relieved to find the *maki-zushi* was quite enjoyable—pleasantly tangy with the slightest hint of salt and not at all fishy.

Richard lifted his glass of beer. "Thank you," he said. "For a day filled with new experiences."

Jenny raised her own drink. "*Kampai.*" Cheers.

It was there again—something in the tilt of her chin, the slight curve of her lips that nagged at him. "Do you have a sister?"

She frowned at the question as she shook her head. "Just a brother."

"Cousins?"

"A few. Why?"

"Because I still can't shake the feeling that you remind me of someone."

"I thought that was just a line," she admitted.

"If I needed one, I could do better than that."

"Yes, I imagine you could," she responded in a tone that challenged the obsequiousness of her words.

She picked up another *maki-zushi* and dipped it.

"Do you have any family in Chicago?" he pressed.

"Not that I know of." She popped the roll into her mouth.

He studied her as he sipped his beer, wondering why she intrigued him so much. It wasn't just the physical attraction or the nagging familiarity, although those were certainly factors. Her intelligence and passion were definite pluses but not the whole answer, either. It was, he finally realized, the whole package that had caught and held his attention. And it was the whole woman he wanted.

He frowned at the thought and reminded himself he wasn't looking for a woman or any kind of personal complications right now.

"You're not eating," Jenny said. "Is your dinner okay?"

He shoved the discomfiting thoughts aside and picked up another piece of fish. "It's fine. I guess my mind wandered."

"Are you thinking about the merger?"

He *should* have been thinking about the merger. Instead, he'd been contemplating a union of an entirely different sort. "Something like that."

"You must be frustrated with the delay."

"A little," he admitted. "Although Helen is even more so. Patience isn't one of her virtues."

"Helen?" she prompted.

"Helen Hanson."

Jenny thought it interesting that he was on a first name basis with his boss. Not that their relationship—business or personal—was any of her concern. Still, she couldn't help prying just a little. "She must think very highly of you to have entrusted you to work out the details of the merger."

"She's a savvy businessperson," he said. Then he smiled. "She's also a good friend."

"I didn't ask," she said.

"But you were wondering."

She shrugged. "I saw her picture in the paper and on the news—when her husband was buried. Although she was wearing big sunglasses that obscured half of her face, it was still obvious that she's a beautiful woman. Beautiful and young."

"Are you looking for a story?"

"Just making conversation."

"Then I'll tell you that she's an incredible person who's managing to hold a troubled company together while still mourning her husband's death."

"Why do you think she's doing it?" Jenny couldn't help but ask. "Why would she care about saving Hanson Media when it's obvious none of her stepsons appreciates her efforts?"

"Only Helen could answer that for certain," he told her.

She shook her head. "They don't know how lucky they are that their father's wife wants to be involved in their lives. There are women who don't want the responsibility of their own children, never mind someone else's." Women like her own mother, who had abandoned her at birth and disappeared from her life completely.

"That's an interesting way of looking at it."

Jenny shrugged to hide the fact that she was uneasy with his sudden scrutiny, concerned that her impulsive comment had revealed too much.

"It's an interesting situation." She sipped her drink. "A business crisis with elements of drama and intrigue."

"Are you a reporter or a novelist?"

"I'm just innately curious."

"So am I," he said. "And I've noticed how adeptly you maneuver every conversation away from questions about you to more impersonal topics."

"That's because my life isn't very interesting."

"You left New York City for a job in Tokyo. I find that very interesting."

"My family's here," she said simply. "My parents, my brother and his wife and their four-year-old daughter."

"No boyfriend?"

She realized she'd been so intent on sidestepping one uncomfortable topic she hadn't seen he was maneuvering her toward another.

"I'll assume there's no boyfriend," he continued, "because I don't think you would have kissed me the way you did if there was."

Jenny was quiet for a moment. "I think we need to clear the air about that," she said at last.

"Are you saying there *is* a boyfriend?"

"I'm saying that I didn't mean to give you the wrong impression. I'm attracted to you." She smiled wryly. "Obviously. But I don't do casual relationships. I can't seem to separate the physical from the emotional, and things inevitably get messy."

"I try to avoid messy if at all possible."

She nodded, understanding that it was a warning as much as a confession and was grateful for his honesty.

"But it's not always possible," he told her.

"We'll keep things simple."

He seemed to consider her suggestion for a moment before nodding. “Simple,” he agreed. He reached across the table to touch the back of her hand. “Does that mean I can’t kiss you good-night?”

She pulled her hand away. “It means no more kissing at all.”

“That’s a pretty strict position to take.”

“It’s smart.” And necessary. Because she knew that if he kissed her again, all her resolutions about keeping it simple would dissolve like *matcha*—powdered tea—in boiling water.

“All right—no kissing. Simple. Smart. Are there any other rules I should know about?”

He was teasing her, trying to lessen the tension.

She smiled to hide the fact that she was just the slightest bit disappointed that he’d given in to her demands so readily.

“That should be good for now,” she said lightly. “And I should be getting home.”

“Do you have a curfew?”

“No, but I have a roommate who worries when she doesn’t know where I am.” And although Samara knew she was spending the day with Richard, Jenny was afraid that knowledge would only cause her friend to have more questions.

“I’ll take you home,” he told her.

“You don’t know where I live.”

He shrugged. “I figure this is a good way to find out.”

“Your hotel’s closer than my apartment,” she pointed out as they left the restaurant. “There’s no reason for you to see me home.”

“I want to be sure you make it there safely.”

"Tokyo is an extremely safe city."

"This is *my* rule," he said. "If we spend the day together, even if it's not a date, I see you home."

"It's really not necessary." She felt silly standing on the sidewalk arguing about it, so she began to walk. "And this is a confusing city to navigate if you're unfamiliar with it. You could get lost trying to find your way back."

"I'll manage."

She didn't try to dissuade him any more, and they walked in silence for several blocks until they reached her apartment building.

"This is it," she said, stopping on the sidewalk.

"Now I'll rest easier knowing my tour guide made it home safely."

She smiled reluctantly. "You still want me to be your tour guide?"

"Absolutely," he answered without hesitation.

"Then I guess I'll see you tomorrow."

"Any hints about what we'll be doing?"

"I'll think about it," she said. "Unless there was anything in particular you wanted to see."

He shook his head. "You're in charge."

She tilted her head back to look at him. "I have to admit, I did expect you would have found an excuse to part ways with me long before now."

"You're surprised by my perseverance?"

"Yes," she admitted.

"Good." He tapped his finger lightly against her chin. "I like knowing that I can surprise you."

She took a step back. "Good night."

"Good night, Jenny."

As she walked inside the building, grateful they'd established an understanding of the rules, Richard watched her, already thinking about breaking them.

Chapter Four

Jenny should have known Samara would be waiting for her. When she opened the door of her apartment, she found her roommate in the living room, thumbing through the pages of a decorating magazine.

Samara glanced up, then at the clock on the wall. "Must have been quite the tea ceremony."

"It was." Jenny dropped her purse and keys on the table.

A moment of silence passed, a few more pages turned before Samara finally asked, "Am I going to have to pry for details?"

Jenny carried two cans of soda from the fridge, passed one to her friend, then popped the top on the other. "I wouldn't know what to tell you," she admitted. "Except that Richard Warren isn't quite who I thought he would be."

Samara closed the magazine and set it aside. "Do you like him?"

"It's too soon to say."

"You just spent the last twelve hours with him—I'd think you'd have an opinion."

She hesitated before admitting, "I enjoyed his company."

"Why do you sound surprised?"

"Because he's smart and charming and far too good-looking."

She was aware that her protests sounded ridiculous, but she also knew that Samara would understand.

Her friend's response confirmed that she did. "He's not Brad Morgan or Kevin Hicks or James Gillett—"

"I know. But he's not that different from any of them either." And she knew that if she ignored her better judgment and let herself get involved with Richard, he would break her heart, too.

"You always said you had great memories of James," Samara reminded her.

"Yeah." Jenny smiled. She'd been twenty years old and completely inexperienced when she'd met James Gillett, and the instant attraction between them had both intrigued and terrified her. He'd been her first love—and her first lover.

"What went wrong?" her friend asked. "Why did you break up with him?"

"Because I finally realized he wasn't ever going to be what I needed, that he wasn't capable of making a commitment." She sighed. "At least that's what I thought until I heard he got married last year."

"James is married?" Samara sounded as stunned as Jenny had been.

She nodded. "Her name's Meghan—she's a doctor."

"You never told me he got married."

"It never came up in conversation."

"If you were pained by it, you should have brought it up."

Her friend's comment made Jenny smile. Although Samara was fluent in English, she still occasionally mixed up similar words. "Why would it bother me?"

"Because you loved him once," Samara said gently.

"Okay, maybe it did bother me a little." She got up to toss her empty can in the garbage. "Or maybe what bothered me was realizing how much I want to be the center of someone's world, like Meghan is for James."

Samara shook her head. "You've been listening to my great-grandmother's stories again."

"She managed to find four men who put her first. All I want is one."

"Some day you'll find him," Samara said, then she smiled. "Or maybe you already have."

Jenny ignored the deliberate hint in the second part of her friend's statement. "Maybe the problem isn't the men," she said. "Maybe it's me. Maybe I'm just not the type of woman who inspires that kind of passion."

"You can't honestly believe that."

"Everyone warned me that James would never commit to one woman. It turns out he just didn't want to commit to me.

"Kevin claimed to love me, then he decided he'd rather be playing his guitar in smoky bars than building a life with me.

"When Brad asked me to move in with him, I thought it was proof we were in a committed relationship. Now I have to wonder if he just wanted someone to water his plants while he was away."

It was the story of her life—always coming in a distant second to someone or something else. And it wasn't just recent experiences that made her feel that way. No, the first seeds of the doubts and insecurities were planted almost twenty-five years earlier when she'd first come into the world and her own mother hadn't even wanted her.

"You've made a few bad choices," Samara said with a shrug. "Who hasn't?"

"Spoken like a true friend." Jenny managed a smile. "But the fact is, not many women have my appalling judgment when it comes to men."

And yet she continued to be drawn to the same type—self-confident and self-absorbed. Men who were not just committed to their careers but obsessed with success, more interested in getting ahead than being with her.

"Maybe Richard's different," Samara said.

She laughed. "Yeah. He's a lawyer instead of a professor, musician or journalist. That doesn't make him any less obsessed with his career."

"He probably bored you to tears talking about legal presidents all day."

"Precedents," Jenny corrected automatically. "And just because he managed to restrain himself from talking law while we were out doesn't mean he wasn't thinking about it."

"You're probably right," Samara agreed, a smile tugging at the corners of her mouth.

Jenny narrowed her gaze on her friend.

"If you want a man who can't think of anything but you, you should date Kimiyasu in circulation. He trips over his tongue every time you walk past his desk."

"He trips over his tongue every time he sees anyone in a skirt," Jenny pointed out.

"Okay, maybe not Kimiyasu. But you should be going out, meeting people."

"I do go out, and I already know a lot of people."

"I meant men," Samara said.

"I know you did—I'm just not interested in dating anyone right now."

"But you're attracted to Richard," Samara guessed.

Her thoughts drifted again to the sizzling kiss they'd shared, and she sighed. "A woman would have to be dead to not be attracted to Richard."

Her friend grinned. "I was beginning to wonder. You haven't dated at all since you moved to Tokyo. And I know it hasn't been from lack of offers."

"I've been busy."

"You've been hiding. Or maybe you've been waiting for Brad to come back."

"If I was waiting for him, I'd still be in New York." Jenny shook her head decisively. "I'm getting on with my life."

"Then why are you so deposed to spending time with Richard Warren? Maybe even having a little fling?"

"Opposed," she said. "And not wanting to jump into bed with another man doesn't mean I'm still hung up on my ex."

"Hmm." Samara propped her feet up on the coffee table, one delicate ankle crossed over the other. "I think the problem isn't that you're not ready to jump into bed with him, but that you are."

She remained silent.

"You're not denying it."

"I'm trying to figure out how many negatives there were in that statement to decipher what you said."

"You want to sleep with Richard, but you know that if you do, you won't be able to go back to Brad."

"I don't want to go back to Brad."

"I bet Richard would be great in bed," Samara continued as if Jenny hadn't spoken.

That was a bet Jenny wasn't willing to take. If his kiss was any indication, Richard wouldn't be great in bed—he would be phenomenal. But she had no intention of telling her friend about the kiss, so all she said was, "That's quite an assumption to make considering that you saw him for all of two minutes."

"What can I say?" Her roommate shrugged. "The man makes an impression."

Jenny couldn't deny the truth of that, either.

Richard did get lost trying to find his way back to his hotel. Although he wasn't entirely sure if it was the lack of recognizable street signs that was responsible for his misdirection or the confusion in his own mind. Because as much as he tried to concentrate on where he was going, he continued to be preoccupied with thoughts of Jenny.

He hadn't realized how structured and predictable his life had become until she'd provided a respite—however temporary—from the tedium of his existence. She intrigued him and challenged him, and she made him feel something he hadn't felt in a very long time—alive.

He wasn't surprised by the attraction he felt. He was surprised that he couldn't seem to put that attraction aside. He'd always managed to divide his life into neat sections: work, family, social. With an admittedly heavy emphasis on work, especially in recent years.

But now he was thinking about Jenny instead of the Hanson-TAKA merger. He was wandering the streets of downtown Tokyo instead of hurrying back to his hotel to review his notes and check his e-mail. And although he'd left her not thirty minutes ago, he was already looking forward to tomorrow when he would see her again.

His thoughts strayed again to the steamy kiss they'd shared in the garden outside of the tea house.

He hadn't planned to kiss her. He'd thought about it—every time his gaze had lingered on the soft fullness of her mouth—but he'd had no intention of acting upon his desire. Until she'd told him to back off in that cool voice that contradicted the heat in her eyes.

It had been an impulse, driven by the need to know which part of her was real.

It had also been a mistake.

Not because he hadn't enjoyed kissing her, but because he'd enjoyed it too much. While he'd suspected there was a lot more to Jenny Anderson than she let most people see, he hadn't expected so much. The depth and intensity of her response had surprised him, proving there was passion beneath the poise and a lot more hot than cool.

He also hadn't expected the wariness he'd seen in her eyes after the kiss had ended. It was that hint of uncertainty that held his own desire in check. He liked women with experience, who wanted only the same things he did. For all her elegance and sophistication, there was a vulnerability about Jenny Anderson that warned him to proceed with caution—or not at all.

She was the type of woman who would want more than he could give her, and he refused to put himself in the position of disappointing her. He'd already failed his mother and his wife—he wouldn't set up anyone else for the same disillusionment.

So he would do the smart thing—he would respect her

wishes and keep their relationship simple. But taking the smart and easy route wouldn't stop him from wanting her.

Thankfully, he would only have to resist temptation for a few more days. As soon as Mr. Tetsugoro was back and negotiations commenced, Richard was confident he would be able to put Jenny Anderson in the back of his mind.

This thought gave him a measure of relief, as did the realization he'd finally found his way back to the hotel.

When he got up to his room, he saw the message light on his phone was blinking. He punched in the code to retrieve his voice mail and found there wasn't just one but four messages waiting—all of them from the acting CEO of Hanson Media Group.

At 10:30 a.m.:

"Hi, Richard, it's Helen. I just thought I'd try to catch you in your room. Obviously you're out, so I'll try the cell phone number you gave me."

11:30 a.m.:

"Richard, it's me again. I tried your cell and immediately was patched through to voice mail. Give me a call when you get this message, please."

2:00 p.m.:

"It isn't like you to be out of touch for so long, Richard. Call me before I really start to worry."

And at 7:30 p.m.:

"Now I'm thinking you've been run over by that bullet train or abducted by aliens. Please call as soon as you get this message. I don't care what time it is."

Richard might have smiled at the content of her last message if not for the obvious concern in Helen's voice. Instead, he suffered the guilt of knowing he hadn't thought to check in with her at all through the day. He glanced at the glowing numbers on the alarm clock and mentally calculated the time difference. It was 8 a.m. in Chicago, which meant he would be able to catch Helen at the office.

"I'm glad to hear you're not dead." It was the first thing she said when she realized he was on the line.

"I'm sorry you were concerned—I was out all day and just got your messages."

"I was only concerned because I've never known you to turn your cell phone off." She didn't sound annoyed so much as puzzled by the fact.

"I had to turn it off for *cha-no-yu,*" he said, a little defensively. "And then I forgot to turn it back on."

There was a long silence before Helen responded. "You…forgot?"

Richard couldn't blame her for sounding incredulous. He'd been shocked himself when he'd unclipped the phone and realized he'd never powered it back up after he left the teahouse with Jenny.

"You must have been quite…distracted."

This time there was amusement rather than surprise in her tone.

"I do have a lot on my mind getting ready for this merger."

She laughed. It was a sound he hadn't heard in a long time—since George's death and the disclosure of the company's precarious financial situation, no one at Hanson Media had much reason to laugh. He was happy to hear her doing so, even if her enjoyment came at his expense.

"You were ready long before you ever stepped on the plane," Helen reminded him.

"There's always more prep work that can be done in a situation such as this."

"That's true." Then she asked, "Who is she?"

"Who is who?"

She laughed again. "The woman you spent the day with."

"You're relentless, Helen."

"One of my finer attributes," she agreed. "Are you going to tell me about her?"

He knew she would continue to badger him until he did. "She's an American journalist who lives and works in Tokyo."

"And she's been showing you around," Helen guessed.

"Reluctantly."

"I can't imagine any woman would be reluctant to spend time with you."

Richard smiled wryly. "You haven't met Jenny."

"Am I going to?" Helen was evidently delighted by the possibility.

"I don't think so."

"Why not?"

"Because I have a job to do here and so does she."

"As long as the business is taken care of, no one would object to you mixing a little pleasure with it. And there isn't much you can do with respect to the merger right now, anyway."

"Unfortunately not," he agreed.

"When are you seeing her again?"

"What makes you think I am?"

"The fact that you didn't come out and say you weren't."

He shook his head. "I assume there was a reason you left so many messages on my voice mail other than to inquire how I'm spending my free time."

"I really just wanted to touch base," she admitted. "You know I get antsy when things are out of my control."

"Then maybe you should have come to Tokyo instead of me."

"With so much going on with Jack and Evan and Andrew, I thought it more important to keep an eye on things here. And I know you're more than capable of handling the negotiations."

"I appreciate your confidence," he said. "When are you coming?"

"You know me so well." He heard the smile in her voice.

"Then you have booked your flight?"

"I'll be there next Saturday."

Chapter Five

Jenny arrived at Richard's hotel the next morning without any definite plans. Since he'd been such a good sport through the tea ceremony and at the theater the day before, she decided to give him a few options. She suggested the Tokyo Tower, the Japanese Sword Museum or the East Garden of the Imperial Palace. His choice wasn't at all what she expected.

"Shopping?" Jenny echoed as she stepped into the revolving glass door to exit the hotel.

Richard smiled wryly as he followed her out into the sunshine. "It's not one of my favorite pastimes," he admitted. "But I need to pick up some gifts and souvenirs while I'm here, and I thought you could help me."

Gifts for his boss? Or a girlfriend back home? It shouldn't matter. If he wanted to shop for a dozen women, it wasn't any of her business. She wasn't going to start acting weird and proprietary just because he'd kissed her yesterday—even if it was a kiss that had made her mind numb and her toes curl.

"Was there anything in particular you're looking for?" she asked.

"Something for an eight-year-old girl and a five-year-old boy."

She turned south, toward the subway station, and asked casually. "Yours?"

"No." His response was quick and vehement. "Caitlin and Tyler are my niece and nephew."

"You mentioned yesterday that you'd been married, so I thought they might be your children."

He shook his head in emphatic denial. "No kids."

There were more questions she wanted to ask: How long were you married? Why did it end? Her curiosity wasn't motivated by personal interest but a simple desire to know what made a person make that kind of commitment—and then break it. Why would a man vow to love a woman forever, then walk away? Why would a mother give her away her child?

But it was evident from Richard's clipped tone that his marriage was a topic he didn't want to discuss, so she let it pass, reminding herself that his failed relationship was just one more reason not to get involved. The next time she opened her heart, she was determined that it would be to a man who could make a promise to her—and keep it. Her only obligation with respect to Richard Warren was to show him around Tokyo.

"If you want a uniquely Japanese shopping experience, there's no place better than Ginza," she told him.

Richard had never been anywhere like Ginza.

As they wandered through the shopping district, Jenny

pointed out famous department stores beside tiny shops selling traditional handmade crafts tucked next to galleries and ultra-modern showrooms. She dragged him from one store to the next, showing him the wares, explaining the history or tradition behind different items.

"You like to shop," he commented, noting the pink flush in her cheeks, the sparkle in her eyes, as she led him through yet another store.

Her smile was easy. "It's a definite vice."

"But is it your only vice?" he teased.

"The only one you need to worry about right now," she said.

"Well, I'm grateful for your help." Following her suggestions and guidance, he'd finished most of his shopping. For his nephew he'd picked up a kite shaped like a carp, which Jenny told him was a symbol of courage and strength and a traditional gift for young boys; for his brother and sister-in-law he'd found a ceramic Murasaki sake set; and for his mother he'd purchased a framed watercolor of Mount Fuji. "But I still don't have anything for Caitlin."

"You will." She took his arm to steer him down a small alley, then over a broken step and through a narrow doorway.

It was a doll shop. A tiny room with floor-to-ceiling shelves lined with white-faced dolls dressed in silk kimonos. He glanced around at the hundreds—maybe even thousands—of dolls, before selecting one at random for a closer examination.

"The workmanship and detail are amazing."

"It's an oyster shell doll. I had one when I was a little girl. My mom bought it for me on our first trip to Japan." She smiled. "I carted that doll everywhere with me until it finally got lost somewhere in our travels."

It was more information than she'd ever volunteered about herself, and he was eager to hear more. Maybe learning about the child she'd been would give him some insight into the woman she'd become. But he knew better than to pry—anytime he asked direct questions, she seemed to shut down.

"I cried when I realized it was gone," she admitted. "But I was almost a teenager by then—too old to be playing with dolls."

She shook her head, as if to shake off the memory, and smiled again. "But eight is just the right age for a gift like this. Still young enough to want to play with it, and old enough to know to take care of it."

"I think you're right," he agreed. "The only problem now is choosing the right one."

Jenny picked up another doll, stroked a hand gently over the hair. "This is like the one I had," she told him. "I still remember the glossy red lips and matching scarlet kimono."

"Then that's the one I'll get," he decided.

After his shopping was done, she took him to the Nissan gallery where he admired the latest offerings from the motor vehicle company, then to the Sony showroom where he played with the latest electronic gadgets.

"My mother always said that the only difference between men and boys was the price of their toys," she told him as they walked out of the store.

He smiled. "I imagine there's some truth in that."

"The truth is in the bag in your hand."

"It's a digital camera barely bigger than a credit card. How could anyone resist that?"

"I can't possibly imagine," she said, tongue in cheek.

He wouldn't give her the satisfaction of knowing that it

had been an impulse buy. He refused to admit that he rarely bothered to take pictures. Instead, he took it out of the box and snapped a quick photo of her.

He checked the display screen, pleased with the image he'd captured. He found the tantalizing glimpses of the woman beneath the surface even more captivating than her beauty, and there was just a hint of that woman in the picture he'd impulsively taken. There was the illusion of a smile tugging at the corners of her mouth and a glint of amusement in her deep green eyes. She intrigued him more than he wanted to admit, enticed him as no other woman had done in a very long time.

He tucked the camera into his pocket, wishing he could so easily tuck away his thoughts about Jenny, and fell into step with her again. They wandered some more, around the Gallery Center Building to look at the art, then through Hankyu and Seibu department stores.

Despite the sexual tension, which had been exacerbated rather than alleviated by the fiery kiss they'd shared the day before, Richard found it surprisingly easy to talk to her. But he noticed that while she was knowledgeable about any number of topics, she didn't offer a lot in the way of personal information. The revelation in the doll shop was the only real insight he'd been given, and he wanted to know so much more.

"Tell me about the story you wanted to write," he said, hoping—despite her loss of the assignment—that it wasn't a topic that would create new barriers.

"I pitched it to my editor as a piece about gender inequality in the contemporary workplace. As I began to research it, however, it became a story about sexual harassment with a prominent corporate VP at its center."

"No wonder you were annoyed when you lost the assignment."

She nodded. "I'd talked to five women—all of whom were either promised promotions if they provided sexual services to the boss or threatened with demotions if they refused to do so."

"None of these women ever complained?"

"He's a powerful and influential man—they didn't see any point."

"How did you get them to talk to you?"

"One of the women is a friend of mine," she admitted. "When she confided in me about what had happened, I guessed she wasn't the first victim. I suggested she approach some other women at work, and they agreed to talk to me, too. They believed that exposing his actions in a public forum—such as the newspaper—would help them get justice."

"How did your friend feel when she found out you weren't going to write the story?"

"She wasn't happy," Jenny admitted. "Especially when my replacement went to the boss to hear his response to the allegations."

"I'm really sorry, Jenny."

She shrugged. "There will be other stories."

"But you weren't just upset because you lost your byline, were you? You were upset because you'd let your friend down."

She was surprised that he'd so readily understood. Maybe, she reluctantly acknowledged, she'd been a little hasty in her judgment of him.

"Tell me about your job—why you wanted to be a

lawyer." She smiled. "Because I'm sure you didn't do so just to please your mother."

Richard didn't smile back. In fact, she thought she saw a shadow pass over his face, but it was gone so quickly she decided she'd imagined it.

"I went to law school because I like to argue," he told her. "And it seemed a good way to get paid for doing something I enjoy."

"That sounds like an oversimplified explanation," she complained.

"What do you want me to say—that I felt a burning need to uphold truth, justice and the American way?"

"Only if it's true."

"The truth is, my parents owned a coffee shop. My dad did the baking and tended the shop while my mother took care of my brother and me. They worked hard to make life easier for us, and I wanted to do something that I thought would make my parents proud."

"I'm sure you succeeded."

"Not entirely. My mother wanted me to become a district attorney."

"Why?"

She was sure she saw the shadow this time, but he only shrugged.

"Instead you chose to wage your legal battles over contract addendums and penalty clauses."

"Pretty much," he agreed.

"What about your wife? What kind of law did she practice?"

"What makes you think she's an attorney?"

"I have friends who are lawyers," she explained. "And

they all seem to be married to one another, having babies who will grow up to be the next generation of lawyers."

He smiled. "I guess there is a fair amount of inbreeding within the profession. And Marilyn—my ex-wife—is also a corporate attorney."

"It seems with so much in common, you'd have the foundation for a good marriage," Jenny noted.

"We thought so," he agreed. "We got married right out of law school, both of us young and ambitious. Six months later, she was offered a great job at a firm in Decatur. She decided to take it, and though we tried to make it work, time and distance eroded our relationship until there was nothing left."

"I don't imagine it was as easy to let go as you imply."

His mouth twisted into something that might have been a smile. "She made it easy when she decided to sleep with her new boss."

"Ouch." Again, she knew his explanation had only skimmed the surface and though she wanted to know more, she was reluctant to pursue what was obviously a painful topic for him. Instead, she glanced at her watch. "I had no idea it was getting to be so late."

"Do you have somewhere you have to be?" he asked.

"Actually, yes," she said. "And if we don't hurry, we're going to miss the first pitch."

The crowd was thick around the amusement park and outside the Tokyo Dome, so Jenny took Richard's hand to ensure they didn't get separated. She ignored the now-familiar tingle that skated through her veins when their fingers linked together. It didn't matter how his touch made her heart race and her heart pound—she was going to be smart and keep their relationship simple.

She led him through the gate, handing their tickets to the attendant. "It's not the White Sox or the Cubs," she told him. "But I thought it might be something you'd enjoy."

"She's smart and beautiful and she likes baseball—that's an almost irresistible combination."

"Only almost?" she teased, refusing to take his words seriously. "Wait until you see our seats."

She led him down section A16, four rows back from the infield, directly facing first base. Close enough to smell the dirt and sweat and feel the tension and excitement as the players stood along the baseline for the national anthem. When the last notes faded away, Jenny sat down beside Richard and breathed deeply to inhale the unique ambience of the ballpark.

"Those are the Yomiuri Giants," she told him, pointing to the home team in the white-and-orange uniforms. "They're the oldest and the most popular professional baseball team around, and they've won more pennants and series titles than any other team in Japan."

"Tokyo's version of the Yankees."

She nodded. "Tonight the Giants are playing against the Hanshin Tigers."

There was a collective cheer as the first pitch was thrown and a strike was called.

"Do you come to the games very often?" he asked.

"At least a few times a year. Samara likes to come with me sometimes."

"Your roommate is a baseball fan, too?"

"She doesn't understand much about the logistics of the game," Jenny confided. "But she appreciates a nicely toned butt in tight pants."

The next pitch was swung on and missed, and the crowd cheered again.

"What's the attraction for you?" Richard asked.

She answered without hesitation. "The crack of the bat when a fastball hits the sweet spot, a diving catch from center field, a well-turned double play, a full-count pitch in the bottom of the ninth of a tie game." Then she smiled. "And nicely toned butts in tight pants."

He shook his head. "I thought you were immune to that sort of thing."

"It's like shopping for a car. I can look without wanting to test drive."

The batter connected with the third pitch—a line-drive straight to the third baseman that was easily snagged for the first out. The fielders tossed the ball around as they waited for the next batter to step up to the plate, and Richard turned his attention to Jenny. "Who do you have to know to get seats like this?"

"It's not the 'who' so much as the 'what'," she admitted. "For these tickets, I had to endure endless hours of tedium and boredom."

The next batter swung at the first pitch, sending the ball deep into the foul territory of right field.

"The shareholder meeting," she explained in response to his quizzical look. "When my parents gave me their proxies, I negotiated for these along with them."

"These are your parents' seats?"

She nodded as the first ball was called, low and outside. "Although, between their business and travel, they don't get to come to many games."

"You said Samara sometimes comes with you—who else do you bring here?"

"Any one of a dozen different men," she lied glibly. She had no intention of admitting that when Samara wasn't available, it was usually her brother who came or, less frequently, a coworker she knew would enjoy the game.

"A dozen?"

"Usually only one at a time."

Ball two, low and outside again.

He slid an arm across the back of her chair.

She eyed him warily.

"And of the dozen men you've brought here, how many went home with you?"

"None—" another swing, another hit, this one into the right fielder's glove for the second out "—of your business."

"Yasushi told me you don't date. Why is that?"

She frowned. "You talked to Yasushi about me?"

"I was curious," he said easily, brushing his fingertips over her shoulder.

It was a casually intimate touch that made her skin burn and her heart pound.

"Now I'm curious about what he'd say if I told him you brought me to a Giants game."

She didn't need to look at him to know he was smiling.

"It doesn't matter because this isn't a date," she said firmly.

"Why aren't you dating anyone right now?"

"Why does there have to be a reason?"

"There doesn't have to be," he allowed. "But there usually is."

"Okay," she relented. "I ended a long-term relationship before I came back to Tokyo a few months ago."

"How long-term?"

"Two and a half years."

"That's longer than my marriage lasted," he admitted.

Jenny considered this revelation as she refocused her attention on the field, surprised to see that the Giants were leaving the field for their turn at bat. And annoyed to realize that she'd been so disconcerted by his casual touch, she'd completely missed the third out.

Richard enjoyed watching the game—at least after he got used to the incessant chanting of the crowd and the unusual background music. Japanese baseball fans might not be as loud as their American counterparts, but no one could claim they were any less enthusiastic.

But even more than the game, he enjoyed watching Jenny. The way her eyes would light up for a well-hit ball or darken with frustration over what she perceived to be an inaccurate call by the umpire, the enthusiasm with which she joined in the cheering, the simple enjoyment she showed in munching down on a hot dog generously slathered with mustard.

He would never have guessed she was a baseball fan. The woman he'd met outside of the TAKA boardroom had caught his eye because she was attractive. In the time they'd spent together since then, he'd realized there was a lot more to her than a pretty package. She was smart, passionate, fun and she didn't interrupt the game to ask about the infield fly rule. She was, quite possibly, the perfect woman.

The perfect woman for someone else, of course, because Richard wasn't in the market for a woman—perfect or otherwise. He was only killing time until Mr. Tetsugoro returned to Tokyo and the negotiations for the Hanson-TAKA merger finally commenced.

* * *

The Giants trounced the Tigers and they did so quickly. As Jenny and Richard filed out of the park with the rest of the crowd, she noted that it wasn't even nine o'clock. She considered suggesting a bar or nightclub, but she really just wanted to get home. As much as she'd enjoyed the day with Richard, she still wasn't completely comfortable with him.

It was the attraction, she knew, that kept getting in the way of what might have developed into a genuine friendship between them. Every time she started to relax, something would happen to remind her of the kiss they'd already shared and the desire that continued to simmer between them. A glance, a smile, a touch—any and all of these silent communications kept her on edge.

She wasn't afraid of him. Although she hadn't known him for very long and certainly didn't know him well, she trusted that he would respect the boundaries she'd set. She was afraid of her own response to him, of the longing that had started to stir deep inside her.

It would be smart to take a step back—several steps even. Because they'd both been honest about what they wanted and while she wasn't interested in a temporary affair, he couldn't offer her anything more.

But he did offer to see her home again. Insisted on it, in fact, and while Jenny tried to object, she was secretly pleased by the courtesy.

When they got to her apartment, he dug into one of the bags he carried to offer her a tissue-wrapped package. "This is for you."

She was surprised, pleased and curious all at the same time, with just a hint of caution dancing around the outside of her other emotions. She couldn't remember the last time anyone had spontaneously given her a gift. Brad certainly hadn't been the type to pick up little trinkets, and flowers had arrived for her only once each year—on Valentine's Day.

"Why?" she couldn't help but ask.

He smiled, as if he'd anticipated the question. "It's both a thank you and a bribe—in appreciation for a wonderful day and to entice you to spend tomorrow with me, too."

"I don't seem to have any other plans," she said.

"Don't you want to open it before you make any promises?"

She tore the paper away, curiosity overcome by stunned pleasure as she unwrapped the oyster shell doll. "But this was for your niece."

He shook his head. "I bought a purple one for Caitlin, because it's her favorite color. This one is for you."

Jenny stroked a hand over the doll's silky hair, her eyes misting with unexpected tears.

"It's beautiful. Thank you." She impulsively rose on her toes and touched her lips to his cheek.

It was intended as an expression of gratitude—an innocent kiss. But the heated awareness that suddenly sparked between them was anything but innocent. She stepped back to find his eyes on her, his gaze dark and intense.

The silence seemed to stretch between them for a long minute before he finally said, "You just broke one of your own rules."

She could only nod, her heart pounding so loudly he couldn't possibly be unaware of it.

"Not that I'm complaining." Richard traced the curve of her bottom lip with his fingertip once, then again. "I was just wondering if it meant that you're ready to throw all of the rules away."

She was tempted, oh so tempted, but definitely not ready.

"I can't." She clutched the doll against her chest and took a careful step back. "I'm sorry."

His smile was wry. "So am I. More than you can imagine."

Chapter Six

Jenny awoke in a rare mood Saturday morning—a fact that was immediately recognized by her roommate.

"Rough night?" Samara asked, spreading jam on a slice of toast.

"No," she responded as she made her way to the coffee pot. She had no intention of admitting that she'd dreamed of Richard last night—of kissing him, touching him, making love with him. A dream inspired by too vivid memories of the kiss they'd shared two days earlier.

It was just a kiss, she reminded herself. Nothing to get all worked up about. Except that it had been *just* a kiss, and that was *exactly* what had her all worked up. She wanted more.

And her imagination was far too creative in supplying the details of exactly what and how much more. She swallowed a mouthful of coffee, needing the jolt of caffeine to shake off the last remnants of the dream and plant her firmly back into reality.

"If it's any consolation," Samara said, "Richard was on his way out last night as I was coming in, and he looked just as frustrated as you do now."

"I'm not frustrated," she denied. "I'm annoyed."

"Oh?"

"It's Saturday and I wanted nothing more than to sleep late and laze around the apartment all day. Instead, I'm on tour guide duty. *Again.*"

"You never sleep late," Samara pointed out.

"I never get the chance."

Samara nibbled on her toast. "I think you need to sleep with Richard."

It was the casual delivery that surprised Jenny even more than the words. She choked on her coffee, sputtered. "What kind of a statement is that?"

Her friend shrugged. "Obviously something has to happen to elevate your sexual tension."

"Alleviate," she corrected automatically. "And I'm not tense."

"Liar."

She refilled her mug with coffee. "Even if I was tense, sleeping with Richard Warren wouldn't help. I have no interest in yet another dead-end relationship."

"Who said anything about a relationship? I was talking about a fling."

Jenny shook her head. "You know I'm not good at remaining emotionally detached."

"And you're falling for him already," Samara guessed.

She shook her head again. She wasn't entirely sure how she felt about Richard, but she was confident she wasn't falling for him. She enjoyed being with him, talking to him, even arguing with him. And each hour she spent with him tempted her to disregard her common sense and open up her heart again, but that was something she wouldn't do. His presence in her life was only temporary and his interest in her would decrease in direct proportion to the increased demands of his job. As soon as he was able to get back to the bargaining table, he would forget about her. She'd be a fool to think otherwise.

And Jenny wasn't going to be a fool again.

They started the morning with a quick tour through the Tsukiji Market then moved on to the Tokyo Tower and the Japanese Sword Museum. It seemed to Richard that Jenny wanted to ensure he saw absolutely everything Tokyo had to offer and was focused resolutely on the task.

She was also, Richard noted, as tightly wound as the spool of string on the kite he'd bought for his nephew during yesterday's shopping excursion.

As she strode briskly down the corridor of the Metropolitan Art Museum, he reached out to touch her arm. She jolted at the contact.

"You startled me," she said.

"I just wanted to ask if you had signed up for some tourist version of *The Amazing Race* with me as your unwitting companion."

"Of course not." But her cheeks colored slightly. "There's so much still to see and you'll be back at work on Monday—"

Her words halted when he took her hand and linked their fingers. He saw her brows draw together, just the slightest hint of a scowl, and he imagined her agile mind rapidly sorting through possible responses to the overture, battling between annoyance and acceptance. If she tugged her hand away, it might place too much importance on a casual gesture. If she left her fingers entwined with his, it might suggest she didn't object to his touching her.

He wasn't surprised when she disentangled her hand from his.

"I just don't think there's anything to be learned by seeing Japan at warp speed."

"I didn't want you to miss anything."

"And I don't want to spend the whole day being dragged from one thing to the next because you think that's what I want."

"What do you want to do?" she asked warily.

"I want you to stop thinking like a tour guide and tell me what you'd most like to do on a day off."

"Sleep in and stay in my pajamas all day."

"It's already too late for the sleeping in part," he said, trying not to think about the second half of her statement. But his errant imagination was already sorting through the options. Skimpy satin, peekaboo lace, seductive silk. The possibilities were endlessly enticing and it took a determined effort to refocus his mind on the conversation. "And I don't believe you're the type to lounge in bed, anyway."

"I didn't know you had to be a certain *type* for that."

"You do," he told her. "And you're not it."

"How do you know?"

"Too much energy and ambition."

She frowned.

"It wasn't a criticism—just an observation."

"You don't know me well enough to leap to a conclusion like that," she said, just a little defensively.

"After spending the better part of three days together, I think I can hazard a few guesses. And I'd know you even better if you'd stop pushing me away."

"I'm here with you now, aren't I?"

"Are you? Because I feel like I'm being shuttled around by Jennifer Anderson, professional ambassador of Japan, rather than the warm, friendly woman who cheered beside me at the baseball game last night."

She wrinkled her nose. "No one calls me Jennifer."

"And that," he said, "is one of the few pieces of personal information you've voluntarily imparted."

"You asked for someone to show you the sights. That's what I've been doing."

"I wanted *you* to show me around because I wanted to spend time with you. Not the reporter or the tour guide, but the real woman. I wanted a chance to know you—your likes and dislikes, your hopes and dreams."

"I'm not as complicated as you seem to think."

He wondered what she was hiding, what she was afraid of. But he knew she'd only withdraw further if he pushed for answers to the questions that lingered in his mind. So he only said, "We can start with how you would spend your free time on a Saturday afternoon." Then he smiled. "We'll work our way up to what kind of pajamas you wear later on."

"A picnic," she said, pointedly ignoring his comment.

"You mean lunch on a blanket on the grass?"

"That's exactly what I mean." She led the way through the exit and into the bright sunshine outside. "It's a beautiful day and I know the perfect place for it."

He tried to remember if he'd ever been on a picnic. He didn't think so. He did business lunches and negotiated contracts over cocktails—dining on the ground in the great outdoors was far outside his area of expertise.

"What's for lunch?" he asked suspiciously.

She already had her cell phone out and was punching in numbers. "We'll pick something up."

Before he could question her about the "something," she was talking in Japanese to whoever was on the other end of the line. After a brief conversation, of which he failed to understand a single word other than her name, she tucked her phone away.

"I had no idea you were so fluent in the language."

She grinned. "It might sound like I am, but I still make the occasional mistake when I'm translating words in my mind. Instead of salad and sandwiches, we might be eating grilled eels marinated in sake."

"*You* might be eating grilled eels," he said. "I'm really not that hungry."

She laughed and tucked her arm through his.

It was a casual and friendly gesture, completely within the boundaries she'd established for their relationship, and yet he felt a jolt of desire, hard and fast, when her breast inadvertently brushed against him.

As they exited the museum, she tilted her head to look at him. "And if you really need to know—I wear flannel."

He sighed with exaggerated disappointment. "You could have at least let me have my fantasies."

She laughed again. "I'll let you share my lunch instead."

Jenny hoped to get in and out of the hotel without anyone but the kitchen staff ever knowing she'd been there, unprepared to face an interrogation from her brother if he saw her with Richard. John Anderson had always been protective of his little sister, but he'd been even more so since her recent return to Tokyo after yet another failed relationship.

It was the newspaper that thwarted her plans.

The headline of the front page caught her attention as she moved past the seating area in the center of the lobby.

"What is it?" Richard asked.

She picked up the paper. "Jiro Mikodashi was fired yesterday."

He looked at her blankly.

"The VP at Kakubishi," she explained. "My sexual harassment story was apparently scooped by the *Herald*."

"I thought your editor had reassigned it."

She nodded. "Unfortunately, Cameron Parks completely missed the point of it. His report on allegations of sexual harassment in the workplace was buried on page twenty of yesterday's paper because it gave no mention of the VP. But the victims must have decided to fight back." Her lips curved. "My editor isn't going to be happy."

"Then why are you smiling?"

"Because I'm hopeful that next time he'll think twice about reassigning a story I've researched." She dropped the paper back onto the table.

"Does that mean you're not still mad at me?" Richard asked.

"It means I've resigned myself to being stuck in the society pages for a while longer. You were really just a convenient target for my frustration this time around."

"This time?" he echoed. "Has this happened before?"

"Twice in the past six months," she admitted.

"Why do you put up with it?"

"Because I don't have a lot of recourse," she admitted.

"Despite my experience at the *New York Times,* I'm one of the youngest reporters on staff here."

"It must make you wonder if coming to Tokyo was a smart career decision."

"It wasn't a career decision at all but a personal one."

"Because of your family?" he guessed.

She felt torn between pleasure and apprehension as she saw her brother making his way across the marble tile of the lobby toward them. "Because of my family," she agreed.

"I heard a rumor you were here," John said when he drew nearer.

She smiled. "Didn't Mom tell us not to listen to rumors?"

"It's not really a rumor if it's true." He bent to kiss her cheek. "You weren't going to sneak out without saying hi, were you?"

"I was trying." But she softened the admission with another smile. "You know I don't like interrupting when you're busy."

"And you know I'm never too busy for you." His cool blue-eyed gaze shifted to fix on Richard. "Or to meet your friends."

Obviously that was a request for an introduction. "John, meet Richard Warren. Richard, this is my brother, Jonathon."

As the two men shook hands, Jenny could almost see the questions flipping through her brother's mind as if they were on cue cards.

"Richard is a lawyer from Chicago working on the Hanson-TAKA merger," Jenny told her brother, preempting what she guessed would be his first inquiry.

That information earned a slight nod. "Room 2212."

"Yes." Richard seemed surprised that the hotel manager would know such a detail; Jenny wasn't.

"Mori Taka keeps one of the penthouse suites reserved

for his personal use," she explained. "And TAKA guests always stay at this hotel."

"I can see why," Richard said. "My rooms are spectacular."

"Has the service been satisfactory?" her brother asked.

He nodded.

"I'm sure Mr. Warren will complete a guest survey card when he checks out," Jenny said.

The corners of John's mouth tipped up a fraction, an acknowledgment he'd got the hint although not a guarantee he would heed her warning. "In the meantime," he said smoothly, "why don't you both join me for lunch in the dining room?"

She shook her head. "We can't. And to clarify, Richard is a business associate and Mr. Taka asked me to show him around Tokyo."

"I didn't ask," John said.

"But you were wondering."

"You're my little sister." He was speaking to her but his gaze was on Richard again as he said, "It's my job to look out for you."

"It's your job to look after this hotel," she reminded him. "I can take care of myself."

"Meiji Jingu is the Shinto shrine dedicated to the souls of Emperor Meiji and Empress Shoken," Jenny told Richard as they passed under the massive wooden torii that gated the entrance to the park. "The grounds of the shrine are covered by a forest of more than a hundred thousand trees donated by people from all over Japan."

He walked beside her along the wide gravel path, conscious of the city sounds fading away as they made their way deeper into the park. "I wouldn't have imagined there was anything like this here," he admitted. "When they show images of Tokyo on the news or in movies—it's always the towering buildings and glittering neon."

"Every city needs somewhere like this," Jenny told him. "A refuge from the frantic pace of urban society."

"And yet you seem to fit as easily into that world as you do into this one."

She shrugged. "When you live in ten different countries before the age of ten, you learn to adapt."

"Not everyone would," he disagreed. "Did you enjoy traveling so much?"

"Most of the time. Then we moved to Tokyo when my brother started high school. My parents wanted him—wanted both of us," she amended, "to be settled and able to concentrate on our studies. It was the first time we'd really had a chance to make friends. But still, as soon as there was a vacation—or even a long weekend—we'd be off to somewhere else again."

"Is that why your brother's so protective of you—because you spent so much time together as kids?"

She smiled as she led him off the path and onto a grassy area partially shaded by nearby trees. "John's a little overprotective, which I have a tendency to rebel against."

"Is that why you don't work at the hotel?"

"I don't work at the hotel because I'm not diplomatic enough to succeed in the hospitality industry." She took a blanket out of the basket he carried and spread it on the grass.

"I imagine there are plenty of positions that wouldn't require you to interact with the guests," he said, helping to straighten a corner.

"True, so maybe my decision was partly based on a

need to be independent—to end the comparisons." She winced. "I didn't mean to actually say that out loud."

"Whose comparisons?" he asked gently.

She knelt and began unpacking the picnic basket. "My own," she admitted. "Ever since we were little, I've tried to be as good as John at something. But he was always older, stronger, faster, smarter. And he'd always wanted to be part of the hotel business, so it made sense for me to find something else, something that was uniquely my own."

"Are you happy with what you're doing?"

"I am. I don't have any desire to be an investigative reporter who gets sent off to some distant country torn apart by war or devastated by natural disaster every time the newswire hums.

"I want to report news that is more relevant and substantial than what I write now for the society pages," she admitted. "But I also want a home and a family, and I want to go home to them every night. I won't ever let it take precedence over my children."

"Is that what you feel your parents did?"

"No," she responded immediately, maybe a little guiltily. "I didn't mean to give the impression that John and I were neglected, because we weren't. There were always nannies and tutors and play dates to keep us busy and out of trouble. But there were occasions when I wished my mom and dad had been around more."

She shook her head. "That sounds incredibly selfish. They gave us every opportunity any child could want, and yet, there were times when all I wanted was to stay in one place."

"It doesn't sound selfish." He took the wine and corkscrew she passed to him and started to open the bottle. "It just sounds like a child who was shuffled around a lot."

Her smile was wistful. “I used to wonder how my life would be different if...”

“If what?”

There was another pause—maybe a hesitation—as she poured the Bordeaux into two crystal glasses, then she shrugged again. “If things had been different. If I’d had parents who were settled in one place.”

He wondered what she’d really been thinking, what had caused the hint of sadness in the depths of her eyes. Because he knew her thoughts weren’t as simple as her response implied.

He sipped his wine as he debated whether to advance or retreat. He wanted her—the more time he spent with her, the more certain he was of that simple fact. And it didn’t seem to matter how different they were or how many reasons they each had for not wanting to get involved. Except he realized he didn’t really know her reasons.

“Tell me about him.”

“Who?” she asked warily.

“Your ex-boyfriend. The one you left before you came back to Tokyo,” he said. “I’m assuming he’s the reason you’re determined to keep me at a distance.”

Jenny picked up her glass, set it back down again without drinking. She didn’t need alcohol clouding her judgment when his mere proximity seemed to do that so effectively.

“You said you broke up with him about six months ago.”

She nodded. Six months, two weeks and five days.

That was how long it had been since she’d left Brad in New York, but it had been longer than that since she’d had sex. And it was sexual deprivation, pure and simple, that was responsible for the power of the attraction she felt for Richard Warren.

"What happened?"

She shrugged, deliberately casual. "I wanted more than he was willing to give me."

"A commitment?" he guessed.

"That's usually what scares a man off, isn't it? And though I'm not denying that I want to get married and have a family of my own someday, all I wanted from Brad was to be a priority in his life."

"That's what he ran away from?"

She managed a smile. "Brad was always running toward the next big headline rather than away from anything else."

"He was an idiot."

"I like to think so." She selected a sandwich but set it down on her plate without taking a bite. "What's your story?"

"What makes you think I have one?"

"Everyone has a story."

"Not necessarily an interesting one."

Obviously he still wasn't going to tell her about his failed marriage. "Okay," she said. "Tell me about the scar on your chin. How'd you get it?"

He rubbed his finger over the spot and smiled. "Making cinnamon buns."

He poured more wine into both of their glasses, giving no indication that he intended to expand on his response.

"You're going to have to explain that," she told him.

"I was five—maybe six years old," he told her. "I always liked being with my dad in the kitchen, but I especially liked the smell of cinnamon buns baking, and he would sometimes let me help make them. One day I was standing on chair beside the counter, helping spread the cinnamon and sugar mixture onto the rolled out dough and I leaned too far, tipped the chair and smacked my chin on the counter."

She winced with instinctive sympathy. "I bet that hurt."

He shrugged. "I don't really remember, but I do remember hearing about it. Mr. Tortelli—a retired judge who lived in the neighborhood and one of my father's most regular and loyal customers tell the story in very dramatic fashion—of The Day Of No Cinnamon Buns At Warren's Café."

She listened, mesmerized by the nostalgia that warmed his voice. Despite the incident, it was obviously a happy time in his childhood.

"Apparently my father was more concerned about the blood than the baking, and he forgot to take the first batch out of the oven before he took me to the hospital. And the second batch, which I had been helping with, had to be thrown out because I'd bled all over the counter.

"I got three stitches and Mr. Tortelli got a tale of woe to share over his morning coffee for the next twenty years or so."

"He doesn't sound like a very nice man," she said, automatically defensive of the child Richard had been.

"Mr. Tortelli was a fabulous character," he explained. "He came in every morning for his coffee and a sweet roll and to grumble about me being underfoot. He'd talk to anyone who would listen about the one time he had to have an apple Danish instead his customary cinnamon bun because I didn't have the sense to keep both my feet on solid ground.

"Mr. Tortelli never had any kids of his own and he liked to claim he never wanted any. But he carried candies in his pocket—the crunchy mint ones with the soft chocolate centers—and he always managed to slip one to each of me and my brother along with a few coins before he grumbled his way out the door again." Richard smiled again.

"My father often said that Mr. Tortelli was the reason

he got up at 3:00 a.m. every morning to bake. He told me that it didn't matter what I chose to do with my life so long as I was there for the people who counted on me to do my job."

"You're close to your dad, aren't you?" she asked gently. "I can hear it in your voice when you talk about him."

He nodded. "I was."

"Was?" She frowned. "What happened?"

The happy memories that had warmed his smile and his voice were gone, replaced by stark emptiness and raw pain. "He was murdered."

Chapter Seven

Jenny immediately regretted her prying. She was always curious about family dynamics—at least with respect to *other* people's families—but she wished now she'd never asked the question.

Richard's gaze was focused on something over her shoulder, or maybe somewhere in another time, and though his words might have been matter-of-fact, she heard the anguish in his tone. She lived with an emptiness deep inside herself from never having known her birth mother. She couldn't begin to imagine the horrible void that had been left inside Richard when his father-a man he'd known and loved—was abruptly and violently taken away.

"It was summer vacation after my first year of law school," he said. "My father was so proud of me—the first Warren to go to college, and on a scholarship.

"Anyway, it was a hot night and he was closing up when a teenage junkie—a skinny fifteen-year-old girl hopped up on some kind of drugs and looking to score some more—came into the café waving a gun around and demanding money. My dad gave her the cash in the register, but he'd already sent me out to make the night deposit so there was only about fifty dollars that he'd kept for the start of business the next day."

He recited the facts evenly, almost dispassionately, but she heard the bleakness in his voice.

"She was furious and still strung out enough to be dangerous. And she put the gun to my father's head and pulled the trigger."

She touched his hand, not objecting when he turned his over to link their fingers together. "I'm so sorry."

"He wasn't even fifty years old, and he'd always been healthy and strong. He was the cornerstone of our family, then suddenly he was gone."

"That must have been horrible." It was an inane and inadequate response, but the only thing she could think of to say in the moment.

He nodded. "It was a shock for all of us. Especially my mother. For months after, she went through the motions of living. Then his killer finally went to trial. My mom sat in the courtroom for the entire proceeding—six days of arguments and evidence and testimony.

"Unfortunately the only evidence the prosecution had was circumstantial. The gun, with the girl's fingerprints all over it, was excluded because it had been found during an illegal search. Without the weapon to tie her to the crime, she was acquitted."

She could only imagine the fury and frustration he must

have felt when the verdict was read in the courtroom. She squeezed his hand gently. "How did your family take it?"

"My mother was devastated all over again. All she'd wanted was justice for her husband. She harassed the D.A., demanding a new trial. She petitioned the courts. She became a crusader—determined to change the laws and the world. When she didn't succeed, she turned her attention to me."

"That's why she wanted you to become a criminal prosecutor," she realized.

He nodded. "I was in my final year of law school by that time and she wanted me to apply for a job with the district attorney's office or for a clerkship with the courts. It didn't matter to her that I had no interest in criminal law—and even less after my father was killed—she just wanted me to make a difference."

"I can understand that she would be angry and disillusioned with the system," Jenny admitted. "But I can't believe she expected you to make it your battle."

He shrugged. "I sent out a dozen applications, including one to the local D.A.'s office. It was a half-hearted measure to appease her.

"I never thought they would actually offer me a job. Maybe it was because of my father that they did. But I also got an offer from Shotwell Cunningham, one of the top ten firms in Chicago. The day I started work there was the same day my mother followed through on her threat to take my younger brother and move away to a little town called Crooked Oak. She said that if I wasn't willing to do my part, she needed to move somewhere she could feel safe.

"And maybe that was a factor in her decision," he allowed, "but she didn't have to move all the way to North Carolina."

"I can't imagine how awful that must have been for you. First losing your dad, then being manipulated by your mother and cut off from your brother."

"She thought I owed it to my father," he explained. "Because he'd made sacrifices so I could go the law school, she thought I had a responsibility to use that education to bring his killer to justice.

"I could see her point, but I couldn't let myself be drawn into her cause, to become part of what was tearing her apart. And she has never forgiven me for letting her down."

"I'm sure that's not true," she said, although the picture she was getting of his mother didn't make her certain of anything except that Mrs. Warren had treated her elder son unfairly.

His smile was bitter. "She didn't even come to my law school graduation."

Unfairly *and* horribly, she mentally amended, trying to imagine how he must have felt not to have such an important milestone acknowledged by his closest family. "I'm sorry, Richard."

"That was eight years ago," he said dismissively. "It hardly matters anymore."

"Of course it matters," she said. "The actions of a parent can have lasting impact on a child's life."

"I was hardly a child. In fact, it was only a few weeks after that Marilyn and I got married."

And she was starting to suspect that the estrangement from his family was a factor in his decision to marry so quickly. "Was your mother at the wedding?"

"I didn't invite her."

No doubt he hadn't done so because he didn't want to be hurt again when his mother declined to share in that special day. She recognized the self-preservation tactic because she'd used it herself. She'd left James because she'd known he wouldn't stay with her, then she'd followed the same pattern with both Kevin and Brad.

But understanding Richard's reasoning didn't blind her to the results. His action had hurt his mother and cemented their separation, and her heart went out to both the parent and child who still bore the scars of a tragedy.

"She sent a card and a gift," Richard continued. "Later, when I called to tell her that Marilyn and I were getting a divorce, she told me she'd known all along that the Crock-Pot she gave us would last longer than our marriage."

Jenny winced sympathetically. "That was harsh."

"She's always known how to make her point most effectively."

"Do you ever see her anymore?"

"Once, sometimes twice, a year. A few years ago I tried to make more frequent visits, as if doing so would somehow bridge the gap between us. But she still can't forgive me for my failure to right the wrong of my father's death."

"What about your brother? You carry photos of your niece and nephew in your wallet, you remember their birthdays—obviously you're close to them."

"Not as close as I'd like, but things are a lot better between us than they used to be. On top of my mother's negative attitude, Steven had his own reasons for resenting me."

"Such as?"

"The fact that I went to law school. After my father died, there just wasn't enough money for my brother to go to college."

"You said you had a scholarship."

"I did, but my parents still helped out with additional expenses. My brother didn't have that option. He was stuck.

Now that he has a successful business as a mechanic and a beautiful wife and two children who adore him, he's happy."

"It sounds as though you envy him," Jenny said.

"I used to," he admitted. "But after my divorce, I accepted that I couldn't have everything I wanted—that my career had to come first."

If Jenny needed any further reminder that he wasn't right for her, it was there in his own words. He might have opened up to her, sharing a lot of his personal history and past hurt, but he wasn't the man who could make her dreams of marriage and a family come true. No woman would ever take precedence over his career—and she had already lived enough of her life in second place.

Richard noticed that Jenny kept casting worried glances at the gray sky as they packed up the remnants of their picnic. It had been a beautiful sunny day when they first arrived, but the weather was changing quickly and rain seemed imminent.

"I don't suppose you have an umbrella in this basket?" he asked as they started to make their way out of the park.

"I wasn't supposed to need one," she said. "The forecast was for clear skies."

She hadn't finished speaking when the clouds opened up and fat drops of rain started to fall. "It was wrong," he told her.

She narrowed her eyes at him. "Obviously."

They quickened their pace, but Richard soon realized why she'd been so distressed by the unexpected precipitation. The blouse she was wearing was white and made of some very filmy fabric that was, within minutes, not just wet but very transparent. Her bra was also white and her nipples were beaded beneath the delicate lace.

Despite the moisture in the air, Richard's mouth was suddenly dry thinking that the young co-eds who participated in wet T-shirt contests during spring break had nothing on Jenny Anderson.

She crossed her arms over her chest. He didn't know if it was because she was cold or because she was aware of the transparency of her garment. He wished he had a jacket he could give her, but he'd opted not to wear one in the ninety degree heat. Then he remembered the blanket. He tugged it out of the picnic basket and draped it over her shoulders.

She turned, her expression reflecting both surprise and gratitude. "Thank you."

He smiled, forcing his gaze to remain on her face despite the urge to let it drop lower. "I can't have my tour guide catching a chill," he said lightly.

"What about the tourist?"

"I live in Chicago," he reminded her. "I'm made of tough stuff. Although I wouldn't object to a cup of coffee to take away the chill when we get back to your apartment."

"That sounds reasonable," she agreed.

Despite the rain, Jenny had enjoyed her day with Richard and found herself reluctant to let it end. As she clutched the ends of the blanket during the short subway ride to her apartment, she worried that she was beginning to enjoy his company too much.

She didn't delude herself into thinking there would be many more days like the last few they'd spent together. Richard's stay in Tokyo was limited. But even so, she knew she was starting to care about him. All it took was one kiss and a few casual touches. Or maybe it was the knowledge of everything he'd been through and his willingness to share it with her that made Jenny want to drop the shields around her heart.

What was wrong with her? Was she so desperately needy that she latched on to anyone who showed the slightest interest? Was she so scarred by her abandonment as a child that she couldn't be alone? She didn't want to think so, but she couldn't think of any other explanation for her inability to control her own feelings.

She hesitated on the sidewalk outside her apartment, suddenly aware that she'd never invited a man inside. As Samara liked to remind her, in the six months since she'd been back in Tokyo, she hadn't even been on a date. And maybe that was the reason for her hesitation—that inviting Richard into her apartment, showing him where she lived and sharing conversation would seem too much like a date.

Not that she wasn't ready to start dating again. Contrary to what Samara thought, Jenny was definitely over Brad and ready to get on with her life. But she wasn't going to date anyone who was the least bit similar to her ex. She was determined to finally break the cycle of dead-end relationships once and for all.

But she had offered him coffee and she wasn't going to renege on that promise. As she unlocked the exterior door, however, she made a point of saying, "Just because you're coming up to my apartment doesn't mean this is a date."

"Of course not," he agreed easily.

Too easily.

She eyed him warily and caught the twitch of his lips as he tried not to smile. She started to question him, then decided she didn't want to know and led the way up the narrow stairs to her fourth floor apartment.

Richard responded to her unspoken query, anyway. "It's not a date until I kiss you."

While Jenny was changing, Richard took advantage of her absence to survey the small living room. There was a sofa and one armchair, an end table, lamp, television. On the table there were thick candles that had burned halfway down set in a shallow bowl filled with decorative stones. The oatmeal sofa was dotted with colorful pillows in various shades of orange and red. It was small but tidy with all the little feminine touches noticeably lacking in his own apartment.

There was a trio of framed photographs on the table. He picked up the nearest one—a picture of Jenny and Samara both in caps and gowns—obviously their graduation day. He set the frame back down and selected another. This one was of Samara and her great-grandmother, and the resemblance between the two women was striking. The third photo was of Jenny and a couple he assumed were her parents. The man had dark hair and dark eyes and the woman was blond with blue eyes. Richard gazed closely at the trio but could discern no obvious familial resemblance among them. He found it strange that she didn't look like either of her parents or her brother, and yet she seemed so familiar to him.

Or maybe Jenny was right—maybe his subconscious was playing tricks on him, giving him a reason for his fixation on her rather than admit it was purely a physical attraction.

She came out of her bedroom dressed in a pair of faded

jeans and a soft yellow T-shirt that clung enticingly to her curves. She'd brushed her hair out so that it hung straight to her shoulders, and he noticed that the ends were still slightly damp.

She smiled at him, a little hesitantly, as if she was suddenly aware that they were alone in her apartment but not quite sure how they'd got there. "You said you wanted coffee?"

"That would be great," he agreed.

While she was making the coffee, he sat at the little table in the kitchen and watched her. After a few minutes, she joined him, leaning over to slide a mug across the table to him. As she did so, her hair fell forward.

He couldn't resist the opportunity, and he reached over to brush a wayward strand off her cheek and tuck it behind her ear. "Did you know that your hair looks like gold in the sun but now, slightly damp, it's more like copper?"

She pulled back slightly.

He smiled. "And when you're nervous, your eyes get dark—like bottomless pools."

She wrapped her hands around her mug. "Do you think a few words of poetic flattery will seduce me, Richard?"

He shook his head. "No, you'd appreciate straightforward honesty more than smooth dialogue."

"You'd be right," she admitted.

"That's why I'm telling you straight out that I want you in my bed."

She set her mug down too quickly, too hard, and coffee sloshed over the rim. She jumped up to get a dishcloth to wipe the spill. "I thought we agreed that wouldn't be smart."

"It's probably not smart," he said. "But I'm starting to think it's inevitable."

"It's not." She shook her head. "You might be content with casual relationships, but I'm looking for something more."

"I won't ever make you any promises I can't keep."

"I'm not asking for any promises. I'm only telling you why it won't happen."

"I guess we'll just have to wait and see about that."

She shook her head, but she was smiling. "You're being pushy again."

"Persistent," he corrected.

"We're completely mismatched."

"That doesn't seem to have diminished the chemistry between us."

"It's the whole opposites attract thing. Maybe we'd have great sex for a while, but it would fizzle soon enough."

"Couldn't we at least enjoy the great sex while it lasts?"

"I need more than short-term physical pleasure," she told him.

"Have you ever had a relationship based purely on physical pleasure?"

"No," she admitted.

He smiled. "Then don't knock it until you try it."

She shook her head. "That little gem of clichéd advice isn't going to make me throw away my long-term goals for the momentary pleasure of having sex with you."

His smile only widened. "It sounds as though you've given this some thought."

He could tell by the troubled expression on her face that she'd given it more thought than she was willing to admit. He wondered if she'd thought about it as often as he had. If the idea snuck up on her at the most inopportune times during the day, if it plagued her dreams at night.

"Only because Samara planted the idea in my mind," she said.

"Your roommate thinks you should sleep with me?"

"She thinks I'm still in love with my ex and sleeping with another man is a first necessary step to getting over him."

His smile turned into a frown. "I'm not interested in being part of your therapy."

"I don't need therapy," she said. "Because I'm not still hung up on Brad."

As much as Richard wanted to believe her, he was disturbed by the possibility that she was still carrying a torch for her ex. Although he was intrigued by the idea of tangling up the sheets with Jenny, he had too much pride to let himself be used as a substitute for another man. "Are you sure about that, Jenny?"

"My relationship with Brad ended more than six months ago—I'm sure."

He nodded. "Good. Now we can both be sure that when you end up in my bed, it will be because you want to be with me and no one else."

"Don't you mean *if?*" she challenged.

He smiled. "No."

Despite his earlier teasing and innuendo, Richard didn't kiss her goodbye.

He paused at the door for a moment, his gaze locked with hers. After a seemingly endless moment, his eyes dropped to her mouth, lingered.

She felt her breath catch in her throat, heard her heart pound in her ears. He lifted a hand, stroked his fingers softly and ever so slowly down her cheek, and said, "Good night, Jenny."

Then he was gone.

She hadn't realized she'd been holding her breath until she let it out after the door closed behind him.

It was a sigh of relief, of course. She was grateful that he was respecting the boundaries she'd established. But at the same time, she was frustrated and disappointed, too.

She turned to see Samara waving her hand in front of her face like a makeshift fan. "Is it hot in here or is it just me?"

"It's just you," Jenny told her.

Samara grinned. "I'm starting to think that Richard Warren is as smart as he is good-looking."

"Why would you think that?"

"Because he knows that if he came on too strong, you'd push him away. Instead, he's taking it slow, drawing you in."

"He's not drawing me anywhere," she denied.

"And he's doing it so cleverly you don't even realize it's happening."

Jenny picked up the remote, flicked on the television.

Her friend perched on the arm of the couch. "What are your plans with Mr. Warren for tomorrow?"

"I'm not seeing him tomorrow."

"Why not?"

"Because the negotiations for the merger are scheduled to resume on Monday and Richard needs to prepare."

Samara sank down beside her on the couch. "Okay, I guess this is where you can say I told you so."

But Jenny wasn't feeling smug, just miserable. Because as often as she'd reminded herself that Richard's interest in her was only temporary, she didn't want it to be true.

Richard stood at the window and looked out into the night at the wonderland of concrete and steel splashed with garish neon lights.

Maybe it was because he'd talked to Jenny about his family today that he found himself thinking about them tonight, wondering what his father would have thought about his son—the lawyer—in this fancy hotel suite in Japan. More than anything, Stan Warren had wanted his children to have an education, to have the opportunities of the world opened up to them. Opportunities he'd never had.

Richard's lips curved as he imagined his father surveying the same scene that was spread out before him now. Stan would have been more puzzled than impressed by Tokyo, although he would undoubtedly have been pleased by his son's success.

His father had once confessed to having had big dreams of his own—plans of going to college, building a career—but then he'd met and fallen in love with Richard's mother. Nancy had ended up pregnant before they'd graduated from high school, and Stan had married her without a second thought. And though she'd lost that baby a few weeks later, he'd known he didn't want to be without her.

Richard had asked him once if he'd ever regretted what he'd given up, the life he might have had. His father had answered without hesitation.

"Sometimes in life you make choices. Sometimes you make sacrifices. Falling in love isn't one of those times—it's not a choice and it's never a sacrifice. It's the greatest opportunity. And if the woman you love loves you back, it's the greatest gift."

His brief marriage had suggested a far different reality to Richard. And though he was certain his father would be proud of what he'd done with his career, he wasn't so sure he'd approve of the mess he'd made of the rest of his life.

Divorced from his wife, alienated from his mother, Richard was—aside from a few close friends—alone in the world.

Usually he took comfort in the fact that there was no one to answer to, no one depending on him. Tonight, it only made him feel lonely.

With a sigh that was both resigned and regretful, he turned away from the window and back to the laptop humming quietly on the antique desk. He sat down and stared at the screen, but he continued to be preoccupied by a certain green-eyed journalist who had the softest, most kissable lips he'd ever tasted.

He'd been with other women. More beautiful women, more experienced women. And yet none of them had ever haunted his thoughts the way that Jenny did.

What was he doing with her? It was a question he'd asked himself at least a dozen times. A question he still couldn't answer except to acknowledge, with more than a hint of regret, that he had no business pursuing her.

By her own admission, she didn't do casual relationships. And Richard didn't do anything else.

Jenny was in the middle of inputting a story for the next day's paper when Richard called her at work Monday afternoon. She hadn't expected to hear from him for at least a few days, knowing he would be immersed in meetings with the TAKA people, and she'd been prepared for the possibility that she might not hear from him at all.

"I was just thinking about you and wanted to hear your voice," he told her.

The words caused an unexpected warmth to flow

through her, but she forced herself to respond lightly. "You must have too much time on your hands."

"I wish I did, but even in these preliminary stages, the negotiations are threatening to be intense."

"You should be thrilled—this is what you've been waiting a whole week for."

"I should be," he agreed. "Instead I'm wondering when I might get a chance to see you again."

"We'll get together some time before you head back to Chicago," she said.

He chuckled softly. "I was hoping to see you several times before then."

"I understand that you're busy."

"But I still need to eat," he said. "And so do you. How about meeting for dinner tonight when I finish here?"

"Actually, I already have plans for dinner," she told him.

There was a pause, then he asked, "A date?"

"A birthday party."

"Are you going with a date?"

Her sigh was part amusement and part exasperation. "No. It's a family thing."

"We could get together after," he suggested.

"I don't know how late I'll be."

"All right," he relented. "Enjoy your cake and ice cream while I'm slaving away."

"I'll do that," she said, although she wasn't so sure she would.

Helen stared at the slim gold pen poised over the linen-textured paper. She'd come a long way since she'd first started writing these letters with a dime-store pen on a page torn out of a spiral-bound notebook. Twenty-five years later, the letters weren't any easier to write. If anything, the ritual had become increasingly more difficult and unexpectedly more painful. Whoever said that time heals all wounds had never had to make the choices she had.

My darling daughter,

She didn't notice the sting of tears, a small discomfort compared to the sharper, deeper ache of emptiness in her heart.

Her hand trembled, smudging the ink a little as she set the point to the page again.

I don't know what to say that I haven't already said a dozen times before. I don't know how to explain—

The phone rang; the pen slipped from her grasp.

She glanced at the call display, frowning at the unfamiliar display of numbers. Then it clicked—Tokyo. The merger. Richard.

She slid the paper aside, took a deep breath and picked up the receiver.

"Hello?"

"Helen, it's Richard."

"Hi." Her voice brightened noticeably. Maybe too noticeably. She tried for a more natural tone. "How are things in Tokyo?"

"Things are moving, if a little more slowly than we'd like," he told her.

"Good," she said, her response proof that she was listening to, if not really hearing, him.

There was a pause before he asked, "Is everything okay, Helen?"

"Why wouldn't it be?"

"Because you're at home at eight-thirty on a weekday morning."

"I just needed to get away from the distractions for a while."

"Is Jack still giving you a hard time about the merger?"

She sighed. "No. For once, this has nothing to do with business."

Which was an acknowledgement that there was *something,* and she'd never intended to admit to even that much.

"Is there anything I can do to help?"

She wished there was a way to delegate the grief and guilt to someone else—if only for a little while. But of course she had to suffer the consequences of her own decisions.

"Just take care of the negotiations," she told him.

Chapter Eight

When Mori Taka called for a morning break to take a conference call, Richard took advantage of the reprieve to track Jenny down in the newsroom. He sat in the chair across from her and gestured to the bouquet of balloons on the corner of her desk. "When you told me you were going to a birthday party, you didn't tell me it was yours."

She lifted one shoulder as she clicked to save her document before turning away from the computer screen.

"Happy belated birthday."

"Thanks."

"Why don't you sound very happy?"

"It was my twenty-fifth," she admitted.

He waited a beat, but no further explanation was forthcoming. "Oh, that's right," he said. "I forgot that twenty-five is the *unhappy* birthday."

She managed a smile. "It wasn't the birthday so much as the celebration."

"Not enough pomp and circumstance?"

"On the contrary," she said dryly. "My parents planned this formal occasion with a catered meal and elaborate decorations. There was even a parade of men."

"Is that some kind of Japanese birthday ritual I don't know about?"

She shook her head. "That's my mother's not-so-subtle way of trying to find me a husband. Most of the invited guests were handpicked for their twin virtues of being single and suitable to marry."

He was starting to understand why she sounded less than pleased.

"I want to get married," she admitted. "But I want to fall in love, too. Not that I expect to be swept off my feet, but a little romance would be nice."

He nodded. "You want love and romance, but no sweeping and no kissing."

Her eyes narrowed as she picked up the cup of coffee from her desk and took a long swallow. "You're making fun of me."

"I'm only trying to keep your requirements clear in my mind."

"Don't bother. It has nothing to do with you."

"Of course not," he agreed. "I'm just an interested bystander. But it might be a good idea to make a checklist."

She shook her head, but the hint of a smile tugged at her lips. "You're not helping."

"Maybe you don't really know what you want."

"And you do?"

He shrugged. "My desires are simple."

Now she laughed openly. "Is that an eloquent way of saying you don't want anything more complicated than a warm body in your bed?"

There was a time that her question would have been valid. That had changed before he came to Japan, but somehow getting to know Jenny had changed him even more. "If that was all I wanted, I wouldn't be here."

"Why are you here?"

"I saw the *Tribune* today." He smiled. "Front page headlines and follow-up on page three. Nice work."

"It wasn't the breaking news I originally hoped for, but I was happy with it," she admitted.

"I was thinking I should take you out for dinner to celebrate."

"Tonight?"

"Actually, I was going to suggest tomorrow. Tonight there's a mandatory dinner meeting."

"And I have to attend a showing at a local gallery tomorrow," she told him.

He considered that before asking, "Business or pleasure?"

"Both."

"Do you have a date?"

"No. Nor do I want one," she admitted.

He smiled. "Would it really be so horrible to drag me along?"

"Why would you want to be dragged along?"

"I enjoy spending time with you. Hard to believe, I know. I guess I'm perverse that way."

She lifted an eyebrow. "Any other perversions I should know about?"

"Not at this point in our relationship."

"We don't have a relationship."

"I'm working on it."

"That's the kind of information you should keep to yourself if you want to go to this showing with me."

"One of the things I like most about you is your honesty. You tell it the way it is. I figured I should return the favor."

"It's formal," she warned.

"I'm sure I can find something to wear."

"All right," she finally agreed. "I'll meet you in the hotel lobby at seven."

"That should be good. Mr. Taka promised we would break early tomorrow because of the late meeting tonight."

"How are the negotiations coming?"

"It looks like this might take a while," he admitted. "I'm starting to think we have a fundamental difference of opinion on certain key issues."

"It's a major step for both companies."

He nodded. It would be a big investment for TAKA but Hanson *needed* the merger, and although Jenny probably knew that, it wasn't something he could talk about. His job was to protect the interests of Hanson Media and advertising their desperation—especially to a member of the press—wasn't a good way to do it.

The phone on Jenny's desk buzzed, startling them both.

"Nigel Whitter is on line four," a female voice announced through the speaker.

"Thanks, Kari." Jenny looked at him apologetically. "I have to take this call."

"And I have to get back to the boardroom." He stood up, ready to go. "I'll see you tomorrow night."

"It's not a date," she reminded him.

He grinned. "We'll see."

* * *

He wasn't going to show up.

For all of Richard's claims about wanting to see her and his determined wrangling of an invitation to the event, it had taken nothing more than a message from Chicago to have him change his plans.

Jenny wasn't surprised—his last minute phone call wasn't unexpected. The disappointment was. She mulled over this realization as she wandered through the gallery, an untouched glass of champagne in her hand.

She'd been looking forward to seeing him. As much as she hated to admit it, it was true. She hadn't seen him since his impromptu visit to the newsroom yesterday afternoon, but she'd thought about him—maybe too much.

He'd apologized profusely for the change of plans; she'd assured him it wasn't a problem. He'd promised to meet her at the gallery; she'd told him it wasn't necessary. And yet, she wanted him to come—she wanted to believe that she mattered enough to him that he would make the effort.

She stopped in front of a vibrant seascape in furious shades of purple and red and wondered what it was about her that she was so ready to fall into the same trap all over again. It was the pattern of her life—to want too much and need too deeply.

She tipped her glass to her lips. The champagne was flat and warm, a testament to how long she'd been holding the drink, how long she'd been waiting.

She moved on to study the next display—this one an abstract of gentle blues, soft greens and subtle pinks. It should have been a soothing picture, but the clash of colors was no less violent because of the muted tones. It was a painting you didn't see so much as feel.

She glanced at the discreet placard noting the title of the work. *Summer Passion.*

Now she understood why the picture seemed to speak to her—it reflected so many of the conflicting emotions inside herself. Desires and denials, frustrations and fears, wants and needs. She swallowed another mouthful of warm champagne and turned away.

As she did so, she caught a glimpse of a dark head and broad shoulders. Her heartbeat quickened, then settled again when she realized the man was a stranger.

He's not going to show, she told herself again. It was foolish to set herself up for disappointment by expecting otherwise. It was equally foolish, she knew, to want him to come. She might not be able to deny the desire that sparked whenever he was near, but she had no intention of giving in to it. She refused to open up her heart to yet another man who would only break it.

But beyond the physical attraction she felt, she actually enjoyed spending time with him. After their initial meeting, she'd been determined not to like him. She was certain he was ruthless and arrogant, single-minded and self-absorbed. But over the next few days they'd spent together, she'd found her initial impressions changing.

She didn't doubt he could be ruthless in his business dealings, but he was also thoughtful and kind, as he'd demonstrated in the pleasure he'd found buying gifts for his family. He could be arrogant, but the cockiness was tempered by his self-effacing humor. And he was intelligent, able to converse easily about everything from baseball to world politics.

Okay, he was still pushy, but he was also an interesting and charming man and she was dangerously close to becoming infatuated.

She decided it was a good thing he'd stood her up.

It was after nine o'clock by the time Richard finished his conference call with Helen and made his way to the gallery. After a long day of meetings, he would ordinarily have wanted nothing more than to loosen his tie and put his feet up. Instead, he'd traded his suit for a tux, any hint of weariness overcome by the anticipation of seeing Jenny.

He pushed open the frosted glass door and stepped inside. The gallery was both smaller than he'd expected and more crowded. Silks whispered, jewels glittered and the scent of money hung heavy in the air.

He stood on the fringe of the crowd and scanned the room, searching for her. If he'd thought about it, he might have been concerned by his eagerness. He only thought of Jenny.

And then he found her.

She was wearing a little black dress that clung enticingly to her subtle curves and a pair of skyscraper heels that emphasized shapely calves. Her hair was swept up in some kind of fancy twist, leaving the long, graceful line of her neck bare. Diamonds sparkled at her ears; a matching teardrop pendant drew attention to the shadowy hollow between her breasts.

He accepted a glass of champagne from a passing waiter and stood back for a moment simply enjoying the view—elegant and sophisticated with just a hint of sexy.

His opinion altered dramatically when she turned to speak to the man standing beside her and he realized the dress was more *little* than anything else. It plunged in the back, dipping almost to her waist and revealing a tantalizing expanse of satiny skin. He gulped a mouthful of champagne, but the cool liquid had no effect on the fiery heat suddenly pulsing through him.

He remained in the shadows, watching as she made her way around the room, stopping to chat frequently with people she knew. She shook hands with some, exchanged air kisses with others, embraced a few.

She was in another man's arms now—a bald man with wire-rimmed glasses—and she was smiling at him, her eyes lit with genuine warmth and humor. She tucked her hand into the crook of his arm and led him over to the buffet table. Her companion shook his head when she offered him a plate, but continued to make conversation with her while she piled hors d'oeuvres on her own.

Richard decided he'd hovered in the background long enough.

He knew the exact moment she spotted him, could tell by the way she stilled as their gazes locked across the room. It was as if every muscle in her body grew taut and every nerve stretched tight. He moved toward her, with every step he sensed her nervousness growing along with the sexual tension between them.

She wasn't comfortable with him, he realized. She didn't relax enough to laugh easily or flirt casually. He decided he liked making her uneasy—at least it proved she wasn't indifferent.

He stepped toward them just as he heard Jenny's companion saying, "I'll see you next week, then."

Her only response was a nod, but she waited until the other man had walked away before she turned to him.

"Hello, Jenny."

Her smile was pleasant, if a little cool. "Richard. I didn't think you were coming."

"I told you I would."

"So you did." She took her time in selecting a stuffed mushroom. "You also said you'd be here around eight."

"I got caught up."

"These things happen."

Her response was casual, her tone wasn't.

"You're annoyed with me."

"Of course not," she denied. "I told you not to worry if you couldn't make it."

"I wanted to see you."

Another cool smile. "And now you have."

He plucked a shrimp from her plate, popped it into his mouth.

"Help yourself," she said dryly.

"Thanks." He smiled as he stole another shrimp. "I missed dinner."

"So did I."

He picked up an olive, held it to her lips. She accepted it automatically, her lips brushing his fingertips as she did so. He saw the flare of awareness in her eyes, the flicker of wariness. She definitely wasn't relaxed now. She was tempted, and fighting the temptation.

"I've actually been here a little while," he said.

"How long?"

He smiled. "Long enough to see you flirting with other men."

"What other men?"

"The bald guy with round glasses, the gray-haired man with the diamond on his pinky, the short guy wearing the red bow tie."

"Not that I owe you any explanations, but Ethan is a friend of mine from way back. In fact, I introduced him to his wife. Saburo is a friend of my parents. And Bruce is a copy editor at the paper."

He nodded. "I see."

She tilted her head back to meet his gaze. "What do you see?"

"That you flirt with married men, old men, and co-workers, but you don't flirt with me."

Her only response was a slight furrow between her brows.

"Is it because I make you nervous?"

"You don't make me nervous," she denied.

"Maybe it's not me," he allowed. "Maybe it's the attraction between us."

"Are the negotiations with TAKA stalled again? Because you really do have too much time on your hands if this is the kind of stuff you're dreaming up."

He brushed the back of his hand over her cheek. "I'm not imagining the way your pulse is racing right now."

She pushed his hand away and picked up a cracker.

He decided he wouldn't push the issue—yet.

"I don't know about you," he said. "But this isn't doing anything to ease my hunger. Why don't we go somewhere for dinner?"

She shook her head. "I can't."

He thought she sounded disappointed, or maybe he'd just imagined it.

"There are still several other people I need to see," she

explained. "But there's no reason for you to stay if you don't want to."

He touched her back between her shoulder blades, his palm tingling where it contacted her silky skin. "I want to."

"Why do I think you're not expressing an interest in the art?"

"Because you're a very smart woman." His hand slid lower, to the small of her back, his thumb tracing the skin inside the V-shape cut of the fabric. "I like your dress."

Jenny had chosen it carefully, determined that if he showed up, he'd know exactly what he was missing. But now that he was here, standing close, touching her, his eyes clearly communicating his desire, she wished she'd chosen differently—more conservatively

But she managed a cool smile and a cooler "Thank you."

His fingers trailed upward again, slowly tracing the ridges of her spine. "I can't help but wonder if you wore it for me—or to spite me?"

"I already told you, I didn't expect you'd show up."

"But you knew it would torture me if I did."

Her lips curved just slightly. "Are you feeling tortured?"

"Among other things." He dipped his head toward her and when he spoke again, his voice was low and his breath fanned across her cheek. "Most notably a desire to take you someplace where I can strip that dress from your body and run my hands and lips over every inch of your bare skin."

"In your dreams."

"It's going to happen. Maybe it won't be tonight, maybe it won't be that dress, but it is going to happen."

The heated promise of his words sent a shiver—part fear, part anticipation—through her veins. Thankfully, before she could throw caution to the wind and throw herself into his arms, she spotted her parents across the room.

She turned back to Richard. "Are you picturing me naked right now?" she asked softly.

"I'm trying," he admitted.

"Well, you might want to put some clothes on that mental image before I introduce you to my mom and dad."

Meeting Jenny's parents was the last thing Richard had expected when he'd finessed an invitation to this event. Not that he had any real objection, but he'd been looking forward to some one-on-one with Jenny, not making small talk with strangers.

He'd heard of Harold and Dana Anderson, of course. They were the force behind Anderson International, a group of hotels renowned around the world for their luxurious accommodations and quality of service. They were the destination of choice for movie stars and professional athletes, politicians and royalty—or anyone who expected the best and could afford to indulge.

He recognized the couple from photographs that had appeared in the society pages of newspapers around the world, discussing not just their chain of hotels but their philanthropic works, as well.

Harold Anderson stood about six feet tall, with the build of a professional football player. His dark hair was liberally streaked with gray, his beard more salt than pepper. He was older than Richard would have guessed, probably in his early sixties, but a man to be reckoned with. Not because of his physical size or the wealth his hotel empire had amassed, but because of the sharp intelligence that gleamed in his dark eyes. Eyes that were narrowed on Richard, shrewdly assessing.

Richard wondered if the man knew he had designs on his daughter or if Jenny's father was in the habit of trying to intimidate any man who came too close to his little girl.

He shifted his attention to Dana Anderson. Jenny's mother was of average height, which meant that she was several inches shorter than her daughter, with chin-length blond hair and blue eyes. She wore a glittery silver gown that highlighted her slender figure and a stunning sapphire and diamond choker.

"Jenny." Dana kissed both of her daughter's cheeks. "You look lovely."

"Looks like she bought only half a dress," Harold grumbled. "Probably couldn't afford the rest because she spends her entire paycheck on rent."

"Dad," Jenny said warningly. But there was genuine warmth and affection in her smile as she turned to kiss him, too.

"There's no reason for you not to live at home," her father said. "Or, if you must live downtown, you could at least let us help you out."

"Harold," Dana piped in. "Let's not get into this in front of Jenny's friend."

It was a deliberate prompt for Jenny to make the introductions, which she finally did. "Dad, Mom, meet Richard Warren. Richard, these are my parents, Harold and Dana Anderson."

He shook hands with each of the senior Andersons. "It's nice to meet both of you."

Dana smiled; Harold didn't.

"I didn't realize you were going to be here tonight," Jenny said.

"Neither did I until about an hour ago," her father responded.

Dana patted her husband's arm consolingly. "Art isn't Harold's thing," she told Richard. "But the artist's mother is a friend of mine, so I thought it would be a good opportunity to show our support for Amaya and see Jenny at the same time."

"We wouldn't have to visit with her at public functions if she still lived at home," Harold said again.

Jenny sighed as she tucked her arm into her father's and tipped her head against his shoulder. The gesture of affection seemed to appease him a little.

"We see a lot more of her now than we did when she lived in New York," Dana pointed out.

Jenny smiled at her mother, a wordless expression of gratitude.

"I guess that's true," Harold finally conceded. "And I do sleep better knowing she's not too far, and especially knowing that she's not with—"

"Look," Jenny interrupted. "There's Jonathon and Michiko."

She smiled as she turned to greet the couple who'd just arrived—her brother and a gorgeous Japanese woman with long, silky black hair, dark eyes and a very obviously pregnant belly.

"Mr. Warren." Jonathon said with a nod.

Richard returned the acknowledgment in kind.

"You know each other?" Harold asked.

"We met at the hotel on Saturday," John said.

Richard imagined father and son would be comparing

notes later, trying to figure out his role in Jenny's life and if he was worthy of her. He wasn't bothered because whatever his role, it was only temporary.

"We haven't met," the woman with Jenny's brother said pointedly. "I'm John's wife, Michiko."

"It's a pleasure." He offered an awkward bow, and she smiled at his attempt of a Japanese-style greeting.

"Where's Suki?" Harold asked the newcomers.

Michiko shuddered. "Can't you imagine the damage she could do in a place like this?"

"I was imagining that she might enjoy comparing her technique with the artist's."

"Harold," Dana admonished in a stern whisper, while the others chuckled.

"There are certain similarities," Jenny agreed. "Although I don't think Amaya would appreciate having those pointed out."

"Suki is?" Richard prompted.

"My niece," Jenny told him.

"An incredibly energetic and active four-year-old who doesn't walk when she can run," John elaborated.

Dana smiled. "She reminds me of Jenny at that age," she said fondly.

Harold put his arm around his daughter's shoulders. "You wouldn't guess that this beautiful young woman used to climb trees, collect frogs and make mud pies, would you, Mr. Warren?"

Richard let his gaze skim over the exquisitely dressed woman who'd captivated him from the first moment he'd seen her outside the TAKA boardroom. "I can't say that I would," he agreed.

"I'm sure Richard isn't interested in hearing stories about my childhood," Jenny said.

"Actually, I am interested," he said.

She glared at him. "In any event," she continued as if he hadn't spoken, "I promised to introduce him to some people."

Then she took his arm and began to lead him away.

"It was nice to meet all of you," he said over his shoulder.

"You, too," Dana said.

Michiko smiled.

Harold and John both nodded, apparently reserving judgment.

"I don't recall you promising to make any introductions," he said to Jenny.

"Then I won't bother."

"So why did you really drag me away from your family?"

"Earlier you said something about dinner," she reminded him. "I'm hungry."

"Were you afraid your mother would pull out an album of baby pictures?" he asked. "Although I don't think that purse was big enough for an album, maybe just one or two photos."

"I'm glad you find this amusing."

He grinned as he followed her outside. "I'll bet you were a cute baby."

"I know where there's a great *teppanyaki* just a short walk up the road," she said, pointedly ignoring his comment.

A *teppanyaki,* he knew from his guidebook of Japan, was a steak house. Although his stomach grumbled its agreement with the suggestion, what he really wanted was some time alone with Jenny.

"I have a better idea."

Chapter Nine

"I'm not sure this is a better idea," Jenny said to Richard, pausing outside the main entrance of the hotel.

"Don't you like the food here?"

"I don't like thinking that my father will probably know I'm here with you before we find a table in the restaurant."

"The staff here are very discreet," he told her.

"Of course they are," she agreed. "I'm just not sure the usual policy of nondisclosure applies to the owners' daughter."

"Then it's a good thing we're not going to one of the restaurants." He took her hand to guide her toward the bank of elevators.

"I'm *not* going to your room."

"It's a suite," he said, as if that made a difference. "And I have no evil intentions. I only brought you here so we could share a meal and conversation without interruption."

She eyed him warily. "This from the man who said what he liked most about my dress was the idea of taking it off me."

He grinned. "It's still true. It's also true that I won't make love with you until you want it as much as I do."

"It isn't going to happen."

"Not tonight," he agreed easily.

Not ever. She wanted to speak those words; she wanted to mean them. But she was no longer certain about anything where Richard Warren was concerned.

The elevator dinged to announce its arrival.

"Are you coming?" he asked.

"Only because I'm hungry," she told him.

He smiled. "I didn't expect anything else."

But Jenny was still wary when she stepped into the car. Not because she didn't trust Richard. He'd been honest about what he wanted from the very beginning, and she believed that he didn't have any ulterior motives for inviting her to his room. She was more worried about her weakening resolve where he was concerned.

"Tell me more about your family," Richard suggested after their meals had been delivered.

"You've met them all except Suki," Jenny said. "What do you want to know?"

"Is your father as protective of you as your brother?"

"He can be even more so," she admitted. "But he and Mom traveled a lot, so John took on a lot of parental responsibility where I was concerned. I think he actually enjoyed intimidating the guys I dated in high school."

"Did he ever beat anyone up for you?"

"Worried?" she teased.

"Maybe."

Jenny laughed softly. "No. In fact, I don't think he's ever thrown a punch. Even when we were kids, John always made smart choices. He never gave our parents a moment's worry, while I tested them constantly. Breaking curfew, sneaking out of the house, smoking, drinking—"

"Why?"

Her smile faded; her eyes clouded. "To prove what I thought I already knew—that I was unlovable. To see if they would give me away, too."

"Give you away?" he echoed, genuinely baffled by her statement. "Why would you ever think they'd do that?"

"Because my mother did." She set her chopsticks down and pushed her plate away.

Suddenly the pieces clicked into place. "You were adopted?"

She nodded. "I always knew it, but I didn't really understand what it meant until I was in sixth grade and a new girl joined our class. Wendy was in foster care because her mother wasn't capable of raising her. She'd been in and out of several different homes over the years. At one time, she'd had foster parents who'd wanted to adopt her. But her mother refused to sign the papers, claiming she loved her too much to ever let her go."

The hurt and confusion were evident in her tone. "And you assumed, because your mother had put you up for adoption, it meant she didn't love you."

"It seems the obvious explanation," she said.

He shook his head, unable to believe that this incredible woman could harbor such deep-rooted doubts about herself. "I don't think it's obvious at all. Maybe she loved you too much to ruin your life by letting you be shuffled in and out of other people's homes."

"Maybe." But she clearly didn't believe it. "In any case, I figured if my own mother could turn her back on me, my adoptive parents would, too. So I started acting out, pushing them to the point where I was sure they would throw their hands into the air and me into the streets."

"But they didn't."

"No. They threw me into counseling instead." She shook her head. "Even then, they didn't abandon me. They sat by my side through each of the sessions, wanting only to help. I yelled at them and swore at them, and they never wavered."

"They love you."

She smiled. "I finally got that. And with the realization came the guilt and a determination to make amends, to make them proud of me so they'd never regret everything they'd given me."

"Was your brother adopted, too?"

"Yeah. He was four years old when his biological parents were killed in a car accident. Two years later, the Andersons decided he should have a sibling."

"And that's when they adopted you?"

She nodded. "I don't know whether it's that he got there first, or maybe it's because he actually looks a little bit like our mom, but he just always seemed to fit into the family while I never quite felt like I did."

"I'm not sure I ever fit into my family, either," he told her.

"But at least you know them. I have no clue about mine."

"Yes, you do," he insisted. "Even though you're not related by blood, you're still a family. That was obvious in the few minutes I saw you together."

She was silent, considering.

"But if you really want to know your biological family,"

he continued, "it seems that would be easy enough to arrange through the agency that adopted you out or—"

She shook her head, cutting him off. "I used to think about it," she admitted. "But then I'd feel guilty for even considering it. I know I'm lucky to have two parents who love me—why would I risk screwing that up by searching for a mother who already rejected me?"

"It seems to me that your doubts and insecurities are screwing up your relationship with your family anyway."

She sighed. "I just wish I was more like Jonathon, more like our parents—quiet and serious. As a child, I had a tendency to do everything at full volume."

He smiled. "You still do."

She frowned.

"You carry yourself with poise and elegance, but there's an energy around you—a constancy of motion even when you're standing still."

"And I thought I'd outgrown that."

He brushed his fingers over the back of her hand. "I don't think passion is a character flaw."

"Passion?" Jenny asked the question skeptically as she pulled her hand away. But even then, she could still feel the warmth of his touch on her skin, and she yearned to feel his touch on every part of her body.

"It's there," he told her. "Tightly controlled and all the more intriguing because of that control. It makes a man wonder what might happen if he ever managed to unleash it."

She pushed her chair away from the table. "I have to go. I have an early meeting with my editor tomorrow."

He stood up with her. "What are you doing Friday night?"

"I'm busy."

"Are you? Or are you trying to put some distance between us?"

"I'm going out with Samara," she said, which they both knew only answered the first part of his question. But she breathed a sigh of relief that she had legitimate plans, because she knew that she was in danger of getting in too deep with Richard and she desperately needed some of that distance he'd mentioned. Better yet, she needed him to finish up the negotiations and go back to Chicago—that would establish a lot of distance.

"Okay," he said. "But that doesn't mean I'm giving up."

"I'm not trying to challenge you."

"I know." He smiled and brushed his thumb over her bottom lip. She felt it tremble, ever so slightly, and could only hope that he didn't notice the instinctive response.

"Come on," he said. "I'll walk you home."

Jenny shook her head. She needed that distance now, before she did something crazy. "I'll take a taxi."

"Are you sure?"

"It'll be quicker," she said. "It's already late and I really want to get to bed. Home to bed. To sleep."

He smiled at the hasty amendments. "Okay."

She exhaled, silently relieved by his agreement. "Good night, Richard."

He caught her hand as she reached for the handle of the door. "Do you really think I'm going to let you go without kissing you tonight?"

"We agreed—"

"The rules are changing," he said.

She didn't have a chance to brace herself before his lips brushed against hers. But even as she yielded to the kiss, she knew nothing could have prepared her for the feel of his mouth on hers, the confident mastery of his lips, the heat of her own desire.

Her lips parted and his tongue skimmed over hers with slow teasing strokes. She couldn't think or reason, only respond. And the immediacy and intensity of her response stunned her. It was more than want—it was an aching need, a desperate yearning.

His hands moved up her back, sliding over the bare expanse of skin from her waist to her neck and back again. She felt her skin heat, her blood pulse, her bones melt.

He pressed her against the door, his body hard against hers, and incredibly arousing. She shivered, suddenly afraid of the growing need she felt inside, and of wanting more than he could give her.

When he finally eased away, she drew in a long, shaky breath and waited for the world to steady beneath her feet.

"What was that?" she asked, sounding breathless and dazed.

The way he looked at her was just as arousing as a touch, unrestrained desire blazing from the depths of his blue eyes. "That," he said, rubbing his thumb over her bottom lip, "was the proper way to end a date."

She swallowed. "I told you it wasn't a date."

His smile was slow and sexy and just a little bit smug. "You were wrong."

Jenny was glad she had plans with Samara and some other friends for Friday night. She'd been spending far too much time with Richard Warren lately, and when she wasn't with him, she was thinking about him. Even more than usual after their evening at the art gallery and the late dinner they'd shared in his suite. Or maybe it was the kiss that was to blame.

It would be easy to explain away her fascination as lust. There was no denying that at least part of the attraction she felt was physical. And maybe, if she'd taken Samara's advice and slept with him a week ago, it might have ended there. It wasn't that simple anymore.

Her feelings for Richard already went deeper than desire. She enjoyed being with him and talking to him, and she found herself missing him when he wasn't around. When he'd asked her about her plans for tonight, she'd been tempted to invite him to join her friends—to show him a karaoke bar as yet another aspect of Japanese culture. She knew no one would have objected to his presence. But she also knew she was just looking for an excuse to see him again. And after the kiss they'd shared in his hotel room—

Well, she'd already spent far too much time thinking about that kiss. What she needed was a night out with friends to forget about Richard Warren.

And it was working, too. Her thoughts strayed to him only once every few minutes instead of a few times every minute. She concentrated instead on the group of people around her. There were about a dozen of them—friends and coworkers and significant others—in the private room they rented once a month to indulge in silly fun without making fools of themselves in front of strangers.

Malcolm had the microphone now and was squinting at the lyrics on the screen and struggling more than a little with the tune of an old Beatles song. Jenny tapped her foot to the beat of the music.

Yes, this was exactly what she needed—time and distance from Richard. Because staying away from the sexy lawyer was the only way to guarantee she would stay out of his bed.

* * *

Richard made his way up the stairs and down the hall to find the correct room number. When he'd called Samara to ask about her plans with Jenny, she'd promised they would be here tonight. He hadn't realized it was a karaoke bar, and he hadn't expected to find Jenny on stage.

He stood at the back of the room for a moment, captivated by her. He recognized the song, vaguely. A pop tune from several years back about believing in life after love. She was belting out the lyrics with obvious enthusiasm, singing as she did everything else—with intensity and passion.

He felt the stir of desire. In the past couple of weeks, he'd grown accustomed to the basic physical reaction of his body to her presence. It was the less familiar and distinctly uncomfortable yearning for something more that bothered him.

It had been a mistake to kiss her again. He'd had a taste, a glimpse—it wasn't nearly enough. He wanted more. He wanted everything.

It was only his promise to her, his reassurance that he would wait until she was ready, that had made him pull away while he was still thinking clearly enough to do so.

She affected him on a level he didn't think he'd ever experienced before and wasn't sure he was ready for. If he was smart, he would turn around now and walk back out the door before she ever knew he was here.

It was further proof of the power she held over him that he didn't turn around. Instead, he made his way across the room, toward a vacant chair in front of the stage where Samara and some others were watching.

He slipped into the empty chair beside Jenny's roommate.

Samara smiled at him. "You made it."

"And I only got lost once."

She laughed and poured him a glass of beer from the pitcher on the table. "That's impressive."

Richard accepted the drink, his eyes on the stage as Jenny finished her song to a smattering of applause.

She bowed, then set the microphone back in the stand and gestured for Samara to take the stage. As her friend did so, Jenny took her now vacated seat.

"You were fabulous," Richard told her.

"Thank you." She accepted the compliment as warily as his presence. "What are you doing here?"

"Samara invited me."

Jenny sipped again. "When?"

"When I called her last night to find out what you were doing tonight." He picked up the pitcher to pour Jenny a drink.

"Thanks." She leaned forward and dropped her voice so only he would hear. "But I'm not going to get drunk and let you seduce me."

"I don't want you drunk," he told her. "I want you coherent and willing."

She sat back again. "You'd have better luck if you tried for drunk."

He smiled and let his gaze drop to her mouth, remembering how soft it had been under his, how incredibly responsive. "I don't think so." He twined an errant strand of hair around his finger and tugged gently. "I do want you, Jenny."

He saw the quick flash of heat in her eyes, but she responded coolly. "Yes, we've already established that."

"I think you want me, too."

"I'm not going to deny there's a basic physical attraction. But I wasn't lying when I said I don't do casual relationships."

"My feelings for you are anything but casual," he told her. "They're powerful and intense and lately they've been driving me to distraction."

The words caused a quick thrill of pleasure to course through her, an instinctive reaction which fueled her annoyance. He was a lawyer—it was his job to find the right words to get what he wanted. She refused to let his words sway her.

"You're just not used to having any woman turn you down."

He shifted his chair closer, his thigh brushing against hers beneath the table. "Could we forget about everyone else and just focus on us for a minute?"

"I'd rather focus on the music," she said. "This is one of my favorite songs."

"Okay." His leg rubbed against hers again. "But we'll get back to this."

It was a promise that made her heartbeat quicken.

Samara finished her song and came back to the table. "Gabe's up next."

"I hope it's a short one this time," Jenny said, then grimaced as the first notes of Don McLean's "American Pie" filled the room.

"We're going to need another pitcher of beer, Kazuo." Samara spoke to the man beside her. Then to Richard she said, "Do you sing?"

He shook his head. "Not in public."

"Everyone has to sing," Jenny said. "It's a commitment you make when you walk through the door."

"It's not exactly a rule," Samara said. "It's more an expectation."

"Of course, if you're uncomfortable with the thought of getting up on stage, you can sneak out now," Jenny told him.

Richard winced as the singer hit a note he'd never heard before. He had some concerns about making a fool of himself, but he was confident he could at least perform better than what they were hearing at present. "I don't think my Japanese experience would be complete without at least a little karaoke."

"I told her you wouldn't buck at a challenge," Samara said.

"Balk," Jenny told her, scanning the list of song choices. "A buck is a male deer or slang for a dollar."

Samara sighed. "Five years of college in America, and I still have trouble with the language."

"Your English is a lot better than my Japanese will ever be," Richard told her.

She smiled her gratitude as the man who'd gone to get more beer returned with two pitchers. He set them on the table, then sat down beside Samara and laid his arm across her shoulders. It might have been a casual display of affection, but Richard recognized the warning in his eyes and knew it was a blatant display of territoriality.

Samara rolled her eyes, obviously interpreting the gesture the same way. "This is Richard Warren," she said. "He's the lawyer from Chicago that I was telling you about. Richard, this is Kazuo."

"You're Jenny's friend?" Kazuo asked.

He wasn't so sure Jenny would consider him a *friend* or that he wanted to be classified as such, but he guessed it was a suitable title at present. He nodded and offered his hand.

Kazuo shook it, his grip more firm than friendly.

"Richard's a karaoke virgin," Jenny leaned over to inform the other man.

He smirked.

"I don't think anyone should have to go it alone their first time," Samara said, coming to his defense.

Kazuo stroked his fingers down her arm. "Maybe Jenny could help ease him into it."

Jenny was shaking her head before Kazuo finished speaking. "I'm sure Richard can handle it on his own."

He set down his empty glass and leaned closer to her. "I can," he agreed. "But I think I would enjoy being initiated by someone with so much more experience."

She glared at him. "You're falling right into her trap."

"I don't mind being trapped with you."

It wasn't the words so much as the tenor of his voice that made her realize there was a lot more going on beneath the surface of their conversation.

"I've got it," Samara announced triumphantly, already punching buttons into the machine to program her selection.

Gabe had finally finished his song and handed the microphone to Kazuo, who passed it to Richard. "You're on."

Richard stood up and took Jenny's hand.

"I'm going to kill Samara," she muttered.

"I like her," he said.

"Then why don't you sing with her?"

"Because I also like all my body parts in the right places, and her boyfriend seemed a little too eager to rearrange them."

She smiled at that. "Kazuo's like a big dog—all bark and no bite."

"Good to know."

"The rest of this crowd is a different story," she warned. "Do you think you can handle it?"

"I'm sure I can stumble along if you lead the way."

Jenny recognized the opening notes of the song and decided that she might forgive Samara for this—someday. At least it wasn't a sentimental ballad about endless love or something equally nauseating. She glanced over at Richard. "You could probably still make a break for the door."

"Not a chance."

There was something in his smile, a distinctly sensual heat underlying the casual curve of his lips. It threw her off balance and made her miss her cue. Then she had to rush the first line to catch up.

Richard's smile widened, as if he sensed her discomfiture and knew he was the cause of it. His gaze lingered on hers for a moment before it shifted to the monitor.

His singing unnerved her as much as the smile. She should have guessed he wouldn't have risked getting up on stage unless he could carry a tune, but she hadn't been prepared for how good he was. He had an incredible voice—strong and sure, even singing the sappy lyrics of an old Sonny and Cher tune.

This time when he smiled, she smiled back.

He was being a really good sport despite having been coerced to participate and it was, after all, harmless fun.

And then he touched her.

In the middle of the stage, under the lights, he'd reached out and stroked his hand down her arm to link with hers as he sang. It was as if the words were intended only for her, and everyone else seemed to fade away.

Suddenly it wasn't just fun anymore. It was fun and dangerous, and the emotions swirling inside her were intense and chaotic—fear and need, wariness and wanting.

She saw the reflection of her own desire in his eyes, but his eyes were unclouded by other emotions. It was simple for him—he wanted her and he intended to have her. He'd already stated that intention clearly and unequivocally.

It wasn't that easy for Jenny. She knew if she allowed

herself to engage in a physical relationship with him, her heart would inevitably become involved. She wasn't capable of separating her body from her emotions.

She sang her lines automatically, as her mind scrambled.

How had this happened to her? How was it possible to feel so much so soon? How had she let herself become involved when she knew he would only be in Tokyo a few weeks? What happened to the distance she'd vowed to establish? The only distance between them now was a few inches, and that space was filled with simmering heat that was already melting the last of her resolve.

It wasn't until the sound of clapping penetrated the heavy throb of blood in her ears that she realized the song was over.

She tore her gaze from his and forced a smile as she bowed to her friends. She heard someone—Samara, she would bet—calling for an encore. But Jenny was already off the stage, dropping her microphone on the table.

She made her way down the stairs, pushed through the door and onto the sidewalk. She started to walk with no destination in mind, propelled by a desperate need to breathe, to think.

But all she could think was that she wanted him. There was no point in trying to deny it any longer. From the moment he'd walked into the bar, she'd known it was too late to hold back any longer.

She wasn't ready for this. She wasn't eager to jump into another dead-end relationship.

Richard was only going to be in Tokyo a few more weeks—a month at the most. But right now she couldn't think of a single reason not to take advantage of every minute they might have together over the next month.

No reason except that her heart had been broken too

many times already. She simply didn't have the experience or sophistication to indulge in a casual affair and her heart was too fragile for anything more.

"Jenny."

She wasn't surprised to hear him call her name. She'd left the bar in a last ditch effort for sanity, knowing that if he followed, there would be no turning away. Not this time.

She stopped, turned to face him. "I just needed some air."

Richard took her hands; her heart stuttered.

In that moment, she knew everything was about to change. She was done fighting with herself. She'd made a list as long as her arm of all the reasons he was completely wrong for her. Okay, it was really one reason that she'd written over and over again—because he would be going back to Chicago soon.

She refused to get involved with someone who would soon be more than six thousand miles away.

But while the rational part of her brain understood that a relationship with Richard was doomed to failure, that part was no match for her need. For days they'd been building toward this moment. The moment when she forgot all the reasons they were completely wrong for each other and let herself get lost in the passion she knew they would discover together.

"What's wrong?"

She shook her head again, one last ditch effort to regain her sanity. "Nothing. Really. It's crazy. *I'm* crazy." She laughed. "It must have been the lights."

"What must have been the lights?" He asked the question patiently, as if he already knew the answer.

Of course, he did. He'd been taking it slow to give her a chance to accept what he'd said almost from the beginning was inevitable.

"Short-circuiting my brain," she answered.

He brushed his thumbs over her knuckles—a casual yet somehow sensual gesture that made her ache to feel his touch all over her body.

She swallowed before admitting, "I was actually thinking of asking you to come home with me."

He drew her closer, one corner of his mouth tilting up in a half smile. "Thinking about it?"

She tipped her head back to look at him and said again. "It was a crazy thought."

After a long moment, he finally nodded. "You're right. And if you'd asked, I would have had to say *no*."

Emotions swirled again. Surprise and regret. Relief and disappointment. Hurt that she could have misread him and the situation. Except that when she lifted her gaze to his again, the stark desire in his eyes conflicted with his response.

She could feel the heat emanating from his body, feel the sizzle of passion that matched her own.

"Because it's crazy?" she asked.

He smiled. "Because my hotel is closer."

Chapter Ten

Jenny pushed Richard's jacket over his shoulders, letting it drop to the floor. She yanked at his tie and tossed it aside. Passion was building, burning, inside her. She started on the buttons of his shirt, fumbling as he dipped his head and pressed his lips to the tender skin at the base of her throat.

She shivered in response to the deliciously erotic tingles that rocketed through her body. His fingers had made quick work of her buttons and his lips continued to trail kisses along the ridge of her collarbone, then over the slope of her breast. Her head fell back against the door as his teeth closed over her nipple through the lace of her bra.

It wasn't enough for either of them. He unfastened the front clasp and pushed the cups aside to cradle her breasts in his palms. His thumbs traced lazy circles around the peaks, moving with tantalizing slowness. She was trembling now, her body pulsating with desire. Then his mouth fastened on her breast, his tongue rasping against the nipple, and the pulse grew stronger, more insistent.

He slid her skirt and her panties over her hips, down the length of her incredibly long legs, adding them to the growing pile of discarded clothing that littered the floor. Then he stepped back to look at her. Except for a pair of stay-up stockings and heels, she was naked, while he still had most of his clothes on. But the blatant appreciation in his eyes obliterated any lingering sense of shyness.

"Richard." It was a demand as much as a plea.

Finally, his lips covered hers in a kiss that was hot and hungry and all encompassing. There was no tentative exploration, no soft seduction. There was just heat and hunger, an escalating passion that could no longer be denied as his tongue slid between her parted lips to tangle with her own.

She reached for him, finished unfastening the buttons on his shirt and parted the material to reveal the firm expanse of his chest. Her palms slid over the smooth hard skin, reveling in the muscular contours she would never have guessed were hidden beneath the business suits he habitually wore.

Her hands moved over him greedily, almost desperately. Had she ever wanted anyone so much? Had she ever been wanted the way he seemed to want her?

She banished these thoughts from her mind. She didn't want to think or question, she only wanted to feel. She slid her hand down into the front of his pants, heard his sharp inhalation as she wrapped her fingers around the hard length of him.

He dragged his lips from hers. "I promised myself that if I actually got you up here, I would take my time with you," he said.

"I just want you to take me." She started to push his pants over his hips.

He put his hands over hers, halting her movements. "Condom," he said. "I've got one in my pocket."

She lifted an eyebrow. "I'm not sure if I'm grateful you're prepared or offended you took it for granted I'd be here."

He dipped his head again, nibbled on the lobe of her ear. "Let's just say I was cautiously optimistic after we said goodbye Wednesday night."

"Then I'll say thank you." She brushed her lips against his as she took the packet from his hand. Her mouth still thoroughly occupied with his, she managed to tear open the wrapper and roll the prophylactic into place. She swallowed his moan as her fingers slid down the length of him.

He broke the kiss to press his lips to the side of her throat. "It seems, Jenny Anderson, that you aren't quite what I expected."

She smiled. "Disappointed?"

His only response was to capture her mouth again as he thrust into her.

She gasped, a combination of shock and pleasure, as he filled her. He lifted her legs to wrap them around his waist. She locked her ankles together, anchoring herself to him. The polished wood of the door was smooth and cool against her back, and she braced herself against it as she tilted her hips to pull him deeper inside.

Richard groaned into her mouth, his fingers digging into her hips to still her impatient rocking. "I'm trying to maintain some degree of control here."

She nipped at his shoulder, then soothed the gentle bite with her tongue. "Control is overrated."

He slowly withdrew from her, then sank in again. She gasped.

"Prove it," he challenged.

He moved out and in, deliberately rubbing against the sensitive nub at her center.

She felt her body tense as her mind struggled to follow the thread of conversation. Her breath was coming in shallow gasps now, her fingernails biting into his back.

"Let yourself go, Jenny."

She couldn't seem to do anything else as the first climax swamped her, the waves of her release crashing one into another, each stronger and longer than the previous, until her skin was damp and her entire body was shuddering.

Richard had never seen anything more beautiful than Jenny lost in the throes of passion. It was almost enough to send him spiraling over the edge with her. But not yet.

He braced his hands on the door and fought to hold on to the last vestiges of his control. The clenching of her muscles around him was almost more than he could stand, but he was determined to show her more. When her trembling had subsided, he wrapped his arms around her and carried her to the bed.

He lowered her onto the mattress and knelt over her, still buried inside her.

"Why—"

He brushed his lips over hers, gently this time. "Because I want to make love with you properly."

She smiled. "I didn't think there was anything improper about what we were doing."

"Maybe not," he agreed. "But I couldn't hold you up and do this..."

He dipped his head and took the peak of her breast in his mouth to suckle deeply.

She moaned.

"Or this…"

He slid a hand between their bodies to the soft tangle of curls at the apex of her thighs.

She gasped.

"Again," he said.

She shook her head. "I can't—I don't—"

"Again," he repeated, driving her ruthlessly up and over the peak again, proving that she could.

He crushed his mouth down on hers, swallowing her cries of pleasure. His own needs refused to be denied any longer, and as he drove into her slick, pulsing heat, he plunged over the final, ultimate peak with her.

"I'm sorry." Jenny's words broke the silence.

Richard propped himself up on an elbow to look down at the woman lying naked beside him. She looked sleepily satisfied, the remnants of a smile tilting the corners of her mouth. She certainly didn't look sorry.

"For what?" he asked.

"Holding out for so long."

He brushed his lips over hers. "I'd say it was worth the wait."

Her lips curved. "Definitely."

"Although that's not to say I want to wait another ten days before we do it again."

She snuggled closer, sliding one long slender leg between his, the tips of her breasts grazing his chest. "What kind of time frame did you have in mind?"

"About another ten minutes," he promised.

Her smile widened and she wriggled against him. His body immediately responded to the seductive movement. He'd barely finished having her, and he already wanted her again.

"Ten minutes?" she challenged.

"Maybe less." He flipped her onto her back and rolled on top of her, capturing her lips, kissing his way down her throat. "I wanted you from the first minute I saw you," he told her. "Just like this—naked in my bed."

She gasped when his lips fastened over her breast, sighed when his tongue swirled around her nipple. "Do you always get…what you want?"

"Usually." He moved to her other breast to minister the same treatment. "Because when it's something that really matters, I don't give up."

Then he kissed her. "You matter, Jenny."

"Don't say things like that," she pleaded softly.

"Why?" He kissed her again, longer, lingering. "Were you hoping this was just sex?"

"Maybe." She shifted, drawing her knees up to bracket his hips, opening for him. "It would make things simpler."

He unwrapped another condom, then groaned when he slid into her and found she was hot and wet, as ready as he was all over again.

"This isn't going to be simple," he promised. "Not for either of us."

Richard awoke to the sound of the curtains being pulled open and the glare of sunlight streaming through the windows. He threw his arm over his eyes. "How can it be morning when I haven't had any sleep?"

"Because the earth continues to revolve whether you're

ready for it or not." Jenny sounded surprisingly awake and cheerful although she couldn't have had any more sleep than he did.

They'd barely let go of one another through the night. If they weren't making love, they were getting ready to make love or cuddling together after just having finished making love. He'd thought it would be enough to have her once. That after he'd had her in his bed he'd be able to get her out of his mind. Instead, he wanted her more.

"And if you opened your eyes," she continued, "you'd see that it's a beautiful day."

"I'd be more willing to believe that if you were still in bed with me," he told her.

"If I was still in bed with you, we might miss out on the entire day."

"Why is that a bad thing?"

She chuckled softly as she tugged the covers away from him. "Come on. I've ordered up breakfast, but you probably have time for a quick shower before it gets here."

He snagged her wrist, tumbled her back down onto the bed beside him. "What's the hurry?"

"It's almost nine o'clock."

"But it's Saturday, right?" He wasn't entirely clear—he'd lost himself in her so completely time had faded away. It could have been hours or days or weeks.

"Yes, it's Saturday." Amusement was evident in her tone. "And there's somewhere very special I want to take you today."

"You could take me to paradise without either of us having to leave this room."

"Let's start with Lake Sai."

"Where's that?"

"It's one of the five lakes of Mount Fuji and it has the most spectacular view."

He smiled. "I'm liking the view from here right now."

"Have you ever seen the sun rise behind Mount Fuji?" she challenged.

"I can't say that I have," he admitted.

"Well, tomorrow morning you're going to. And I promise it will be unlike anything you've ever seen."

Somehow she managed to make the prospect of getting up at daybreak appealing. Or maybe it was just the idea of being with her. And if that was how she wanted to spend her weekend, he would oblige her.

Then it hit him—Saturday.

He swore softly.

Jenny frowned. "What's the matter?"

"It's Saturday."

"Yes, I believe we've already established that."

"Helen's coming into town today," he said. "And I'm supposed to go with her to some cocktail party thing tonight."

"Oh." She smiled, but he could tell it was forced. "Well, we'll go some other time then."

"I'm sorry, Jenny."

"It's okay. I shouldn't have assumed that you were free."

But he could see the disappointment in her eyes and felt like a heel for putting it there.

"If I had a choice—" he broke off.

Why didn't he have a choice? Why did he need to be at this reception? It was a purely social event—there would be no business decisions made, no legal expertise required. And it certainly wasn't as if Helen needed him to hold her hand. She might not be pleased by his last-minute change of plans, but he'd rather face her displeasure than the resignation in Jenny's eyes.

From what she'd told him about her childhood and her previous relationships, he knew that her biggest insecurity was feeling as though she was always second best. No one had ever put her first and now, after one night together, Richard was doing the same thing—subordinating her wants to the demands of his career. And the worst part of it was that Jenny wasn't even surprised or angry, as she had every right to be. She'd simply accepted his decision, as if she'd expected he would disappoint her.

The knock at the door signaled the arrival of their breakfast. Richard signed for the meal, then sat at the small table across from Jenny.

She toyed with her food, sipped her coffee.

"How do you get to Lake Sai?"

She frowned at the question as she refilled her cup with coffee. "Car or train."

"Do you have a car or should we rent one?"

"I have a car."

He nodded. "Okay, then I'll take my shower so we can get going."

"Going where?"

"To Mount Fuji to see the sunrise."

"I thought you had plans—"

"I can change them."

He watched the emotions that crossed her face—surprise, pleasure, a flicker of guilt, before she pushed away from the table.

"But your boss—"

"Helen will understand." He stood up and crossed the room to where she was standing.

"I appreciate the offer," she said, "but you don't have to—"

"I want to," he interrupted.

He put his arms around her "—I want to spend the day with you—" pressed his lips to hers "—and the night—" kissed her again "—and all of tomorrow."

Jenny negotiated the tight curves of the winding road with an ease that indicated familiarity—and a speed that made Richard nervous. "This road seems awfully narrow for two-way traffic."

"Don't worry," she told him. "It's a private lane and no one else will be here this weekend."

"Didn't you tell me that we were going to a hotel?"

She shook her head. "I said we were staying overnight."

It was a clarification that told him little. "Staying where?"

They rounded another curve where the trees suddenly gave way to a clearing, highlighting the long low building made of rough-hewn logs.

Jenny pulled up beside the building and parked her car. "My parents' cabin."

He eyed the structure warily. "Did you happen to mention to your parents that you were coming up here?"

"Not specifically." She opened her door and stepped out of the car, linking her hands together over her head, stretching her arms toward the sky.

Richard reluctantly got out of the car, accepting it was necessary to continue their conversation even though he wasn't convinced that the smartest course of action might not be to turn around and return to Tokyo. "What if your parents decide to come up here this weekend?"

"They won't." She popped the trunk; he grabbed their bags. "My brother or I use it a lot more than they do. And with Mich being so close to the end of her pregnancy, she and John haven't been venturing too far out of the city."

He could only hope she was right. He knew neither her father nor her brother would take kindly to finding her snuggled up in the cabin with Richard. On the other hand, spending the weekend snuggled up with Jenny might make any consequences worthwhile.

"Come on," Jenny said, leading him around to the front of the cabin.

They dropped their bags inside, then went through the cabin opening up the windows. There were three bedrooms, one obviously a master with a king-size bed and ensuite, another with a double bed and dresser, and the last contained a set of narrow bunks, a toy chest and a bookshelf. There was also a second bathroom, a moderate-sized kitchen/eating area, and a spacious family room with a stone floor-to-ceiling fireplace. It was rustic and simply furnished, yet also warm and inviting.

"It's not fancy but it's private," Jenny told him.

"I like it," he said.

"You haven't even seen the best part yet."

Richard followed her back outside, down a well-worn path through the trees toward the lake. Although the mountain was visible from his hotel window on a clear day, that distant glimpse hadn't prepared him for the spectacular majesty of Mount Fuji up close. As they stepped into the clearing at the water's edge, his only thought was—she was right about the view.

"It's…incredible."

She smiled, obviously pleased by his reaction. "I've never been anywhere that fills me with the same sense of peace and tranquility as this spot right here."

Considering how much of the globe she'd seen, that was quite an endorsement. His travel experience was much more limited, but he agreed with her assessment wholeheartedly.

The smooth and glossy surface of the lake gave the impression of a mirror provided by nature solely for the purpose of reflecting the towering mountain above. The trees stood tall and proud all around, silent guardians of this natural paradise where the only sounds were the crickets chirping and the birds singing, and the only scents were of damp earth and fresh pine.

Richard didn't consider himself a religious person, but there was something almost spiritual about this place, a sense of magic surrounded it.

"I can see why you love it," he said. "I imagine your friends are always angling for invitations to come here with you."

"Except for Samara, I've never brought anyone with me," she admitted.

He didn't ask why, and she didn't volunteer that information. Perhaps they were both wary of the answer, unprepared to deal with the implications. Instead, he said softly, "Thank you for sharing this with me."

"You're welcome."

She smiled at him again, a smile of warmth and companionship and affection. And in that moment, she was simply too tempting to resist.

Jenny's breath caught in her throat as his lips brushed over hers. Unlike the insatiable passion they'd shared through the night, this was different. Softer, gentler, deeper. Or maybe it wasn't so much the kiss as the emotions churning inside her.

She hadn't known it was possible to feel both secure and vulnerable, except that in the warm strength of his arms she couldn't separate one feeling from the other. It was exhilarating and intimidating, tempting and terrifying all at the same time. It was also frustrating that no matter how hard she tried, she couldn't seem to keep her emotions in check.

She knew he cared about her, and that he would take care with her. But she also knew that she had no protection against him, no shield for her heart. She was in danger here—teetering on the edge of love, desperately trying to regain her balance. But every minute with Richard pushed her a little further toward the precipice.

She'd thought she had a choice, that she'd made a conscious decision to be with him. But after having spent the night in his arms, she knew the truth. There had never been a choice, only a destiny.

Being with him, loving him, were inevitable—as necessary as breathing.

Losing him was, she knew, just as certain.

Chapter Eleven

Richard didn't know what time it was when Jenny nudged his shoulder, he only knew that when he cracked open an eyelid it was still dark and, therefore, obviously not morning. He tugged the sheet up and snuggled deeper into the mattress.

"If you don't get up, you're going to miss the sunrise," she warned.

"It'll happen again tomorrow."

"But we won't be here tomorrow," she reminded him.

When he failed to respond, she nudged him again.

"I'm getting the impression that you're not a morning person," she said, but she sounded more amused than dissuaded.

"I'm not." He pulled the pillow over his head. "Wake me up at noon."

"Okay. But you'll miss seeing me dance naked on the lakeshore."

He shoved the pillow aside. "Naked?"

She laughed. "Come on, I've got coffee on."

"Naked sounded a lot more appealing than coffee," he grumbled, but he sat up and swung his legs over to the floor.

"Let's start with coffee," she said.

While Jenny was gone, he pulled on a pair of shorts over his briefs, then tugged a T-shirt over his head. He sniffed the air, inhaling deeply the fresh aroma of java.

"Thanks." He accepted the mug she offered and gulped several mouthfuls of coffee before he could focus his sleepy gaze on her. She'd already showered and was dressed in a long, flowing skirt and a sleeveless V-neck blouse. She looked wide awake, refreshed and stunningly beautiful.

He didn't care what time it was, he'd wake up happy every morning if he woke up with Jenny beside him.

The thought jolted him awake more effectively than a whole pot of coffee. Whatever fantasies had snuck into his subconscious while he'd slept beside her in the night needed to be exorcised. He wasn't in a position to commit to anything more than a temporary affair—a mutually pleasurable diversion—and they both knew what was between them couldn't last. His business in Tokyo would be concluded in a few weeks, then he'd be on his way back to Chicago. Except that the prospect of going home wasn't quite so appealing to him now.

He gulped another mouthful of coffee and renewed his resolve not to think beyond the present. "Let's go see this sunrise."

But when he followed her out of the cabin, only the

slightest hint of light defined the edge of the horizon, leaving everything else in complete darkness.

"This is sunrise?" he muttered.

Jenny took his hand and led him down toward the water. "Don't be such a spoilsport."

He refrained from further comment as she lowered herself to the ground. She hugged her knees to her chest, and he sat behind her, wrapping his arms around her so that her back was against his front, her hips cradled between his thighs.

She leaned her head back against his shoulder and sighed contentedly.

"Don't you dare fall asleep," he growled.

She laughed. "I'm not going to fall asleep. I'm just relaxing."

He tightened his arms around her. "Maybe this isn't so bad."

"It hasn't really started yet."

"I didn't mean the sunrise," he said. "I meant being here with you. I like the way you fit into my arms."

"I like being in your arms," she admitted.

"You could have been in my arms without leaving the bedroom."

She laughed again. "Just watch the sky."

So he did. They sat together, silent and content, as the sun peeked over the horizon, a spill of brilliant color that spread over the dark canvas until it had obliterated the black and night became day.

It was an awakening of the earth and all its creatures, and Richard was now very much awake.

He lowered his head and pressed his lips to the base of Jenny's throat. She sighed softly. He could smell her shampoo, and the subtle essence of her skin warmed by the early-morning sun. It was a scent that was enticing, arousing and uniquely Jenny.

He pushed the neck of her shirt aside to trail his lips over the ridge of her collarbone as his hands moved beneath the fabric to skim up her sides. He found the clasp at the front of her bra, opened it. The silky weight of her breasts filled his palms.

She moaned when his thumbs scraped over her nipples. "I didn't think you were a morning person."

"You've changed my mind."

"We could, uh, go back to the cabin."

His teeth closed gently over her earlobe. "How isolated are we out here?"

"The nearest neighbors are—" she gasped as his hands continued to tease and his lips nibbled "—miles away."

"We're completely alone?" He shifted to lower her to the ground, his fingers nimbly working the buttons down the front of her shirt.

"Completely," she agreed.

He lowered his head to take one breast in his mouth.

She gasped again as he suckled; moaned again when his hand slid beneath her skirt and between her legs. She was ready for him, and he was hard with wanting her.

He couldn't see the cabin from here. In fact, he couldn't see anything but the lake and the trees and the sun rising over the mountain. It was a place far removed from the world he knew—untouched, uncivilized, untamed. And it stirred within him the most primitive of urges—to mate, to claim, to possess.

Jenny seemed to be driven by the same basic needs. She was as frantic as he was now, as she pushed his shorts over his hips. Her fingers wrapped around him, teasing him, guiding him. As she took him inside, surrounding him with slick heat, something inside him snapped so that even the illusion of control was shattered.

He plunged deep, again and again, in a frenzied pace that she eagerly matched. On the soft emerald grass, under the brilliance of the morning sun, they made love frantically, passionately, recklessly.

He didn't realize how recklessly until he'd emptied himself into her.

He swore softly as he rolled off of her. "I forgot protection."

Jenny reached for her shirt. "Is that something you've done before?" she asked hesitantly.

"No," he told her. He wasn't in the habit of having unprotected sex. In fact, since his divorce, he'd never been with a woman without the protective barrier of a condom between them. "The only concern is pregnancy."

Which was a big enough worry. And if she got pregnant, he knew it would be his fault. Dammit—he knew better than to take such chances. At least he always had before. But in the moment, he'd thought of nothing but his need for her, and now they both might have to face the consequences.

Jenny watched the play of emotions across his face. Panic, frustration, resignation. She knew he was the kind of man who would insist on being there for his child—even if the child was unplanned and unwanted. Thankfully, she took her own precautions. The last thing she wanted was a man tied to her for all the wrong reasons.

"Then there's nothing to worry about, Richard."

"How can you be sure?"

"Because I'm on birth control," she said softly.

"Oh." He exhaled, obviously relieved.

"I got carried away in the moment, too," she admitted. "But I wouldn't risk bringing an unwanted child into this world."

"Unplanned doesn't always mean unwanted," he said gently.

"Maybe not," she agreed. "But as much as I want children someday, I wouldn't let any baby of mine ever think it was a mistake."

"I still owe you an apology."

She shook her head. "We're both equally to blame."

"I just don't want you to think that I'm in the habit of overlooking something so basic."

She managed a smile. "I think your immediate reaction proved otherwise."

Richard sighed. "I've never wanted anyone the way I want you."

"You don't sound happy about it."

"It scares me, that I could need you so desperately I would forget about everything else."

Her heart warmed at this reluctant admission.

"And it scares me," he continued, "that you want things I can't give you. I'm not in a position to think about marriage or a family."

Some of the warmth dissipated now, but she asked lightly, "Have I asked you for any of those things?"

"No. But I know you want them."

She nodded. "But I don't expect them from you. I knew from the beginning that our relationship would have boundaries—I accepted those the night I went back to your hotel room."

"Maybe that's what bothers me," he said. "You deserve more."

"And some day I'll have more," she said. "For now, I only want to be with you."

Although the drive back to Tokyo was filled with easy conversation and comfortable silences, Jenny's heart grew heavier with each mile. She always regretted having to leave the cabin, but her disappointment was even stronger this time because she knew that when they reached the city, the magic of her weekend with Richard would be gone.

She parked in her usual spot beneath the hotel. It was a reasonable walk—or a short subway ride—to her apartment, and it was a lot cheaper to keep her car here than to pay the premium for a parking space closer to her residence.

While they were at the lake, neither had broached the topic of what would happen when the weekend was over. As Jenny unlocked the trunk, she felt awkward wondering whether it would be more appropriate to say good-night or goodbye.

Before she could decide, Richard spoke.

"Will you stay here with me tonight?"

She hadn't anticipated the question, and though she was pleased that he'd asked—grateful to know that he was as reluctant as she to let the weekend end—she knew she should say no. She should go back to her apartment, to give herself some time and space to think. But even knowing their relationship had no future, she wasn't ready to give him up just yet.

"We both have to work in the morning," she said.

It wasn't a yes or a no but an indication that she was willing to be persuaded.

He hefted his duffel bag onto one shoulder, snaked his

other arm around her waist. "There are a lot of hours yet between now and then."

His smile was slow and sexy, filled with promises she knew he could fulfill. She felt her insides quiver.

It terrified her, this reaction to him. He didn't even have to touch her. All it took was a glance, maybe just the hint of a smile, and she was overwhelmed with need for him.

It had never been like this for her before—so completely all-encompassing. She'd never needed anyone as she needed him.

No—she shook off the thought. It wasn't Richard. It was just the newness of their relationship, the fresh blush of desire finally realized.

But even as her mind struggled to rationalize her feelings, she knew it wasn't true. Because she'd been in relationships before—starry-eyed with infatuation and full of confidence for the future.

This was different.

Partly because she already knew there could be no future for her and Richard. Partly because she knew, in her heart, that nothing that had come before compared to what she felt for Richard now. Mostly because she was afraid she would never feel this way again.

Why did she always have to dream the impossible dream? Why couldn't she simply accept what was without wanting more? Why couldn't she enjoy the time she had with Richard now and not worry about what would happen when he was gone?

She had no answers to these questions, no way to soothe the uneasiness in her heart.

It scared her to think how much he'd come to mean to her in such a short amount of time, to realize she was already in danger of falling in love with him. She knew it just as surely as she knew that she would be the one left alone and hurting when he was gone. But that was a problem she could worry about tomorrow.

"I'll stay," she said.

Within minutes they were in his suite, their clothes making a trail from the door to the bedroom.

He'd lost count of the number of times they'd made love since that first momentous occasion Friday night. Every time he thought he was satisfied, desire stirred anew. Then desire would give way to demand. It was as if he couldn't get enough of her. No matter how many times he had her, he wanted her more.

He wanted her now.

He forced himself to take it slowly, exploring every inch of her body, lingering where he knew it pleased her, reveling in the sound of her soft sighs and moans.

He made his way down the length of her body, exploring her with his hands, his lips, his tongue. He paused at her hip, touched the small heart-shaped mark. "Is this a tattoo?"

"No." She laughed softly. "Just a birthmark."

"I like it." He lowered his head and pressed his lips to the spot, then traced the outline with his tongue.

She squirmed, the instinctive movement arousing him beyond belief. He gripped her hips, holding her still while his mouth moved lower. He heard her suck in a breath as his tongue flicked over her, then a gasp as he brought her to the brink of climax, and a long, throaty moan as he pushed her over the edge.

Monday morning, Richard got an extra key card from the front desk for Jenny. He didn't know how long he was going to be tied up in meetings during the day, and he liked the idea of her being there when he got back to his room. He wanted to spend every minute that he could with her.

It was almost eight o'clock when he got in Tuesday night, and she was there as she had been the night before, sitting at the desk, her fingers clicking away on the keys of her laptop. The sight of her tugged at something inside him.

She glanced up when he entered, her lips curving. "Hi."

He dropped his briefcase inside the door and crossed over to her. "Hi, yourself." Then he bent his head to kiss her, long and lingering.

He pushed the chair away from the desk and drew her to her feet, all without taking his lips from hers. She came into his arms willingly, her body melting against his. He knew he could have her naked in his bed in about thirty seconds flat, but he was learning to draw out the pleasure of just being with her and enjoying every minute.

When he finally eased his lips from hers he asked, deliberately casual, "How was your day?"

She tipped her head against his chest and sighed. "Well, it could have been worse."

"What happened?"

"I ran into my sister-in-law-in the lobby."

He was silent, waiting for her to elaborate, because so far he wasn't seeing the problem.

"At 7:00 a.m."

"Oh."

She nodded.

"What was she doing here at that hour?"

"John forgot some kind of report or something at home, and she came by to drop it off."

He massaged her shoulders gently, loosening the tight muscles. "Are you worried that she'll tell your brother?"

"I'm twenty-five years old, Richard. I hardly need his permission to sleep with you."

But the tension in her shoulders told a different story.

"And anyway, I don't think Mich will go running to tell him."

"But the possibility concerns you," he guessed.

She hesitated. "I'm just worried that my family will think our being together means something."

He had no right to take offense at her words, but he couldn't deny that her casual dismissal of what was between them bothered him. He dropped his hands from her shoulders and took a step back. "And of course it doesn't mean anything, right?"

"I just don't want my mother thinking about wedding bells when we both know we don't have a future together."

Frustration tangled with the hurt and anger. "Why do you keep bringing up the end of our relationship as if it's a foregone conclusion?"

"Because you'll be going back to Chicago when the negotiations are finished."

He didn't know why he was pushing her. He should be grateful she'd accepted the parameters of their relationship. Instead he said, "Neither one of us can predict the future."

Jenny moved to wrap her arms around him. "I know, and I don't want to waste the time we do have together arguing about this."

"Okay," he agreed. "Let's argue about something else."

She exhaled wearily. "Obviously you have something specific on your mind."

He nodded. "Why do you sneak out of here at 7:00 a.m.?"

This time she stepped away. "I don't sneak."

He wasn't going to debate semantics. "It doesn't make sense that you have to get up an extra hour early every morning to go home and change before work."

"I can hardly wear the same clothes as the day before," she pointed out logically.

"You're deliberately missing my point."

"I just don't see why it should matter to you."

"It matters because I can think of more productive ways to spend the time than on the subway."

"I don't mind."

Maybe she didn't, but he sure as hell did.

She'd told him from the beginning that she didn't do casual relationships. For the past several years, he hadn't been capable of anything more. But he'd pursued her anyway, selfishly and relentlessly, and he'd got what he wanted.

Except that suddenly he wanted more.

"Why don't you want to bring any of your stuff here?"

She hesitated, just a second, before responding. "I don't want to take anything for granted."

"Or is it that you don't want me to take anything for granted?"

"We both know this relationship is only temporary."

And so their disagreement had come full circle again.

He sighed, accepting that he wasn't going to be able to change her mind about a point he'd made so clearly from the start. Instead he said, "If we only have a few weeks together, I want to spend every minute I possibly can with you."

She hesitated a moment before nodding. "I'll go home after work tomorrow to pick up a few things."

"Thank you." He brushed his lips over hers again. "I could meet you at your apartment, make dinner for you."

"Are you growing bored with the hotel menu?" she asked.

"Maybe I just want to cook for you."

"That's an offer I won't refuse," she told him.

Jenny was surveying the contents of her closet, trying to decide which clothes she should take to the hotel. Nerves skittered inside her belly, not because it mattered what she wore to work the next day but because the idea of moving in with Richard—however temporarily—terrified her.

She hadn't expected so much to change so fast.

Friday morning she'd been firm in her resolve to keep Richard at a distance. Friday night she'd spent the night in his bed, in his arms. Every night since then had been the same.

Now it was Wednesday, she'd left him less than twelve hours earlier, and she was missing him already.

She finally decided on a navy pin-striped skirt and a sleeveless silk blouse. She found matching shoes and threw them into a bag along with her underwear and toiletries.

Pushing the closet door shut, she decided that one outfit was enough. *One day at a time.*

Her heart leaped at the knock on the door, and she chided herself for the reaction. This wasn't high school and she wasn't waiting on her date for the prom. She was a grown woman and it was Richard—there was no reason for her sudden jitters. The pep talk did little to settle the quiver in her belly.

He greeted her as he'd got into the habit of doing, with a long slow kiss that made everything inside her melt into a puddle at her feet. There was no doubt that Richard Warren was a first-rate kisser and she sighed, blissfully, contentedly, as she gave herself up to the mastery of his lips.

Tonight, it was a hands-off kiss as he had a bag of groceries in one hand and a flat, wrapped parcel in the other.

"How did you manage at the market?" she asked, when the kiss finally ended.

"I took Yasushi with me," he admitted. "I could tell he was curious as to where I'd be cooking dinner, but he's too polite to ask."

"I'm curious, too," she told him. "About what's in the package."

"It's a present."

"For me?"

"Yes, for you." He offered it to her. "But you have to let me put this food away before you open it."

She helped him unpack the groceries, her curiosity growing by the minute.

Richard sensed her mounting excitement, as well as her careful restraint. He remembered her surprised pleasure when he'd bought her the oyster shell doll and wondered if no one had ever given her presents just for the fun of it.

"Okay," he said, when he'd closed the fridge door. "Open it."

She tore at the plain brown paper with unbridled enthusiasm, then gasped as the painting was revealed.

"Summer Passion." She murmured the title softly, recognizing it immediately. Then she looked up at him, stunned. "How—"

"I saw the way you looked at it, that night at the gallery, and I knew I had to buy it for you."

"It's—wow—I never expected anything like this."

He grinned. "And I never expected to find you at a loss for words."

"I shouldn't accept this," she said, but her fingers gripped the edge of the frame as if she would never let it go.

"Why not?"

"Because I saw the price tag and—"

"Do you like it, Jenny?" he interrupted to ask patiently.

She sighed. "You know I do."

"Then that's all that matters."

"I was going to buy it," she murmured. "But when I went back the next day, it had a sold tag on it."

"I bought it that night but agreed to let the gallery keep it on display through the weekend."

She frowned. "We weren't even lovers then."

He smiled. "But I knew we would be."

"That was quite an assumption to make."

"I was right," he reminded her.

"And I'm too thrilled to have this painting to be annoyed by your smugness." She tore off the last of the paper and tucked the picture under her arm. "Come on. I know exactly where I'm going to put it."

He followed her to the bedroom. She closed the door behind him, leaned the painting against the wall, then started to peel away her clothes.

He watched, his initial fascination quickly supplanted by growing arousal. She was so incredibly beautiful, stunningly passionate, perfect. Okay, he knew she wasn't actually perfect, but she was perfect to him in all the ways that mattered.

She unclipped her bra and added it to the pile of clothing already on the floor.

He swallowed, hard. "I thought you were going to show me where you wanted to hang the painting."

"I will." She smiled as she tugged him down onto the bed with her. "After I show you how grateful I am."

Jenny gulped down a second cup of coffee as she hastily scanned the financial section of the *Japan Times*. Although it was a competitor of the *Tokyo Tribune* and, therefore, not a newspaper to which she subscribed, it was the morning daily that was provided to guests of the hotel and she justified her reading of it as a way of keeping up-to-date with the stories and style of the other paper.

Richard held out a hand as he joined her at the table, and she automatically handed him the front section. If she'd thought about it, she'd be surprised how quickly they'd established a comfortable morning routine. It was almost as if they'd been together for months instead of just ten days, and it was all too easy for Jenny to envision a life with Richard, a home together.

A few more of her clothes hung in the closet now, her toiletries stood next to his in the bathroom, and the novel she was currently reading sat on the bedside table. But the embroidered insignia on the towels and the meals delivered by room service were constant reminders that this was a hotel rather than a home. They were conveniences that reminded Jenny she didn't belong here—and that she didn't belong with Richard.

With that thought weighing heavy on her mind, she passed the rest of the paper to him. "I have to run or I'm going to be late."

"What's your hurry today?"

"Meeting with my editor." She brushed her lips over his. "I'll see you later."

She escaped from the hotel, chased by the guilty knowledge that she'd deliberately lied to him. She wasn't running to a meeting—she was running away from the feelings she could no longer deny.

She tried to remember that she'd only known him a few weeks, but time seemed irrelevant. The only thing that mattered was the rightness she felt with Richard, the sense of belonging that filled her heart whenever she was in his arms.

It couldn't last—she knew that. And she knew it would end with her heart broken if she wasn't careful. She had to believe that she could still protect her heart. She liked Richard, she had fun with him, but she wasn't in love with him—yet. And she wasn't going to let herself fall in love with him.

Except that every minute they were together, she felt herself sinking in deeper. It was too intense, too everything. And yet it wasn't nearly as much as she wanted it to be.

That was why she had to end it.

Chapter Twelve

While Jenny was rushing off to see her editor, Richard was reviewing the files for his meeting with Helen. Mori Taka had announced a day away from the bargaining table, insisting that he had other pressing business to take care of. Richard wasn't sure if it was a legitimate explanation or a tactical move to demonstrate that he had the upper hand in the negotiations—as if everyone at Hanson wasn't well aware of that fact.

It was that knowledge, as much as the delay, that seemed to dishearten Helen, so Richard had suggested an informal meeting in his room to discuss the situation. Not that they hadn't already discussed everything in the greatest detail, but he knew she needed a distraction.

Inviting her to his suite, however, turned out to be the wrong kind of distraction. He realized his mistake as soon as she excused herself to use the washroom after lunch. Sure enough, she returned a few minutes later, a small smile curving her lips.

"I never imagined you'd have a pink toothbrush," she teased. "Or is the green one yours?"

"They're both mine—I'm fastidious about oral hygiene."

Her smile widened. "You know, for a lawyer, you don't lie very well."

"Thank you," Richard said dryly.

"There's that dinner tomorrow night," she reminded him. "Why don't you bring Jenny?"

He'd already planned to invite her, but now he reconsidered. "Why—so you can interrogate her directly?"

"So I can meet her," his boss corrected.

"Why?" he asked again.

"Because I've never known you to be so completely captivated by a woman."

He frowned but couldn't deny the truth of her statement.

"Oh, my," Helen said softly. "You really are serious about her."

"No." But his denial was too quick, almost desperate.

Her smile was sympathetic. "You don't want to be, but you are."

She was right, of course—especially the part about him not wanting to be serious. He'd thought he had everything he wanted: professional respect and financial security—the hallmarks of a successful career he'd dedicated nine years to building. Most importantly, he was content. Or he had been until Jenny Anderson came into his life.

Now he'd found a woman he looked forward to seeing every day. A woman he wanted to fall asleep beside every night and wake up with every morning. A woman who made him think about the future.

He was still thinking about Jenny after Helen had gone. Maybe it was because she'd been on his mind that he wasn't surprised when she walked through the door.

He could tell, though, that she was startled by his presence. She glanced at the pile of papers on the desk in front of him. "I thought you'd be at TAKA," she said. "I didn't want to interrupt."

"I gave you a key card so you could come and go as you wanted," he reminded her. "And I'm glad you're here because it turns out that I'm finished for the day, and I was hoping I could talk you into playing hooky with me."

"I can't." That was her response—abrupt and final with no further explanation.

He noticed that she'd made her way to the other side of the room, and he suddenly suspected the distance she was establishing wasn't only physical.

"Are you going to tell me why you came back then?"

"I've been doing a lot of thinking," she told him. "And I realized that I can't do this anymore."

He felt his chest tighten. "Do what?"

"Be with you."

The tightness increased. "You didn't seem to have any objections last night. Or this morning."

She looked away, her cheeks flushing. "If it was just sex, there wouldn't be a problem."

"What is the problem?"

"Can't you just accept that I don't want to maintain this charade of a relationship any longer?"

The words were deliberately hurtful, but Jenny was not

a cruel person. It was this knowledge that made him realize there was more going on than she was admitting to.

"No," he said simply.

"No?" she echoed, clearly not having anticipated his objection.

"I'm not going to let you ruin a good thing without at least explaining why."

She crossed her arms over her chest. "I don't owe you any explanations."

"If you don't want to talk about us, why are you here?"

She remained stubbornly silent.

"You came to pick up your things," he guessed.

"Yes, I did." She lifted her chin defiantly and moved past him into the bedroom.

He followed, leaning against the doorjamb as he watched her gather up her belongings, hoping his nonchalant pose would mask the growing uneasiness in his gut. "Why?" he asked again.

"Do we really need to catalog the reasons?"

"I think so," he said, proving his stubbornness could match hers.

Her weary sigh made him want to take her in his arms and comfort her, but he knew she wouldn't welcome any overtures right now.

"I warned you from the start that I don't do casual relationships," she said.

"We've gone way beyond casual. You know how much I care about you, Jenny."

She laughed shortly. "You care about me and I'm already halfway in love with you."

He was still puzzled. "Why is that a problem?"

She moved into the bathroom to retrieve her toothbrush,

shampoo and the scented cream she rubbed on her skin after a shower. "Because I've been through it enough times to recognize the signs, and I can't do it again."

She started toward the door.

"Whoa. Wait a minute." He stepped in front of her. "You're walking away now because you don't want to fall in love with me, is that what you're saying?"

She nodded. "I won't let my heart be broken again."

"That's the stupidest thing I've ever heard."

Her chin came up, her eyes narrowed. "No—stupid was ever getting involved with a man who can't be what I need."

"We both knew the situation from the beginning. Nothing has changed."

"Maybe not for you," she said. "For me, everything has."

For him, too, although he didn't fully realize it until she'd walked out the door.

It had been a difficult but necessary decision for Jenny to make, as she tried to explain to Samara as they were on their way to work the next morning. Her roommate's response wasn't at all what she expected.

"You're an idiot," she said bluntly.

"Thanks for your support."

"Anyone with eyes can tell the man is hung up on you."

"I don't think Richard Warren gets hung up," Jenny denied.

Samara shook her head. "He has major feelings for you and he isn't going to let you go that easily."

"He already did."

"You just caught him off guard. Once he's had a chance to think about it, he'll be back."

This time it was Jenny who shook her head, remembering what he'd once said about not chasing women who weren't interested. Besides, he was tied up now with the merger, too busy finalizing the details to worry about sleeping alone, and probably already looking forward to finishing up his part of the process so he could go back to Chicago.

Except that when she walked into the newsroom and saw the huge bouquet of flowers on her desk, her heart did a funny little flip inside her chest. She wouldn't have thought Richard was the kind of man to make grand romantic gestures, and the initial surge of pleasure was quickly replaced by apprehension.

"I think this proves my tip," Samara said.

"Point," Jenny said automatically, although she wasn't sure it did.

She couldn't imagine Richard choosing such an elaborate and obviously pricey display of roses and lilies and orchids. He would be more likely to show up with a bunch of daisies in hand. But that was the biggest clue—if Richard wanted to give her flowers, he would be there. He wouldn't expect a bouquet—no matter how stunning—to make his case for him.

Jenny pulled the card out of the display.

"Well?" Samara demanded impatiently. "What does it say?"

Jenny stared at the message, at the confirmation of what she'd already known. "They're not from Richard."

Her friend frowned. "Then who—"

"Surprise."

The flowers were a surprise. The presence of Jenny's ex was a shock. Even more astonishing was the way Brad smiled, completely charming and supremely confident, before he planted a firm kiss on her mouth.

"Hey, babe."

Jenny could only stare, baffled and speechless.

Hey, babe. As if she'd been expecting him. As if they'd never even broken up.

She carefully disengaged herself from Brad's embrace and stepped behind her desk.

Samara, who had met Brad only once but had never been a fan of his or his relationship with her friend, had already disappeared. Jenny knew she would face a barrage of questions later, but for now she'd been left alone to face her ex-boyfriend.

"What are you doing in Tokyo?" she asked him.

"I came to see you."

"Why?"

His smile never faltered. "Because I missed you."

She shook her head. She couldn't believe this was happening to her. Not now when she'd finally taken steps to move forward with her life without him, when she'd been on the verge of falling in love with yet another unsuitable man and was still feeling raw about the end of that relationship. "You can't just show up here after more than six months and expect to pick up where we left off."

He walked around the desk, breaching the physical barrier she'd deliberately placed between them. "I spent a lot of time during those six months thinking about you."

"And I spent those six months getting over you."

For the first time, his supreme self-confidence seemed to waver. "You don't mean that, Jenny."

"Yes, I do."

"We've got three years of history together," he reminded her.

"Two and a half years that became history more than six months ago."

Her phone buzzed and Jenny reached for it eagerly. Any interruption was a welcome one right now.

"Richard Warren is here to see you," Kari said.

Almost any interruption, she amended.

"Should I send him in?"

"No, I'll be right there," Jenny said to the receptionist. She didn't know why Richard was here, but she had no intention of introducing him to Brad—especially when she still had no satisfactory explanation for his being in Tokyo right now.

"I'll be back in a minute," she told him.

"I'll be waiting."

As she made her way to the front lobby, she was struck by the irony of the fact that Richard—a frequent visitor to the newsroom over the past couple of weeks—had been stopped at the desk while Brad—a stranger—had walked right in. The difference, of course, was that Brad had a media pass, and the combination of his press credentials and his glib charm would get him in almost anywhere.

All thoughts of her ex dissipated as soon as she saw Richard. Her heart ached, yearned, but she forced a cool smile. "Hi."

His only response to her greeting was to say, "I've got five minutes before I need to get back to my meeting."

"Okay." She didn't know what else he expected her to say.

He took her arm to lead her away from the reception desk and Kari, who was blatantly eavesdropping on their conversation. If the few stilted words they'd exchanged could even be considered a conversation.

There was a definite sizzle in the air when he touched her. Obviously the sexual attraction was still there, no matter how much she might want to pretend otherwise.

He dropped her arm and took a couple of steps away, then came back to her again. He dragged a hand through his hair. She thought he looked tired—or maybe she was just imagining it. Because she'd spent a mostly sleepless night without him was no reason to suspect he'd done the same.

"I can't say everything I need to in five minutes," he finally told her. "There's a dinner tonight at Okumura. Mr. Taka's hosting so I can't get out of it, but you could come with me."

She shook her head. "I can't. I meant what I said—"

"The food is supposed to be first-rate and—"

"You know it's not the menu I have a problem with," she interrupted him this time.

"You blindsided me yesterday," he said quietly.

And she'd hurt him. She could see that now and she regretted it, but it only confirmed that she'd done the right thing in ending the relationship before either of them got any more involved. "I'm sorry for that."

"But not sorry for what you said," he guessed.

She shook her head.

"We need to talk about this."

She started to shake her head again.

"If you won't come to Okumura, I'll come to your place after dinner," he forged ahead, ignoring her protest.

His cell phone rang; he muttered an oath under his breath as he glanced at the display. "I have to go. The meeting's about to resume."

He touched her again, just a brush of his hand over hers, but that simple contact nearly obliterated all of her resolve. "I'll see you later."

She watched him go, already thinking about what plans she could make for the night ahead. It didn't really matter what she did so long as she wasn't home when Richard stopped by. Because she knew she wasn't strong enough to resist him.

She'd forgotten about Brad until she got back to her desk and found him sitting in her chair, looking as if he had every right to be there. Of course, he probably thought he did.

She bit back a sigh and said, "I have work to do."

He turned the chair so that he was facing her, but didn't move out of it. "Who is he?"

"Who is who?"

"The guy in the lobby."

Her eyes narrowed. "Were you spying on me?"

"Of course not. I just passed by on my way to the men's room."

She pointed to the other side of the newsroom, in the opposite direction from the reception area. "The washrooms are there."

He smiled, shrugged. "I didn't know. I've never been here before."

She wasn't sure she believed his explanation but didn't see any point in making an issue of it. "I really have work to do," she reminded him.

"Okay." He stood up. "What time do you think you'll be finished here?"

"I don't know."

"I'd like to see you tonight, Jenny."

She started to refuse, then hesitated. She didn't want to give Brad any false encouragement, but she wanted to argue with Richard again even less. If she went out with Brad, she wouldn't be home when Richard came to visit, and he would have to accept that she wanted their relationship to be over.

"All right," she said at last.

"Great. We'll pick up something for dinner and go back to your place."

Except the whole point of agreeing to see Brad was so she wouldn't have to face Richard. "I'd rather go out," she told him. "I know a place that—"

"Let me make the plans," he interrupted. "I want to surprise you."

As she watched him go, she wondered why such benevolent words unnerved her.

Jenny's vague sense of foreboding solidified when she figured out where Brad planned to take her for dinner.

"How did you find this restaurant?" she asked.

"I overheard someone talking about it in the newsroom."

Someone—or Richard? Was it possible Brad had overheard Richard inviting her to join him for dinner with the TAKA people?

No, it was a coincidence—an unlikely and unfortunate coincidence—and there was no reason for her to be concerned. It was a big restaurant and still somewhat early for dinner. If she was lucky, she and Brad might be gone before Richard ever arrived.

Still, she hesitated on the sidewalk. "I'm not really that hungry," she said. "Why don't we just go for sushi?"

"Because I'm starving," Brad told her. "And I have a reservation here."

Of course he had a reservation. It was next to impossible to get a table at Okumura without one.

She ignored her discomfort and followed him into the restaurant, inwardly cringing when she saw that the Hanson-TAKA party was already there. The maître d' led them right past the long table where Richard was seated to a smaller, more intimate setting in the corner.

She wondered again if Brad had planned this. But even if he'd somehow known that Mr. Taka had chosen the same restaurant, he couldn't have arranged for them to be dining in such close proximity. Just as Jenny couldn't have guessed that she would feel not just uncomfortable but guilty when her eyes met Richard's across the room.

Dammit, she had no reason to feel guilty. Neither of them had ever made any promises, nor asked for any. It had been casual, easy, temporary. And now it was over.

If she'd had any doubts in that regard, the cold fury in Richard's gaze eliminated them.

Jenny really wasn't hungry, but she dutifully picked at her food, going through the motions without tasting anything. She was conscious of Richard on the other side of the room, of his eyes on her.

She wanted the meal to be over so she could go home. It had been her intention to stay out late, to ensure she wouldn't be there when Richard stopped by. But she knew now that he wouldn't be coming anywhere near her apartment tonight.

"Did you want dessert?" Brad asked.

She shook her head and set her napkin back on the table. "I couldn't eat another bite."

He frowned. "You barely touched your dinner."

"I told you I wasn't very hungry."

He seemed about to say something else, apparently changed her mind. "How about another glass of wine?"

She shook her head again. "No, thanks. I really just want to go."

Annoyance flickered in his eyes. "What's the hurry?"

"It's been a long day, and I'm tired."

"It's barely nine o'clock," he pointed out. "And I brought you here because there's something important I wanted to talk to you about."

She didn't want to talk—she just wanted to go home and cry the tears she'd been holding back since she'd walked out of Richard's hotel room the previous afternoon. But there was one question she felt compelled to ask. "Did you know that Mr. Taka was bringing the Hanson people here?"

His hesitation answered her question before he spoke, "Maybe I did. Maybe I'm not happy about the way a certain lawyer from Chicago has been sniffing around you."

"How do you know anything about Richard Warren?"

"It's my business to find the story," he reminded her. "When I saw you with him this morning, I made a point of asking some questions."

His audacity might annoy her, but it didn't surprise her. Giving Brad the smallest bit of information was like giving a starving dog the scent of a meaty bone.

"Did you get the answers you wanted?" she asked coolly.

"All but one."

"Which one?"

He pinned her with his gaze. "Have you slept with him?"

"I guess I should be grateful you're asking me rather than polling the newsroom."

"Have you?" he asked again.

She couldn't lie to him. She didn't want to lie to him. "Yes."

His mouth thinned. "I can't say I'm happy about that."

"Do you expect me to believe you haven't been with anyone else in the past six months?"

"There have been other women," he admitted. "But only because I was trying to forget about you."

Women—plural. And he was all bent out of shape because she'd been with one other man.

He took her hand again. "It didn't work. I couldn't stop thinking about you, missing you."

"And yet it took you six months to contact me."

"You know me, Jen. I pride myself on my independence. I didn't want to admit that I needed you." He reached across the table for the hand that was resting on the base of her wine glass. "Did you know that I haven't been back to New York for more than a few days at a time since you left?"

"Your six-week assignment lasted six months?"

"I was finished on schedule," he said. "But when I got home, it didn't feel like home anymore. Without you, it was just an empty apartment. So I took another assignment. And another after that. Until I realized, consciously or not, I'd been making my way toward Tokyo."

She remained silent, not sure what kind of response was appropriate.

"But I knew if I came to see you, if I hoped to convince you of my feelings, I couldn't show up empty-handed." He pulled a cellophane-wrapped fortune cookie out of his pocket. "So I brought this for you."

"From China?"

He frowned, obviously missing the subtlety of her point. "From London, actually. I know a guy there who owns a company that makes these." He set the it down in front of her. "Open it."

She opened the wrapper, wondering what kind of fortune he'd dreamed up for her and wishing he hadn't bothered. But she broke open the cookie, then stared speechless at the ring that fell out.

Chapter Thirteen

Jenny thought she'd been shocked when she'd seen Brad in the newsroom, but that moment of incredulity didn't begin to compare to this.

"I want you to marry me," he said.

She didn't know what to say.

She'd never expected, after so many months apart, that he would want not just to reconcile but to move their relationship forward—to take that next final step he'd always seemed so wary of. To offer her everything she'd always wanted.

And it was everything she wanted.

So why wasn't she leaping out of her chair to throw herself into his arms? And why was she now, as he was sliding the ring onto her finger, fighting the urge to pull her hand away?

She knew the answer to all of those questions was the same. Richard.

She heard the scrape of chairs and glanced up as the Hanson-TAKA group started to move toward the door. Richard's mouth was set in a thin line as his gaze moved toward her, disappointment evident in his eyes.

What had she expected—that he would pull her into his arms and beg her to marry him instead of Brad? Yeah, that was as likely as the Yomiuri Giants winning the World Series.

She turned her attention back to Brad and realized that he'd been watching her watch Richard. She felt a twinge of embarrassment, but she refused to feel guilty for having moved on with her life during the time she and Brad had been apart. And she had moved on. She didn't want Brad anymore, she wanted Richard.

How could she possibly accept what Brad was offering when her heart was still aching for Richard?

"I was thinking a fall wedding would be nice," Brad continued.

"This fall?"

"Of course," he said. "We've been apart for too long already."

He was saying the right things, but she knew the real reason he wanted to marry quickly wasn't that he'd missed her so much. She stared at the dazzling marquise diamond on her hand for a moment, then looked up at him.

"Were you even going to tell me about TCR?" she asked softly, referring to the company she knew he'd invested in heavily—a company that had recently declared bankruptcy.

She saw the flicker of surprise on his face, the shadow of guilt in his eyes.

"What does that have to do with anything?" he demanded, a trifle defensively.

"I'm guessing everything."

He frowned. "I love you, Jenny."

"And yet, during the whole two-and-a-half years we were together, living in the same apartment, you never once voluntarily mentioned the word marriage."

"I wasn't ready."

"You're not ready now," she said.

She'd loved Brad once, had even dreamed of marrying him. But all she could think about now was Richard. How her heart had raced when Richard touched her. How her mind had spun when Richard kissed her. How her body had tingled when she'd made love with Richard.

She pulled the ring off her finger. "I can't accept this."

"I thought this was what you wanted."

"A year ago it was," she agreed.

He frowned. "Are you saying no?"

"Yes," she said, with absolutely zero regret. "I'm saying no."

Richard knew the man he'd seen Jenny having dinner with was her ex-boyfriend, but not because she'd told him of her plans. No, during their brief conversation earlier that day, she hadn't even bothered to mention that he was in town. He only knew about Brad because he'd happened to cross paths with Samara as he was leaving the *Tribune* building. She'd been happy to tell him about the unexpected and unwelcome visitor.

But while Samara obviously didn't like her friend's ex, it was Jenny's feelings that mattered. Richard figured the ring on her finger made those feelings pretty clear.

He told himself it shouldn't bother him so much. She'd been honest from the start about wanting a husband and a family, just as he'd been honest about not being the man to give her those things. He should be happy that she was finally getting what she wanted.

Instead, he was selfish enough to be miserable.

Just when he'd started thinking about how they could maintain a relationship after the Hanson-TAKA merger was finalized, his hopes had come crumbling down around him. Even before the ex-boyfriend returned, Jenny had left him, and any hope he might have had of changing her mind had been obliterated by Brad's proposal.

Richard had once worried about her vulnerability. It turned out the joke was on him. She was the one who'd walked out. He knew it hadn't been an easy decision for her to make, but she'd done so anyway, and he'd been the one left with his heart torn open.

Or maybe it was his pride that was in tatters, only his ego that was wounded by her easy dismissal of him and everything they'd shared.

In any case, he had other things to think about. Now more than ever, he wanted this damn merger finalized so he could go back to Chicago and forget he'd ever met Jenny Anderson.

He popped the locks on his briefcase and pulled out Hanson's latest financial reports, determined to put her out of his mind and focus on his work. But the letters and numbers blurred before his eyes and his mind insisted on wandering.

He pushed away from the desk and moved to the window to look out at the street below, his father's words coming back to him again.

And if the woman you love loves you back—

He severed the thought with a laugh that reflected more derision than humor.

Jenny claimed she'd ended their relationship because she was falling in love with him. Following that same logic, he figured she must be completely head-over-heels for him now. It was the only reason he could think of for her to marry another man.

Keiko Irene Anderson came into the world at 10:37 p.m.—a seven-pound fifteen-ounce bundle of wrinkly red skin and spiky black hair with a very healthy set of lungs.

When Jenny finally left the hospital, after cooing over the latest addition to the family and taking her turn to hold her brand-new niece in her arms, she intended to go home. She needed to think, to process everything that had happened in the past twenty-four hours, and she needed to sleep.

But instead of going home, she found herself in front of the hotel. Had she planned to come here all along?

She didn't know. But now that she was here, she knew she couldn't leave without seeing Richard.

Still, nerves skipped in her tummy as she made her way to the elevator, up to the twenty-second floor, then down the corridor. The last time she'd come had been to tell him that their relationship—barely begun—was over. She hadn't expected that she'd have reason to come back to the hotel while Richard was still here. And she wasn't sure it was reason so much as need that had compelled her to come now.

She just wanted to explain about Brad. She could only imagine what he thought, knowing she'd been in his bed only days before receiving a proposal from another man. And she thought he might want to know about the baby.

Or maybe she was just making excuses.

She ignored this niggling thought as easily as the Do

Not Disturb sign hanging on the handle and rapped her knuckles against the wood.

She waited a minute, maybe two, and had lifted her hand to knock again when the door was yanked open.

"You're the absolute last person I expected to see tonight," Richard said to her.

She twisted the strap of her purse around her hand, suddenly aware that she had no idea what time it was. She didn't know when she'd left the restaurant or how long she'd been at the hospital. Whatever the hour, Richard clearly hadn't been sleeping.

He was still dressed in the suit he'd been wearing at dinner, although the jacket had been discarded and the tie loosened. His hair looked slightly rumpled, as if he'd run his hands through it. His jaw was shadowed with stubble and his eyes were dark. He looked sexily disheveled and just a little bit dangerous.

That thought gave her pause. *Dangerous* wasn't a word she would ever have associated with him before. Then again, he'd never looked at her quite this way before.

She ignored the quiver of nerves to ask, "Can I come in?"

His only response was to step back to allow her entry.

He closed the door behind her, then moved across the room to pick up a glass of amber liquid. She guessed it was probably the whiskey that was responsible for the edgy glint in his eyes.

"You're not wearing his ring," he noted, lifting the glass to his lips as she stepped past him.

"I—" she cleared her throat "—no."

"Did you turn down his proposal?"

She wished he'd offer her a drink or invite her to sit down—anything to ease this uncomfortable situation.

But he did neither, merely standing across the room watching her.

"Yes."

He seemed surprised by her response, but quickly recovered to ask, "Why? I thought you wanted to get married and have a family. Isn't that, after all, why you dumped me?"

She winced at the anger in his tone. "My decision to end things with you had nothing to do with Brad. It still doesn't."

"Because what we had between us would never have been enough for you."

He was right. What they'd shared together, as wonderful as it had been, wouldn't have been enough. She would eventually, inevitably, have wanted more. She knew herself well enough to have anticipated that, and she knew Richard well enough to know that he couldn't give her what she needed. It was the reason she'd ended their relationship.

I care about you, Jenny.

The memory of his words evoked both joy and pain. Joy because she knew that he did care; pain because caring wasn't loving. And she'd promised herself that she would never settle for second best again.

But she couldn't deny that she missed him. She felt the tightness in her throat, the threat of tears she hadn't yet let herself shed. "I'm not sure what I want anymore," she admitted.

"Then why are you here?" he asked again, more gently this time.

"I, ah, came to tell you that that Michiko had her baby. Another girl." She smiled. "Keiko."

"When?"

"Tonight. She's beautiful." Jenny smiled. "She wasn't

an hour old when I got to hold her in my arms—this brand-new baby, a tiny perfect human being."

She could still feel the slight weight of the fragile bundle in her arms and the pang of longing so deep inside it made her want to cry.

"I do know what I want," she said.

"A baby," he guessed.

"A family," she corrected. "All my life, I've never quite felt as though I fit. I love my parents and John and Michiko and their beautiful little girls, but I've always felt a little disconnected—as if they'd been given to me to share but weren't really mine. I want a family of my own."

It was a dream he'd once had, too. But that dream had faded a long time ago. His father's death had been the first blow, a hard lesson in the fragility of life; his mother's abandonment had confirmed the capriciousness of love; finding his wife with another man had only solidified his doubts and questions. No, a family wasn't something he'd dared dream about in a long time.

Except when he'd been with Jenny, then he'd found himself wanting more than he should. He'd found himself thinking about a future with her in it. Even as he'd reminded himself it was a fantasy—a dream that could never be reality because her life was here and his was in Chicago—he'd convinced himself the obstacle of distance wasn't insurmountable if they both wanted to be together.

Of course, her dumping him effectively destroyed those illusions.

"If you want a family of your own so much, why didn't you accept Brad's proposal?"

She didn't answer.

"Okay," he said when she remained silent. "Why don't you tell me why you're really here?"

"Obviously I made a mistake." She started toward the door.

He grabbed her arm and turned her around to face him again. "Did you come to see if I'd be willing to make the same offer? How far are you willing to go to entice me?"

His lips hovered above hers. He saw her eyes widen, felt the soft exhale of her breath. He pressed his body against hers, let her feel his arousal. As angry as he was with her, as frustrated as he was with the situation, he couldn't deny that she still turned him on. And having her back in his arms, even like this, aroused him beyond belief.

Apparently he wasn't the only one affected by their nearness. Jenny moaned as she shifted instinctively, cradling the ache of his arousal between the softness of her thighs.

He bit back a groan of frustration as he tried to remember that she'd dumped him, trampled right over his heart on her way out the door. But right now, with her back in his arms, he didn't seem to care. Or maybe he cared too much.

He crushed his mouth down on hers. He was furious and frustrated and hurting more than he was willing to admit, and all of that pent-up emotion poured into the kiss.

He expected her to slap him—he deserved to be slapped. At the very least, he expected that she would pull away. Instead she moaned, her lips parting for the ruthless onslaught of his tongue. Her hands weren't pushing against him but holding on, her fingers curled into the fabric of his shirt. Her body molded to his, soft curves yielding to hard angles, her heart beating in frantic rhythm against his.

Somehow, without either of them being aware, anger gave way to ardor and passion transformed to tenderness.

She trembled. Or maybe he did.

He was no longer certain where she left off and he began; it no longer mattered. The taste of her seeped into his blood, more potent than any whiskey. His hands moved over her body, no longer punishing and demanding but seeking and giving.

His lips skimmed over her cheeks, tasted the saltiness of her tears. Whatever point he'd intended to make was lost in the realization that he'd hurt her, and that was the one thing he'd never wanted to do. He leaned his forehead against hers. His voice, when he spoke, was thick with emotion, regret.

"Give us a chance, Jenny."

She brushed the tears off her cheeks, moved toward the door. "I already did."

He had maybe a few seconds before she walked out on him again. A few seconds to find the words that could change the rest of his life. No closing argument he'd ever made before a judge had been so important.

But what could he do? If she'd already made up her mind, what was left to say?

I love you.

The answer seemed obvious, but the words stuck in his throat. He couldn't do it. Even if it was true, he couldn't use those words to manipulate her.

All he said was, "You wouldn't have kissed me the way you just did if this was over."

She looked up at him, her eyes filled with equal parts sadness and determination. "It has to be over."

"Why?" He heard the desperation in his voice, but he was beyond caring.

A single tear trembled on the edge of her lashes before

it spilled over and tracked slowly down her cheek. "Because if I give you a chance, you'll break my heart. And I don't want to hurt anymore."

Richard had tossed back several more glasses of whiskey after Jenny's visit before accepting that no amount of alcohol would cleanse the taste of her lips or banish her image from his mind. Then, when he'd finally crawled into bed and slept, he'd dreamed of her. Dreams in which he'd been able to see her but was unable to reach her. Dreams in which he'd been running toward her while she slowly faded away. He didn't need a psychiatrist to figure out she was lost to him. Not just in his dreams but forever.

When he awoke, he felt as though a jackhammer was pounding into his skull, but even the pain in his head couldn't make him forget the emptiness in his heart. A long shower and a handful of aspirin did nothing to improve his disposition. Though he wasn't in the mood to make pleasant conversation, he had no legitimate excuse to cancel the breakfast meeting Helen had set up the night before and he was at her suite by 8 a.m.

"You look like hell," she said upon opening the door.

Richard moved past her to pour himself a much-needed cup of coffee from the service that had been set up in her sitting area. "I knew I should have gone with the blue tie."

"It would match the circles under your eyes," she agreed.

He swallowed a mouthful of hot coffee. "I was up late."

"Working?"

"What else?"

She refilled her own cup and sat down. "I'm glad I'm not paying you by the hour or we'd be bankrupt already.

Not that I believe for a minute that the merger caused you to lose sleep last night."

"The merger is the only thing that matters right now." He perused the tray of pastries. It was easier to pretend he was hungry than to face the pity in Helen's eyes.

When it became obvious to her that he didn't intend to say anything more, Helen sighed. "I thought we were friends, Richard."

"We are," he agreed.

"Then why won't you tell me what's going on?"

He selected a cherry Danish he didn't really want and set it on a plate. "Because I'm a man, and we don't like to admit our mistakes."

"Then you're admitting you made one?"

He nodded. Although whether his biggest mistake was in ever getting involved with Jenny Anderson or letting her walk out of his hotel room last night, he didn't know. In any event, she'd made it clear that whatever they'd shared was over.

But what choice had he given her? What had he offered other than a few weeks of his life and a good time in his bed? Of course she wanted more. She deserved more.

He didn't want ties, commitments, obligations—and he definitely didn't want to fall in love. What was love anyway but a four-letter excuse for hurting those you claimed to care about?

Marilyn had said she loved him, but that hadn't stopped her from sleeping with another man. Not even parental love was dependable. His father had died and his mother had withdrawn her affection from her elder son. No, he didn't ever intend to put his heart on the line again.

Jenny was better off with someone who wanted the same things she did. Someone who would put her needs first, who would love her and give her the future and family she wanted. But the thought of her with any other man—exchanging vows with him, making love with him—he couldn't let himself think about it. The idea of her in any other man's bed drove him insane.

"Do you think you'll ever get married again?" he asked, surprising himself as much as Helen with the question that tumbled out of his mouth.

A smile played at the corners of her mouth. "Are you proposing?"

"No," he said quickly, then winced at the vehemence of the denial.

She laughed. "It's lucky for you I'm not easily offended."

Richard decided to keep his mouth shut until his brain started functioning normally again.

"I know there's been a lot of speculation—public and private—about my marriage to George. But regardless of what anyone says or thinks, I married him because I loved him.

"Maybe I was idealistic," she admitted. "Maybe even a little naive. But I had hopes and dreams like any young bride when I made my vows."

She shrugged. "Some of those hopes faded, some of my dreams changed. That happens not just in marriage but in life.

"But to answer your question, yes." She smiled, a little wistfully. "If I ever fell in love with someone who could believe in my dreams—I would get married again.

"However, I think the real question you need to answer is—would *you* get married again?"

Richard raked a hand through his hair and sighed. "I don't know."

A month ago, he wouldn't have had any difficulty answering that question with a resounding no. But a month ago, he didn't know Jenny. Now, he couldn't imagine his life without her.

If he had to choose between making a commitment and losing her forever, he would marry her.

But his pride wouldn't let him ask—not now.

He wanted her to choose him not because he was willing to put a ring on her finger, but because she loved him.

As he loved her.

The realization should have come as a shock, maybe even sent him into something of a panic—instead, the acceptance of his feelings filled him with an unexpected warm contentment.

He was scared, too, but as much as he feared putting his heart on the line and having it rejected as both his mother and his ex-wife had done, he was even more afraid of losing Jenny forever.

Chapter Fourteen

Jenny stopped by the hospital to see Mich and the baby on her way home from work the next day. The visit with her sister-in-law and new niece was a bittersweet reminder of the dreams of a family of her own that continued to elude her. She was on her way out when her brother and Suki were coming in.

John left his elder daughter with her mother and baby sister to follow Jenny outside.

"I heard Brad proposed to you," he said.

Jenny didn't bother to ask where he'd heard. Her brother had contacts everywhere in the city. Instead, she nodded.

"Please tell me you're not going to marry him," John said.

"I'm not going to marry him."

He frowned at the immediate response. "Do you mean that or are you just humoring me?"

She smiled. "You don't have a sense of humor."

"Not about something like this," he agreed. "Because I don't want to see you get hurt again."

"I'm old enough to make my own decisions," she reminded him gently. "And to face the consequences of those decisions."

He sighed. "I know, but just because you've grown up doesn't mean I can stop wanting to protect you."

"Old habits die hard?"

"Something like that."

Despite his general agreement, she could tell he had something specific on his mind. And she was sure she knew what it was.

"You found out about TCR, didn't you?"

His startled glance confirmed she was right—somehow her brother had learned that Brad's big investment had turned out to be a big dud.

"I didn't realize you knew about it," he said.

"I'm not an idiot, John. Don't you think I wondered why Brad was suddenly so anxious to marry me?"

"I don't think you're an idiot," he assured her. "But I did think that your history with him might have clouded your judgment."

She just shook her head.

He took her hand, squeezed it affectionately. "I'm glad. You deserve so much better."

She felt her throat tighten, and she knew she had to change the subject quickly before she embarrassed both of them by breaking into tears.

Before she had a chance, however, John spoke again. "I thought for a while, before Brad came into town, that you and Richard Warren—"

"I don't want to talk about Richard," she interrupted.

"I'm sorry," he said gently. "When I saw the two of you together, the way he looked at you, I got the impression he really cared about you."

Which was the same way Richard had described his feelings, but her heart ached for love too much to settle for anything less.

"I didn't get a chance to talk to Suki," she said in an obvious effort to change the topic of conversation. "How's she liking her new sister?"

John's gaze held hers for a long moment before he answered. "I think she's still undecided at this point. She was excited about the idea of a sister, but I don't think Keiko is quite what she had in mind."

"It must be a difficult adjustment for her," Jenny said. "To go from being an only child to being the older sibling of a baby who's getting all the attention."

"Yeah, it is." He grinned at her.

"As if you remember," she scoffed.

"I do." He tugged a strand of her hair playfully. "Actually what I remember most was the way you used to follow me around. Everywhere I went, wanting to do everything I did. It drove me nuts.

"Then you started to grow up, make friends of your own, do your own thing. You hardly paid any attention to me anymore. That's when I realized how much I missed you."

"You missed bossing me around," she teased.

"Yeah, that, too. Although it will take Suki another couple of years to appreciate that benefit of having a little sister."

Jenny shook her head despairingly, but their discussion about Suki had given her an idea.

"Why don't I take Suki to the lake for the weekend?"

she suggested. "It will give you and Mich some time alone with the baby and give Suki some special attention."

"Suki would love that," he agreed.

Jenny was glad she'd suggested coming up to the cabin with her niece. Although she couldn't help being reminded of her last visit with Richard, she was determined not to dwell on it. This had always been her favorite place, and she wasn't going to let recent events ruin the enjoyment for her.

After dinner, she and Suki went for a walk in the woods, then they popped some corn and sat in front of the TV to watch one of Suki's favorite cartoon programs. Jenny loved her niece's company—she was honest and straightforward and uncomplicated.

"I thought it would be fun to have a sister," Suki confided, munching on a handful of popcorn. "But Keiko doesn't do anything except sleep and cry."

She smiled as she stroked a hand over the little girl's silky hair. "That's all you did when you were a baby, too."

Her niece was obviously skeptical. "Really?"

She nodded. "And then you started to crawl and walk and run. And now there's nothing you can't do."

"I can't drive a car," Suki said wisely, reaching into the bowl again. "And I'm not allowed to use Mommy's scissors unless she's helping me."

"That's a good rule," Jenny agreed.

Suki was silent for a few minutes, watching the television, before she asked, "Are you going to have a baby, Aunt Jenny?"

The ache she felt inside was getting to be familiar—a bone deep yearning mixed with too much uncertainty. "I hope so," she said. "Someday."

Suki nodded. "But you've got to get a husband first."

Not technically, but Jenny didn't bother to correct the little girl on that. As she'd told Richard, if she was going to bring a baby into the world, she wanted him or her to have a mother and father who loved one another and were committed to raising their child together.

"If you don't get a husband," Suki continued, "you could borrow me. I could be your little girl sometimes."

She hugged the child closer, touched by her niece's generous heart. "Like we're doing now?"

"Just like this." Suki snuggled into her lap, and within a few minutes, she'd closed her eyes.

Jenny waited until the program was over to make sure the she was completely asleep, then lifted her carefully to carry her to bed. She'd just finished tucking the covers around her when she heard a knock.

She hurried to the door before a repeat of the sound could wake her niece. She'd thought it might be one of the distant neighbors, or somebody who'd gotten lost and needed directions to get back to the highway. It never even crossed her mind that it might be Richard.

He brought his hand from behind his back, offering her a tentative smile along with a bunch of wilting daisies.

The flowers completely disarmed her, because they were exactly what she'd once envisioned he would choose if he were to give her flowers. She accepted the bouquet automatically, her throat tightening as she touched a soft white petal. But she couldn't let Richard know that she weakened so easily, so she continued to stand in the doorway, not inviting him inside. "What are you doing here, Richard?"

"I wanted to apologize for the other night. When you came to my hotel."

She sighed. "There's nothing to apologize for," she told him.

"Then why did you run away?"

"I didn't run away," she denied. "I simply came up here to spend some time alone with my niece."

"I've missed you," he said softly.

She'd barely managed to rebuild some of the walls around her heart, and he was already tearing them down. She wished she were strong enough to turn him away, but she'd missed him, too. She sighed and stepped away from the door. "You can come in for a few minutes."

He followed her into the family room, sat beside her on the sofa, his body turned so he could look at her. "I've been thinking about what you said the other night," he told her. "About wanting a family of your own."

"You don't have to tell me again that you don't want the same thing," she told him.

His fingers stroked down her cheek, a gentle caress. "I didn't think I did," he admitted. "But I've started to realize that wants can change—or maybe it's the people who come into our lives who make us want different things."

She felt her heart leap, but forced her voice to remain calm. "What are you saying?"

He was silent for a long minute before he finally said, "I want to help you find your birth mother."

Okay, that wasn't quite what she had expected.

"I told you before, I'm not interested in looking for a woman who wasn't interested in me."

"How do you know she wasn't interested?" he challenged.

"She gave me away, didn't she?"

"And now you're rejecting her because she rejected you first, and you keep waiting for everyone else to do the same thing." He shook his head. "Actually, you don't wait. You leave so that no one can leave you."

"That's ridiculous."

"Is it? It seems to me that's exactly what happened with us."

"Did you come all this way to psychoanalyze me?"

"No, I came all this way to tell you I love you."

She stared at him, stunned.

He smiled wryly. "I didn't expect it, either."

She pushed herself up from the sofa. "I'm going to have a glass of wine, do you want one?"

He followed her to the kitchen area. "Does that offer mean you're not going to kick me out tonight?"

She shrugged as she took two glasses from the cupboard. "There's a spare bedroom."

He waited patiently while she uncorked the bottle then poured the wine. He accepted the glass she passed to him before asking, "Aren't you going to say anything?"

"My mind is still spinning."

"Mine, too." He set his wine down, then pried hers from her fingers and placed it on the counter beside his own. He took her hands, linking their fingers together. "I didn't think I would ever fall in love again. I know I didn't want to. But you changed everything for me, and I don't ever want to be without you again."

She still didn't say anything, but he felt her fingers tremble slightly in his grasp. He squeezed them gently before he let her go.

"Give me another chance—give *us* another chance, Jenny."

"I haven't kicked you out," she said. Then added, "Yet."

He smiled. "I'm grateful."

"That doesn't mean I'm not thinking about it."

"Of course not."

He was being agreeable again and smiling that smile that made her knees weak. She wanted more than anything to give him another chance—to give *them* another chance. It was because she wanted it so much that she forced herself to take a step back.

She'd been on an emotional roller coaster the past few days and didn't know if she could trust anything she was feeling right now. "I'm too tired to think about this right now. I need to go to bed."

"Okay." He reached for her hand as she started to move past him, halting her in her tracks. "But there's one more thing you need to think about."

Then he lowered his head and pressed his lips to hers.

It was the briefest touch, a test, a taste.

Then his mouth brushed over hers again. She sighed and her eyelids fluttered closed as she tried to remember if he'd ever kissed her like this before—with endless patience and gentle persuasion. The passion was still there, she could feel it simmering just beneath the surface, but there was also tenderness and affection, and a hint of something warmer, softer, deeper. She was just starting to sink into it, allowing herself to be seduced by him, when he eased back.

"Sweet dreams, Jenny."

Richard was awakened to the sound of a steady, rhythmic thump against the wall directly behind his head. He pushed himself up in bed, taking a moment to orient himself in the unfamiliar surroundings.

He was at Jenny's parents' cabin. She hadn't spent the

night with him—which wasn't a surprise but still a disappointment, but she'd let him stay—which was a relief as much as a surprise. He hoped it meant that she hadn't written him off completely. He hadn't expected the declaration of his feelings to break down all the barriers between them, but he hoped it would at least be a step toward building a life for them together.

The continued thumping drew his attention again. He pulled on his clothes and went to investigate.

The door of the room beside his was open, and there was a child on the bottom bunk. She was lying across the narrow mattress, her head hanging over the edge, her feet swinging back and then forward, thumping against the wall.

Well, that explained the noise.

"You must be Suki," he said.

She tumbled off the bed, her face splitting in a wide grin as she nodded enthusiastically. "Auntie Jenny's making breakfast."

"Is that why you woke me up?"

She shook her head, wide-eyed, innocent. "I promised not to wake you and not to go into your room."

Richard couldn't help but smile. "I guess you didn't do that," he agreed. "But now that I'm awake, why don't we go find out what's for breakfast?"

She nodded again, obviously approving his suggestion, and placed her hand inside his much larger one. "I'll show you the kitchen."

Richard had offered to cook dinner for all of them, but after a day of hiking, Suki almost fell asleep at the table before he'd even boiled the water for the pasta. Jenny gave her a bowl of cereal and got her ready for bed.

While the sauce was simmering, he opened a bottle of wine and set the table.

"Looks like you thought of everything," Jenny said when she came back into the room.

He handed her a glass of wine. "I seem to have forgotten candlelight and soft music."

She took a long sip of the merlot. "Candles are a fire hazard and music inhibits conversation."

"Are you really so unromantic?"

"I appreciate romance at the right time and place," she said. "But this isn't it."

"Sometimes you have to make the time and place." He lowered his head to hers and kissed her softly. He felt rather than heard her sigh and though he was tempted to deepen the kiss, he forced himself to pull back. Her eyes were soft, clouded, her lips still slightly parted.

"I've been wanting to do that all day," he told her.

"I've been thinking that I should have sent you back to the city last night."

"You're not going to get rid of me that easily this time," he told her.

"What if I start using words like commitment or marriage and babies?"

"Try me," he said.

She studied him for a moment, then shook her head. "I'm not sure this is a good idea."

"This?" he asked.

"You and me."

"I think it's a very good idea." He dumped the pasta into the pot, set the timer, then came back to where she was standing and kissed her again. "The best idea I've ever had, in fact."

"I should send you back to the city now."

"It's too late."

She sighed. "I know."

But she didn't sound happy about it, so he steered the conversation to more neutral topics as he finished dinner preparations and throughout the meal. They worked together clearing up afterward, and then Jenny went to check on Suki.

"She hasn't moved since I tucked her in," she told him.

He took her hand and led her over to the sofa. "I remember your mother commenting that Suki reminds her of you. I think she's right."

Jenny laughed as she sat down beside him. "The resemblance is uncanny, isn't it?"

"Not that she looks like you, but she has your spirit—your tenacity and endurance. She's a great kid."

"Yes, she is."

"And you're going to be a great mother someday."

"Maybe." Her voice was wistful. "Someday."

He was surprised by how much he wanted to give Jenny the gift of a child, to see her belly grow round with their baby inside it. "How many kids do you want to have?"

"Two or six or a dozen." She smiled, then shrugged. "At least two."

It was easy to imagine her surrounded by children, obvious that she had enough love for twelve of them.

And he knew now that he wanted to give her what she wanted, because he'd finally realized it was what he wanted, too. Not marriage and family in an abstract sense, but to marry Jenny and have children with her. To live with her and grow old with her. To be with her forever.

It was suddenly so clear to him, but he knew she would

need some time to trust he'd changed his mind before they could make those kind of plans. Still, he couldn't help asking, "When you think about the future, do you see me with you?"

"Why are you asking me that question?" She sipped her wine. "Aren't you going back to Chicago in a few weeks?"

"Most likely," he agreed. "There are things I'll need to deal with on that end to get this merger off the ground."

She nodded.

"Any chance you would go with me?"

Her eyes widened. "To Chicago?"

"Just until the details are worked out, then we could come back here."

"You want to come back to Tokyo?"

"I want to be with you, Jenny—whatever that takes."

"Why?" she asked softly, the question tinged with both hope and skepticism.

"Because I love you," he said again. "And I'd like to think that wherever the future takes us, we can find a way to be together."

Again, she sidestepped the declaration of his feelings, shifting so that she was straddling his lap, her knees bracketing his hips. "Let's not worry about tomorrow." She touched her mouth to his, nibbling gently. "Not tonight."

He bit back a groan as she rocked against him. He really wanted to talk to her, to make plans with her, but the sensual movements of her body were making it difficult for him to even think. "Your, uh, niece is sleeping down the hall," he reminded her.

"Suki is a very sound sleeper." She was already tugging his shirt out of his pants, sliding her palms up over his chest.

He loved the coolness of her fingers on his skin, the eagerness of her touch. "That isn't what you said last night."

"Last night I wanted you to suffer—at least a little." She pressed her lips to his chest, swirled her tongue around his nipple. Then she tipped her head back, her lips curving in a seductive smile. "Tonight, I want you to suffer a lot."

Helen was becoming increasingly frustrated by the delays. She was even more frustrated by the realization that she wasn't in any position to make demands. TAKA was in control of every step of the negotiations and then had final say over whether or not the merger would even happen. There was nothing she hated more than being on the weak end of such a power imbalance—it made her feel like she was sixteen years old again, knowing she couldn't have the one thing she wanted more than anything else in the world.

Twenty-five years later, she felt just as helpless. She forced herself to push those feelings aside as she poured another cup of coffee and waited for Richard to arrive.

She forgot about ancient resentments and current concerns when he walked through the door. He looked different—she noticed that right away—more settled, and happier than she'd ever seen him. Definitely happier than the last time they'd had a morning meeting like this.

"Looks like somebody had a good weekend," she said.

"It was a great weekend."

"Then you worked things out with Jenny?"

"Not all the details, but those will come."

She was genuinely pleased for him. With everything else in chaos around her, it was comforting to believe in the healing power of love.

"I'm going to marry her," Richard announced.

Helen had started to lift her cup to her lips, then set it down again. "When you decide to move, it's always full speed ahead. When's the wedding?"

"Soon." He smiled. "Jenny doesn't know yet."

"When are you going to let her in on this plan?"

"Soon," he said again.

"Last time we spoke about marriage, you were reluctant to even consider making that kind of commitment again," she reminded him.

"That was before I fell in love. Now I don't want to imagine ever waking up without her."

Helen's heart sighed at the emotion in his words, and at the same time it ached knowing that she could only dream about being loved so deeply and completely.

"The only thing that scares me now is the thought of the dozen or more children Jenny wants to have," Richard said.

She pushed her own regrets aside to respond to his concern. "I think you'll be a terrific father."

"I hope so," he said. "But you know from your own experience with Jack and Evan and Andrew how much grief kids can give you—and they're not even your own."

She felt the familiar pang and accepted it. "No, they're not."

"I'm sorry," he said. "I didn't mean to sound insensitive."

"You didn't. It's true. I've tried to be their mother, but I'm not." Maybe they might have felt closer to her, opened up more easily, if she'd had George's baby—a tie of blood to join them together—but years of trying had been both unsuccessful and heart-wrenching.

"Did you ever wish you'd had a child of your own?"

She swallowed the regrets, the grief, the guilt, before responding softly, "I did have a child."

His eyes widened, reflecting his shock.

He couldn't be any more surprised than she was. Her child wasn't something she ever talked about, but the baby she'd given up had been on her mind almost constantly since the twenty-fifth anniversary of that date. Maybe it was time she unburdened herself of the secret she'd carried for so long. "A little girl," she admitted softly.

"You've never mentioned having a daughter."

"I was only sixteen when I got pregnant. It seemed the best thing to do—for both of us—was to give her up for adoption."

"I'm sorry, Helen. I know that must have been hard for you."

She nodded. "Hardly a day's gone by since then that I haven't thought about what might have been different if I'd kept her, wondered if giving up my baby was the right decision.

"It was twenty-five years ago on August second," she told him. "And I still remember every detail. I got to hold her in my arms for only a few minutes before they took her away, but I'll never forget the soft downy hair, the perfect little fingers and even tinier fingernails, the heart-shaped birthmark on her hip."

Richard froze. "A birthmark?"

Helen smiled as she blinked the moisture from her eyes. "It wasn't very big. Maybe it wasn't even a heart. But I thought it was. And I told her it was a symbol of my heart that she could carry with her forever, so she would always know she was loved."

He thought back to the bouquet of balloons he'd seen

in Jenny's office—the admission that it had been her twenty-fifth birthday on the second of August. He knew that she had a heart-shaped birthmark on her hip, and now he knew why she always looked so familiar to him.

Jenny was Helen's daughter.

Chapter Fifteen

"I used to believe I'd find her," Helen continued, lost in her memories. "During the first year after my baby was born, I looked into every stroller I passed, searching for the slightest hint of familiarity. I can't count how many times I thought—maybe it's this child, maybe it's her."

"Have you tried to find her?" Richard asked.

"I considered it," she admitted. "But I figured, having given her up once, I had no right to interfere in her life later. I also figured she would have tracked me down if she wanted to."

And she hasn't.

The unspoken words echoed in the silence of the room.

"Do you want to find her?" he asked softly.

"More than anything else in the world. I want to see my little girl again."

"Your little girl is twenty-five years old now," he reminded her gently.

"I know." She managed a tremulous smile. "Objectively I understand that. But despite the passing of time, in my heart, I still think of her as the baby I held so briefly in my arms."

Richard didn't respond. He could hardly tell Helen that her daughter had grown into a beautiful young woman—a woman who had made it clear she had no interest in finding the mother who had given birth to her and given her up.

Jenny was pleasantly surprised when Kari buzzed through to tell her that Richard was there to see her. He came through the newsroom a few minutes later carrying two bento box lunches.

He smiled at her, but she sensed the tension in him.

"I thought you would be tied up in negotiations at TAKA all day," she said.

He set the boxes on her desk. "We seem to alternate between periods of intense negotiation and twiddling our thumbs."

Today he was obviously twiddling his thumbs, and she guessed the inactivity with respect to the merger was responsible for his tension. She knew he was anxious to finalize the deal. Was he also anxious to return to Chicago? Did he still want her to go with him?

He hadn't mentioned the possibility since they'd returned from the lake, and she was wishing now that they'd talked about it more while they were there. But she'd been taken aback by the suggestion, thrilled at this evidence that he wanted their relationship to continue, and equally scared to hope that it could. There were a lot of obstacles to overcome if they were to build a future together and after having her heart broken so many times before, she was almost afraid to let herself believe they could make it work. But she wanted to try. She wanted to be with him.

One day at a time, she reminded herself again.

"I did see my boss this morning, though," Richard told her.

"Did that meeting go well?"

He smiled, but she still saw the hint of shadows in the curve of his lips. "Helen wants to meet you."

"She does?" Jenny was both surprised and a little apprehensive.

"She's curious about the woman who's stolen my heart."

"You didn't tell her that?"

This time when he smiled, it came more naturally. "I didn't have to. She said it was the smile on my face that gave it away."

Jenny felt her cheeks flush as her own lips curved.

"She invited us both to have dinner with her tonight," he said.

"Do you want to?" she asked, sensing there was something about the suggestion that was causing him to hesitate.

"I would really like you to meet Helen," he admitted. "But there's something you need to know before you decide whether or not you want to."

"What's that?"

He paused, cleared his throat. His obvious hesitation made her tummy flutter with apprehension.

"Just tell me," she said.

"During our conversation this morning, Helen mentioned that she had a baby a long time ago, and she gave her up for adoption."

She considered the revelation as the slow, throbbing ache of longing she'd learned to deny so long ago began to beat inside her breast again. Jenny was adopted; Helen had given her baby up for adoption. She wasn't sure if that gave them something in common or set them apart. She guessed Richard was wondering the same thing. "And you think, because I was adopted, I'll hold that against her?"

"I wish it was that simple," he said.

She frowned.

"I think you're Helen's daughter."

Jenny could only stare at him, stunned. Then she shook her head. "That's impossible."

Richard reached across the desk for her hand, but she pushed her chair back and stood up.

"Helen's daughter was born on August second twenty-five years ago," he told her.

She shook her head again. "It's just a coincidence."

"I'm not telling you this to upset you," he said gently. "But I think this could be a great opportunity for you to finally know your biological mother."

She turned away. "I don't want to talk about this. The idea is just too ridiculous."

"I know it seems unlikely—"

"I doubt I'm the only child born on that day who was given up for adoption," she interrupted.

"You're probably right."

The easy agreement and soothing tone didn't help to ease the panic building inside her. Somehow she knew there was more to come.

"And if it was only your age and date of birth, I wouldn't have jumped to any conclusions," he told her.

"What else is there?" she demanded.

"You look like her."

"She's blond," Jenny said automatically.

"Which is probably why I didn't make the connection immediately," Richard said. "But the first time I saw you, I thought you looked familiar. I realize now, it's because you look like Helen.

"It's not an obvious resemblance," he continued. "But your bone structure is the same, your eyes are the identical shape and color, even the way you move is similar."

"That's hardly conclusive," she scoffed.

He nodded. "There's something else Helen mentioned."

She swallowed, not wanting to ask the question and yet not able to hold it back. "What's that?"

"A birthmark."

Her hand went instinctively to her hip.

"The baby Helen gave up for adoption had a heart-shaped birthmark exactly where yours is."

She couldn't lie about the birthmark or deny its existence—he'd seen it, touched it, kissed it. Maybe that's why she felt so betrayed by these disclosures now. How could he do this to her? How could he even suggest something so ridiculous—especially when he knew she had no interest in her birth mother.

She stared at him through eyes blurred with tears, and asked, "Why are you doing this, Richard?"

"Because I think the only way you're going to overcome your doubts and insecurities is to face the past."

"*You* think? How could *you* know anything about my doubts and insecurities?" she challenged. "How could *you* understand what it's like to be unwanted? How could you possibly imagine what it's like to be discarded and forgotten?"

"You weren't unwanted or forgotten," he said softly.

"Maybe that's what *you* think—but the reality tells a different story."

"Why don't you meet Helen before you jump to any conclusions?" he suggested.

She shook her head, hating that he sounded so damn logical and reasonable when the jumble of emotions inside her was anything but. "I don't want to meet her."

He studied her for a long moment, and she somehow sensed that he was disappointed in her response.

"Okay," he said at last.

Okay?

She eyed him warily.

"It has to be your choice," he said. "And when you're ready, I know you'll make the right one. You just need some time to think about it."

She thought about it.

Throughout the afternoon, Jenny sat in front of her blank computer screen unable to do anything but think about what Richard had told her.

Could it possibly be true? Could Richard's boss be her birth mother? Jenny didn't think so. But why would Richard even suggest it if he didn't believe it could be true? As much as she wanted to continue to deny the possibility, her curiosity about Helen Hanson was piqued.

She did an Internet search, found a few articles, some more pictures. Usually Helen was with George Hanson, the media mogul, and gazing through adoring eyes at her much older husband. He was a handsome man, Jenny had to admit, but she wondered if the woman had been attracted by his looks as much as by his much more impressive wealth. Then he'd died, and Helen had found out the wealth wasn't quite what she'd expected it to be.

Maybe that was why she'd cooked up this story about an adopted child now. If Richard mentioned Jenny's name to his boss, it would have been easy enough for Helen to find out that she'd been adopted—and by a very wealthy family. With that information, she'd probably decided it would be easier to claim a long-lost daughter with a hefty trust account than to try and save her husband's failing business.

After the debacle of Brad's recent proposal, it was the scenario that made the most sense to Jenny. It certainly made more sense than believing it was a simple coincidence that her lover's boss could be her biological mother.

"Every time I'm here, you're clicking away on that computer—and you accused me of being a workaholic."

Jenny jolted at the interruption.

As if conjured by her thoughts, Brad was suddenly there.

"I thought you'd be back in New York by now," she said.

"It seemed a shame to come all this way and not take the time to see Tokyo. I spent the weekend sightseeing."

At least she didn't need to worry that she'd broken his heart when she turned down his proposal.

"I'm heading back tomorrow," he told her. "But I wanted to say goodbye before I left."

He glanced past her to the computer monitor. She inwardly cursed herself for not thinking to close the window when he'd shown up.

"What are you working on?" he asked.

"Just doing some research for a story on the TAKA merger with Hanson Media."

"Doesn't sound very interesting."

"It's not a natural disaster or civil war, so I guess it wouldn't seem too interesting to you," she agreed.

"Wow." Brad ignored her comment, his attention focused on the picture on the screen. "The Hanson widow looks remarkably like you."

Now she did click to close the window. "They say we all have a twin somewhere in the world," she said lightly.

His gaze narrowed on her. "Yeah," he agreed at last. "That's probably it."

She forced a smile. "Have a good trip back."

"Maybe I'll see you in New York sometime?"

"Maybe."

He hesitated a moment before bending to kiss her cheek, then he was gone.

She exhaled a shaky sigh of relief. Unfortunately, it wasn't so easy to get rid of the thoughts about Helen Hanson that plagued her mind.

She hadn't given Richard an answer about dinner with Helen. She wasn't sure what her answer would be. Her initial instinct had been to refuse—as if considering the invitation would give too much credence to the possibility that Helen was her birth mother. Then she resolved to accept, if only to prove that the claim was completely erroneous. Brad's reaction to Helen's picture made her rethink this position. What could meeting Richard's boss possibly prove except that there were some similarities in their appearance?

She was still undecided when she showed up at his suite later that afternoon. He'd given back the key card she'd returned last week, but she took a deep breath to steady her nerves and knocked.

* * *

Richard felt the strain in his smile when he opened the door and saw Jenny standing there. His brain scrambled for an out from what he already knew was an impossible situation as he heard himself say, "You're early."

Her smile was warm. "I couldn't wait to see you."

Normally the admission would have filled him with satisfaction. But there was nothing normal about the situation she was about to walk into, and he felt only trepidation as she stepped past him and into the room.

She halted abruptly, and he knew she'd spotted Helen standing on the other side of the room. She looked at him—shock, hurt and a hint of fear in her eyes.

Before he had a chance to say anything, Helen turned.

He heard her suck in a breath as her eyes locked on the younger woman. Her eyes widened and her face went pale, as if she was seeing a ghostly apparition—or the daughter she'd given up.

"Oh, my God."

Jenny was the first to look away, silently pleading for his help. But he didn't know what to do. As much as he'd wanted the two women to meet, he hadn't wanted it to happen like this.

"You promised that it would be my decision," she said. Her words were barely more than a whisper, but he heard the echo of her hurt, her distress, the belief he'd betrayed her.

"I didn't plan this, Jenny."

"Just another unlikely coincidence?" she asked, her tone laced with skepticism.

"It is," he insisted.

Helen had remained silent, listening to their exchange, but she finally spoke to Jenny. "You're my daughter."

Jenny shook her head. "My mother is Dana Anderson."

"She's your adoptive mother," Helen clarified.

"She's the only mother I have—the only one that matters."

Helen flinched as she absorbed the harsh words that were more a reprimand than a statement of fact. But it was the stark pain in Jenny's eyes that squeezed Richard's heart.

While revealing the truth seemed to him the obvious—and maybe the only—way to start to heal the wounds of the past for both of them, he hadn't wanted it to happen like this. Yes, Jenny needed to hear why Helen gave her up, to know that she wasn't unwanted. And Helen needed to know the woman her child had become, to understand that she'd made the right decision all those years ago. But he wished he hadn't found himself tangled up in the middle.

"I didn't mean to upset you," Helen said softly. "I'm just so glad to finally meet my daughter."

"I'm *not* your daughter," Jenny said. But the denial was shaky and her eyes were filled with tears when she turned toward the door.

"Jenny, wait—"

But she was already out the door.

She went to her parents' house. With her entire world crumbling around her, Jenny couldn't think of anywhere to go but home.

Dana was pulling weeds out of her flower beds when she arrived, but one look at her daughter's face and she peeled off her gardening gloves and went to her. "What's wrong?"

She couldn't answer. Her throat was tight, her eyes swimming with tears.

Her mother took her hand and led her over to the porch. Jenny followed without protest, sitting down on the step beside her. It wasn't until her mother took her in her arms that Jenny let the tears fall. She couldn't hold them back any longer. Dana cuddled her as she had when she was a child, and Jenny cried as she hadn't cried since she was a child.

She cried until her eyes were swollen and her throat was raw, until she felt as if she didn't have any tears left inside.

Dana rubbed her hand over her back. "You're really starting to scare me, honey."

She lifted her head from the comfort of her mother's shoulder. "Sorry."

"I don't want you to be sorry, I want you to tell me what's wrong so I can help you."

"You've always been there for me," Jenny said. "Always, even when I didn't deserve it."

"You've always deserved it."

She managed a watery smile. "Even when I was a teenager, testing your patience?"

"Especially then." Dana kissed both of her daughter's tear-streaked cheeks. "No matter what, your dad and I will always love you."

Jenny blinked back fresh tears as she nodded, finally accepting it was true, acknowledging that the family she'd wanted so desperately had been there for her all along.

Richard checked her apartment and the newspaper, but couldn't find Jenny at either of those places. That left only one possibility that he could think of—her parents' home. While he wasn't anxious to face either Harold or Dana Anderson, his need to see Jenny left him with no other option.

Samara had given him the address, and Dana Anderson opened the door almost immediately after he pressed the bell.

"I need to see Jenny," he told her.

"She doesn't want to see you right now, Richard."

He wasn't surprised by the response, but he wouldn't let it deter him, either. "I'm not going anywhere until I talk to her."

Her lips curved ever so slightly. "I wonder if your stubbornness is any match for my daughter's."

"I'm not going to give up on her."

"You probably already know that Jenny doesn't do anything in half measures. When she loves, she loves completely. And when she hurts, she hurts deeply."

"I never wanted to hurt her."

"But that's what happened, isn't it?"

"I regret that Jenny met Helen the way she did," he said. "But I still believe she should know her birth mother."

"Because it's what your boss wants?" she challenged.

"Because it's what Jenny needs. I know you're her mother in every way that counts," he continued. "And Jenny knows that you love her, but she still has insecurities because of her adoption."

"You think knowing her birth mother will change that?"

"I think it's an important step."

"Even if it's not what she wants?"

He hesitated, then nodded.

"I happen to agree with you."

His surprise must have shown, because Dana smiled.

"Harold and I expected there would come a time when Jenny started asking questions about her adoption," she said. "But she never did. We knew she *had* questions—that was obvious in so many ways—but she never voiced them, at least not to us. I think she felt it would be disloyal to show any interest in her birth mother, or maybe she thought we would be hurt if she wanted to find her."

She sighed. "I saw how much she was hurting herself by keeping it all bottled up inside, and I tried to talk to her. Harold and I both did. But Jenny adamantly refused to discuss her birth mother and we never succeeded in forcing the issue."

"I don't think anyone forces Jenny to do anything."

"You do know my daughter."

"I love her, Mrs. Anderson."

Dana sighed again. "You're lucky Harold is in Singapore on business right now. He would have called the police and had you hauled off to jail for hurting his little girl."

"Am I safe in assuming you won't?"

"I won't," she agreed. "I also won't tell you that Jenny likes to sit by the pond out back when she needs to think."

Jenny was there, as her mother had said she would be.

Sitting alone on the grass, her chin resting on her bent knees, her arms wrapped around them. She looked like a child—lost and alone.

She didn't hear him approach, so Richard stood silent for several moments watching her, trying to find the words to repair the damage that he'd done. Her eyes were puffy and red-rimmed from crying, and he felt the sharp kick of guilt in his chest.

It didn't matter that he hadn't deliberately set up the meeting with Helen. What mattered was that he'd set everything in motion, and he was responsible for hurting her.

He sat down on the grass beside her.

She stiffened but gave no other indication that she was even aware of his presence.

They stayed that way, side by side and silent for several long minutes before he broke the silence. "How long do you think you can continue to ignore me?"

"Until you go away."

He shook his head. "You once accused me of being pushy. Well, I'm going to keep pushing until we deal with this."

"There's nothing to deal with."

He watched as a tear slid down her cheek, then another.

"I love you, Jenny."

She shook her head fiercely. "Don't you dare say that to me now."

"It's true."

"If it was true, you wouldn't have ambushed me."

"I didn't invite Helen to my hotel suite. I wouldn't do that to you. But now that you've met her—"

"I didn't want to meet her." She stood up, finally turning to face him. "I thought I made it perfectly clear that I had no interest in finding my birth mother—and that applies to anyone claiming to be my birth mother, too."

He was silent for a moment before he said, "You should have heard her talking about the baby she'd given up—the grief in her voice."

"You should have heard *me* when I said I didn't want to know the woman who gave me away."

"I heard you," Richard admitted. "I just couldn't believe you really meant it. I can't believe you don't have questions."

"About the mother who abandoned me at birth?" she asked scornfully.

"About her *reasons* for giving you up."

"Well, I don't."

He still didn't believe her, but he knew it would serve

no purpose to press the issue now. "Then I'm sorry," he said, accepting that he did owe her an apology for the way events had unfolded, for causing her pain even if it had been inadvertent.

He reached for her, wanting to offer her comfort, wanting to draw her closer. She seemed so distant now—her hurt and anger a tangible barrier between them.

She pulled away from him.

"Please don't let this come between us."

"You put it between us," she said coolly. "When you put Helen's needs before mine."

"Dammit, Jenny. That's not how it happened."

"Isn't it?"

"No. I was only thinking about you."

But his words didn't sway her. He could tell she didn't believe him. In her entire life, no man had ever put her first. Certainly none of her ex-boyfriends had, and he couldn't blame her for being skeptical now.

"You need to talk to Helen," he said gently. "You need to hear from her why she made the decisions she did. Maybe then you'll finally stop feeling like you've always been second best."

She shook her head. "I'll stop feeling that way when other people stop treating me that way."

Then she turned and walked back to the house.

Jenny felt numb. The hurt and anger and confusion had all been washed away by the flood of tears, leaving her feeling only empty inside. Her emotions now spent, her mind started to sift through the bits of information she'd been given, forcing her to face new questions she wasn't sure she was ready to have answered.

Dana knocked softly on her door before entering the bedroom. The mattress dipped slightly as she sat beside her daughter. "I saw Richard leaving."

She didn't respond.

"Do you feel better knowing you hurt him, too?" The gentle tone failed to mask the censure in the question.

Jenny scowled. "I can't believe you're taking his side."

Her mother sighed. "It's not about taking sides, but I do think he wants what's best for you."

"Best would be not having Richard Warren make decisions for me."

"What about Helen Hanson?" Dana asked. "What are you going to do about her?"

She shrugged. "Nothing."

Dana waited.

"Despite her claims, I don't believe she's the woman who gave birth to me."

"Why not?"

"It's just too unbelievable that our paths would happen to cross the way they did. It's like something out of a bad movie."

"It does seem unlikely," Dana said.

Jenny wondered why her mother's agreement failed to appease her.

"And I don't need some stranger coming into my life at this stage and making such outrageous claims," she continued.

Dana nodded. "If her claim is truly outrageous."

She frowned. "Do you believe it could be true?"

"Are you asking that question because you really don't believe it—or because you don't want to know?"

Jenny wasn't sure how to respond.

"Because if you want the truth—" Dana placed an envelope on the bed "—you'll find it in there."

She stared at the label, noted that it was addressed to Harold and Dana Anderson, but didn't touch the package. "What is it?"

"It's the report of a private investigator your father and I hired to find your birth mother."

"When—why—" She shook her head, trying to organize the questions that were swirling around inside her head.

"About ten years ago," Dana said. "Because we thought there would come a time when you wanted to know. Because we thought you should know."

"Is it…Helen Hanson?"

"The investigator told us he found her and he'd send the report. But we never read it. It was for you, Jenny, not for us."

She picked up the envelope with trembling fingers, turned it over. She traced a fingertip over the seal, but made no move to open it.

"I don't think Richard would have even suggested the possibility that there was a connection between you and Helen if he wasn't absolutely certain," Dana said. "But you can stay mad at him and take comfort in not knowing for certain, or you can open the envelope."

Chapter Sixteen

Jenny took the envelope with her when she went back to her apartment. She put it on the dresser in her bedroom, where it seemed to mock her while she tried to sleep. Finally, at around three a.m. when she finally gave up the pretense, she climbed out of bed and carried it into the living room.

She turned on the small lamp beside the sofa and sat for several long minutes with it in her hand. She knew it wasn't going to stop nagging at her unless she either opened it or burned it. At the moment, she was in favor of fire—she wanted only to obliterate this evidence that had the power to turn her whole life upside down.

But she knew that wouldn't really change anything. It certainly wouldn't make the questions go away.

She slid a shaky finger under the flap, tearing the seal.

Her heart was pounding as she pulled the pages out of the envelope, her throat dry as she unfolded them.

She felt as if she was on a roller coaster, waiting for the big dip.

Re: Jennifer Anderson.

As her eyes scanned the black typeface on the paper, her heart settled into a familiar rhythm. There were no rises or heart-stopping falls, no quick bends or stomach-clenching turns. There was no shock or disbelief or even any anger left, because the words confirmed what she'd already known in her heart.

She folded the papers up, tucked them back into the envelope and fell asleep on the sofa.

Richard was on his way out the door when he spotted Helen striding briskly down the hall toward his room. Her face was paler than usual, her eyes dull—almost defeated.

He stepped back to let her inside, instinctively knowing that whatever had brought her to his room this morning when they both should have been on their way to TAKA was something they wouldn't want to talk about in the hall.

"Mori Taka is threatening to pull out of our deal."

She made the announcement without preamble when he'd closed the door behind her.

Richard frowned. "He can't do that."

"He can if there were material misrepresentations," she said.

"What are you talking about?"

She handed him a copy of the morning paper. He felt the beginning of a chill as he looked at the pictures of

Jenny and Helen side by side, a chill that grew colder upon scanning the headline. "Unexpected Family Reunion or Deliberate Corporate Plant?

The icy feeling spread as he read further.

> That is the question TAKA executives are pondering this morning in wake of the revelation that one of their own employees, American-born journalist Jenny Anderson, is the biological daughter of Hanson Media Group's CEO, Helen Hanson.
>
> Ms. Anderson came to Tokyo from New York City shortly after the death of Helen's husband, George Hanson, at about the same time it was discovered that the U.S. media giant was in extreme financial trouble.

Richard folded the paper. He didn't need to read any more to know that the article would hurt Jenny deeply and could be disastrous for the merger. As unhappy as she'd been to find out that Helen was her mother, he could only imagine how she'd feel having that information announced to the public—especially with the implication that she was working behind the scenes to help facilitate the merger with TAKA.

He wished he could be there for her, but Jenny had shut him out. She wouldn't even talk to him—never mind let him help her come to terms with the revelation. The only thing he could do now was focus his attention on the merger. It was the reason he'd come to Tokyo—and the only thing he had left.

Jenny dumped the paper into the recycle bin. She'd always been a private person and she felt sick at the thought of the intimate details of her personal life splashed across the newspaper for public consumption. And she was furious at the implication that she would let herself be used by anyone—even her biological mother—as an inside spy. Beneath the hurt and the anger, she was also determined. She might not be able to undo the damage that had been done, but she could track down the reporter and find the "anonymous inside source" who was responsible.

But aside from her parents and Helen, Samara and Richard were the only ones who knew the truth. She trusted her best friend implicitly and never entertained the possibility that she would leak such a hurtful story. She was just as convinced that Richard wasn't responsible for the headlines. Even though she was angry with him right now, she didn't believe for a minute he would do something like this. Besides, he had nothing to gain from the publicity and a whole lot to lose. If TAKA used the revelations as an excuse to pull out of the merger, the repercussions for Hanson Media Group would be a lot worse than her personal angst.

While Jenny didn't have any ready suspects, she was a reporter and she did have contacts in the newspaper world. The *Herald* had got the story from someone, and she was determined to uncover that source.

Helen returned to Chicago and tried to go about the day-to-day business of running a company whose future was increasingly uncertain. She could blame George for leaving Hanson Media in a hell of a mess, but she knew her own actions since taking the helm had only compounded the problems.

She'd been reluctant to leave Tokyo—for a lot of reasons, but especially because she didn't want to lose the daughter she'd just found. She'd tried contacting Jenny, by calling her apartment and visiting the newspaper. But Jenny refused to see her and in the end, she'd accepted that her presence was needed at home. Richard had remained in Japan to continue discussions with TAKA.

The phone on her desk buzzed and she sighed. Just one more interruption in a never-ending series of them.

"Yes?" she asked wearily.

"Jenny Anderson is here to see you."

The weariness was immediately replaced by equal parts anticipation and trepidation. The way things had played out the last time she'd seen her daughter—the first time since she'd given her up—she'd believed it might very well be the last time she saw her.

She didn't know what it meant that Jenny was here now, but she was anxious to find out. "Send her in."

Helen pushed her chair back and stood up, brushing her hands down the front of the navy skirt she wore, smoothing imaginary wrinkles. Her heart was pounding furiously and her chest was tight.

Then Jenny was there, standing in the doorway, and the love for her child that she'd kept bottled up inside for so long spilled over.

Don't rush, Helen reminded herself. Don't push for too much too soon. She'd made that mistake once already.

Jenny was here—she'd taken that first step. For now, that was enough.

"Hello, Jenny."

Her daughter hovered on the threshold between the corridor and Helen's office, hesitant, uncertain. "I probably should have made an appointment with your secretary to set up a more convenient time to see you."

"Of course not," she denied immediately. "Please, come in."

Jenny took two steps into the room, the distance of at least ten feet and twenty-five years still separating them.

"I didn't know you were planning a trip to Chicago."

"I wasn't." She took another tentative step forward. "It was my parents' idea."

Her parents being Harold and Dana Anderson, of course. Helen wondered if the choice of words was deliberate or not.

"They thought I should talk to you," she continued. "And I agreed."

Helen waited.

Jenny was clutching the strap of her purse so tightly her knuckles were white. Helen wanted nothing more than to comfort her child, ease her obvious pain. But she didn't delude herself into thinking this was a reunion—it was a confrontation. Her daughter's next words proved that.

"I'd like you to answer some questions. I would have asked them earlier, but you left Tokyo less than forty-eight hours after dropping the bomb that blew apart my life."

Helen looked away. "You wouldn't take my calls. I couldn't stay in Japan indefinitely, hoping you would talk to me."

"Why did you leave?"

"The news created a crisis for Hanson and since I was responsible, I needed to deal with the repercussions of it personally."

"What would you know about responsibility? It seems to me you're best at walking away from it."

It was a well-aimed blow and Helen took the hit, accepting there would be a lot more before she and Jenny came to any understanding of the past—if they ever did. "I can't blame you for thinking that, but you don't understand the circumstances that existed twenty-five years ago."

"You didn't want to be bothered with a child." She shrugged. "It doesn't seem all that complicated to me."

Helen's own hurt was forgotten as her heart broke open for the obvious pain hidden deep within her daughter's deliberately casual response. "If that's what you really believe, why are you here?"

She shrugged again. "I guess I just wanted to hear you admit it."

After too many years of wondering, Jenny wanted only to put the questions and doubts behind her. She'd spent too much time wondering about her birth mother, imagining various scenarios to explain why she'd been given away.

What she'd read in the private investigator's report gave her some answers but no explanations. Helen had been sixteen when she got pregnant, and although Jenny could muster some sympathy for a teenage girl with no education or resources to care for a baby, she didn't understand the twenty-five years of silence that had followed. In that time, Helen moved away from her controlling parents, went to college and married a wealthy and successful businessman—all without expressing any interest in the child she'd given up.

"I can't tell you that," Helen said softly. "Because the truth is that I wanted you more than anything else in the world."

Jenny refused to be swayed by the tears she saw shining in the other woman's eyes—eyes that she could admit now were almost exactly like her own.

"But I was still in high school and my family refused to support me if I kept my baby. I didn't want you growing up in that kind of home, anyway. I wanted you to have a loving home—a real family."

She remained silent.

"You're still skeptical," Helen said.

"I don't know what I expected you to say," she admitted. "And I guess there's a part of me that can't help thinking you've had twenty-five years to come up with a good story."

Helen opened the bottom drawer of her desk and pulled out a stack of envelopes. She pushed them across the desk toward Jenny. "You're right," she said. "I've had twenty-five years. And those are the letters I wrote on your birthday on each of the past twenty-five years. I want you to have them. Maybe then you'll understand that I spent every day of those twenty-five years wondering if I'd made a mistake. Questioning if there might have been some way I could have made it work. Hoping you were truly happy with the family you'd been given."

Jenny picked up the bundle of letters, noted that the envelope on top had the current year inscribed on it.

"I was happy," she said. "My parents are wonderful."

Helen nodded.

"You would have known that if you'd made any effort to find me."

"I'd relinquished my rights—along with my responsibilities—when I gave you up."

Jenny hesitated before asking, "If you really wished you could have kept me, why didn't you ever have any more children?"

"I wanted children," Helen told her. "More than anything, I wanted a baby to hold in my arms, to fill the emptiness in my heart that had been there since the day I gave you up. And we tried. George had three sons and I'd had you, so there didn't seem to be any reason we couldn't have a child of our own."

She looked away. "We tried everything, until I finally accepted that not being able to have another baby was my punishment for letting go of the one I'd been given."

Jenny felt the sting of tears in her own eyes. Regardless of what she wanted to believe, there was no denying the emotion she heard in Helen's voice.

She swallowed around the tightness in her throat. "It was Brad Morgan who leaked the story to the press."

Helen frowned. "The reporter?"

"And my ex-boyfriend," she admitted.

"Why did he do it?"

"To get back at me for rejecting him. I think he knew I decided not to marry him because of Richard, and it would have been a way to get back at him, too. But his primary motive was probably financial. I heard he was paid well for the exclusive."

"What is the situation with you and Richard?" Helen asked gently.

"There is no situation," she said.

"You're still angry with him, too," she guessed.

"No. Maybe." She sighed. "It doesn't really matter."

"Of course it matters."

Jenny shook her head.

"He loves you, Jenny. And you wouldn't still be hurting so much if you didn't love him, too."

She felt a sharp pang of regret, but accepted that the end of their relationship had always been inevitable.

"He called me yesterday," Helen continued.

Jenny didn't ask why. She told herself she didn't want

to know. It still hurt too much to think about everything they might have had.

"TAKA has agreed to resume negotiations," she explained, "and Richard needed my consent to put another condition on the table."

Helen paused, as if waiting for some kind of response, but she remained silent.

"He wants a position with Hanson in Tokyo when the merger goes through."

Jenny's gaze flew to Helen's; the other woman smiled.

"I told him it seemed like a reasonable request," she continued.

"Why?" Jenny asked softly.

"Obviously he wants to stay in Japan, and I can think of only one reason he would do that."

"He's starting to like sushi?" she asked weakly.

Helen laughed, then turned serious. "He loves you, Jenny, and he wants a chance to prove it."

Jenny tried to sort out her thoughts and feelings about Richard throughout the thirteen-hour flight back to Japan, but when the plane finally landed, she was still no closer to any answers. Despite Helen's assertion that Richard wanted to stay in Tokyo, she was afraid to let herself hope they could get past all the misunderstandings and build a future together.

She'd called her mother from the airport to let her know she was coming home. Dana had told her that she and Harold were going up to the cabin for a few days but would make arrangements for a car to pick Jenny up and drive her there. She was already looking forward to the peace and serenity of the lake, hoping the answers that eluded her might be found there.

It was almost nine p.m. when the car finally pulled into the narrow laneway that led to the cabin and Jenny was struggling to stay awake. Even though she'd only been gone a few days, her internal clock was having difficulty adjusting to the time difference, and she was looking forward to falling into bed and sleeping for twelve hours straight.

She didn't see him on the porch. She'd walked right past him, her hand reaching for the handle of the door, when the first notes of the music registered.

Her heart skipped a beat, then began thudding frantically against her ribs when she turned and saw Richard.

She swallowed, tried to speak, but her throat was tight. As the music played, memories of the night they'd sang this song together—the first night they'd made love—flooded over her, swamping her with emotion. It was the same night—though she wouldn't admit it until a long time later—she'd fallen in love.

Richard took a step toward her. "It's about time you got here."

She couldn't deny she was a little disappointed. She wasn't sure what she'd expected him to say, but after everything they'd been through, after coming home and finding him here, she'd expected…more.

"Have you been waiting long?" she asked, matching his casual tone.

He smiled as he took her hand in his, linked their fingers together. "I've been waiting for you forever."

And with those words, her heart simply melted. It wasn't just the incredibly romantic words, it was the sincerity in his voice and the love shining in his eyes. It was the "more" she'd been hoping for, and then some.

"I love you, Jenny."

Her throat was tight again, but she managed to respond. "I love you, too."

"Enough to marry me?" he asked. Then, with his free hand, he pulled a box out of his pocket and flipped open the lid.

She gasped softly and took an instinctive step back.

"That's not quite the reaction I was hoping for," Richard said.

Her gaze darted from his face to the gold band sparkling with diamonds, and back again, while the music continued to play in the background. "You can't mean it."

"Why can't I?"

"Because you don't want to get married."

"I've got a ring right here that says otherwise," he told her.

"You don't have to do this, Richard."

"I *want* to."

She swallowed. "Why?"

"Because I love you, and I'm hoping you'll overlook all the things I've done to screw up our relationship and marry me anyway."

This time her heart did sing with joy, but she forced herself to show some restraint. She didn't want him to feel pressured or coerced in any way. She needed to know that he wanted this as much as she did.

"We both screwed up," she said softly.

"Yeah, but that doesn't make a very romantic sounding proposal."

She smiled. "You have a point."

"And you still haven't answered my question."

"I don't remember actually hearing a question."

His gaze was unwavering, the love he felt shining clearly in his eyes. "Will you marry me, Jenny?"

She exhaled an unsteady breath.

"You better mean it," she warned him. "Because if I put that ring on, I'm not ever taking it off."

He reached for her hand and slid the circle of diamonds onto her finger.

It fit perfectly.

Jenny didn't know what time it was when Richard shook her awake, she only knew that when she opened her eyes it was still dark and, therefore, obviously not morning. She closed her eyes again.

"If you don't get up, you're going to miss the sunrise," he warned.

"It'll happen again tomorrow," she reminded him.

"I want to see it today," he said. "And if you don't get up and get dressed, I'll carry you outside naked."

She didn't doubt it. After last night, she wasn't sure there was anything he wouldn't do. She pushed herself up and tried to stifle a yawn. "I thought you weren't a morning person."

He smiled. "I wasn't—until I had the life-altering experience of making love with you as the sun rose."

"Life-altering?" she said skeptically, tugging on the clothes that had been hastily shed beside the bed the night before.

"Absolutely." He brushed his lips over hers. "Come on, I've got coffee on."

She stifled another yawn as she followed him down the hall. She took her cup of coffee outside, cradling it in her hands as she snuggled against Richard's chest. Despite her teasing, she understood what he meant about life-altering experiences, and she knew that meeting him had been such an experience for her.

He'd helped her to face her past and inspired her to look forward to their future. He'd shown her what it was to truly love and be loved. He'd done so much for her, she'd wanted to do something for him in return. It had seemed like a good idea at the time, but now she wasn't sure if he'd appreciate her effort or think she'd overstepped her bounds.

In either case, she wasn't going to embark on a future with any secrets between them.

"There's something I meant to tell you last night—before we got distracted."

"What is it?"

"When I went to the States, I didn't just go to Chicago."

"Where'd you go?"

"Crooked Oak, North Carolina."

She felt the tension in the arm that was wrapped around her, although his voice was neutral when he spoke. "I didn't know you knew anyone there."

"I didn't," she admitted. "Not until I met your mother."

He didn't say anything.

"I thought, since it was a trip about mending fences, that I would make the effort."

He sighed. "I appreciate what you were trying to do, Jenny, but you don't know my family."

"She misses you, Richard. She knows she was wrong to say the things she said, to make the demands she made. She just doesn't know how to bridge the gap she's created between you—or even if you want her to." She turned to face him. "She didn't even know you were in Japan."

He shrugged, but she saw the flicker of guilt in his eyes. "I haven't talked to her in a while."

"You should call her."

He hesitated briefly, then nodded.

"Will you?" she asked, pressing for verbal confirmation.

"I'll call her," he agreed.

She smiled and leaned forward to press a brief kiss to his lips. "Thank you."

"I should probably be thanking you," he said. "But I'm not convinced this is going to work."

"It will," she said confidently. "If I can overcome the barriers of twenty-five years to patch things up with Helen, you can reconcile with your mother."

"This really matters to you, doesn't it?"

She nodded. "Because you reminded me how important family is, and I know how much yours means to you." She smiled. "And because I want a big traditional wedding and they're your family."

"Except that you couldn't have known I was going to propose when you went to see my mother."

She shrugged. "Maybe I figured I owed you some interference after you made me confront my past."

"You can spend the rest of your life interfering in mine," he told her.

"I will," she said. "Forever."

Gold and crimson light spilled into the sky as their lips met—the signal of a new day and the promise of a new life together.

* * * * *

MERGERS & MATRIMONY

BY
ALLISON LEIGH

Chapter One

She was never going to be happy again.

Why couldn't she stop that thought from circling her head?

Helen Hanson quietly rose from her chair and made her way from the wedding reception. Not a single person sitting at the crystal-bedecked table gave her a second glance. Why would they? They were all virtual strangers, connected strictly because of their connection to the bride, who'd already departed the reception with her devoted groom.

The ballroom was *filled* with people who were virtual strangers. And the ones who weren't strangers—most of them, anyway—would probably be glad of Helen's absence, should they happen to notice.

Her knees felt weak. Her heart was thudding. She very much feared she was beginning to sweat.

Perhaps she was having a hot flash.

She was only forty-one, but that didn't mean much. Menopause? Perimenopause? Simple insanity?

She pasted a pleasant smile on her face as she nodded blankly at the gazes she happened to intercept while she wound through the tables.

She might be falling apart, but she'd be damned if she'd let it show.

She was never going to be happy again.

"Stop it," she whispered to herself as she slipped out into the solitude of the corridor. The narrow heels of her Manolos sank into the thick ivory carpet and she pressed her palm flat against the silky-sheened wallpaper, steadying herself.

A young couple, laughing, rounded the corner at the end of the hall and Helen lowered her hand, managing another smile.

"Mrs. Hanson," the young woman, Samara, greeted her. "Didn't Jenny look beautiful?"

Helen nodded. Samara had been Jenny's maid of honor. "She did. As do you."

The girl flushed prettily and waved a little as her date dragged her back to the reception.

Alone again, Helen's smile faded and she walked down the hall. She wanted nothing more than to escape. To close herself in her hotel room where she could replace her couture gown with her soft fleecy sweats that were about a hundred years old and bury her head in her pillows. There, she wouldn't have to maintain the smile, the pleasant facade, the veneer of confidence that was meant to assure everyone that she knew what she was doing.

Damn you, George.

Wasn't anger one of the typical stages of grief? If it was, she didn't feel as if she'd ever get off that particular tread-board.

Her eyes burned and she started to duck into the ladies' restroom, but the sound of feminine laughter coming from inside stopped her, and she kept walking down the hall, turning corners, this way and that, only reversing her direction once again when she'd reached the kitchen and realized she was getting in the way of the busy catering staff.

She hauled in a shaking breath, smoothing her hands over the sides of her drawn-back hair.

Get a grip, Helen.

This is a happy day.

Jenny's wedding day. Your *daughter's* wedding day. To a man, a truly good man whom Helen considered a friend, even.

She closed her eyes for a moment.

It *was* a blessing. Jenny and Richard were married. And Jenny had *wanted* Helen to be there. The baby girl that she'd given up so very long ago had welcomed her.

Helen had no reason for tears.

They burned behind her eyes, anyway.

"Mrs. Hanson."

The voice was deep. Only slightly accented. It could have belonged to any man, anywhere.

She still recognized it, and it made her spine go ramrod straight.

She wasn't just anywhere. She was in Tokyo.

And he wasn't just any man.

She blinked hurriedly, then angled her chin toward him, sending him a pleasant smile. "Mr. Taka," she greeted. "I hope you and your guest are enjoying the festivity."

Morito Taka—she knew some called him Mori, but those who did were close to him, which she was not—did not have an expression of happiness on his stern countenance. He looked the way he'd looked in every business meeting he'd grudgingly taken with her. Disinterested, aloof and completely dispassionate.

"Jenny and Richard, all of us, are honored by your presence this evening." The words were as sincere as she could make them. Not only was Jenny employed by a TAKA-owned newspaper, but it had been Helen's idea for Hanson Media Group to climb into bed with TAKA. It was the only way to save the company her husband had left in shambles. But that didn't mean she had enjoyed a moment of the experience.

"You seem...disturbed." He made the comment almost unwillingly. His gaze—so dark a brown it was almost obsidian—was unwavering.

She'd seen an occasional picture of the Japanese mogul before they'd met face-to-face—all part of her research—but it had in no way armed her for just how disconcerting that gaze was, even now after months of warily circling a business deal she'd managed to engineer. A deal that would either justify George's only real desire of her, or put her family's business entirely within this man's power.

The man himself was disconcerting, when it came down to it. And she couldn't exactly pin down the reason why. Morito Taka didn't stand as tall as George—he certainly didn't top six feet the way her late husband had. At forty-seven, he was also a couple of decades younger than George had been. His dark hair was very closely cropped, as were his mustache and goatee, the latter of which sported the slightest hint of gray.

She supposed some might consider the man handsome.

She, however, was more concerned with the intentions behind those hawkish eyes.

"Women cry at weddings," she demurred. "I'm sure that isn't a habit owned wholly by Americans."

He almost smiled. She hoped. She couldn't quite tell. Not with the way the man's features were so strongly carved. There was nothing particularly friendly about Morito Taka's looks. He didn't possess the nearly constant smile of hospitality and hopefulness to please that his associates did.

Probably why she'd dreamed about him the other night. The man was a warrior. And she'd been the enemy who'd been more of a not-entirely-unwilling quarry.

Today, he wore a beautifully tailored tuxedo, in honor of the occasion. In her dream, he'd worn—

She brushed away the unwelcome thought, the way she had been for weeks. The man was only showing up in her dreams because of the power he held. It meant *nothing* more than that.

"You are not sitting with your family," he observed smoothly.

She didn't allow her smile to waver. Her three stepsons and their significants were scattered about the table seating in the reception. It might be a social event, but none of them could afford a missed opportunity for networking with the TAKA powers-that-be. But as the reception had worn on, as the champagne had flowed ever more freely, it had been natural for the family members to begin congregating.

She was always pleased to see the family together. She liked to think that during the long months since their father died, George's boys had become closer as a result of having to work together to save their heritage—Hanson Media Group. They'd all, each of them, even found happiness and love.

She also liked to think that she might have played some part in that.

But she wasn't naive, either. The boys—none of them truly boys, but that was how George had thought of them—tolerated her presence because they had to. Not because they particularly wanted to.

Jenny and Richard's reception was no exception.

"I was sitting with friends of Jenny's family."

"But not your sons."

Thank you for pointing that out. She somehow managed not to flinch. "My husband's sons," she clarified, even though he knew that fact perfectly well. He knew most every personal detail about her, including the fact that she'd had a child—Jenny—when she was little more than a child herself. When the scandal of that secret broke, he'd tried putting the kibosh on the TAKA-Hanson merger.

First of all, Jenny was an employee of TAKA. But once it had been established that she was *not* a plant of Hanson Media's, there'd still been the scandal of it.

And heaven forbid scandal touch the pristine TAKA juggernaut. Nevertheless, good business sense had obviously overridden Morito's distaste for dirty laundry, because the TAKA lawyers were still meeting with them.

"Your husband's sons," he allowed. "It must be difficult."

She waited a moment, not entirely certain which "it" he was referring to. "I'm sorry, I don't know—"

"Your loss. It is recent. Clearly, it still affects you."

George had died nine months ago. Morito undoubtedly knew that, just as she knew how long ago he'd taken charge of TAKA from his father, Yukio—a transition that hadn't gone entirely smoothly, though she'd had to dig a little to learn that fact. "Yes, it does affect me," she agreed quietly. "You lost your wife, too."

"Many years ago."

"I'm sorry."

He inclined his head a few bare inches, but it was enough to acknowledge the sentiment. She was vaguely surprised. He didn't usually seem even that human. "Your guest will be missing you," she said, hoping that he would go, and go quickly, back to the side of the very beautiful young woman who had accompanied him to the reception.

"You left because you were unwell?"

"No. I'm not unwell. I'm fine."

"One rarely seeks privacy for...happy crying. You seemed distressed."

The fact that it was this man, of all men, to notice that particular detail didn't thrill her.

The fact that her eyes started burning all over again delighted her even less. She swallowed and was very much afraid that her smile was unraveling around the edges.

His eyes narrowed and he made a soft sound under his breath. "Come." He extended one hand, long-fingered, slightly bony and definitely masculine below the perfectly short cuff. "I know a quiet place."

Now that she wasn't blocking the kitchen entrance, the corridor *was* fairly quiet. She didn't want his sympathy, or his comfort. She wanted the miracle the merger with TAKA would provide. Only then would she ever feel some semblance of contentment again.

Only then would she have proven she had at least *some* value.

His fingers touched her elbow.

Human contact. From him again, of all people.

Her eyes burned hotter. She ignored it. She should be used to ignoring her own pain; she'd been doing it for weeks. Months. Years.

She glanced up at him, the "thank you" on her lips disappearing as silently as a popping soap bubble.

His eyelashes were thick, she noted inconsequentially.

"Thank you," the tardy words emerged, soft and husky.

He bowed briefly, impersonally.

But his gaze dropped briefly, tellingly, to her lips.

She managed to keep herself from stumbling over her own high heels as he guided her along the corridor. Maybe she *was* losing her mind. She was accustomed to the way men often looked at her.

She'd never expected such a look coming from Morito Taka.

Definitely losing her mind.

Music drifted after them. They could have been in any luxurious hotel in any part of the world. But they were in an Anderson hotel, owned by the man who'd adopted her baby girl a lifetime ago.

They entered a silent elevator, yet he didn't release

her elbow. She was privately shocked, both by that fact, and by the fact that she was grateful for the support.

Even if it did come from him.

She didn't ask where they were going, or why he wasn't returning to the woman who'd accompanied him.

Instead, she stared blindly at the gleaming number display as they ascended. Her stomach felt weightless.

The elevator's doing.

Only the sensation didn't abate when the elevator stopped, and they stepped out, directly into some sort of atrium.

Plants grew in lush abandon, so different in tone from the gardens she'd become accustomed to on her visits to Tokyo. Those gardens were undeniably beautiful in their scrupulous detail and precision. This indoor garden was beautiful, but wildly so.

"Please sit." Morito directed her to an iron bench, padded in scarlet silk, placed beneath the draping fronds of some weeping tree she couldn't hope to identify.

She sat and his hand finally fell away from her elbow. He, however, didn't sit. He moved away several feet, and focused his intense attention on another tree that stood at least fifteen feet tall.

She looked upward. The ceiling was there, eventually. Most of it was glass. Her gaze moved back to Morito. His long fingers were touching a tree leaf.

Caressing it.

She looked away. Focused beyond the clusters of bushes to realize the atrium wasn't only an atrium. A hotel suite lay beyond.

"Is this your room?" She hoped the muted light masked her flush from the abrupt question.

"Hai." He gave her an inscrutable sidelong glance.

It wasn't merely a room. Nor a luxurious suite. It was a penthouse the likes of which even she was unaccustomed. And she'd grown accustomed to plenty as the wife of George Hanson.

The trophy of George Hanson.

The words circled inside her mind, mocking her.

She rose. "May I look around?" She nodded toward the living area beyond the small jungle. A winding stream of water flowed cleverly beneath the floor, enhancing the room's delineation.

"Hai."

She crossed the floor that was really a bridge over the water, and eyed the wall display opposite her.

Swords. Masks. Vases. Artifacts that looked as if they belonged in a museum somewhere rather than a hotel. She walked closer to the swords. They weren't encased under protective glass. She had the sense that she could have reached up and removed one from the wall, if she'd wanted. She stepped closer, studying the detail on the handle.

"It was my great-great-grandfather's. One of the last of the samurai."

Not just a hotel penthouse, then, but Morito's penthouse? The irony that Jenny's family owned the hotel where Mori Taka evidently *lived* struck her.

She wasn't going to wonder where his lovely companion, presumably still waiting downstairs for him, figured into the equation. "It's remarkable. The entire collection is remarkable. Also family heirlooms?"

"Yes."

"The only thing my family has of my great-grandparents' is the family bible." A bible that would have contained Jenny's name, if Helen had been stronger in the face of her father's anger. "All the births are recorded in the front of it," she elaborated.

He slid the sword off the wall. "Tradition," he murmured, studying the weapon. "It is important. Many families are forgetting that."

He held the sword comfortably. Confidently. The deadly blade was nowhere near her, yet she still felt a nervous jolt inside her. The way of the samurai had passed…hadn't it?

"And do you conquer your adversaries with the sword, still?" She kept her voice light.

His gaze transferred from the sword to her face. "Then the attorneys, yours and mine, would be left with no enjoyment at all."

It took her a moment to realize he'd made a joke. The corners of his lips were curved ever so slightly upward.

She smiled. "Very true."

Silence settled, and she realized she was still looking at the smile that so subtly touched his lips. Well-defined lips in a well-defined face.

He'd wielded a sword in her dream, too.

"Well," she said suddenly, "I should get back downstairs before they begin wondering where I've gone."

"Hai."

She was grateful he didn't voice the suspicion that nobody was likely to miss her presence no matter *how* long she was gone. "Thank you for your time, Mr. Taka. It was very kind of you."

"I am rarely kind, Mrs. Hanson." He replaced the sword on the wall. "I am certain you know that. Perhaps

I, too, needed a reason to excuse myself from the celebration."

"I can't imagine a man like you wanting to excuse yourself from someone as lovely as your companion." A companion who was undoubtedly twenty years—or more—his junior.

Which was the same thought most people had had upon seeing her with George.

"She is lovely," he agreed noncommittally. He walked with her across the bridge and pressed the button for the elevator. The doors immediately opened. "Your sons should be ashamed of themselves."

Whatever relaxation she might have obtained in this odd garden-penthouse-museum immediately fled. She could feel the vertebrae down her spine slipping into stiff alignment. "I don't believe my stepsons have done anything of which they should be ashamed."

She only wished they knew—could accept—just how proud she was of them. They'd all come a long way since George's death, but to say they had a warm, familial relationship was grossly overstating reality.

Helen was determined to face reality. She'd spent enough of the last several years living in something that had been anything but.

"They have a duty to you, yet they have openly shown disrespect," Morito stated.

"They are grown men who are free to express their opinions." Her tone went a little thin. Jack, the eldest, was only six years her junior. "Perhaps what you've interpreted as disrespect is merely open communication among the Hanson Media Group family. It was something my late husband valued," she added, mentally crossing her fingers. While alive, George had never valued anyone's opinion except his own. She may have realized it during his lifetime, but it wasn't until after his death that she'd had to truly face the consequences of it. "You're a businessman, Mr. Taka. I'm sure you understand the value of many ideas being brought to the table, even when those ideas are dissenting."

"A wedding is not a meeting being held around the thirtieth-floor conference room table," he countered. "Perhaps if your husband were still alive, he would—"

"But he's not alive," she responded evenly. "I understand you would have preferred to deal with my husband, Mr. Taka." Ironic, since George had been keeping a separate set of books on Hanson Media Group, disguising the fact that the company was on the verge of ruin. "Or that you would prefer to deal with my stepson, Jack." She stepped into the elevator and turned to face him. "However, I hold the controlling interest in Hanson Media Group, so—as we say in my country—I'm afraid you're stuck with me."

His hand lifted, holding the doors from closing. "Ah, Mrs. Hanson. Do not forget." His lips curved upward again, but the motion only heightened the hardness of his high, squarely sculpted cheekbones. "Currently, you are not in your country. You are in mine."

He moved his hand and took one step back.

Helen stared at the dull reflection of herself in the doors as they closed. Her breath slowly leaked out.

"Oh, George," she whispered. "I gave you my heart and you gave me...this."

A floundering family who'd never wanted her, a sinking company and the responsibility for saving both.

Maybe she never *would* feel real happiness again. Not the kind that Jenny and Richard were experiencing. Maybe she'd never felt that in the first place, and the delirious emotions she'd felt when she'd first married George had been nothing more than a figment of her imagination.

But she'd just been firmly reminded that she didn't have the luxury of worrying about it. Not when so much stood at stake and the man who could make or break them was a modern-day warrior named Morito Taka.

Chapter Two

Trophy Wife to Media Madame?

Helen sighed, reading the headline plastered across the front of the oversize magazine.

Would the gossip never end?

The headline was accompanied by a splashy photograph of her and George from years earlier. She looked exactly what the headline proclaimed—the epitome of trophy wifedom. Not a blond hair out of place from the big, wavy affair that stretched down her back. Diamonds glittering from every point—ears, throat, wrists, fingers. The black dress was hardly sedate, either. It was cut down to there, and cut up to there. And the man beside her, George, had looked like a beefy gray bear with his proprietary arm heavy on her shoulder.

She eyed his image. She'd changed since that photo

had been taken, admittedly, mostly during the past year. No longer did she favor the big hair that George had claimed to adore. The jewelry he'd bestowed upon her, except a few narrow bracelets, her favorite watch and a tasteful necklace or two, had all been relegated to the safe back home and she didn't care if she ever wore the rest again. There were days lately when she felt as if she ought to have locked away her wedding ring, as well.

George had placed the ring on her finger all those years ago in a ceremony on an exotic beach that neither his family nor hers had even known about until after the fact.

She needed to take off the ring, yet wearing it was a reminder of what she was doing—and why.

She brushed her finger over the printed photograph. Yes, she'd changed mightily. But George hadn't.

She waited for the familiar wave of grief, but it didn't come.

She sighed again and turned the cover to the article inside, but her mind wasn't really on the rehashed story of the problems Hanson Media Group had found itself embroiled in.

Hanson Media Group had proved themselves innocent in the recent porn scandal involving their Web site, so why couldn't the gossip rags catch up with that?

She slapped the magazine closed and shoved it aside. The plate of fresh fruit and yogurt she'd ordered for breakfast held little appeal and she pushed that aside, as well, picking up her cup of coffee instead.

She probably should have stayed at her own hotel. Had her breakfast in her suite.

But she'd felt restless, particularly since Evan, Meredith, Andrew and Delia had departed for Chicago earlier that morning. Jack and Samantha had accompanied them all to the airport.

And somehow, Helen had ended up back at the Anderson hotel.

All around her, morning diners were rushing in and out of the dining room. Businessmen hunched over laptop computers while they sucked down coffee and talked on cell phones. Families waved travel brochures about and argued which sights they wanted to see that day. It was no different than any other morning she'd spent in Tokyo, yet that morning *was* different.

Jenny and Richard were married and had headed off for a brief honeymoon—all that they would allow themselves at this critical juncture of the TAKA deal—despite Helen's assurance that they should take however much time they desired.

And Helen had ended the prior evening by not endearing herself any to the exalted Morito Taka.

She rubbed her fingertip over the pain that throbbed beneath her right eyebrow. There was yet another meeting scheduled for the following afternoon with Morito and his merger and acquisitions people.

She wished it were scheduled sooner. Having to wait around more than twenty-four hours for Morito Taka to pull the plug because of her behavior the night before was wearing on her. She'd hardly slept at all and she was definitely feeling it. She wanted to snap at every person who came within five feet of her, and it was such an unaccustomed crankiness that she annoyed even herself.

She propped her elbow on the horrid gossip magazine and sipped her coffee. At the table beside her, two teenagers were trying to convince their parents that an amusement park was more appealing than the Imperial Palace garden.

Pick the garden, Helen silently commented. Amusement parks—fun though they were—abounded elsewhere, after all.

"Doing your morning reading, Mrs. Hanson?"

She jerked, spilling a drizzle of coffee over the white linen table cloth. Swallowing a curse that would surely have convinced him that she was just as coarse as he seemed to believe, she looked up at the man standing over her.

He was uncommonly tall for a Japanese man, she thought, not for the first time, and resisted the urge to stand. She might feel on more equal footing if she had, but asserting herself at the moment was probably not wise.

"Good morning, Mr. Taka." Helen summoned a pleasant smile from somewhere inside her and pinned it on her face, taking in both him and his companion—the young woman from the reception. The girl looked even more perfectly beautiful and perfectly young in the unforgiving morning light that streamed through the tall windows than she had the evening before. "Can I offer you both some coffee?" She settled her hand atop the fine silver coffeepot that sat in the middle of her table.

"I never acquired the taste for coffee," Morito said. His gaze was still on the gossip rag. His expression showed little, but Helen nevertheless sensed his disapproval.

It was the same sense she'd gotten from him since their first meeting.

The woman with him settled her long, slender hand on his arm, speaking softly. Helen's Japanese was still too shaky to follow what she said, and she made no attempt to try. Instead, she pretended not to notice the short response Morito gave to his companion, or the unmistakable credit card he removed from his pocket and handed to her. The woman bowed, expressed a musical "goodbye" to Helen, and then glided out of the dining room, her sheaf of gleaming brown hair swaying around her slender waist.

Helen looked back at Morito. "I'm sure it would take only a moment for tea to be brought, if you'd like."

"Thank you, Mrs. Hanson, but I will decline. I have business to attend to." His voice was polite, but cold. "Please enjoy your morning and your…reading."

Her molars clenched a little. "I wasn't actually enjoying this reading," she said just as politely. "But an older man in the company of a younger woman always seems to strike a popular note." Her gaze transferred briefly to his departing companion. "I'm sure you've experienced that yourself." She couldn't believe the words came out of her mouth.

His expression didn't change, but she knew with uncanny certainty that the unsubtle jab had hit its mark.

She felt no pleasure in it, however. Only more annoyance with herself for letting the man needle her. She—Hanson Media Group—*needed* this man. Why was she having such difficulty lately remembering that?

"I would feel no shame being photographed with my cousin." His voice was smooth. "As you have said, she is a lovely young woman. Now, if you will excuse me." He inclined his head and moved away before she could summon an apology.

She didn't bother cursing, now. She simply pulled out

enough yen from her minuscule purse to cover the check that had not yet been delivered, and strode after him.

Her heels clicked on the gleaming floor, joining the morning cacophony. She quickened her step, following right after him as he left the building. She was probably breaching the rules of etiquette in a dozen ways, but she couldn't let herself worry about it as she practically sprinted after him. If she didn't catch him before he entered his waiting vehicle, she wouldn't have a chance at this until their meeting the next day.

She already felt on the defensive during their meetings—she didn't need to add to it.

"Mr. Taka." She reached out and touched his arm from behind.

He stopped on the sidewalk, five yards from the teeming road, and gave her fingers a seemingly deadly look.

She let go, knowing she'd made yet another gaffe. "*Sumimasen*. I'm sorry. I made an unforgivably rude comment, Mr. Taka, and I apologize. I hope you'll accept it."

Mori stared at the blond woman standing close beside him. She seemed ignorant of the throng of people flowing around them like water separated by an annoying boulder. "Why?"

Her eyebrows drew together. She had a very narrow face, he thought. Everything about her seemed narrow. Tall. White.

She often dressed in white.

He wished he were not as aware of her as he was. He wished she were not insistent on attending every meeting concerning the takeover. She could have delegated the responsibility to someone else as she had done earlier in the process.

"Why should you accept my apology?" Her voice was low. Smooth. It possessed none of the lilting notes of the voices of the women in his life. And her gaze met his straight on. Another uncommon trait. Not just among women, but among men.

He should have found her bold gaze rude.

Instead, he found himself comparing the color of her eyes to the jade paperweight that his daughter had given him for his last birthday.

He did not like women such as Helen Hanson. But the female standing before him intrigued him, nevertheless.

His driver was waiting nearby on the sidewalk, prepared to open the door for Mori the moment he stepped toward the car. Mori ignored him. "Why does it matter to you? Our negotiations are beyond the point of worrying over small offenses." This was not strictly true. He held the power to pull out TAKA at any point he chose.

Despite his father's dissenting opinion, Mori did not yet choose to take that action.

"Then I hope you'll accept my apology because I'm not ordinarily rude." Her gaze didn't waver. "To anyone."

"So you chose to practice on me?"

A tide of pink flowed over her cheekbones. "I was irritated. Because of the magazine I was reading. I shouldn't have taken it out on you."

He understood what she was saying, but remained silent, still studying her. She wore trousers like a man, and a jacket like a man. But the white silk was closely tailored, following her lithe figure as finely as his custom-made suits fit him, and what it covered was *not* a man.

From his vantage point, he could see the pearl suspended by a thin gold chain where it rested a bare inch above the buttoned lapel of her jacket, and practically sense the velvety moistness of her skin in the morning humidity.

She took his silence for misunderstanding, though. "What I mean is that I shouldn't have turned my irritation with that ridiculous article toward you."

"The article was untrue?"

Her lips pressed together for a moment. "It was gossip."

"Fabricated?"

"Trivial, outdated and slanted. I'd hoped that publications like that would have moved on to some other topic by now rather than continuing to dwell on the past travails of Hanson Media Group."

"*Are* they in the past?" An Internet porn scandal. The revelation of a secret baby. Neither were things which he wanted even distantly associated with TAKA. No matter how advantageous it would be for TAKA to acquire Hanson's not inconsiderable U.S. assets.

She angled her head. She had high heels on her narrow feet and was only slightly shorter than he as a result. "I'm confident that they are well past, as you must be, Mr. Taka, or I doubt you and I would be having this conversation at all."

"We are having this conversation because you wanted to assure yourself of not causing me offense," he reminded.

"An assurance I still don't have," she observed. But there was no heat in the words. And her gaze still didn't swerve from his.

He found himself smiling a little. He was Japanese to his soul, but he'd had a European education. Something about the woman reminded him of those days when he had been...freer. "You are considered bold in America?"

Now, she looked wry. "I'm quite average, I'm afraid."

"That I do find difficult to believe," he admitted. If she really were an average American businesswoman, her narrow feet would not have made it past TAKA's lobby. "I accept your apology. And now you must accept mine for excusing myself." He actually felt reluctant to do so.

"Of course." She stepped back, reminding him of a tall white candle the way she stood among the navy uniforms of the cluster of schoolchildren marching by. "Until tomorrow afternoon, then." One of the children nearly bumped into her, and a quick smile lit her features as they avoided collision.

The vestiges of the smile crinkled her nose and revealed a faint dimple in her cheek as she looked from the child back to him.

The smile was quite unlike the smoothly practiced ones she usually exhibited.

Instead of moving to his car, he stood there. He had seen the untouched plate of food on her table when he and Misaki had stopped. The *single* plate of food.

When they were sitting in a conference room, Helen Hanson was a woman surrounded by family and business associates. But to share her morning coffee and fruit, she'd had no one.

Again.

"You did not finish your meal."

Now, her bold gaze dropped. He knew, in her case, it was not a sign of respect, but an indicator of avoidance.

"I'd had enough," she said. "Thank you, Mr. Taka, for your time. I look forward to meeting with you again." She placed her hands on her legs and bowed.

He had things to do. Responsibilities. There was no reason to prolong their impromptu meeting.

"As do I," he replied automatically. "Do you have plans for today?" Whatever they would be, they would not involve any member of TAKA. They did not have another meeting scheduled until the following day. Mori expected to spend at least a portion of his afternoon allaying his father's latest battery of concerns where the takeover was concerned.

Helen had straightened and once again, her expression showed some slight bewilderment. Not surprising. He was not given to pointless conversations. It was not his way to be rude, of course, but neither was it his way to waste time. He had no time to waste, generally.

"I thought I might do some sightseeing," she said. "I read about a festival being held this week. I—I'm afraid I can't recall the name of the location. I have it written down back at my hotel."

"Rarely a week passes when there is not some kind of festival."

"It has something to do with the leaves beginning to change."

"Ah." He nodded. "Your sons will accompany you?"

The bewilderment cooled, and he found himself regretting his voiced assumption when her smile went from spontaneous to practiced.

"My stepsons have their own plans," she said, backing away yet another step. "As well they should. I've delayed you long enough, Mr. Taka. Again, my apologies."

His life had been an endless series of social courtesies where apologies were rote. For an American woman like Helen Hanson, he doubted that was the case. "I have some free time this morning. Perhaps you would allow me to be your guide?"

Her lips parted in surprise, but he gave her credit for recovering quickly enough. "I would be honored, Mr. Taka."

He was fairly confident that honor had little to do with her acquiescence. She wanted his cooperation in the TAKA boardroom.

"Very good," he said. "My driver and I will take you to your hotel to retrieve your necessities."

"Thank you, but that won't be necessary." She held up a tiny clutch, not much bigger than a wallet. "I have everything I need in here. My room key and passport and such. Not that it's a key, of course. Just one of those credit-card type things. I'm forever having to get a new one at my hotel. I seem to demagnetize them or something." The rush of words halted abruptly. Pink color rode her cheekbones again and she stepped toward the car.

His driver immediately opened the rear door and Mori watched Helen slide into the limousine. She sat down first and then drew in her legs.

Her pant legs rode up a few inches as she did so, treating him to a brief glimpse of very slender, very delicate ankles.

He stared over the hood of the vehicle, not seeing any of the traffic quietly congesting the street or the pedestrians streaming along the sidewalks.

Evidently, he had gone insane, just as his father kept accusing.

He restrained the urge to loosen his tie and haul in a

deep breath as he moved to the car and climbed in beside Helen.

She sent him a smile that looked as uneasy as he felt.

Then Akira closed the door softly, and there was only Mori and Helen, seemingly shut off from the rest of the world.

He flicked open the buttons holding his jacket closed and stared straight ahead.

The smell of her—something sophisticated but oddly light—filled his head.

He had been accomplished in the art of small talk since he had worn short pants. But summoning inane banter just then seemed to require tremendous effort. "Have you done much sightseeing?" He managed to glance her way, politely enquiring.

Her hands were folded neatly together in her lap. She wore an enormous diamond ring on her wedding ring finger.

"Not as much as I'd like," she admitted. "I feel as though I've spent more time on airplanes traveling back and forth from Chicago to Tokyo than actually staying put long enough here to see as much as I've wanted to."

"You…enjoy Tokyo?"

"It's a fascinating city. I'm always so surprised that it's as quiet as it is." She looked away, out the side window. Her hair was pulled back in a ponytail that revealed the nape of her neck.

"Quiet?" He faced ahead again and when she turned forward once more, his gaze seemed to meet hers in the subtle reflection provided by the smoked partition separating them from the driver.

"For such a large city, I find it remarkably quiet.

There is traffic noise, certainly, but rarely have I heard a horn honk. It's nothing like Chicago."

"No, it is not."

"You've been to Chicago?"

"Occasionally. It, too, is an interesting city."

She smiled faintly. Even in the dim partition, the reflection of it was bright. "Are you being polite?"

"Yes."

"What did you *really* think about Chicago?"

"Noisy. Intrusive." He switched his gaze from the reflection to the real thing. "Impolite."

Her eyes glinted with humor, which surprised him.

Ordinarily, she was very circumspect, highly intelligent and mostly aloof.

Until he had found her hiding tears, that was.

Then, she had seemed wholly human.

"I find it vibrant and endlessly entertaining," she argued pleasantly.

"Also true."

Her eyebrows rose. "Really?"

"I enjoy Chicago when I visit."

"How often do you get to the U.S.?"

"A few times a year. I am in London more often."

"On business or pleasure?"

"Ah. To me, Mrs. Hanson, business *is* pleasure."

Her sudden frown was quickly smoothed away. "That's something my husband used to say."

"You miss him a great deal?"

Her lashes swept down for a moment, hiding those jade eyes. "Of course." Then she turned and looked out the window again. "I love Chicago, too. But I must say I'm becoming quite fond of Tokyo."

"Have you always lived in Chicago?"

"Oh, no." The moment of awkwardness seemed to ease. "I come from New York state, originally. I moved to Chicago when I was a young woman."

"You are still a young woman."

"Kindly put and appreciated. Particularly by a woman who's just watched her—" she faltered only slightly "—grown daughter get married."

"You will be a beautiful woman when you are eighty," he said diplomatically. Truthfully.

Her lips twitched a little as if she were trying not to laugh. "I'd accuse you of flattery, but that seems out of character."

For the first time in longer than he could remember, *he* chuckled. The sound startled her as much as it did him. "True."

After a moment that lasted longer than it should, they both looked away from each other.

The limousine pulled into the park, where a throng of people had already gathered. When Mori stepped out of the car, a breeze had sprung up, helping in a small way to alleviate the humidity. He turned back and took Helen's hand to help her from the vehicle.

She stepped out beside him, and he released her, pretending not to notice the way she rubbed her palms together, as if she, too, felt the lingering heat. Above their heads, leaves from the trees flitted in the air like gently burnished confetti.

She craned her head, avidly taking in the small, orderly garden that was lined with Japanese maples. "It is so beautiful here." The words were little more than a sigh.

"Yes."

Only Mori was not looking at the trees.

He was looking at her.

Chapter Three

They walked together.

Mostly in silence at first, which suited Helen just fine. She wasn't accustomed to feeling tongue-tied, yet being in Morito Taka's presence definitely had that effect.

"In a few weeks, the turning of the leaves will be at its peak," he told her. His hand lightly touched the small of her back as they stepped around a cluster of young women and children.

In a few weeks, she hoped the merger would be complete. "We have the fall colors at home, too. My home is surrounded by trees, in fact." An architectural magazine had once described the grounds around George Hanson's estate as the forest protecting the media king.

Only recently had Helen admitted to herself that staying alone in the house had become more than she could bear. It had been one thing when she'd only been grieving the loss of her husband.

As if such a thing could ever be an "only."

But when she'd believed she'd *only* been the woman called late one night and told that her husband had suffered a massive heart attack in his office, it had been simpler.

Not that George had betrayed her with another woman.

In a way, that might have been simpler, too.

No, George had betrayed her with the very company that he'd charged her with saving. The company that had been his *real* love.

And when she'd learned that fact, staying alone in his mausoleum of a house had become increasingly difficult.

Being near his personal effects—she still hadn't had the heart to clear them away—had become a mockery instead of a comfort. The house with the soaring, gleaming windows that afforded one a spectacular view of their own personal "forest" had become more of a prison than a haven.

"Mrs. Hanson?"

She dragged her thoughts together with more effort than it usually took. Morito was clearly waiting for her to accompany him along the walkway which forked in front of them.

"Call me Helen," she said, not particularly caring if she were committing yet another breach of etiquette or not with the request. She stepped forward, catching her heel on the edge of the pavers.

His hand steadied her. "Are you all right?"

No. She was insane. She was stressed. She was… alone in a world crammed full of people. "Perfectly," she lied, her voice bright. "Is that row of lanterns hanging from the trees decorative, or do they ever light up?"

"They are lit every evening." His dark gaze didn't transfer from her face to the lantern display, however. And she felt herself flushing.

Like some foolish schoolgirl.

It was embarrassing.

"I imagine it's beautifully picturesque."

But he clearly wasn't interested in the visual appeal of the lanterns. "Why is it that you choose to involve yourself in your late husband's business when you could be doing anything else that interests you?"

"Is that why you offered to play tour guide? To try and scare me off the merger?"

"I was under the impression that nothing scared you—" his hesitation was barely noticeable "—Helen."

Her throat constricted on a swallow. *Be careful of what you ask for, because you might get it.*

She unbuttoned her jacket and slid out of it, folding it over her arm. When she looked up at him, he was looking at her silky white camisole. It was a perfectly decent garment, with double spaghetti-straps and a neckline high enough to afford zero cleavage.

She still felt naked under that look of his.

But donning her jacket once more was out of the question. First, it was too warm and humid. Second, he would then know he unsettled her.

The man had the upper hand all too often and she was tired of it.

Would it equalize them if he knew *she'd* been at the root of bringing the American company known as Hanson Media Group to TAKA's attention in the first place?

Would he respect the bold action, or would he detest it *for* that very boldness?

"I have plenty of fears," she assured. "And I'm in charge at Hanson Media Group because my late husband believed that's where I should be." Only after he was gone, though. Never while he'd been alive.

"Is it where *you* want to be?"

"Is heading TAKA where *you* want to be?" she returned.

"It is my duty."

"As Hanson Media Group is mine." The conversation wasn't going anywhere she wanted it to go. "But enough of duty." She smiled brightly. "What do you do for enjoyment?"

"Walk in a garden with an interesting woman."

Her breathing hitched a little. But she was too mature to be swayed by pretty words. In the beginning, George had had plenty of lovely sentiments. Ultimately, though, they'd meant nothing. "You're too polite to describe me as what you really think."

He was definitely amused. The lines fanning out from his eyes crinkled slightly into evidence. "And that would be?"

She gave it a moment of thought. "A jarring woman."

"Jarring?"

"Like the sound of metal scraping over concrete."

"Ah." He caught a blowing leaf right out of midair. "No. I do not think so." Holding the leaf by the stem, he twirled it slowly between his fingers. "You are not the norm."

"Not in Japan."

"Not in Japan," he confirmed.

She supposed it was progress that he didn't lecture her about what was the norm in his world.

"I enjoy my own garden," he said after they'd walked a while. "My daughter. Though her insatiable curiosity and sense of mischief is a trial at times. Mountain climbing. And, surprisingly—" he gave her a sidelong look "—sparring with an interesting woman."

Then, while she was feeling rather speechless over his uncharacteristically personal comments, he handed her the leaf.

"It is time we return."

She nodded silently, and they turned back in the direction of the waiting limousine.

It seemed only minutes before she was dropped off at her own hotel. As he'd done at the park, Mori waved off the chauffeur and alighted from the vehicle first, then turned and gave his hand to her.

She steeled herself, then placed her palm against his. His long tanned fingers closed around hers, and she joined him on the sidewalk. The moment she was upright, he let go of her, which was a good thing if she wanted to be able to continue breathing in any sort of normal fashion.

She moved her jacket from one arm to the other, keeping hold of the leaf, as well, then repeated the bow that she'd spent quite some time privately perfecting. "Thank you again, Mr. Taka, for your time. I look forward to our next meeting tomorrow."

He bowed, as well, and stepped to the car, looking like some sort of lithe tiger as he sank down on the sleek leather seat. He looked at her from the darkened, air-conditioned interior. "Please call me Mori."

Then he pulled the door shut and the limousine pulled from the curb to be swallowed among the stream of nonstop traffic.

"Do you require assistance, Hanson-san?" The uniformed doorman approached her.

Helen dragged her attention from the departing vehicle and shook her head, giving the doorman a distracted smile as she headed into the hotel. "Thank you, no."

The attorneys always seemed to be the first ones to arrive. When Helen stepped into the TAKA conference room the next afternoon, there were half a dozen of them already there. Including Jack. He noticed her arrival and headed toward her, lowering his head a little when he stopped beside her. "You weren't in your room last night."

Curiosity had her lifting her eyebrows. "I went to the gym."

"Samantha tried reaching you for a few hours."

Helen hadn't received any phone messages. "Is something wrong?"

His handsome face looked slightly uncomfortable. "We thought you might join us for dinner."

Bless Samantha. Helen knew the invitation would have to have been instigated by her old friend, now married to Jack. "I'm sorry," she said sincerely. "I would have been happy to join you." Instead, she'd sweated for an hour with free weights and stretched herself into contortions with Pilates. She'd wanted to wear herself out enough to sleep well, and for the most part, she'd succeeded.

She'd slept quite well.

She'd also dreamed quite vividly. Even now, remembering, she could feel warmth beneath her skin.

"You're looking flushed." Jack's sharp gaze missed nothing. "Are you sick?"

Not so long ago, Helen would have believed that Jack would be happy if she'd said she was, for then he could insist she miss the meeting. It had been bad enough that he'd been thrust into helming Hanson Media after his father died, an act that had pulled him away from his own successful legal career. But it had been an even more bitter pill to have the stepmother he'd never had any use for become, essentially, his boss when George's will had left her with the majority interest in the company.

In the past few months, Jack had not necessarily become fond of her, but he'd at least realized she wasn't the dimwitted blond bimbo he'd once believed her to be. The merger with TAKA had been her idea, and he'd seen the value in it.

Hanson Media Group could not continue to function on its own. George's mismanagement had been too devastating. But the merger with TAKA would ensure that the family business would continue to exist. His heritage would not be lost. It would certainly be changed, but they *would* continue. Hundreds of Hanson employees would keep their jobs. George's boys would still have their inheritance, as would their children, once they began arriving. And considering that Delia, Andrew's bride, was quite pregnant, that wouldn't be far off now.

"I'm fine, Jack, just anxious to get this underway." She glanced around the room, then at her watch. "Everyone is here but Mori." The man wasn't usually late.

"Mori?" Jack repeated. "Since when is he *Mori?*"

"Ever the lawyer," Helen tsked lightly, patting his arm. No one would be seated around the table until the head honcho appeared, so she nodded toward the tea tray set up on a sleek ebony credenza. Today, the tray was manned by a thin woman who was as adept at fading into the background as the other voiceless attendants had been. "Do you want to start off with some tea?"

"I could float a steamer on all the tea I've drunk lately," Jack muttered under his breath.

Helen hid a smile. "The details shouldn't take much longer to finalize, then you can get back to normal life."

He looked disbelieving.

She didn't feel so much like smiling then. Was he so jaded that he couldn't believe that he wasn't sentenced to Hanson Media duty for the rest of his days?

She flipped open her leather notepad and drew out the gold pen that had been in her possession ever since she'd plucked it and a sealed envelope bearing her name out of George's personal effects in his desk. She jotted a note on her daily journal to try reaching Judge Henry again back in Chicago, and as she did so, Mori entered the room, three young men dogging his heels as they nodded and listened intently to whatever it was that he was saying. His Japanese was too rapid and low for Helen to follow, but the words certainly had his minions scurrying when he finished.

His gaze traveled impersonally over the occupants of the room—all of whom had seemed to stand just a little straighter when he'd appeared—as he walked straight to the head of the conference table and rested his fingertips on the highly glossed ebony surface.

If Helen had hoped for his glance to linger when it reached her, she'd have been sorely disappointed. He gave her no more regard than he did the tea attendant who silently placed a tall glass of water beside him after he'd seated himself.

She told herself she wasn't disappointed and that was that.

This *was* a business meeting, after all. Not an unexpected stroll through a park.

The rest of the attendees arranged themselves around the table, reminding Helen, not for the first time, of soldiers assuming battle positions. She was sitting to Mori's left, with Jack nearest the man. The rest of the left side was occupied by her team. The right side of the table was comprised of TAKA representatives.

She wondered what the right side would do if the left pulled out a handful of rubber bands and began shooting them across the wide, wide table.

She grabbed the gold pen and banished her silly thoughts. Each place setting around the table had been furnished with a packet of materials bound within a slick cover that featured only the TAKA logo.

After a nod from his brother Mori, Shiguro Taka, a more familiar face at these meetings than Mori, smiled across the table and reached for his packet. "Good afternoon. We will turn to your marked pages, and continue from our last meeting. Mr. Hanson—" his attention focused on Jack "—you will note that the changes you required have been incorporated in this revision. They are so noted." The explanation was redundant, since they'd all been down this road before. Helen didn't bother pointing out that the last round of revisions had been at her demand, not Jack's.

As long as the concessions had been made in favor of Hanson, she was happy. The last thing she wanted to do was lose even twelve percent of their Chicago staff because of outsourcing their accounting department to TAKA headquarters.

She followed the text of the voluminous document as Jack and Shiguro laboriously went point by point through the pages. The afternoon light was lengthening through the tall windows lining the wall when, nearly thirty pages later, she silently reached over to Jack's copy and circled an item.

Shiguro kept reading aloud as Jack glanced at her. She shook her head, mouthing "No."

He nodded and looked across the table at Shiguro. "I'm sorry, Mr. Taka. Our position with regard to the philanthropic budget remains unchanged. These funds are raised and administered by employees within the Chicago headquarters. It is an employee-driven effort that benefits the community and Hanson Media has always given a dollar-for-dollar match."

Shiguro's pleasant expression didn't change. "A four-million-dollar employee giving campaign is an admirable accomplishment, Mr. Hanson, one that requires no additional corporate contributions."

"Since its inception, Hanson Media Group has pledged equal support to that of its employees," Helen spoke before Jack could. "It is that kind of involvement in our local communities that has helped Hanson maintain its strong foothold in the marketplace. The consumer buying one of our publications believes we're in partnership with them in making a better community. It's not just good citizenship—it's good marketing."

"Expensive marketing," Shiguro countered, clearly willing to argue the point.

Helen was prepared for it, though. Goodness knows she'd argued with Jack and her own team over the matter often enough. Four million dollars a year *was* a lot of money, particularly for a company that had just narrowly avoided bankruptcy.

Mori murmured something to Shiguro, and the other man's expression tightened. But he nodded. "A fifty-percent match."

Jack started to speak. Helen touched his arm. "One hundred percent," she said.

"Mrs. Hanson." Shiguro shook his head almost pityingly as he sat back in his seat. "You must not understand the situation."

"Sixty percent," Mori said, cutting off his brother.

Helen looked Mori's way, and found his gaze focused on her. She wished she'd accepted the tea or glass of water when the girl had offered it, since her mouth felt impossibly dry. "Ninety."

She heard Jack murmur her name under his breath. "Be reasonable," he added quietly.

She remained silent.

"Mrs. Hanson," Shiguro interjected. "TAKA believes in contributing to its community as well. Our charitable giving—"

"—reached an incredibly generous three point seven percent of the proceeds for your last three fiscal years."

Shiguro clearly did not appreciate being interrupted,

least of all by her. "Sixty percent." He repeated his brother's concession.

She shook her head.

All around the table, members on both the right and left sides began shifting.

"If we agree to table this item for today," Jack suggested, "we could continue?"

Helen could have sat there all evening and argued her side, but she knew in the scheme of things, the point was a relatively minor one to most everyone but her. "We can resolve it another time," she agreed. The practice wasn't uncommon to their negotiations.

Shiguro glanced at Mori, and seemed to take his silence for assent, because he focused once more on their agreement. "We will continue, then, in the following section." Papers rustled around the table as pages were turned.

"The changeover in all branding to the TAKA brand will be accomplished within twelve months," Shiguro read, glancing at Jack over the top of the reading glasses he'd pushed onto his nose.

Helen carefully set her pen down on the center of her notepad.

Shiguro continued. "All media relations regarding the acquisition of Hanson Media Group will be directed through the Tokyo office."

At that, even Jack started shaking his head. "That is neither feasible nor practical."

"It is TAKA's belief that—"

"This is not an acquisition," Helen reminded him, for what felt like the millionth time. That was the tightrope they constantly walked—to retain as much control of Hanson Media as they possibly could while availing themselves of the power and positioning of the Japanese juggernaut. "The *branding* of Hanson Media Group carries more weight with Americans than TAKA does. By exchanging one for the other, we'll be alienating the very people who keep us in business. These are the people who purchase HMG periodicals. Listen to HMG radio stations. Subscribe to HMG online services. To them, TAKA is just another name. HMG is part of American culture."

"As TAKA is not acquiring your radio stations, we are not concerned with that," Shiguro said. "And while I'm sure your opinion is heartfelt, every acquisition of TAKA bears the TAKA name."

"Until now. And could we refrain from using the term *acquisition?* This—" she hefted the bound document up a few inches and let it drop heavily on the table "—is a merger."

Shiguro gave her a condescending look before transferring his focus to Jack, then to the raft of legal eagles to Helen's side. "This *acquisition* will be handled in the same manner as we've always—"

"Mrs. Hanson is correct." Mori's words stopped Shiguro's midstream. "A study was commissioned a few years ago on the importance of branding in the American marketplace. Perhaps Hanson Media Group is not up to the level to which some soft drinks or photocopiers have risen, but it was nevertheless one of the most widely recognized corporate names in that area of the country."

Helen slowly picked up her pen again. She had a print out of the salient points from that particular study tucked in a pocket of her notepad. Now, she wouldn't even have to pull it out.

Her gaze lingered on Mori, but she directed her comment toward the other side of the table. "Hanson Media Group may have had some faltering moments this past year—" a mild understatement "—but that does not negate the positive public image it has held for decades. TAKA will be benefiting more in the U.S. under our brand, and there is not one person around this table who does not recognize that fact." She let her gaze travel that table, resting briefly on each person in turn. "We would, however, consider changing the name to Hanson North America. With the divestiture of our radio division prior to the merger with TAKA, we could roll out the amended corporate name and play on the broadening to an international status."

Mori gave a slight nod. Nobody argued with her suggestion. Shiguro was surprisingly quiet.

"Hanson North America. I will have our PR department get in touch with yours to coordinate the details. The item regarding branding will be amended," Mori said and that was that. They moved on to the next paragraph.

Jack gave her a sideways look of approval and Helen wanted to sit on her hands to keep from shaking with triumph. Instead, she just kept a tight grip on George's gold pen.

There was no sunlight pouring through the windows by the time the meeting ended. Helen had a stiff ache in the small of her back from sitting for so long. She'd taken pages of notes, and argued several more points, not all of which she won, but overall, she was intensely satisfied with the accomplishments of the day.

And the evening.

"I suppose I'm going to have to go out and drink with

these people again," Jack murmured to her as everyone rose and began talking about anything under the sun as long as it was not mergers and acquisitions. "I'd rather get back to Samantha."

Helen didn't doubt it, but she knew there was no point in reminding Jack that if he was invited out, he couldn't possibly refuse, for to do so would be offensive.

Shiguro was making his way toward them, his customary smile back in place. He did not present the physical presence that his brother did, but he was nevertheless a striking man. "My brother wishes a moment with you, Mrs. Hanson, if you would be so kind?"

Helen ignored the surprised look she received from Jack. "Of course." She excused herself and headed toward Mori. Behind her, she heard Shiguro courteously ask Jack and the rest of the Hanson team—all men—to join him for drinks. She didn't let it bother her that she was not included in the invitation. It wasn't the first time she'd been excluded, and she had no real desire to beat the bars for several hours before engaging in an argument over who would take care of the check, which—according to Jack—was how most of those excursions ended. That particular debate was primarily an expected exercise in courtesy. TAKA always picked up the tab in the end no matter how many times Jack insisted on getting it "next time."

Mori stood near the door, in conversation with two other men. The assistant who'd accompanied him, and who'd been the minute-taker of the meeting, was standing just behind him, taking more copious notes.

Helen waited to the side, not wanting to interrupt him. She was well aware of Jack still watching her even as he conversed with Shiguro. Of course he would be curious why Mori would request to speak with her. It wasn't a common occurrence. In fact, it was a first-time occurrence.

Her eldest stepson caught her eye. More than curious, she decided, giving Jack an almost imperceptible shake of her head. Jack was definitely…disapproving.

And, sadly, that *wasn't* uncommon at all. She ought to have been used to it by now. George's boys had never accepted her marriage to their father despite her best efforts at forging some sort of relationship with them. She really ought to have developed a thicker hide by now.

"Mrs. Hanson." Mori touched her elbow and she nearly jumped right out of her skin.

She laughed a little, meeting his intensely dark gaze. Mrs. Hanson. Not Helen. So much for progress. "You caught me woolgathering, I'm afraid."

He tilted his head slightly. "Daydreaming."

"Ah…well, yes."

His lips lifted ever so faintly. "I hope they were pleasant, then. The daydreams." His gaze flicked briefly to the darkened windows before returning to her face. "Though the day is already sleeping."

She could feel Jack's gaze boring a hole in her back. "Was there something specific you wished to speak with me about?"

"Yes." He looked beyond her. "Your son must have made a formidable attorney. He looks fierce."

"Jack is well-suited to the law," she understated. Jack *had* been formidable. He still was, for that matter. No more than the man standing beside her, however.

"You are tired?"

She hesitated, thrown by the directly personal comment. "It's been a long day." Preceded by many long days. "But I'm pleased with the results."

Now, there was a definite glint in his eyes. "I'm certain that you are," he said mildly. "Shiguro is perhaps less pleased."

Helen smiled faintly, not commenting. They watched Shiguro and his group make their way out of the conference room, Jack among them.

When their voices no longer could be heard in the corridor, however, the vast quietness of the conference room pressed in on Helen.

As did the fact that she and Mori were very much alone.

"Did you wish to join them?"

Once again, she was surprised by his perception, and then annoyed with herself for *being* surprised. The man was far too observant. "No," she admitted.

"Shiguro has a liking for karaoke that not everyone shares."

The image of Jack in a karaoke bar made Helen's lips lift. But she still didn't know what had prompted Mori's request to speak with her.

"You are…feeling better?"

Caution leaked into her. "I'm quite well, thank you."

"Our negotiations have progressed more slowly than we expected."

She considered reminding him that he was the primary reason for that, with his objections that had nearly derailed the deal more than once. "Things worthwhile aren't often come by easily."

He nodded slightly. "I tell my daughter that when she does not want to study."

It was hard envisioning the severe businessman as a father, though she'd already known he was one. "How old is your daughter?"

"Twelve. For another few months, anyway."

"Ah. Almost a teenager. Are you prepared for that?" she asked lightly.

"Dreading," he deadpanned. "Will you dine with me?"

Her pen slipped from her fingers.

He stooped and retrieved it before she could, and held it up to study. "I have noticed that you are never without this. What do the initials signify?"

She took it when he handed it to her, and slid it into her portfolio. "My husband's name." She didn't really want to talk about the pen she'd given George or its significance. "Was there something particular about the merger you wanted to discuss?"

"Over dinner, you mean."

"Yes."

"Not everything concerns business."

"Right now, for me it does." The admission came without thought.

He slid the portfolio out of her surprised hands. "That is a pity."

She eyed him when he cupped her elbow and urged her toward the door. "Why?"

"You are a beautiful woman."

She didn't presume that he meant it as a compliment. "I suppose you believe I should be more concerned with nonbusiness pursuits?" They'd arrived at the elevator and he released her elbow as he pushed the call button. "Maybe you think I'm only suited for finding another husband who can keep me in diamonds and Botox."

"You prefer a marriage of emotion, I suppose."

The elevator doors slid open and she stepped inside. "Contrary to popular belief, I did marry for love. And, quite honestly, I can't imagine feeling that way again."

Mori followed her into the elevator and pressed the button. "My daughter claims she never wants to marry."

"She is only twelve."

"When I was her age, my parents had already arranged my marriage." He looked from the lights of the floor display to her. "Kimiko wants only to move to America and be famous."

"Doing what?"

He seemed to shrug without ever truly moving a muscle. "I think she has not decided on that, yet. As long as it is very…American."

Her stomach swooped a little, a result of the elevator's rapid descent. "And you disapprove."

"She would do better to apply her passionate interest to her schoolwork than to whatever fad currently has your country in its grip."

At least his voice had lightened. She smiled in response. "Now *that* sounds like a typical twelve-year-old."

He smiled a little, too, but didn't comment.

She could guess what he was thinking, though. Probably the same thing she was. That her only experience with twelve-year-old children had been when *she* was one. They both knew she'd never been involved in her own daughter's life when she was twelve.

The elevator slowed abruptly and the doors slid open to the silent, cavernous lobby. The only occupants were three security guards, who stood and greeted them as they passed and stepped out into the evening.

The same car as the other day waited curbside and Mori headed toward it. "Come. We will eat and not discuss business. That can wait for the next time we sit around the conference table."

Her stomach swooped again, but this time she couldn't blame it on the elevator. "Then what will we talk about?"

He lifted his hand toward her, palm upward. His hooded gaze settled on her face. "Something will come to us."

Involvement with this man over anything that *wasn't* business—even something as simple as a walk in the park or dinner—was a mistake.

She knew it. She *knew* it.

But she stepped forward anyway and put her hand on his.

Chapter Four

Mori was not certain what had prompted him to ask the woman to dinner. The same nonsensical thinking that had prompted him to accompany her to the park.

Both decisions were inexplicable.

Except that he could not rid himself of the image of Helen, alone once again.

She was silent as Akira drove them away from the TAKA building. Was she merely looking out the window at the passing lights, or was she wondering as much as he was *what* they were doing there together?

Business did indeed make strange bedfellows.

"I thought we would go to the Anderson hotel." He finally broke the silence. "The restaurant there is admirable." International food and international clientele. Helen would be quite at home.

"Yes, it is a lovely restaurant. I've eaten there several times."

There was nothing in her voice to indicate dissatisfaction, nothing in the composed expression revealed by the on-off flicker of neon as they drove. For some reason, he still sensed it.

"It is uncomfortable for you to go there? The Andersons are—"

"Oh, no," she cut in quickly. "I'm very comfortable at the hotel's restaurant."

Even if it was owned by the man who had adopted her daughter.

She did not voice the words, but Mori added them anyway.

She made a little sound. "With you having a suite there, I certainly don't have to tell you how wonderful the restaurant is. But it's been comfortable for me. Very...Western. I don't have to worry about showing off how inept I still am eating with *o-hashi.* It's silly, and nothing for you to concern yourself with, truly. I just...well, I find I'm missing my own kitchen."

"You cook?"

She turned a little, until she was facing him more squarely. Her hair gleamed like a beloved pearl in the dim light. "I've been known to attempt it." Her voice was slightly dry. "I wasn't always married to a man who had a raft of household staff. George never understood that I actually liked fixing meals. That was Cook's job and that was that."

"Sumiko—my wife—preferred to be the organizer."

Her smile widened. "Plan the meals, but leave the actual preparing of it to the chef?"

He did not know why he had mentioned his wife. Particularly when he so rarely thought of her. "Yes. It is refreshing to have a meal at home." His words were sincere. Though he had not been to his own home outside the city in many weeks. "I also enjoy the kitchen. When are you planning your return to the United States?"

She took the abruptness of his question in stride. "Looking forward to getting rid of me?"

"Shiguro may be feeling some anticipation."

She laughed softly, then waved her hand. "I'm sorry. I know I shouldn't laugh. Your brother is a credit to the TAKA organization."

Shiguro was. But Mori was not unaware of his brother's annoyance with having Helen involved in their negotiations or that he was an easier mark for their father when it came to influencing him against the Hanson deal.

"Actually, I was thinking how long it had been since I was at *my* home."

"Where is that?"

"A few hours north of Tokyo. A very small village where I was born."

"The original Taka-ville?"

He smiled faintly. "Something like that. Nesutotaka. My mother's home is there though my father prefers to spend most of his time at their apartment here. He finds it difficult to be too far away from the office."

"You succeeded him only a few years ago?"

He nodded. "We agreed to speak of other matters," he reminded.

"So we did. Tell me about Nesutotaka."

"You would consider it...old-fashioned. It is wooded and very green. No proper roads."

"No concrete high-rises?"

"The only high-rise is the mountain that overlooks the village."

"It sounds lovely."

"Kimiko, my daughter, loathes it."

"Kimiko." Helen sounded the name softly. "What does it mean?"

"Essentially, beautiful child."

"Kimiko," she repeated again, nodding. "What a wonderful name. I suppose for a twelve-year old girl, Nesutotaka is pretty tame."

"Dull was the word she last used, I believe. She is most happy to stay at her school, or at my father's home. He does not indulge her liking for the more modern culture, but he has television, at least."

"Does she stay with you at all here in Tokyo?"

"My duties are not very interesting to her, either," he said drily. "She stays with me very rarely."

She fell silent for a moment. "You must miss her."

"Yes."

"Well, perhaps she'll grow up and work side by side with you at TAKA. Be the first women in a senior management position there."

"She will make a suitable marriage."

Helen made a soft sound. "Have you already picked out her groom?"

"There are families I would consider." His father was already greatly displeased that the matter had not been fully arranged.

"And what about what Kimiko wants?"

"Kimiko will please her father."

Her brows rose a little. "Oddly enough, you just sounded like *my* father. He was adamant about what I would or wouldn't do, as well."

"It is a father's duty to see to the well-being of his children."

"I'd rather think of it as a father's privilege." Her voice had noticeably cooled.

"You are American. You have no reason to understand this thinking."

"I understand that my father ruled his family with an iron fist, because that was his *duty.* I don't think he once considered what was truly best for our welfare."

"Our?"

"My mother. My brother. Me."

"You are close?"

She shook her head. "My mother died several years ago. My father still lives in a small town in upstate New—" She broke off when the phone in the console discreetly beeped.

"Please excuse me." He answered, knowing he was not going to like the results as soon as he heard the voice of Kimiko's headmaster. He listened, watching Helen from the corner of his eyes.

She had looked out the window again in a polite attempt at offering him some privacy.

"I will come by tonight," he cut off the headmaster's stream of excited chatter and disconnected the call.

Yes, he missed his daughter, but he did *not* miss Kimiko's present path of mischief.

"Problem?"

"An inconvenience."

"If you need to pass on dinner, I'll understand."

Canceling at this juncture would be unacceptable. "The headmaster of my daughter's school. He will wait."

"Is she all right?"

Did he seem so cold that she thought he would ignore Kimiko if she *were not?* "Until she must face her father, she is."

"And it is none of my business. I'm sorry if it sounded as if I were prying."

Her voice had regained its formal cadence. The pearl that glowed from human contact now looked cool and distant. No less lovely, but far less valuable.

"The school is near here. If you would not mind delaying our dinner a short while, I can attend to the matter, and we can dine after."

She made no movement, yet her demeanor immediately softened again. "I don't mind in the least. But your daughter may wish to have dinner with you."

He doubted it. He pushed the intercom button that connected the rear of the limo to Akira. "Stop at Kim's school."

"Hai."

"I hope she isn't in very much trouble," Helen said after a moment. "Your expression is…fierce."

He realized he was frowning and tried to stop.

A smile played around Helen's lips as she witnessed his effort. "There is an expression. 'Turn that frown upside down.' Have you heard it?"

"No."

She made an exaggerated frown and touched her finger to the corner of her lip, nudging upward. The frown became a smile.

"Silliness." Kimiko would undoubtedly be enthralled with the woman.

"I think everyone needs a little silliness in their lives. Particularly men with twelve-year-old daughters."

"And what is the silliness in *your* life?"

"Well..." Her hands lifted slightly, then fell back to her lap. "Maybe I've been a bit remiss in that area in my own life, lately."

He touched his finger to his mouth and pushed up.

Her head tilted. "You should get an A for effort," she assured, amused.

"And a D for results."

At that, she laughed.

And he felt the frown finally ease from his face. "You are an interesting woman, Helen."

"So you've said. I still am not entirely certain why."

"I find you...curious."

"Like a bug to be studied?"

He found he did wish to study her. For unfathomable reasons. Yes, she was a beautiful woman. But he had beautiful women available to him whenever he chose.

What was different about *this* woman?

The car pulled to a stop in the curving drive that fronted his daughter's boarding school. "There is a small garden if you would like to wait there," he told her when Akira opened the door.

"Yes, please."

The headmaster, a short, fastidious Briton named Mr. Hyde-Smith, had spotted the car and was hurrying toward them.

Mori spotted his daughter hanging back, near the heavy wooden gate that guarded the garden in the forecourt. Though it was dark, there was enough illumination from the lanterns to see that her appearance was, indeed, as shocking as Mr. Hyde-Smith had complained.

He headed toward the other man, wanting to avoid discussing his daughter's behavior in front of Helen. She had revealed herself to be a challenging opponent in their negotiations. For her to see that he was unable to control one small twelve-year-old girl would only weaken his position in her eyes.

Mr. Hyde-Smith bowed deeply as Mori reached him. "I didn't wish to disturb you, Taka-san, but as you can clearly see, Kimiko has broken our personal grooming requirements. Something must be done before the other students see her. Why, she could start a revolt!"

"Revolt is a strong word." Mori gestured to his daughter, who begrudgingly made her way to his side. She would not meet his gaze and he touched her hair that had been a gift from her mother—a deep brown silk—that was now as pink as bubble gum. "She can stay in her room until someone can be summoned to fix it."

"I'm sorry, Taka-san. We do not allow our students to make their hair vile colors, nor do we allow visible piercings or tattoos."

His mouth tightened. "Piercings?"

Kim rolled her eyes. "I don't have any piercings, Papa."

"The tattoo!" Mr. Hyde-Smith jogged Kimiko's arm and his daughter huffed and lifted it to her father's inspection.

The thing covered the entire length of her inner arm, from narrow wrist to inner elbow. An American flag.

He had last seen his daughter less than a week earlier.

Her arms then had still been untainted. "Go wait with Akira." His voice dropped.

Fortunately, she had the good sense not to argue.

When she was gone, Mori pinned his irritation on the headmaster. "What sort of supervision is occurring here that she not only has time to turn her entire head *pink,* but can have that thing applied to her arm?"

Mr. Hyde-Smith gulped a little. "It was a free day today, Taka-san. You were supplied the schedule at the beginning of the school term. We expect our pupils to monitor their own behavior, particularly when they reach Kimiko's age."

Mori knew what was coming even before the headmaster got there.

"Perhaps Kimiko would be happier in a different educational setting."

Mori wanted to gnash his teeth together. For the past year, the man had been hinting that his daughter would be better off elsewhere. "I will return my daughter in the morning," he told the man evenly. "Thank you for your trouble."

Mr. Hyde-Smith opened his mouth, but closed it again. He bowed. *"Domō arigatō gozaimasu,"* he murmured.

Mori was already heading back to the car.

Helen had remained seated inside, and he could see Kim leaning over, talking rapidly, her hands gesturing.

The gnawing headache settled in for a nice long visit. How long after a tattoo was given could it be removed?

Mori curtly told his daughter to stop disturbing Mrs. Hanson and to get into the vehicle.

She gave him a long look, but did as he bid.

Once they were inside, Akira drove away from the

small, prestigious boarding school. Kimiko was sitting between him and Helen. "This is Mrs. Hanson, Kimiko."

"Dōzo yoroshiku," his daughter mumbled.

"I'm pleased to meet you, too," Helen replied, in English. "Is that one of those stick-on tattoos?"

Kim held up the arm in question as if it were truly a thing to be admired. "I bought it in the marketplace this morning," she said.

"It is *temporary?*" His relief was so great he wanted to box her ears all over again.

"Yes," Kim said, as if he were dimwitted. "It washes off with soap."

"And will your hair wash back to its usual color?"

Her expression clearly told him it would not.

"You look like you have dipped your head in Day-Glo pink."

"It took three bottles," Kim said, then ducked her chin, evidently realizing that he was not as impressed with that fact as she.

"You have to dye it back."

His daughter remained stonily quiet.

"Why pink?" Helen asked, as if there were no tension congesting the vehicle at all.

"To match the dress I want to wear at my thirteenth birthday party."

"That is not for some time yet," Mori said evenly. "And long before then I expect my daughter to possess the color of hair with which she was born."

"When I move to America, I will make my hair every color of the rainbow." Kimiko looked up at Helen. "Maybe even gold as the sunrise. Could I have the color you have?"

"Well..." Helen's gaze flicked over his daughter's head for a moment, meeting his. "I'm afraid mine is pretty much what I was born with." She tugged the length of her thick ponytail over her shoulder. "It's darkened only a little since I was a girl. I always wanted to have beautiful, rich brown hair. Like a sable. But I never had the courage to try it."

"Changing it would be a waste." He eyed his daughter. "Now I have to find a professional to fix this mess. At this hour."

"I don't see why I have to change it at all."

"There are rules to be followed."

"It's a dumb rule."

He let out a sharp breath. He would not engage in an argument with his daughter in front of Helen. "Since you have delayed Mrs. Hanson's dinner long enough, you will join us for our meal. I will deal with you, afterward."

"It'll be even later then. To find a hairdresser, I mean." Helen's voice was cautious. "Perhaps we can take a rain check on dinner."

"Rain check?"

"A promise to do it another time."

Kimiko suddenly looked abashed. "Please, I do not wish to interrupt your meal, Mrs. Hanson. I am happy to do as my father requests."

"It is settled," Mori stated.

Helen was looking at his daughter. "And I am happy to have such a lovely girl join us for dinner."

Kimiko put a self-conscious hand to her hair.

It seemed that it took a woman to make her question whether or not her choice of hair color was wise. What her own *father* thought was another matter entirely.

Fortunately, they soon arrived at the Anderson hotel, and Mori escorted his companions to the restaurant. The maître d' greeted them all effusively and managed not to stare at Kimiko's head as he showed them to a table near the windows that overlooked the city lights.

Despite the excessively late hour, the restaurant was more than half full. Helen declined wine with a polite excuse, which surprised Mori, as did the order she made for a medium steak. Most of the women he knew—American or not—seemed to subsist on salads and little else.

He ordered a fruit tray for his daughter, who had already eaten her own dinner earlier, then his own preference—which happened to be nearly identical to Helen's.

The waiter disappeared as quietly as he'd appeared and Helen lightly touched Kimiko's colorful T-shirt. "Do you like fish?"

Her shirt was patterned with dozens of tropical fish. "I have an aquarium in my room at school," she said. Her English was only slightly accented. "Some day, my father may let me learn to scuba, so that I may see the fish without a cage."

"Scuba diving is a wonderful experience, but I haven't been in years. I've always loved watching fish in aquariums, though. There is something so peaceful about them."

"What kind of fish do you have?"

Helen shook her head. "None, I'm afraid."

"Papa, you must show Mrs. Hanson *your* fish." Like a Ping-Pong ball, Kimiko's attention bounced back and forth between the adults. "Bettas," she told Helen. "Very beautiful ones. My father has bred many of them. But the males have to be kept separate. They would fight."

"I've heard that." Her eyes were amused, but she did not seem to be bothered by Kimiko's rapid conversation. If anything, she appeared to be rapt.

The result of missing her own daughter's company at that age?

He decided he was speculating far too much about Helen's motives and her state of mind. "Kimi-chan," he murmured softly, silently warning her to cease her chatter.

His daughter's lashes swept down, hiding her expressive eyes. If it had not been for the yard-long skeins of pink hair streaming to the seat of her chair, she would have looked quite demure.

He knew better.

"Where have you been scuba diving?" he asked Helen.

Her fingers were slowly sliding up and down the stem of her water goblet. "Mostly the Caribbean. My husband used to enjoy it. When we first were married, we went often."

"Family holidays?"

Her fingers hesitated for just a moment, hardly long enough to be noticed. "Unfortunately, George's boys didn't accompany us. Have you been diving?"

He nodded.

"Papa prefers mountain climbing." Kimiko pressed her lips together, as if she had realized she may have been too free with information with their foreign guest.

"Kimiko is correct. I do prefer mountains to water. But, I have enjoyed many interludes beneath the surface."

Helen's smile widened. "What a lovely way of phrasing it."

What was lovely was the way her jadelike eyes sparkled when she smiled.

If she were merely a woman he had happened to meet, he would have had no qualms in pursuing the attraction. But she was in his country for professional reasons. That alone put her in a class where some men would feel perfectly comfortable in pressing their attentions on her, wanted or not.

He was not some men, however.

She was, for now, an opponent. When the acquisition of Hanson Media Group was complete, she would be a business associate—albeit one far removed from his center of operations here in Tokyo.

Attractive she was. Too wise to fall prey to it, he was, as well.

A phalanx of waiters arrived, bearing their array of dishes, and for a while, silence reigned over the table as Mori and his companions ate.

Kimiko finished her fruit in short order and, unable to overlook the tiredness in her eyes, he sent her up to his suite. "Wash the tattoo," he added, in case she had any ideas of leaving the colorful emblem in place.

He caught her rolling her eyes, but she went without debate.

Which left him alone with the puzzling and disturbing Mrs. Hanson.

"A few bottles of color from the drug store, and she'll be brunette once again."

"She does not stop to think about the consequences of her actions."

"She is twelve."

"More than old enough."

"When was the last time she was able to spend time with you?"

Too long. The thought had him frowning. "Why?"

"Maybe the pink hair is more a tactic to be with you than to satisfy her fashion urges."

He started to deny that, but stopped. They had already spoken too much of his family. "Kimiko is happy at school."

"Yes, I believe you mentioned that." Her voice was smooth. "It looked like a very old building. Beautifully maintained, but old. Did you, by any chance, attend there?"

"Yes."

She smiled softly. "Did you ever try some mischief to get beyond the walls?"

He and Shiguro had been terrors. But she need not know that. "No."

She merely chuckled, shaking her head. "And I never intentionally missed my ninth-grade English class, either."

He could easily imagine her as a young teenager. She had probably been the epitome of blond and carefree. "Do you wish to have a coffee?"

"I'd love one. But—" she looked regretful "—I must decline. If I have coffee at this hour, I'd be awake until dawn."

"You are tired." Though it did not show in her face. "I have kept you too long. Please forgive me."

"Not at all. It has been my pleasure."

"Akira will, of course, drive you to your hotel."

"It's not far. I can walk."

"That would be dangerous. A woman alone on the

streets at this time of night. If you will not allow Akira to drive you, then I will accompany you."

She stilled, her gaze measuring. "I am in the position of having to agree to your terms, aren't I? To do otherwise would be ungracious of me. Even though I am perfectly capable of finding my own way there."

"You have not been ungracious since we met." The truthful admission felt raw. He *much* preferred it when she did not speak her thoughts so freely. "If I were to acknowledge your capabilities, would you acknowledge that it would be safer for you to be transported to your hotel by someone I trust?"

Her head tilted slightly to one side. "Always the negotiator, Mr. Taka?"

"Earlier, it was Mori."

"So it was. *Mori.* I would be most happy to accept the offer of your driver," she capitulated. "Your daughter needs your attention tonight more than anyone. Thank you very much for the dinner. The food was delicious and the company delightful. Please tell your daughter I very much enjoyed meeting her."

Judging by Kimiko's equally rapt attention to Helen, the feeling had been mutual.

A disturbing fact, given his daughter's already inflated infatuation with Western ways.

"We will meet tomorrow."

"Around the conference table," she finished.

"Yes."

"I look forward to it." She bowed slightly, then walked out of the restaurant.

Watching her go, he knew he, also, was looking

Chapter Five

"What's this I hear about you and Mori Taka having dinner together last night?"

Helen paused, lifting her scone halfway to her mouth. How quickly word spread. "Good morning to you, too, Jack."

His lips tightened as he entered the living area of her suite. "You can't charm your way through the merger, Helen."

She gave him a long look. "I'm so flattered that you think I might try." Her tone was cooler than she intended. But, really, how long was she to be painted with the trophy-wife paint? "It was merely dinner, Jack."

"Mori doesn't *have* dinner with us, Helen."

"Well, he didn't with *you,*" she agreed drily, which

was all she intended to say about the matter. "How is Samantha this morning?"

"Samantha is fine." The woman in question sailed into the room. "Jack, I hope you haven't been grilling Helen already. It's far too early for barbecue." Samantha leaned over and brushed her cheek against Helen's. "He's in a bad mood," she whispered sotto voce, before straightening again and sending her husband an impish smile.

No matter how irritated Jack might be with Helen, he still reacted to his wife's cheerfulness. The man was completely in love, and it pleased Helen in ways she could never adequately convey to her stepson. "Too much sake last night with Shiguro and the boys?"

Jack threw himself down on the couch opposite her. "We've got another week of meetings, at the very least, before we can sew this up. Then, what? Two or three months to make sure the transition goes smoothly?"

"Probably. Of course we'll be having the gala to celebrate the final signing well before that." She hoped that all of the boys would be in Tokyo for it. There would be *plenty* to celebrate, not least of which was the merger.

Samantha sat next to Jack, her hand smoothing over his thigh. "Jack found out this morning that one of his former law partners was appointed to the bench."

Understanding swept through Helen. "Things will work out, Jack. I know this has been frustrating for you, but, trust me. They *will* work out."

"Aren't you little Mary Sunshine."

"Jack," Samantha hushed.

"It's all right, Samantha." Helen took a small bite of her scone, but her appetite had waned. She leaned over the glass-topped coffee table and dragged her portfolio close enough to flip open.

Some of the time with Jack—most of the time—it was best for her to focus on facts.

She pulled out her latest sheet of notes, which she handed over to him. "Items I'd like to get cleared away with TAKA today."

He took the sheet, sitting forward.

Even with his dissatisfaction over being thrust into the management of his father's company, he wasn't going about it halfway. George had always been proud of Jack, though he'd been miserable at telling his eldest son that. Unfortunately, Helen was aware that expressing *her* pride in him wouldn't make up for his father's failings.

"You want to get back into the charitable giving again?"

"It has to be settled, Jack. If we don't do it now, we'll never get approval from the new board to continue a full match when the merger is complete. Not when TAKA will have a weighted presence."

Jack folded her notes and tucked it in his lapel pocket and stood. "Fine. I've got a conference call set up shortly with Evan about spinning off the radio division. We need to time it before the merger to keep the FCC happy. I'll see you before the meeting." He brushed his hand over his wife's hair and left just as abruptly as he'd arrived.

Helen looked over at Samantha. "It will be hard for him to stick out the transition period here."

"It isn't that he dislikes Tokyo," Samantha assured. "Quite the opposite, in fact."

"He misses his law practice."

The young woman nodded. "But, on a good note, we're considering finding a real place to live while we're here. Living in a hotel all that while doesn't appeal to either one of us. Having a place of our own, even temporarily, would be nice."

"I'm sure it would be. You and Jack haven't had a chance to really settle anywhere yet. There just hasn't been time with all the company issues in the way."

"Company issues that brought us back together in the first place." Samantha looked like the cat who got the cream as she grinned. "So…dinner with Mori Taka? What was that all about?"

"It was about nothing. His daughter was there, too."

"Introducing you to his family." Samantha nodded, slyly humorous. "Getting serious, already, eh?"

Even though Samantha was only teasing, Helen still felt her cheeks warming. "I'm sure he would have much preferred to keep his daughter far, far away from me."

"I don't believe that for a minute."

Helen just shook her head and waved her hand, trying to dismiss the matter. Too bad she couldn't dismiss it from her mind, however. Morito Taka was taking up much too much of her thoughts of late.

"He's a striking man." Samantha splayed her hand, studying her fingernails. "Intelligent, obviously. Rich, clearly. A woman could do worse."

Samantha *had* experienced much, much worse, at the hands of her first husband. "I'm *not* in the market for a man." Helen's voice was firm. "It hasn't even been a year since George died." But it had been far longer than that since she'd felt the interest of a man.

Perhaps that was why she couldn't get Mori out of her head. She'd been alone in her bed for too many years.

"Maybe you should be in the market," Samantha

countered, obviously not at all cowed by Helen's insistence. "There's no time frame on falling in love."

"Love?" Helen stood up so quickly she knocked her portfolio right onto the floor. "Believe me. The last person I would fall in love with is someone like Mori Taka. He's—"

Samantha had sat up, and was watching Helen closely. "He's…what? I know you're not going to say Japanese, because I won't believe for a second that the differences in your cultures would bother you in the least."

If anything, Helen found the differences as appealing as they were frustrating. But that was not the point. She picked up her portfolio and dropped it on the coffee table. "He's too much like George," she finally admitted.

"Jack's told me about his father," Samantha said slowly. "I don't see how the two are similar in the least, and I'm not talking about their ages."

She wished she hadn't said anything at all. Thinking about George was still painful, and not for the reasons Samantha would expect. Her friend believed that George had been the love of Helen's life. Helen had believed it, too, until the truth of George's feelings for her had capsized her life. "It doesn't matter, anyway. Once we finalize the merger, I doubt I'll have much interaction with Mori afterward. He'll be running TAKA from here, and I'll be back in the States."

"You still plan to be involved with the company, though."

Helen couldn't bring herself to lie, outright. Not when, with each passing day, she was wanting more and more to escape.

Ironic, given how many years she'd been disappointed in George's refusal to allow any involvement on her part in Hanson Media.

"Have you heard from Andrew or Delia? Do you know how she's feeling after the long flight back to Chicago?"

"Like she's ready to pop with the baby," Samantha answered. "Which she feels like despite international air travel. And she still has a few months to go. What are you not telling me, Helen?"

"Don't start imagining things." Helen pushed the tray of scones toward her. "Have you eaten yet?"

Her young friend made a face, but she dutifully picked up a scone and let the matter drop.

Helen was too wise to believe the subject would remain dropped, however. But for now, she was glad for the reprieve. "So, tell me. What kind of place do you and Jack want to find? A house? An apartment?"

Samantha smiled and began debating the merits of each. Helen focused her attention as best she could.

But it was hard, when her thoughts kept slipping to the unwanted appeal of Morito Taka.

Helen needn't have worried that she would not have all her wits about her that afternoon when facing off against Mori and his minions.

He wasn't there.

Shiguro offered no explanation over Mori's absence other than extending a profuse apology before taking Mori's seat at the head of the table and proceeding to be more obstreperous than ever before.

She actually found herself wishing that Mori *was* there, even though, up to now, he'd been a much more difficult prospect than Shiguro.

By the time they'd debated issues for two hours with no concessions whatsoever made on Shiguro's part, Helen had a raging headache.

Even Jack looked like he was on the verge of telling Shiguro to take a flying leap. When Shiguro actually retraced steps about the number of board positions that would be available to Hanson—a matter that had been firmly resolved already—Jack actually started to stand.

Helen saw the glint of satisfaction in Shiguro's eyes and without thought, cried out, distressed.

Heads swiveled her way as she swayed slightly, pressing a shaking hand to her cheek.

"Helen?" Jack looked concerned as he leaned over her. "What's wrong?"

"I'm so sorry." Her voice was weak. "I just felt faint. I—I'll be fine." She sat up a little straighter. "Please. Let's continue. Pay me no mind."

"Of course we will cease, Mrs. Hanson, if you are unwell." Evidently, Shiguro drew the line at taking advantage of a seemingly ill woman. He spoke sharply to the secretary taking the minutes, and the woman jumped up and scurried from the room. "I have sent for a physician."

Oh, Lord. This is what she got for acting without thought. "Please, I do not wish to cause an inconvenience. If I could just have a few minutes of rest."

Jack was eyeing her oddly. Naturally. The man was such a straight shooter.

Something she'd always tried to be, too. But desperate times called for desperate measures, and she'd been proving that for months now.

"She may rest in my office," Shiguro said.

It wasn't quite what Helen had hoped for, but beggars

couldn't be choosers. "Thank you very much for your kindness," she said weakly. "Jack, you'll help me, won't you?" She held her hands toward him.

He bent over her as he helped her out of her seat. She stumbled a little, resting her head against his shoulder, tossing in a pitiful moan for good measure.

"What are you doing?" he whispered as he half carried, half walked her toward the door.

"Hush."

He did, until they were closed in the relative privacy of Shiguro Taka's office.

Jack dumped her on a chair. "Have you lost your mind?"

Helen straightened her jacket. "Did you want to continue that farce of a meeting? There was no other way we could call a halt without—"

"—causing offense." He exhaled roughly. "I feel like we've taken two months' worth of work and tossed it out the damned window. What did you do with Mori last night, anyway, that he blew off the meeting today?"

She hated the defensiveness that swelled inside her. But she wasn't sure that she *hadn't* done something to set today's debacle in motion.

"I didn't *do* anything with him," she said truthfully. "You know as much about Mori's whereabouts today as I do." And getting angry served no good purpose. "I didn't know what else to do at the meeting, all right? If we were at home, I would have just said it was time to break, but you know that doesn't work here. Shiguro would take it as a sign of weakness on our part or a lack of respect for TAKA, or both. Either way, we'd be on the short end of the stick. But if they think I'm unwell, it's an excuse we can all forgive."

"You think they believed that little act of yours? You may be good at gaining the interest of wealthy men, Helen, but you are *no* actress."

She stomped down the pain inside her. She'd been acting for months and nobody had even known it. "It doesn't matter if they believed it or not, Jack. The point is, we're not going to let Shiguro call the shots, and he'll have gotten that message today, without having his nose rubbed in it."

"Games," Jack snapped. "It's playing games."

"Negotiations are a game," Helen said tiredly. Lord knew that George had taught her that quite well. "It's just one where the stakes involve more than a gold-plated trophy."

He raked his hand through his hair and paced the confines of Shiguro's office. It was surprisingly modest in size. "Now what do we do? Hang around for the next few hours waiting for them to get some doctor in here?"

"Don't worry. It'll only be a few minutes before they'll send someone in to check on us. We'll apologize most sincerely for the inconvenience I am causing and reschedule the sit-down. No harm, no foul."

He looked highly dissatisfied with the entire matter.

She couldn't blame him.

She wasn't feeling particularly satisfied with anything at the moment, either.

"If this merger falls through this late, Hanson won't be able to recover."

How well she knew that. "Hanson wouldn't have recovered if it had fallen through earlier, either, Jack."

He stared out the window, his hands shoved in his pockets. "Nice of my father to leave us with this mess, with no warning, no plans for how to save it all."

He'd had a plan, all right, Helen answered silently. Her headache seemed to worsen at the thought, and when Shiguro arrived with a physician in tow—one who spoke not one word of English—she didn't have to work very hard at feigning illness at all.

Helen sat there portraying "wan" and the men organized her return to her hotel, just as she'd known they would. And Jack, bless his heart, insisted on accompanying her, when Shiguro suggested resuming the meeting without her.

The man was not pleased, and as she spent the rest of the afternoon and evening alone in her hotel suite, going over the latest reports from Chicago, she couldn't help but wonder if Shiguro was suddenly manipulating things on his own accord, or if he'd been instructed to do so by the absent Mori.

She was sleeping when the phone rang.

She sat up with a start, blinking at the bright reading lamp beside the couch where she'd dozed off.

The clock read 2:00 a.m.

The phone rang again and she snatched it up, alarm in her voice. "Yes?"

"I heard you were feeling poorly."

The adrenaline pulsing through her abated slightly. Spread across the coffee table were the reports she'd been studying all evening.

They'd lulled her to sleep.

"Helen? Are you there?"

"I'm here. Mori? What are you calling at this hour for? Is there a problem?"

"You tell me."

She rubbed her hand down her face, trying to jump start her sluggish brain. "Where were you today?"

"My father-in-law died."

Shock provided more than the necessary spark to her brain. "Good heavens. I'm so sorry. Shiguro didn't say anything about it."

"I have heard reports from the meeting."

She could only guess what sort of slant they'd have if they'd been provided by his brother. And, she still wasn't convinced that Mori hadn't set up the entire thing—though it seemed oddly backhanded for a man who'd been perfectly upfront about his objections in the past.

"Are you all right?" she asked.

He was silent for a moment, as if her question surprised him. "Why would I not be?"

"Your wife's father?"

"It was...not unexpected. I did expect Shiguro to reschedule the meeting."

"You *did?*"

"He and my father believed it was more important to proceed."

The father with whom she knew Mori was often at odds. "I'm afraid we didn't get much accomplished."

"Because you were taken ill."

She covered her eyes with her hand, unable to form the lie. "Was it your decision to reduce our board positions from three to one?"

"The physician my brother provided. Was he helpful?"

In other words, no, the reduction hadn't been his

idea. If it had been his decision, he would have just said so. But he couldn't very well tell her that his brother had chosen to act without his approval.

"The doctor was very solicitous," she assured him. "Will you be needing to change the scheduled meetings, then? Because of your loss?"

"It would mean a delay of a week or longer."

Better a delay than to give Shiguro another opportunity to press his own agenda. "Then we will have a small delay," Helen said. "How is your daughter? Was she close to her grandfather?"

"She is back at school. Brown-haired again and broken-hearted over that more than the loss of a man she barely knew."

"Did your wife have siblings?"

"No. I am the closest family member. Sumiko's mother will need my assistance. I'll be in Takayama for several days."

"Of course. Mori, I am sorry. I'm glad you called."

"I should have waited until a more suitable hour to speak with you."

Why hadn't he? She badly wanted to ask, but refrained. "It's fine that you called me now."

"You were awake?"

"Well, no. But that's all right."

"I startled you."

He'd startled the life out of her. She couldn't get a call at such an hour anymore and not be reminded of the night she'd been phoned with the news that George had suffered a heart attack in his office. "A little," she admitted. "But I'm still glad that you called."

There was no denying the personal nature of his

doing so, though. "Is…is there anything I can do?" She knew the offer sounded ridiculous. She was a *gaijin*—a foreigner in his country. A person with whom he was associated only because of business purposes. Her question made about as much sense as him calling at such a late hour.

"No. Thank you."

She stared at her bare feet, hesitant to bid him the good-night that would be the sensible course. "So, Kimiko's hair is back to normal. Did the tat wash off?"

"Tat? Ah. The flag. Yes. It is gone. I am keeping you from your sleep," he said abruptly.

Since she'd met Mori, her sleep had been interrupted by him. He just wasn't privy to that fact. "Well, good night, then."

"Kombanwa."

Helen hung up the phone. She didn't shut off the light and move to the bedroom, though, until she realized she was picturing Mori sitting on his end, staring at the phone the same way she'd been.

She hadn't brought very many personal items with her to Tokyo. Only clothes and accessories that she would need to get through the meetings with TAKA.

But she had brought her jewelry case.

Not the enormous locking monstrosity that George had once insisted she use to store the jewelry he liked her to wear when it wasn't in the safe, but a much smaller, simple wooden box. She lifted the lid.

Once, the box had contained only letters. Unsent letters that she'd written to her daughter. One every year since her birth.

Jenny had those letters now. Reading them had

helped to show her that she *hadn't* been unloved by her natural mother. That Helen hadn't shunted her off as a baby to the quickest taker just because it was the easiest solution for Helen.

Now, the jewelry box contained one narrow tray, partially filled with Helen's few necklaces and bracelets—and a dried leaf that she had kept for reasons that still escaped her.

But it wasn't any of those that drew Helen. It was the single folded sheet of paper beneath the tray.

She pulled it out. Unfolded the weighty stationery. Embossed at the top were George's initials.

Such familiar paper.

She'd given the stationery to him for their last anniversary, along with the gold pen she now used.

Quite a testament to one's marriage, wasn't it? A gift of personalized stationery and an engraved pen.

There had been no romantic evening for them to celebrate. Those had gone by the wayside years earlier, about the same time that George had told her he was not interested in having a baby with her, after all.

Back then, she'd blamed his decision on weariness over their failure to conceive, despite availing themselves of every conceivable technological advance in the area.

Now, Helen knew better when it came to George's motives. Their life together hadn't been based on love, at all. Not even from the beginning.

She unfolded the letter, her fingers smoothing along the creases.

Helen, it began. Not even a *dear,* or *my darling* to soften the words to come.

Helen,
I knew when we met that you'd make me an admirable wife. Beauty and intelligence is an appealing combination, so despite your modest beginnings, I knew your presence at my side would serve me well. The smartest thing I did was to marry you. I've watched you these years and you've never failed in meeting the purposes for which I chose you, whether it was charming my associates or hosting my friends. You were disappointed that I didn't publicly avail myself of your business acumen—the very thing that brought you into my world when you were nothing but a bright intern—but that didn't stop you from offering your thoughts all these years, even when they were unasked for. You have tenacity, Helen. And grit. I've always liked that about you. But now, you'll have to use those traits to undo what I've done. I always knew you'd outlive me, Helen. If you're reading this, then you'll know I was right in my thinking. Now I'm trusting you to take care of Hanson Media. You'll know what to do when the time comes.

It's all I have to give the boys, even though they never seemed much to want it. Maybe, as they get older, they'll be smarter than their old man, and put value where it is due.

Now, there's only one thing left for you to do, Helen.

Save the only thing that matters to me: Hanson Media.

It was signed, simply, *George.*

* * *

She could have recited the words by heart, so often had she made herself read it since she'd found it—sealed and addressed to her along with the pen he'd probably used to write it—waiting for her to discover in his personal papers at the office.

But the one word that the letter did not contain, the one word that would have meant the world to her, was the one he'd deliberately withheld.

Love.

George hadn't married her because he'd loved her. He'd married her for just exactly the things people had whispered.

Her youth.

Her looks.

Her intelligence, which he only wanted in evidence when they were in private.

It hadn't been love that prompted him to sweep her off her feet when she'd been a lonely intern with a fresh MBA. It had been his calculated mind that had seen which attributes would best serve his needs that had motivated their marriage. Unfortunately, Helen's love for him had blinded her to the truth. George hadn't really wanted her as a wife. She'd *been* a trophy because she'd allowed him to make her one. Yet he'd died trusting that she would be able to pull his company out of the fire.

She folded the letter and shoved it back in the box, flipping the lid closed. There were times she wished she'd burned the letter. Set a flame to it and watched it go up in smoke, just the way she'd felt the marriage she'd committed herself to out of *love* had gone up in smoke.

But she was what George said she was.

Tenacious.

Only now she had to prove to herself that she wasn't *only* what George had made of her—a wife chosen for her assets, rather than her heart.

If she had to work with TAKA in order to do that, she would. But once Hanson Media was secure again, joined at the hip with the juggernaut that TAKA was, she'd be happy never to think again of the man who hadn't loved her, after all, *or* his company.

Chapter Six

"You have a visitor, Helen."

Helen dragged her focus out of the month-ends and looked up. Her assistant, Sonia Townsley, stood in the doorway of her office. "I thought my only appointment was later."

"It is. Three-thirty with the broker who wants to list your house."

Helen pressed her fingers to her temple. She hadn't made up her mind yet what she would do with the house. But Darryl Waters was an old friend of George who'd been pushing for the listing. Since she was back in Chicago while Mori handled his father-in-law's matters, she'd agreed to discuss the matter with the broker, but only *discuss*. "Then who is here?"

Sonia slipped into the office, looking almost clandestine. "Morito Taka," she whispered.

Helen stared. *"What?"* She hadn't spoken with Mori since the night he'd called about his father-in-law, a week earlier. Because of the delay in negotiations, she'd decided to return to Chicago to attend to matters there while Jack and Samantha had remained in Tokyo.

"Not what. *Who.* Morito Taka." Sonia waggled her hand in front of her. "And if I might say so…holy cow. Wow." She collected herself when Helen just waited. "Everything is in such a mess up here that I put him in the conference room."

What would Mori be doing in Chicago? Unannounced, yet?

"Helen?"

She realized she was staring at the round fishbowl on the corner of her desk. The Betta seemed to be staring back at her as he slowly swished his brilliant blue tail. He'd arrived by courier a few days after her return.

A gift from Mori. A gift for which she worked hard at not placing too much importance. The Japanese were notorious for gift giving. The fish was nothing more than a polite courtesy. Nothing more significant than the collection of funky hair ornaments that she'd sent to him for Kimiko.

"The conference room is fine," she said.

"He'll want a tour, I suppose. I can give the departments a heads-up."

"Of course. Right. Good idea." She stood and smoothed back her hair as Sonia headed to the door. "No. Wait."

Her assistant stopped, her eyebrows lifted. "Yes?"

Why would he make such an unprecedented visit? Was it another attempt to call off the merger?

Just because the final negotiations had been temporarily halted, did that mean he wanted to halt them permanently?

She looked at the fish, her mind teeming. Mori the man. Mori the opposition. Which was real? Which did she trust?

She closed her eyes for a moment, shutting out the sight of the exquisite fish. The debate going on inside her head wasn't so easily avoided.

"Don't call anyone," she said. "Mr. Taka will have his tour. There's nothing at Hanson that isn't up to snuff." She tugged the hem of her jacket and headed out the door. "Don't worry, Sonia," she assured. "Go back to what you were doing. And call Darryl for me to reschedule."

"Shouldn't I call Evan or Andrew? Or David?"

"There's nothing to call them about," Helen said. "If Mori thinks he's going to find us less than prepared, he's wrong. Period."

Sonia looked uneasy, but she nodded, and Helen made her way to the conference room.

Despite the several days since she'd last seen Mori in Tokyo, the sight of him still had her catching her breath. He was standing at the window, looking out.

She moistened her lips, wishing she'd taken a few minutes just to freshen her lipstick, then was annoyed at her own insecure vanity.

She straightened her shoulders and entered the room. "Mori. This is a surprise."

He turned. As always, he wore a suit. This one was a dove gray that ought to have given him a more approachable look than his typical black. It didn't. He was as unreasonably attractive as ever, too.

"Not an unwelcome surprise, I hope," he replied smoothly.

"Of course not." She crossed the carpet toward him, hand extended, which he shook. Thankfully, the disturbing contact was brief. "Quite the opposite," she assured, hoping she wasn't telling a blatant lie. "It will be a pleasure to finally show you our shop here."

"The reports from my associates who have been here have always been most complimentary." His voice was so diplomatic she had the sudden urge to laugh. She knew good and well that his associates had returned to him every nitpicking detail about the Chicago office in order to increase TAKA's bargaining power and decrease Hanson's.

"Well, you've seen the view—" she nodded her head toward the bank of windows "—so, shall we see the rest?"

"You have the time?"

"Actually, no," she admitted wryly. "I'm in the middle of pulling together month-ends for a certain CEO."

His lips lifted in one of his rare smiles. "A tyrant?"

At that, she did laugh. Softly. The man definitely had a way of surprising her. "An excellent negotiator," she corrected. "We'll start here on this floor and work our way down."

"And will you show me every nook and cranny?"

"Every dusty corner," she assured lightly, and exited the room ahead of him.

She was painfully aware of the warmth of him as he followed her, which was ridiculous given the circumspect distance he maintained between them.

They made their way along the corridor, and Helen pointed out each office, stopping to make introductions along the way. She knew it was unaccustomed behavior for him—he negotiated deals at the highest level. He wasn't one to take note of every employee under the roof.

But Helen was. That was the way Hanson Media worked now, and Mori might as well learn that fact, for good or bad. And, she was relieved to see, nobody quailed at meeting the big man himself. To a one, her staff members were dignified, professional and welcoming. Unfortunately, David, George's younger brother, who was in charge of PR; and Evan, George's middle son, were both out of the office at meetings. "Andrew," she told Mori, as they passed his empty office, "is with his wife, Delia. Do you remember her from Richard and Jenny's wedding?"

"Yes. She is carrying your first grandchild."

She hesitated only momentarily, before answering with a smooth smile. The truth was, she didn't have any expectations that Andrew would want his and Delia's child to think of her as a grandparent.

She was just grateful that she was truly happy for Delia, who—at thirty-seven—was carrying a baby when at the same age, Helen had been unable to conceive. She'd been somewhat afraid that she'd be envious of her. Instead, she'd only felt pleasure and anticipation.

Thank goodness.

But that didn't mean Helen was certain that *she* was ready to be thought of as a grandparent, either.

They finished exploring the floor and then returned to her office. Mori glanced around, not seeming particularly interested in the furnishings or the view beyond the sparkling windows. He bent slightly and looked at the fishbowl, however.

Helen had not only sent him a written thank-you for the gift, she'd personally calle,d as well. "The fish was a very thoughtful gift," she said. "Again, I thank you."

"You did not tell me he was your officemate."

"Well, I'm here more than I am at home. Captain Nemo would get lonely at home."

"Captain Nemo?"

"From *Twenty Thousand Leagues Under the Sea.* The book."

He straightened. "Yes. I know it."

She folded her hands together, hoping she hadn't inadvertently insulted him. "Shall I show you the rest of our offices? Do you have time constraints?" She ought to have asked that earlier. The man could have a dozen reasons for being in the States that did not concern Hanson Media Group in the least. "Perhaps Evan and David will be able to make a late lunch with us."

"My time is yours."

A few weeks earlier and she would have found that idea daunting. Now she found it…disturbingly appealing. "All right, then. Back to seeing those nooks and crannies." She headed out of her office. "Sonia, check David's and Evan's schedules and see if we can't get in somewhere for lunch."

Her assistant nodded. "Will do."

Satisfied, Helen headed toward the elevator. Mori touched her elbow as they got on, just a slight grazing of his fingertips, and she stopped, looking up at him.

His faint crows feet crinkled. "I find I have missed our conversations."

She couldn't have moved then if a train had been bearing down on her. "I'm not sure if you're pulling my leg, or not."

He glanced down. "Lovely though they are, I must refrain."

The laughter rose in her throat before she could stop it. If a man were to say such a thing to a woman in the workplace nowadays, he'd be accused of harassment. "How fortunate for me," she returned humorously and managed to keep herself from smoothing a self-conscious hand down her skirt.

The fact of the matter was, she wasn't altogether sure she wouldn't like his hands on her legs. Very much.

And wasn't that quite the admission standing in her husband's office building?

George is gone.

She banished the whispered reminder from her thoughts and left the elevator when the doors opened. Mori followed.

Was he looking at her legs?

Stop thinking like a schoolgirl.

She walked a little more quickly, heading toward the print division. His long legs easily kept pace beside her. "When did you arrive in the U.S.?"

"This morning."

She slowed, glancing up at him. "Aren't you tired?"

"Not particularly."

She found the trip between Tokyo and Chicago exhausting.

"I am almost a day younger here, after all," he continued. "Is that not the ultimate quest of the Americans? To find their youth?"

"But you'll regain the day when you return home," Helen reminded. "And I might miss the days when I didn't…creak quite so much when I get up in the morning, but I can't say returning to *my* youth is all that appealing."

She pushed through the double doorway and entered a cacophony of voices and computer keys. "Speaking of youth, however, how is your daughter?"

"Still brown-haired. She sends me e-mail photos of herself wearing the hair decorations you sent. She is most pleased with them. I will forward a few to you if you would like to see them."

Helen managed not to smile too widely as she paused inside the doorway. "I would love to. I'm glad she is enjoying them. She was delightful, even with the pink 'do.'"

"She looked…common."

"She's only experimenting, Mori. She struck me as incredibly bright and creative."

"She can be bright and creative when she is in university. Until then, she needs to focus on her studies."

"Never underestimate the importance of education," Helen agreed. It had taken her longer than usual to obtain hers, but she'd finally put herself through college working nearly any job she could get to pay for her MBA.

And then she'd met George and her career aspirations had taken a backseat.

She lifted her arms, encompassing the pack of cubicles and desks and the people who worked at them.

"The heart of the newspaper," she said, raising her voice a little. "This is where Hanson Media Group all began." She continued her stint as tour guide, entering the fray, making introductions and briefly describing each person's role.

It had taken her nights of study to learn all the names and responsibilities. But it had been well worth it when she'd been able to knowledgably discuss the staff that first day after George's will had put her in charge.

Hanson had endured heavy layoffs shortly after Jack had come on board and discovered the seriousness of his father's mismanagement. By knowing the people who remained, Helen had been able to earn their otherwise reluctant trust.

There was still an element of fear underriding most everyone who worked at Hanson Media, but it didn't have the crews heading for the nearest porthole, ready to desert a sinking ship. They were sticking tight and well, not certain how the entire merger would work out, but willing to wait and give it a chance.

Mori, she noticed as they finally made their way through the other divisions—even radio, which he didn't have to show an interest in since that had to be separated from Hanson Media Group before they could become part of a foreign company—seemed much more approachable than he did walking the corridors of his own castle.

He just smiled faintly when she dared comment on it once they returned to her office. He'd seated himself in one of the side chairs around the small round table in her office. "If I were to engage in conversation with the salary men, word would quickly spread that I had lost my sanity. I would no longer have their respect."

Sonia popped her head in. "David can meet you at Benny's at two. I haven't been able to reach Evan. I've left a message for him."

"Thanks, Sonia."

Her assistant smiled and disappeared again, closing the door behind her.

Helen wished Sonia hadn't done that. It seemed to add too much privacy to her meeting with Mori. So, she busied herself pouring them both glasses of water from the pitcher Sonia had placed on the table while they'd been touring the building. "How is your mother-in-law doing?"

"She is well. She is visiting my mother's home for a few days."

"Your two families are close, then? They live some distance from each other, don't they?"

"Hai." His long fingers slowly circled the glass, but he did not lift it. "The Yamamoto and Taka families were the oldest in Nesutotaka. My mother and Sumiko's mother were like sisters growing up. Sumiko's mother moved away when she married, however. But they still remained friends."

"And they liked the idea of their children marrying?"

"It was not a sentimental decision," Mori explained. "Sumiko's lineage was desirable to my father's family. TAKA had provided my family with great wealth, but it is the Yamamoto family that once had ties to the emperor. My mother and father's marriage was decided upon for similar reasons. Each generation has made an advantageous match."

"And you think your daughter should do the same, when she's older."

"You have that look of disapproval in your eyes, Helen."

She looked down at her hands. She was holding her glass in the same way that Mori was. Only a few inches separated their knuckles. "People, even Americans, marry for all sorts of reasons. But I'm old-fashioned enough to wish everyone would marry only for love."

"I think that is more a romantic belief than an old-fashioned one. Even Americans have had arranged marriages, and not so many generations ago."

She couldn't dispute the truth of that. "Well, these days marriage here is so easily entered and exited that I think it takes a deep emotional commitment to make it last. And if the people don't care about making it last, then what is the point of marrying in the first place?"

She looked up to find him watching her with that mesmerizing stare of his, and felt her cheeks heat. She laughed lightly. "And if that isn't getting away from the purpose of your visit, I don't know what is."

"You had this deep emotional commitment to your late husband?"

She inhaled a little. "I did."

His eyes narrowed a little and she knew he'd caught her unconscious emphasis of "I." But he let the matter pass without comment, for which she was profoundly grateful. "The purpose for my visit was not to tour Hanson," he said. "Though I did find it enlightening."

Enlightening? She stifled her wariness over that particular statement. "Then what is the reason you're here?"

"To offer you my apology."

Her heart dove right down to her toes. She couldn't have drawn a breath if she'd been a red flag waved in front of a bull's nose. "You're calling off the merger."

His eyebrows shot together. "You have gone as pale as moonlight. Drink your water."

If she drank, she'd vomit. All these months of maneuvering, of planning, negotiating, of sleepless nights and endless days had been for naught.

She'd failed.

He made a sound under his breath and wrapped his hand around hers on the glass, lifting it toward her mouth. "Drink," he ordered. "I am not, as you say, *calling off* anything. The acquisition is proceeding."

There was an odd buzzing sound inside her head. Water filled her mouth and she swallowed before it spilled over her chin. "Merger," she mumbled.

His lips twitched. "Better." He lowered their hands and set the glass on the table. "Do not faint. I would not know what to do with you."

"I have the feeling you *always* know what to do," she murmured. She realized his hand was still covering hers, and his fingers felt warm and...comforting.

She didn't want comforting. She wanted the merger inked so maybe her life would lose the nightmarish tinge it had developed. "What do you mean by apologizing, then? You've done nothing that requires one." Certainly not something that would necessitate a trip from Japan to offer it.

"My father does not wish for TAKA to become involved with American business," he said. "He strongly disapproves of it."

"Your father is no longer CEO of TAKA, though. You are." If Yukio Taka had still been in control, she *never* would have gone to TAKA.

"It is not our nature to dishonor one's father."

"Well, I can certainly understand that. And I respect that. But I still don't—"

"You will let me continue?"

She clamped her lips shut and nodded.

He sighed a little. "My father met with Shiguro on the day that I was unable to attend our scheduled meeting."

"When your father-in-law passed away."

"*Hai.* That day. My father convinced Shiguro to try to renegotiate some of our previously approved items."

"The number of board seats."

"*Hai.* Shiguro, he is a good man. A good…son. I regret that his good intentions to our father were insulting to you and your associates. Shiguro offered to come here himself, as he should. But it is I who is ultimately to blame."

"You weren't responsible for what your brother decided to do, Mori."

"Everything that occurs in the house of TAKA is my responsibility. I wish to assure you that the Hanson seats are unchanged."

"Well. I'm relieved to know that we won't have to battle *that* out again. It was difficult enough in the first place. Of course, I accept your apology."

"Though you find it unnecessary."

His fingers were more tanned than hers, the backs of his hands slightly dusted with hair.

Masculine hands. Strong hands.

She'd seen him casually wield the sword in his hotel suite. Would his hand be as deft without a weapon?

She swallowed.

"Perhaps unnecessary, but welcome all the same," she assured, casually pulling her hand free of his by reaching for the pitcher and refilling the glass. "It is reassuring to have confirmation that Shiguro's actions that day hadn't been at your request."

"I do not force my decisions through other parties."

"No, you don't. You say right up front that something is or isn't acceptable. It's very honest. I admire that."

"Honesty isn't always a part of business."

She shook her head. "Or life." Then, because that seemed too dreary altogether, she looked at her watch. "We should go if we're going to catch David at the restaurant. It's a popular haunt of Hanson people, just a few blocks from here, if you don't mind walking?"

"No, I do not mind."

She retrieved her purse from the drawer in the desk and after confirming that Sonia had been able to change Helen's appointment with the real estate broker, she and Mori left the building.

It was a particularly stunning day outside, just breezy enough to lend a coolness to the day, and a hint of approaching autumn weather. As they walked, Helen pointed out directions for some of the more famous landmarks—the Sears tower, the Hancock Building—and before she knew it, they were entering the dark, cavelike entrance to Benny's. Several steps down, the light moderated some, and the jazz trio playing in the corner could be heard.

It was quite unlike any place that TAKA had hosted them at in Tokyo and she couldn't help but wonder what Mori's reaction would be. She spotted David already seated, and wove her way through the closely set tables to him.

Her brother-in-law stood as she approached and stuck out his hand to Mori as she made the introductions. "David was George's younger brother," she told him, even though Mori would certainly be aware of the relationship. "Hanson's PR department is incredible and it's all because of David."

"Helen gives me too much credit," David said easily. "We have a great public relations department because we have a great group of people who make it so."

They sat and a waitress sidled by, depositing a tray of warm rolls and cold crudités in the center of their table. "Drinks?"

"Iced tea for me," Helen said. David and Mori both nodded and the waitress disappeared again.

"So, Mr. Taka, what prompted your visit to Chicago?" David's question was congenial, but she certainly knew what he had to be thinking beneath it. The same thing she'd been afraid of.

"Mostly social," Mori told him and his gaze was on Helen as he said it.

Her mouth went a little dry and she wished the waitress would hurry with the iced tea.

"Well, if you want to see anything of the city, Helen's your girl. She knows the place like the back of her hand."

"Does she?" A faint smile played around Mori's sharply carved lips. "How…convenient for me."

"David is too modest," Helen countered. "He's lived here longer than I have."

"Maybe," David conceded, "but I wouldn't make as entertaining a guide as you. Plus, if you get tired of the typical tourist attractions, you might enjoy seeing the house. George and Helen's place. It's considered one of the finest properties in the city."

Helen found her gaze trapped by Mori's. "Then I must not miss seeing Helen's place," he stated.

Forget dry-mouthed. She was dying, purely and simply.

From somewhere, however, she dredged up an agreeable nod. "I would be pleased to show you my home, Mori."

And then his smile widened, and she wasn't sure that receiving an invitation to her home hadn't been his intention, all along.

But why?

Hosting business associates at their place had been one of the things George had evidently married her for. She'd done it often and done it well.

So why did the idea of Mori Taka being under her roof send every nerve she possessed into a fit of the screaming meemies?

Chapter Seven

Helen's shrieking nervousness was still well in play later that evening as she put the finishing touches on the table.

She'd set two place settings at one end of the mile-long dining table. On any given day, the table could seat twenty, and while Helen might have felt safer putting Mori at one end and her at the other, she did realize that doing so would look as infantile as it felt.

It's only a business dinner.

She kept telling herself that while she straightened the blown glass vase containing a tight bouquet of Sterling roses. It's only a business dinner. Only.

"Mrs. Hanson?" Gertrude, the housekeeper, who was the only staff person whom Helen had kept on, spoke from the dining room entrance. "I've selected a few wines from the cellar for your dinner. Would you like to look them over?"

Helen shook her head. Gertrude had worked for George even before their marriage. Helen hadn't had the heart to suggest she retire, and these days, it was only the two of them who floated around the enormous house. Helen had left it up to Gertrude to hire a cleaning service to help her, and had been grateful when the older woman finally, grudgingly, allowed a strictly supervised crew to come in monthly and do the "heavy work" as Gertrude called it. "I'm sure whatever you chose will be perfect."

Gertrude hesitated a little, her light blue gaze somewhat curious. "This *is* a business dinner?"

"Yes." Helen turned the vase an inch.

"For two."

Another quarter inch. "Yes."

Gertrude sniffed a little and came more fully into the room. "Pardon me for saying so, Mrs. Hanson, but it *is* okay for you to have a date."

Helen jerked and stared at Gertrude. "Excuse me?"

"You're a young woman. You shouldn't be alone."

Her cheeks flushed. "I don't feel all that young, I'm afraid."

"Oh, garbage." Gertrude patted her ample hips. "*I* am not all that young, and even I have a gentleman caller from time to time."

Helen raised her eyebrows.

"Now, don't look so surprised, Mrs. Hanson. I'm a woman, after all."

"Yes, you are, Gertrude. And one I'd be lost without." She looked at the table. "But this really *is* a business dinner."

Gertrude looked regretful. "Well, all right. If that's the case, then I really should stay to serve and clean up after."

"No, you shouldn't. All I have to do is pull things out of the oven and fridge because you're so organized. Go." She smiled. "Call up your gentleman friend and go wild."

"You go ahead and laugh," Gertrude replied blandly, "but you just might be surprised what a woman my age can get up to."

Helen chuckled. "I'm not laughing at you, my friend. You give me hope."

Gertrude patted Helen's shoulder. "Go put on something pretty."

Helen looked down at her clothing. "What's wrong with this?"

"Even if it is a business dinner, you don't have to wear an iron gray suit."

"You make it sound like I look like a prison matron," Helen murmured. "This is a designer suit."

"I suppose I could scare up some handcuffs and a baton for you," Gertrude replied, "but something a little softer might be more appealing, fancy designer name or not."

The doorbell chimed softly.

And for all of Helen's insistence that this dinner was strictly business, she froze.

Gertrude, bless her soul, refrained from saying "I told you so," but her arch expression conveyed it anyway. "Skedaddle up those stairs to your room. I'll let in your guest and show him into the library. Cozier there than the living room, don't you think?"

Helen didn't know what to think. She just went up the stairs at a rapid clip, hearing Gertrude head to the door behind her.

In her closet, Helen stared at the racks of clothing. What would she wear? She grabbed a hanger.

A skirt that left *way* too much of her thighs bare? No. That was from the George days.

She tossed the hanger aside and grabbed another.

Suits, suits, suits. She owned dozens of them. Found them to be her safety net in fashion, and had ever since she buried her husband along with his desire to see her in the latest fad, even when *she* had felt ludicrous wearing such revealing items.

Her heart was thudding in her chest, and she could actually feel herself beginning to perspire.

"Get a grip, Helen."

She turned away from the side of her closet filled with suits, and the side still filled with her George-days wardrobe. Jeans were much too casual, as were her plethora of capris and workout garments.

From downstairs she could hear the faint sound of the heavy front door closing and imagined Mori walking through her home, escorted by Gertrude to the library. There wasn't a fire burning in the fireplace down there, but it still would offer a decidedly intimate feel for Mori.

Why hadn't she told Gertrude to put him in the living room?

She groaned and grabbed a sleeveless white sweater and a pair of loose silk slacks. In seconds, she'd replaced the iron maiden. She hurried out of her room, dashing down the stairs and practically running to the library.

She stopped outside the arched doorway and, smoothing back her ponytail, drew in a long breath, grabbed composure with a desperate grip and entered the room. "Mori, I'm so sorry to keep you waiting."

He wasn't wearing a suit, either, she thought inconsequentially. A thin cashmere sweater the color of nutmeg covered his chest and chocolate brown slacks completed the look.

Very chic.

Very…handsome.

Very…un-Mori.

The man had probably been born in a suit. How could she continue convincing herself they were having dinner in her home for purely business reasons when the man didn't even have the decency to dress for the occasion?

"You did not keep me waiting," he said, interrupting the flow of insanity inside her brain. "I was studying your book collection. It is very eclectic."

"Most of it was George's."

He pulled out a narrow leather-bound volume. "Emily Dickinson?"

"Not all of the collection was George's," she qualified.

He smiled faintly and slid the book back into place.

Her palms felt moist. She curled them over the back of the upholstered love seat that faced the stone fireplace. "Did you settle in to your hotel all right?"

"Yes." His gaze continued traveling over the room, and finally settled on her.

She should say something. She was a grown woman. A sophisticated woman. Everyone said so.

So why couldn't she find a single coherent thought inside her entire stupid head?

"Thirsty?" she blurted. "I mean, would you like a drink?"

"Beer, if you have it."

She pressed the tip of her tongue against the inside of her teeth. "Have a seat. I'll be right with you."

He nodded, but turned back to the towering shelves filled with books. As soon as she saw him pulling one out, she made herself move sedately from the room.

Good as her word, Gertrude had already departed. Probably because she'd taken one look at the very sexy Mori Taka and decided that she could be absent for *this* particular business dinner. Helen yanked open the stainless steel refrigerator door and crouched down, studying the contents, hoping there would be a beer or two lurking in the cavernous confines.

There wasn't.

Her breath hissing between her teeth, she quietly darted through the house and into George's home office. Sure enough, there were still bottles in the small refrigerator hidden in the wall. She grabbed a few and ran back to the kitchen where she poured herself a short, squat glass of ice water. She set everything on a silver tray, added a bottle opener and a pilsner glass from the cupboard and carried it back to the library.

He was sitting on the love seat.

Somehow, his choice made her uneasy.

Not uneasy in a fearful way, but uneasy in a woman-man sort of way.

She really was losing her mind.

She smiled at him and set the tray on the table next to the love seat. There was no coffee table between it and the fireplace; only an exotically thick off-white Flokati rug covered the carpet.

There were three other chairs near the love seat and

she chose the closest one to him before opening the beer to pour into his glass. "I hope import is okay." She handed it to him.

He looked amused as he reached over and wrapped his hand around the tall, skinny beer bottle she still held. "It is a Japanese beer. To me, it is not an import."

She laughed and shook her head at herself. *"Sumimasen."*

He handed her the remaining glass and lifted his in a toast. *"Kampai."*

She took the glass from him, grateful that she'd stuck with water and not anything alcoholic. Her head was already swimming enough. "Cheers."

They drank.

Then, not wanting another awkward silence to descend between them, Helen stood. "Please excuse me. I just need to check the oven for a moment. I hope you like chicken." She didn't say it out of courtesy. She was suddenly very aware that during the dinner they'd had that one night, he'd ordered beef.

"I do."

She was appalled at the relief that rolled through her. "I'll be right back."

He smiled faintly.

She took off, rolling her eyes at herself. The man was clearly amused at her.

A fine thing for someone she wanted—needed—to have some measure of respect for her when it came to the bargaining table.

The chicken was perfectly fine when Helen peeked in the oven. How could it not be, with Gertrude having prepared it, and the state-of-the-art oven that shut itself off at the precise time, merely keeping the contents at an optimal temperature?

"It smells good."

She slammed the oven door shut and turned. "I…yes. It does. We can thank Gertrude Singer for that. My… um, my housekeeper. And cook, and everything else I need, pretty much."

"But you say you like to cook?"

"I do. But, somehow, I thought homemade pizza might not be your cup of tea."

He set his beer on the granite island that consumed the center portion of the window-lined kitchen. "I do not prefer anchovies on my pizza, but otherwise, Kimiko keeps me well acquainted when she is with me." He pulled out one of the iron-legged barstools on the far side of the island and leaned against it. "You are nervous."

And thank you for pointing it out. "Not at all."

He tilted his head slightly, looking down at the floor. "You have no shoes."

She looked down.

Lord. She'd forgotten to put on shoes.

"Perhaps I don't wear street shoes in my home."

"I doubt that is your custom here," he said wryly.

She wanted to curl her bare toes against the slate tile. "I…forgot," she admitted. "It had nothing to do with nervousness. Just rushing."

If she were Pinocchio, her nose would be a foot long by now.

"Here. Drink."

She realized he'd also brought in her glass of water. "Thank you." She took it and swallowed it down, realizing belatedly that he probably assumed she'd just chugged a half-full glass of vodka or something. Well, that was too bad. At every meeting they'd had in Japan involving the dinner hour, alcohol had flowed freely, even though she'd rarely drunk much more than appearances required.

She just didn't have a head for it.

"Dinner is ready, if you'd like to eat now. Or perhaps you'd like me to show you around the house?" That was, supposedly, the excuse for this tête-à-tête. For him to see the marvel that was George Hanson's abode.

"You can give me the tour after."

"It will be my pleasure. The dining room is this way." She started from the kitchen, only stopping once she reached the formal dining room and held out her arm. "Please. Have a seat."

He looked up at the high frescoed ceiling then around the large room. "An impressive room."

"That seems to be the impression most people have."

"And you?"

She tried looking at the room with fresh eyes. "It is impressive. And large. And—" she rocked her head from side to side "—and…large."

"Very large."

She felt a smile budding around her lips—a real smile. "Well. We *could* eat in the kitchen."

"Would that scandalize you?"

Surprisingly, her grin broke right out at that. "Mori, if you haven't realized it yet, scandal is becoming second nature to me." Then she held her breath, because, though she was *almost* getting to the point where she could speak lightly of painful things that had been mucked about in the press about her, she wasn't at all certain he would feel the same.

But a dimple slowly appeared in his cheek as he smiled. "The kitchen it shall be." Suiting words to action, he crossed to the table and deftly stacked the plates.

She hurried after him, picking up the flatware and linens and stemware.

They reset their table at one end of the island. Mori disappeared for a moment while she was busy serving up the roast chicken and setting out side dishes.

She was just finishing when Mori returned. He wasn't carrying the foot-high vase, but he was carrying one of the roses.

She set the wine Gertrude had chosen on the counter and eyed the flower. The barely unfurled blossom looked delicate and silvery against his fingers.

Then he handed her the rose. "If you would please hold this?"

She took it, watching curiously as he picked up his beer bottle. He looked very serious then as he shook out his ivory linen napkin, made a fold or two, followed by a few deft twists that she could barely follow, and swaddled the bottle in ivory linen.

The finished product looked like a flower itself, and then he took the rose from her and dropped the stem into the center of his creation.

She slipped onto one of the stools. "Well, my goodness. Does the TAKA board know what highly developed skills you're hiding?"

"You would not be so impressed if you saw what Shiguro can do with a cherry stem."

It took her a bare moment longer than it should

have to realize he was joking because his expression was so deadpan.

She smiled and pointed at him with a stern finger. "You're a tough one, Mr. Taka. But I know your secret now. You *do* have a sense of humor."

"Do not let my senior management hear that."

She pressed her lips together and mimicked twisting the key. "The secret will go with me to my grave."

He lifted the wine bottle and filled their glasses. "However, now that you know my secret, you must share with me yours, or we shall be on uneven footing again when next the lawyers crack their whips."

"Ah." She sipped her wine, watching him over the rim of her glass. The man was too attractive by far and drinking wine would only lower her defenses against him. "All of my secrets have been splashed about already. Part and parcel of that scandal thing, you know."

"That is not an answer."

"I kind of thought it was," she countered lightly and set down the wine to reach for the carving knife. "Light or dark?"

"Light."

She quickly carved a slice of succulent chicken and slid it on his plate, then repeated the process for herself.

"You are delaying."

She lifted her eyebrow. "A woman should never divulge her secrets so easily."

"Negotiation." He nodded, seemingly thoughtful. "You like the negotiation as much as you do the end result."

She thought of some of the endlessly tedious meetings she'd endured with TAKA. "Not *every* step of the negotiation."

"Still, you delay."

She pressed her lips together and shot him a long look, which he ignored as he took over serving duty and filled her plate with more food. "I won't be able to eat all of that," she finally said.

"Negotiation is good for the appetite."

She smiled sweetly. "You're an amazingly annoying man, do you know that?"

"So I have been told. The secret?"

She took a fortifying sip of wine. "All right. Sometimes I wish I could chuck all of the business and run away to hide. Just for a few days." To forget she was a widow, that she was fighting tooth and nail to prove her own worth. "Now, see? That was much more *secret* than you expected."

"This is why I go to my home in Nesutotaka. To escape."

"You need to escape? I thought you thrived on the pressure of heading up TAKA."

"Sometimes a man just wants to be a man." His hooded gaze no longer seemed amused as he focused it on her face. "Just as a woman simply wants to be a woman."

Her mouth went dry again and she doused it with another fair dose of the grape. Her half glass was down to a fourth. "And when you escape, do you work in your garden? Mountain climb?"

"You remember our conversation that day."

"I remember everything," she murmured.

"And forgive nothing?"

She hesitated, caught by the question. "No. I'd like to think I forgive."

"Others or yourself?"

The conversation was becoming far too personal for comfort. What would Mori Taka know about matters so intimate to her? Was he taking a shot in the dark, or did her failures show that clearly on her face and in her life?

So she just smiled confidently and picked up the wine bottle. "More?"

He nudged his empty glass within reaching distance of her pour, yet when she finished and set down the bottle, he didn't pick up his glass.

Instead, he caught her hand in midair.

She stilled, looking at his hand on hers. His fingers were warm as he tilted her hand. The diamond setting on her wedding band had turned slightly on her finger and he pressed his thumb against it, moving it until the ring was centered once more. The diamond caught the light and sent gleaming prisms dancing around them.

"You do not eat enough," he said. His thumb nudged the setting once more. The prisms died as the ring slid much too easily around her finger. "What is it you worry about?"

She managed a light laugh and tugged her hand free of his. "Well, I won't worry that my Pilates trainer is ineffective."

"Pilates?"

"It's a type of exercise."

"You need less Pilates, and more food."

"Gosh. Thanks, Mori. Every woman wants to be told she's too skinny. It's right up there with being told she's too heavy."

His slashing eyebrows pulled together over his nose. "I am not wishing to tell you these things. I am expressing concern."

"You have no reason to be concerned," she assured, but her voice didn't hold the ring of authority she'd have preferred. "I'm not suffering from consumption. I'll summon strength enough to celebrate the merger when it's complete, believe me."

"As I told you before, not everything is about business."

She needed to remind him of her response to that, but for some reason she just didn't have the energy to do so. She reached for her wineglass only to realize it was empty. Their plates were empty, too.

When had they managed to polish off most of Gertrude's meal?

Her head was most definitely swimming. "Can I get you anything else, Mori? Gertrude has left a fruit tray if you'd care for something sweet."

"No, thank you."

She began clearing away the dishes, moving them to the sink, and Mori rose, helping her. She couldn't recall George ever doing such a thing, and they'd been married for ten years.

Then, when Mori rolled up his sleeves and began filling the sink with hot water, she decided she must have had *way* too much wine. "What are you doing?"

He'd discovered the narrow compartment beneath the sink. "Soap." He pulled out the bottle of liquid soap and squirted some beneath the running water. "Aids in cleaning," he explained blandly.

"Mori, you're not going to wash dishes."

He reached for a wineglass and without thought, she took hold of it, too. "You're a guest, for goodness' sake."

"And we will work faster together, than alone." He

surrounded her wrist with his free hand and gently worked the glass free of her grip to set it in the soapy bubbles. Without looking, he reached out and flipped off the water.

He did not release her wrist.

She felt parched again and swallowed, moistening her lips. “Mori—” But she didn’t know what to say, so she fell silent.

“We will be concluding the merger soon.” His voice was deep. Low.

“Yes.” Her answer was little more than a whisper. “I…look forward to it.”

“Do you?” With barely half a step, he closed what was left of the distance between them. His thumb smoothed slowly back and forth against her wrist, pressing gently against the pulse that beat there.

“Yes.” This one was even more faint.

His hand slid up from her wrist to her forearm. Her elbow.

“This…isn’t wise.”

His hand grazed beyond her elbow to her upper arm and even higher, cupping her shoulder. “No,” he agreed and lowered his head, slowly covering her lips with his.

A soft sound rose in her throat and time seemed to grind to a halt as he explored the shape of her lips, teasingly light, tempting, exploring.

Wine, she thought hazily. He tasted slightly of wine. She leaned into him, sucking in a breath when his hand slid to the small of her back.

Then there was nothing exploratory, nothing teasing. There was only heat and thick, drowning want.

She clutched his arms, feeling a need to steady herself, when there really was no need, for his arms were strong and warm and surrounding.

"Helen?"

She moaned a little, angling her head, wanting more of Mori's kiss, more of *Mori.*

"Helen? Are you here?"

Mori lifted his head, his eyebrows drawn fiercely together. "There is a woman calling for you."

"Helen?" The voice drew nearer.

Mori had barely set her away from him, putting some semblance of propriety between them, when Delia stepped into the kitchen. Andrew was right behind her.

"There you are," Delia said. "Didn't you hear me calling?"

"Sorry." Helen crossed to the woman who'd captured the heart of her youngest stepson, and kissed her cheek. "You're looking wonderful," she said truthfully, before either Delia or Andrew could question her further. "Pregnancy just seems to agree with you more every day."

Delia pressed her hand down her abdomen that seemed particularly pronounced given her petite size. "Thank you." Her blue gaze traveled beyond Helen to Mori. "Mr. Taka, it is a pleasure to see you again."

"Yes, it is." Andrew moved over to shake the man's hand. "Welcome to Chicago. My uncle told us you were having dinner here tonight." Though Andrew's voice was perfectly genial, Helen still felt his censure. "I trust my father's wife has treated you well."

"Helen is a most gracious hostess," Mori replied.

"I was just ready to set out fruit and make some coffee. You'll stay, of course? Delia, be a darling, would you, and show Mori and your groom to the library, while I finish up a few things in here."

Delia was no fool. She clearly knew she'd interrupted something. The tinge of sympathy in her eyes as she smoothly redirected the men out of the kitchen told Helen so.

The moment they were gone, Helen turned toward the sink, grabbing the edges of the counter hard enough to bruise her palms.

Get a grip on yourself, Helen Hanson.

"Helen? Are you all right?"

She straightened like a shot at the sound of her stepson's voice. "Of course, Andrew. I'm sorry that I didn't think to call you, and Evan and Meredith, as well, to join us for dinner." She quickly reached for the porcelain canister that contained ground coffee. "I don't know where my mind has been these days." She rapidly filled a filter and set the coffeemaker into action. "Did Delia's checkup go all right this afternoon?" She yanked open the refrigerator door and grabbed the fruit tray that Mori had already declined.

"Delia and the baby are both fine." Andrew eyed her closely. "You look frazzled. What's wrong?"

Nothing that some time alone with Mori wouldn't cure.

The thought had her cheeks turning hot. "You'd be frazzled, too, if you had the head of TAKA Incorporated in your home with hardly any warning," she said and thrust the tray into his hands. He had to either take it, or let the beautifully laden crystal tray fall to the floor. "Take that to the library, would you? I'll be right in with plates and napkins and such."

But Andrew, as stubborn as he had been since he was

eighteen and not at all keen on the idea of her as a stepmother, didn't budge. "Has he upset you?"

She stopped and stared. Yes, she and Andrew had made progress in the last months, just as she'd made progress with his brothers. But she hadn't taken to convincing herself that they'd made an about-face in the family love and loyalty department.

Yet Andrew—his deep brown eyes narrowed—looked truly concerned.

For her.

And the fact of it had her throat tightening. "No," she assured gently. "He hasn't upset me."

"Then why are you flushed?"

"The kitchen." She waved nonspecifically. "The oven. You know. Now, go. I'm sure Mori would like to hear about the rash of accounts you've landed this month."

"Helen." Impatience tightened the already-sharp angle of his jaw. "You *would* tell me if something were wrong."

Oh, Lord. Why did the man choose *now* to show the interest that she would have given her right arm to have in years past? She did the unthinkable and reached up to kiss his cheek. "You're a good man, Andrew. Your father would be proud of you."

A statement that only made his slightly thin lips twist. "That isn't an answer, Helen."

"It's the one you're getting," she told him, moving to a tall cupboard that housed serving trays. "Now, please. I need a few minutes of peace. I'll be right in."

"I don't like this. Something is—"

"Everything is fine." She began assembling cups and saucers on the tray she'd pulled out.

He sighed, and left with the fruit platter. She rapidly

finished preparing the coffee service, remembered in the nick of time that Mori didn't drink it, and hurriedly boiled water for tea. While she did that, she sent a hasty call to Meredith, to see if she could get her and Evan over to the house in the next few minutes.

She could, and they did, arriving only minutes after Helen carried the coffee and tea into the library. Not only had her middle stepson and his significant other come, but David and his wife, Nina, arrived with them.

Suddenly, it seemed as if the house was full of people. Someone had turned on some low music and the atmosphere had turned festive.

She busied herself refilling cups, greeting Meredith and Nina, and generally letting the Hanson men do their thing.

But across the room, Mori's gaze met hers and it made her breath grow short, all over again.

What would have happened had Delia and Andrew not interrupted them?

The look in Mori's eyes answered that.

Chapter Eight

"Helen? This is Richard. I need to know when you're going to be back in Tokyo. There is noise that Yukio Taka is planning to make a move to unseat Mori as CEO of TAKA. We need to talk."

Helen listened with disbelief to the message on her voice mail. Richard and Jenny had returned to Tokyo from their honeymoon while she was back in Chicago. She'd only spoken with them once, and had been truly glad for the conversation. She'd also wanted to call a dozen times since, but was very aware that the new relationship she was forging with Jenny was still tender. Delicate.

Now, she dialed Richard's number in Tokyo, completely disregarding the time difference. When he finally answered, his voice was full of sleep.

"'Lo?"

"Richard, it's Helen."

"It's two in the morning."

"I'm sorry. Tell Jenny I'm sorry, too. I just heard your voice mail."

"I left it yesterday."

She'd been with Mori yesterday. "I was…tied up."

"Yeah. With Mori Taka, according to Jack, who heard the news from about ten sources at Hanson. What's going on?"

She pressed her fingertips to her eyes. "That's what I'd like to know. How serious a threat is Yukio to Mori's position at TAKA?"

There was a faint delay. "Serious," Richard finally said. "He's managed to have a special board meeting called."

"On what grounds?"

"Mismanagement, conflict of interest. He may have tossed in another couple of allegations, but those are enough."

Stunned surprise struck her dumb for a long moment. "But TAKA has grown under Mori's tenure as CEO. How can that be mismanagement? And conflict of interest over *what?*"

"His personal involvement with a principal of Hanson Media Group."

She groaned, wanting to kick herself. After all the hurdles they'd run into when it came to the merger, she hadn't *once* thought of her…what—friendship?—*whatever* it was that had been growing between her and Mori as a hindrance on TAKA's part. If anything, by becoming personally involved with Mori Taka, she was more afraid of giving the man an edge *against* Hanson Media.

"There's no personal involvement," she told Richard evenly.

Mori had left that morning to return to Tokyo. He hadn't been in Chicago even twenty-four hours, and he'd been with *her* even less than that.

He'd left for his hotel when Andrew and Evan and the girls had left, since Evan and Meredith offered to drive him to his hotel.

There had been no more kisses, no more tantalizing touches. No more anything, except a call that morning to bid goodbye and to tell her that negotiations would be resumed in a week.

"What do we do about this, Richard?"

"Jack and I have an appointment in the morning. We'll draft a statement countering the allegation, but quite honestly, the TAKA board isn't looking at *us*. They're only concerned at the moment with Mori."

"But if he's unseated and his father is reinstated, Yukio will kill the merger. He's made it very plain that he doesn't approve of it. That's why Mori came to Chicago in the first place—to apologize for his father's latest tactic at the meeting Mori missed."

"Helen, you do realize that his trip there is being used as proof of Yukio's claim."

"There's nothing inappropriate going on!" But there probably would have been, had they not been interrupted. She squashed the little voice that prodded her conscience with that particular fact.

"You and he had dinner, alone, a few nights before you left Tokyo."

"His daughter was with us! Are there people *following* us?"

"Daughter present or not, Mori Taka can't make a move in Tokyo without someone taking note. Particularly when he's in the company of a beautiful blonde." Richard's voice was matter-of-fact. "At this point, TAKA stands to lose plenty if the deal is killed. They've already invested a lot of time, effort and money. Yukio may still have some pull with the board, but Mori is also on solid ground. He was second in command for fifteen years with an impeccable record, and has only seen successes in the past two since he became CEO."

"Does Mori know what's going on? He's probably in the air right now."

"He knows. Be sure of it. And he's undoubtedly taking countermeasures. Yukio Taka may have gotten the board to agree to a meeting, but that doesn't mean he has enough votes in his pocket to swing a coup against his own son. Plus, the very act of him attempting makes TAKA look bad. You know how well that's going to go over with their highly traditional board members? It won't. Don't worry, Helen. We've weathered worse and the ship hasn't yet sunk. It's not going to now, either."

"I hope you're right. I hadn't planned to come to Tokyo until the weekend. But I think I should get there now."

"Being at Mori's beck and call isn't going to help the situation."

"I'm *not* concerned about Mori." It was a blatant lie and she knew it. "Other than that—ironically—he's our best chance at finalizing the deal. But if that board thinks they're going to besmirch anything concerning Hanson—including me—I want to be there to face it."

"Well. You're the boss." Still, he sounded somewhat reluctant. "Just remember, my friend, that this isn't

Chicago. Having a woman of power challenge them has been tough as it is. We don't want to exacerbate the situation."

"Spoken like a lawyer," she said. "Look, kiss your wife for me and go back to sleep. I'll call when I get into Tokyo."

He laughed softly. "Kiss her for *you?* What about for me?"

"I have complete confidence that you've already taken care of that."

After Richard hung up, Helen sat there staring at the phone in her hand.

What would she do if the merger fell through? What would George's boys do? And Samantha and Meredith, both of whom held valuable positions with Hanson Media?

She didn't doubt for a moment any one of their abilities in finding positions elsewhere. To a one, they were talented and committed.

But they shouldn't *have* to make such a move!

She hung up the phone and picked up the gold pen she'd given George. Using it, carrying it with her, was as much talisman as reprimand. "George, what if you were wrong?"

"Wrong about what?"

She jumped, dropping the pen. It rolled across the desktop. "David. I didn't realize you were here. What can I do for you?"

He entered the room and leaned casually over the back of one of the wing chairs that sat in front of her desk. "Maybe I should be asking what I can do for you."

"I don't know what you mean."

"Look, Helen. I know George wasn't…the best of husbands. And I didn't do a whole hell of a lot to make things easier for you while he was alive."

Her stomach tightened. "David, of all people, you were probably the easiest one to get along with."

"Sure, because we hardly had any involvement at all. I just wanted to tell you that I know it hasn't been easy for you. And I'm sorry. You've been more loyal to Hanson Media than anyone—hell, even George, considering his mismanagement and cover-up of it—and I want you to know that you're doing a good job."

She wasn't about to start bawling in the office, but she definitely felt like it. "Thank you, David. I appreciate that. But Jack would have come through if he'd been given an opportunity."

"Jack and Andrew and *particularly* Evan, after being left out of George's will, would have been happy to dump the place out of pure frustration and their feelings for the man who was their father but hardly acted like one."

"Maybe they'd have wanted to," Helen agreed softly, "but I don't think it would ever have come to pass. They'd have gone down with this ship, because it *is* Hanson."

"I'd like to think you're right. I know they would *now,* but I'm not so sure they would have eight, nine months ago. In any case, I figured it was time I said how I felt."

"You've heard from Jack, I suppose."

He nodded, and of course, he knew the ramifications if Yukio were to succeed. "Who would have thought that we'd be in a position to *want* Morito Taka in place, when he seemed to be our biggest obstacle to overcome?"

She nodded, unable to get a word out of her tight

throat. She would never forgive herself if she aided, even unknowingly, in Mori's downfall.

"So." David eyed her. "When are you leaving for Japan?"

"As soon as Sonia can book me a flight."

He nodded. "Well, have a safe flight, and I have confidence that we'll all be in Tokyo in a few weeks' time celebrating the completion."

"You'll be bringing Nina and the kids, right?"

"Wouldn't want to go anywhere without them." He lifted a hand and left her office. Only a few months had passed since he'd been a devoted bachelor. Now, he was very much a devoted family man and Helen had no worries that he'd be a distant parent like his older brother George had been.

For one thing, David adored Nina and her two children. He'd married her for the *right* reason—love.

She pushed the intercom for Sonia. "Book me the earliest flight for Tokyo."

"I'm already looking into schedules," her assistant came back. "Give me five more minutes and you'll be all set."

Satisfied, Helen grabbed the phone and her personal phone directory and made some notes to leave with Sonia. She sorted through the paperwork and files and tasks on her desk, rapidly selecting those she needed to take with her, and those that could wait until her return or be assigned to someone else.

She was just closing her jammed briefcase when Sonia entered. She handed Helen a printed itinerary. "Plane departs in three hours. I've ordered a car for you. It should be downstairs as soon as you leave, so you can run by your place and pick up some clothing. You have your passport?"

Helen nodded, skimming the itinerary. "Thanks. It's in my briefcase already. Here." She handed her assistant the notes that she'd made. "I need you to make those calls for me. And—" she patted a stack of file folders topped by a thick report "—if you can get Evan to handle this, I'd appreciate it." He was officially head of the radio division, but he'd also been pretty much acting as her replacement whenever she'd been in Japan and he'd been doing a tremendous job of it.

"This—" she tapped the middle stack "—you can take care of."

Her assistant pulled a face, but Helen knew she was perfectly willing and capable of handling the assignment. "These are the invitations that you wanted me to look over." She handed them back to Sonia. "Just send my regrets on all of them."

"Even Judge Henry's birthday celebration?" Sonia flipped through the dozen or so letters and cards.

"Send a gift…" Helen thought for a moment. "Make it a basket of chocolates. Dark, milk, white, whatever, but make sure they're individually wrapped. Small pieces that he can keep up at the bench with him. He's always telling me how he wishes he had chocolate to sweeten his disposition when he's hearing cases." She had a longstanding friendship with the elderly man dating back to the first time they'd sat on a philanthropic committee together. She was sorry to miss his party. She'd wanted to talk to him more in person about Jack's career.

"How do you remember this stuff?"

"Years of practice as the wife of George Hanson."

She slipped on her raincoat and grabbed her briefcase and purse. "Meredith's been trying to get Devlin Catering on line for the merger celebration. It might help if you give Cynthia Devlin a call. Her number's in my desk. She's a silent partner in her sister's catering firm, and she and I go way back."

"Are you sure we should start making those plans? Devlin will want a hefty deposit, given the short notice."

"Cynthia and I got our MBAs at the same time. Plus, she owes me about a million favors and that's why she won't quibble over the short notice. We want Devlin Catering because, quite simply, they are the best. And yes, I'm sure we need to plan." Her voice was determined. "Everyone in Hanson Media will be celebrating when this thing is finished. If anything else comes up, send it to Evan. Otherwise, you know where I'll be. Oh. And don't forget to feed Captain Nemo."

Sonia picked up the fishbowl. "I'll move him out there with me. He'll be in good hands. Have a safe flight."

But Helen barely heard her assistant. She was striding out of the office, her mind mostly consumed with one thing, and it wasn't the merger.

It was Mori Taka.

She reached him by phone while she was on the plane. It would be very early in Tokyo, but she suspected he'd already be at the office, and he was.

"How are you?"

He didn't pretend to misunderstand. "I have had better days."

"Mori, I'm so sorry this is happening. I feel responsible."

"Unnecessary. My father has been looking for an excuse, and he focused on the merger and you. What is the phrase your old Western movies were fond of? Rounding the wagons?"

"Circling the wagons."

"*Hai.* Circling the wagons. That is what I am doing."

"That's great, just as long as you have enough wagons," she murmured.

"I am not without some influence here," he reminded drily.

"Considering it's your own father that has taken this route, you're sounding remarkably calm."

"Should I run screaming through the hallways of TAKA?"

She almost smiled at the unlikely picture of that. "No."

"Where are you calling from? The reception is thin."

"I'm in flight."

"You are coming to Tokyo?"

She could have been flying anywhere, yet he'd automatically assumed Japan. "Yes."

"I will be glad to see you." His voice held a note that sent her pulse thudding.

"Mori—"

"You are *not* responsible for the actions of my father."

She closed her eyes, pressing the phone hard to her ear. "How do you seem to know what I'm thinking?"

"It is why I earn the large dollars."

She smiled. "You mean the big bucks."

"*Hai.* That is what I said." He was silent for a moment. "I must attend to matters here, but I will see you when you arrive."

She couldn't help the anticipation that warmed inside

her, even though she tried to steel herself against it. "That might not be the wisest course," she cautioned.

"I will see you when you arrive," he repeated.

And she didn't have the willpower to argue.

Well, wasn't she haring off to Tokyo? She might as well forget she'd ever *had* any willpower. "All right. Until then."

"Sayonara."

She disconnected the call and leaned her head back against the high seat.

"Mrs. Hanson, would you care for a cocktail?" The flight attendant stopped next to Helen's seat.

"Just coffee, please."

The beautiful girl smiled and moved to the next row in first class, repeating the spiel.

How many times would she be making this flight to Japan?

For a moment, she envied Jack and Samantha for their plan to remain in Tokyo at least for several months.

They won't need to if the merger fails.

She shushed the negative little voice. The merger could not fail.

And neither could she.

"The TAKA board is meeting tonight." Richard announced the moment Helen cleared customs. He took her carry-on suitcase from her.

"So quickly?" *Everything* seemed to be happening at breakneck speed.

"Yukio isn't wasting time. He knew Mori would still be busy dealing with his father-in-law's death. If it weren't so nasty, I'd have to give the guy points for hitting Mori at an optimal time." He glanced her way. "You look tired."

"Thanks. You look good. Marriage must agree with you." She knew his first marriage certainly hadn't, though. And while she'd definitely benefited from his intense drive focused solely on his career for as long as it had been, she was delighted he'd found a way to slow down enough and not let love pass him by.

"Jenny's anxious to see you," he said, as if he'd read her mind.

"Anxious as in worried, or anxious as in looking forward to?"

Richard looked sympathetic. If it weren't for him, she would never have known that Jenny Anderson was the baby girl she'd long ago given up. But he'd recognized the similarity and the coincidences when he'd become involved with Jenny and had put the puzzle together.

Helen would be forever grateful to him for that.

"Looking forward to," he assured. "She has a massive photo album from the honeymoon that she can't wait to share."

Helen's heart squeezed. "I can't wait to see it."

Richard's pace ate up the distance as he led the way through the very busy airport, skirting business travelers and tourists with ease, and it wasn't long before they were outside and he was heading for a waiting car.

A familiar car.

Helen's feet dragged as she recognized Mori's driver, Akira, standing alongside the long vehicle.

Richard turned when she slowed. "What?"

"That's Mori's car."

"Handy, since he's inside."

She swallowed, suddenly nervous as a teenager. She'd been traveling for the last fifteen hours. Her hair was mussed, her suit wrinkled and if she had a lick of makeup left on her face, it would be a minor miracle.

"Well?" Richard raised his eyebrows. "Come on."

When Mori had said he would see her when she arrived, she hadn't taken him quite so literally, but painfully aware of the way Akira and Richard—and Mori, for all she knew given the darkened windows of the vehicle—were watching her, she moved forward as if she'd never hesitated at all.

"Konnichiwa," she greeted Akira when he reached out to take her heavy briefcase.

He bowed, murmuring in stilted English, "Good afternoon, Hanson-san." He quickly stowed the briefcase and the suitcase he took from Richard in the trunk then opened the rear door for them.

Helen climbed inside.

It seemed foolish, but she was grateful for Richard's presence on the facing seat when Akira closed the door and moments later the limousine began moving.

"Richard tells me the board meeting is tonight," she said, noting that Mori looked as urbane as ever in a black suit, and not at all worried about the outcome of the meeting. "You've probably got more important things to be doing than picking me up at the airport."

"I am doing exactly what I choose to be doing. Your flight was turbulent."

"How did you…never mind." Mori had his ways, and she wasn't going to wonder too hard just now about it. "It was bumpier than usual. There was a storm we had to go around, otherwise the plane would have been on time." She assumed that if Mori knew the flight conditions, he'd also known about the delay and hadn't sat, cooling his heels, in the loading zone all that time.

"Kimiko sends her greetings."

His right hand rested on the long leather seat. It was a full ten inches from her left hand, also resting on the seat.

And still, her hand felt tingly warm.

"How is she?"

"Well."

"How did you and Richard come to be together this afternoon?" She finally voiced the question that had been hovering inside her.

"Mr. Warren and I were discussing a few points of the transition."

So, they were still in an all-systems-go mode. That was good.

Knowing it didn't alleviate Helen's worry, though. It would be there, lurking under her own forcibly positive attitude until Mori's board had met.

"What points?"

"Nothing for you to be concerned with."

Helen looked across to Richard, waiting.

"Really," he assured, "it was small potatoes."

The CEO of TAKA didn't spend his time on frivolous details. And she'd foolishly thought that she and Mori were past the days when he clearly hadn't wanted to discuss even major business matters with her.

She folded her hands in her lap and looked out the window, hiding the sting she felt.

Fortunately the limo arrived quickly enough at the TAKA building. "Akira will drive you to your hotel," Mori told them. "We will speak later."

"Good luck this evening, Taka-san," Richard told him.

Mori bowed his head. "Thank you." His gaze slanted to Helen. "I am glad you are here."

She wanted badly to ask him *why,* but kept the words inside. "Good luck."

A faint smile touched his lips, and then he was gone, a tall, striking man striding into the skyscraper that bore his name.

Helen eyed Richard. "*What* little details?"

He huffed out a noisy sigh. "I knew you weren't going to let that slide."

She lifted an eyebrow. "Richard?"

"He had some questions about you, okay? That's all."

"Questions?" Her voice was not growing any warmer. "About what? And why ask you?"

"I was delivering the statement Jack and I worked on this morning and happened to mention I was picking you up from the airport. He already knew when you were arriving, and offered the car. I was pretty surprised when the guy came along, too. Just what *is* going on between you and Taka, Helen? It's clear that something beyond business has occurred."

"Well, that's terrific," Helen observed, "since it will lend credence to Yukio's ridiculous claims against Mori."

"Are they ridiculous?"

"I've said so, haven't I?"

"And I've believed you. But—"

"But *what?*"

Richard paused, very much the attorney framing his words. "The man looks at you, Helen."

She felt her face flush. "At the risk of sounding extraordinarily conceited, I'm afraid men have often *looked* at me."

Now, Richard just looked impatient. "He looks at you the way I probably look when I watch Jenny."

"That's…impossible," she said.

It was Richard's turn to raise his eyebrow. "Is it?"

Chapter Nine

That evening, Jack, Samantha and Helen went to Jenny and Richard's apartment for dinner.

Despite the cheerful face everyone put on, and the true enjoyment Helen felt when Jenny pulled out the photograph albums of the honeymoon, it felt more like a wake than a family get-together.

They were *all* waiting on word from the board meeting.

Jenny eventually turned on the television and they watched the news channel to see if there would be mention of a TAKA coup. She also made a few calls to her associates.

No one seemed to know anything.

By eleven o'clock that night, Helen was simply dragging.

She had slept a few hours on the flight, but other than

that, she hadn't put her head on a bed pillow in more than twenty-four hours.

"Much as I'd like to stick it out with you youngsters, I've got to get some sleep."

Richard snorted. He and Jack were both only a handful of years younger than she. "Nice try, Helen. You're still not gonna pass for a gray-haired granny, even when we make you one."

Her gaze flew to Jenny's, who blushed and shrugged. "Not yet," she said, "but there have been some negotiations."

The first real smile Helen had felt since the previous morning hit her face. "I think that sounds great," she told Jenny, and couldn't keep herself from hugging her.

Her eyes stung when Jenny hugged her in return.

Then they were gathering jackets and purses and heading out into the cool evening to hail a taxi.

Count your blessings where they are, Helen reminded herself. Whatever happens with the merger, she'd found Jenny and the boys had found their loves.

Wasn't *that* more important than anything else?

Alone in her hotel room, she took a shower, realized she'd forgotten to pack any nightclothes and wrapped herself in the plush white bathrobe provided by the hotel.

Despite her exhaustion, though, she couldn't relax enough to climb into bed.

She stepped between the heavy drawn curtains and the window and looked out at the city lights.

Was the board meeting still in progress?

She imagined that she could see the shape of the TAKA building, but knew it was unlikely. Her window faced east and the TAKA building was west.

Sighing, she rested her forehead against the windowpane. It felt chilly to the touch.

They were supposed to sign the final paperwork any day now. A gala celebration would shortly follow for the employees in both Japan and Chicago, the media and every mucky-muck in both countries.

Would that still come to pass?

Her head hurt from thinking about it.

Tugging the lapels closer around her, she slipped from between the heavy drapes and headed to her bed, but a soft knock on her door stopped her.

Jack or Samantha, she thought, immediately crossing the room and throwing open the door. "Have you heard—"

She stared at Mori, her words drying up.

He looked like hell. His face was tired, his eyes bloodshot.

His tie was loose, his jacket bunched in his fist.

Without thinking, she stepped back, silently inviting him inside.

He entered, pulling his tie even looser.

She closed the door, leaning back against it, and watched him cross the room. He tossed aside his jacket and went immediately to the bar and opened the small refrigerator that was stocked with every known assortment of alcohol.

She'd never bothered touching it.

But given Mori's countenance, she strongly considered the need for a stiff shot of something.

He pulled out a bottle she didn't recognize the name on, and dumped the contents in one of the squat crystal glasses that sat atop the bar.

When he'd finished, he turned, drink in hand, and looked at her.

Her hands balled in the deep pockets of her robe. "Are you all right?"

"My father saw the wisdom of retracting his request." He drank half the contents of his glass in one long drink, then moved to the couch and sat on it.

His head bowed and he stared at the drink held loosely in his hands.

She went over and sat beside him. "That ought to sound like good news," she said softly. "But you look like a man who has lost the war, rather than winning it."

"There is no winning when my father has made known to everyone that he has no faith in me."

She started to put her hand on the back of his neck and realizing it, curled her fingers, drawing back before touching him. "You say he took back his request of the board, though."

"Hai."

"Didn't they wonder why?"

"Hai." His voice turned very dry. "My father claimed illness prompted his behavior. He, who has never been *ill* in his life."

"So there was no board meeting at all?"

"There was a meeting, during which I received many votes of confidence."

"Well, that's good, right? Your position is still secure?"

"You need not worry. The board will not overturn the decision to acquire Hanson Media Group."

She stiffened. Yes, she'd been rightfully concerned about the merger, but the moment she'd seen Mori looking so *un*-Mori, she'd only had thoughts of him. "Merger," she reminded him evenly.

His dark gaze turned to her. *"Sumimasen,"* he said. "Pardon me. *Merger.*" He quaffed the rest of his drink and leaned forward, setting the glass with inordinate care on the gilt-edged coffee table. "Your father is still alive, is he not?"

"Yes," she said warily. "Why?"

"You do not have a good relationship?"

"No, we do not." She pushed to her feet, tightening the belt of her robe. "And I suspect that you, with your wealth of ways, know why that is."

"He forced you to give up your baby when you were little more than a baby yourself."

"I was sixteen. At the time I didn't feel much like a baby."

"Kimiko is twelve."

"At that age, four years' difference might as well be a lifetime." She truly didn't know where this was going, but she knew she wasn't comfortable with it.

She hadn't spoken with her father since the day he'd held her arms when she'd tried running after the adoption representative carrying away her child. And though she'd kept in touch with her brother while their mother was alive, the contact had been inevitably awkward. *She'd* wanted to make her mother's life easier—what good was the wealth Helen had surprisingly married into, if she couldn't bring more comfort to the people she'd loved?

They seemed to think she was only trying to lord it over them. Her brother had been barely willing to pass on the financial assistance she'd sent for her mother to have in the guise of a gift from him. If it were anything other, she knew her father would have made sure their mother would not accept it. Now, in the years since Helen's mother had passed away, she'd spoken to Walt only twice. He'd made it clear he had no use for her, just like their father.

"My father left me no choice about the baby," she said. "But bringing a child into *that* family wasn't something I wanted to do. It was bad enough for my brother and me. I wasn't going to subject any child of mine to an atmosphere like that."

"Like what?"

She smoothed back her hair only to catch her fingertips in the thong holding it in a ponytail. She pulled it loose and stuck it in her pocket. Her hair slid over her shoulder. "Controlling. Unloved. My father and mother *had* to get married when she became pregnant with my older brother, Walt. The day I told my parents that I was pregnant, my dad looked at Mom and told her that it was all *her* fault. I was just like her, trying to trap another innocent guy."

"Unwed pregnancies have been occurring through the ages, even in my country."

"And causing plenty of scandal," she reminded pointedly.

His gaze didn't waver from hers and she knew that he still didn't feel badly for halting the negotiations when the truth about Jenny came out.

"Did your husband know about the child?"

First her father, now George. "Why does it matter to you, Mori? It's all water under the bridge." Dark, churning water.

"Did he?"

She couldn't fathom what possessed her to answer. "No, he didn't."

"Why did you not tell him?"

"This has nothing to do with tonight's board meeting."

He pushed to his feet and headed toward her. Slowly. Deliberately. "It has to do with *you*."

"Obviously, considering your questions are *about* me. Why do you care?"

"I do not know!" His voice rose slightly and he grimaced. "Why do I jeopardize everything I have worked for my entire life to visit you here, at this hotel, when anyone could have seen me enter the doors and speculate which room I visit? I could have a dozen lovers and not surprise a soul, but I visit with Helen Hanson, head of Hanson Media, and I am looked at with suspicion by men who have worked with me for decades."

She winced. "I'm sorry they all find me so offensive."

"You are not offensive, Helen, you are a *gaijin* businesswoman, playing on *their* field, and they do not like it when they suspect I have joined your team. TAKA is not accustomed to negotiations like this. You are surely aware of it. TAKA takes *over* companies. Yet *you* have kept us at the table while still managing to prevent that from happening. It is…remarkable."

At any other time, she would have been deeply pleased by the comments—not exactly praising given his position, but definitely giving her full measure. "This whole thing is insane. You and I are *not* involved, except across the bargaining table."

He touched her cheek. "Are we not?"

She swallowed. "This is what's getting us into trouble in the first place."

"Yet here I am, even though most people would consider me to be the most practical and traditional of men."

"Well, maybe just like many men, you only want to get me in the sack. *Bed,*" she clarified at his blank look.

"Do you *sack* with many men?"

"I don't think that's any of your business."

His thumb slid beneath her chin, then along her jaw until he held her face captive.

Her heart bounced around unevenly. She lifted her chin, just to prove that she could move away if she chose.

His hand didn't move.

"No," she finally said huskily. "I don't *sack,* as you say, with men. I was married for ten years. And before that, way before that, was Jenny's father. So do not even try to lecture me."

Mori's eyelids drooped a fraction more until only a thin gleam of brown showed between his thick lashes. "Did he lecture you a lot?"

"Who?" Now was not the time to get confused by the man's intense physical appeal. "My father? He was an unending lecture."

"Your late husband."

"The only thing George lectured me about was my waistline, the length of my hair and why he wanted me to stay out of Hanson Media."

"He was a fool not to recognize he held a pearl in his hands."

"Don't stand there and pretend that you welcomed me in the conference room with open arms, Mori. You detested me."

"You disturbed me," he corrected softly, closing the distance between them by half. "But it is true that you are not the typical person with whom I deal."

"You have business dealings in other countries than Japan," Helen reminded. "You don't have female associates in London?"

"In London, yes. But they do not come to my country and challenge me under my own roof."

"Just because I want what's reasonable and fair for Hanson Media doesn't mean I'm challenging you."

A faint smile hovered around his lips. "You are challenging me even now."

"I—" she pressed her lips together for a moment. When she thought she could speak without debating yet another point, thereby proving the man correct, she tried again. "What exactly do you want, Mori?"

"In general, in life, or in this moment?"

"This moment."

"I want you."

Her mouth dried. Well, she'd asked, hadn't she?

"Despite all the reasons why I should not, why it would be better that I did not, I still want you. And I keep choosing to see you because of it."

Her lashes lowered. Her hands twisted in the sash of her robe. "You said you came to Chicago to apologize for your father and Shiguro."

"And I spoke the truth. I also came because I wanted—needed—to see you. Apologies *can* be offered over the telephone." He closed his hands over her fidgeting ones. "Do you not wish to see me, also?"

"Mori—"

"Do you?"

"Yes." The word was more a breath.

"One day—" he lowered his head close to hers, whispering softly against her ear "—it will be just you and me. A woman and a man. No contracts, no lawyers. Only us. Only this." His lips touched her jaw. His hands lifted hers until they were caught between their torsos.

Her knees felt weak. She spread her fingers and they tangled in the trailing ends of his magenta tie. She slowly pulled the knot loose. "And what about *this* day?" Her voice was faint.

"This day I am TAKA and you are Hanson Media."

It was frightening how badly she wanted him to stay. How hard it was to focus on the reasons why he should not.

The only times in her life when she'd put reason and common sense behind a locked door, she'd ended up paying a high price. The first, she'd been just sixteen when she fell in love with a jock named Drew Sheffield. He hadn't stood beside her when she'd needed him—he'd run hightail to his parents, who'd quickly moved him out of town lest he have his aspirations tainted by poor little Helen Needham.

The second time, she'd married George Hanson, a man twenty-seven years her senior who'd swept her off her feet so quickly she hadn't even *tried* to find her common sense.

Drew had just been a boy too young to face the consequences of their actions and George had used her love for him for his own purposes, only acknowledging her business acumen when he'd had no other recourse.

What would throwing common sense to the wind do now?

Could she even take a chance at finding out?

"You have had a long day," Mori murmured, brushing his lips over hers, successfully eroding another layer of sensibility. "You need sleep. Tomorrow we resume the negotiations. I have had messages sent to all the parties involved. We have much work to do to become back on schedule."

She was painfully aware of all the work they had yet to accomplish—points on which they had yet to agree. "I thought we would be waiting until next week because of your father-in-law's passing."

"Do *you* wish to delay still?"

She shook her head. The closer they got to the end, the worse the pressure got. She wanted the deal signed and delivered.

Only then would she feel like the last ten years of her life had actually *meant* something.

"No, I don't want any more delays." Because she didn't think she'd rest again if she didn't, she leaned up and pressed her mouth against his.

His hand slid through her hair, cupping the back of her head, fingers flexing against her scalp.

She could have purred, and was gratified that when they pulled apart, his breath was as short as hers.

"You have to go," she told him huskily.

"I know."

Her head fell forward, resting against his chest. "I don't want you to." The admission felt raw.

His arms closed around her back and he held her so close that she suddenly felt like crying.

Which only served to remind her of the night of Jenny's wedding when he'd caught her in tears.

"I do not want to leave you, either," he said.

"It's a mistake. The last two days are proof of that."

"What do you worry about more, Helen?" Mori's chest rumbled beneath her cheek as he spoke. "Undoing the merger, or being with a man other than your husband?"

She didn't want to think about George anymore. "My husband and I hadn't shared a bed in several years."

"Because of his age?"

"He might have been sixty-eight, but he was a *young* sixty-eight."

He tilted her head back until her face was exposed. "He had other women?"

How many times had she wondered that, herself? "I don't think so. George's only mistress was Hanson Media."

"Then why?"

She closed her eyes. "I'm not asking you questions about the relations you had with your wife."

"We lived together as man and wife only long enough to conceive Kimiko."

"At least you were lucky enough to *conceive* a child."

He was silent for a moment and she made the mistake of opening her eyes. He was watching her with that disturbing intensity—seeming to see into her very soul.

"You wished to have another child," he surmised.

Her throat was tightening up again. She didn't want to feel all that emotion. If she had to feel anything, she wanted it to be the drugging pleasure he caused—even if that *were* the height of folly given the circumstances.

"Helen?"

"Yes. For the first six years we were married, we tried

everything, every conceivable treatment, even nontraditional methods. There was nothing physically wrong with George, nothing physically wrong with me."

"Yet—"

"No child." She pulled out of his arms, feeling too naked and vulnerable to stay so close to him. "Maybe that was my karma. I'd given away one child, so I wasn't to be allowed another."

"I am not certain that is an accurate definition of karma," he said softly, and the simple gentleness in his voice had her eyes flooding.

"How about God's punishment, then?"

His head tilted slightly. "It was just not meant to be. My wife killed herself because of her lack of interest in the life she had and for the child she'd borne."

Helen was shocked out of the painful memories that sucked at her. "I had no idea."

"Why would you?"

Because she'd investigated very thoroughly every aspect of TAKA and its principals before she'd put her plan for Hanson Media into action. "What happened?"

"Sumiko was not a strong woman like you are." He tapped his finger against his head. "Here."

Helen wrapped her arms around herself. She didn't feel particularly strong. She felt shaky and hopelessly without common sense.

"When Kimiko was still an infant, her mother began spending more time away from her. Traveling. Going out at night with friends. I was too immersed in TAKA to see what was happening at first. When I realized she was addicted to alcohol and drugs, I made sure she had treatment, and she became better for a while. But it did not last. Eventually, her body could not sustain the abuse she heaped on it."

"Kimiko was only a baby."

"Yes."

She shook her head. "I'm so sorry, Mori. What an awful thing to have happen to all three of you."

"If I were to use your example of karma, I would believe that I will never be able to be a husband again, because I had already failed to keep safe the wife I did have."

She pressed her lips together for a moment. "You wish to marry again some day?"

"I do not wish to be alone for the rest of my life," he answered.

Which wasn't really an answer at all.

"I was responsible for my wife, but I have realized that I could not force her to change her life. She had to want change from within badly enough to put up a fight and take the help she was offered from all sides. But she did not."

"Did you love her?" She realized she was holding her breath and made herself let it out slowly when he took his time answering.

"I loved her for the child she gave me."

"Then at least there was that."

"You still grieve for the man that did not share your bed."

"I grieve for the marriage I thought I'd had." The truth burned. "I loved my husband, and I thought he loved me. Turns out I was wrong, and I'm afraid I'm finding that reality more difficult than accepting his death."

"Why do you believe he did not love you?"

She didn't know what possessed her to reveal such

matters. Was it because he'd shared the facts about his wife?

Were the details of his past any less painful than hers?

She went into the bedroom and picked up the jewelry case from the dresser and started to carry it back out, but he stepped into the bedroom after her.

Her nerves tightened even more.

"I *know,* because he told me." She set down the case and pulled out George's letter to her. It was the devil inside her that handed the sheet of stationery to him. "Everything I'd believed about myself, about my marriage, turned out to be nothing more than wishful thinking."

Mori glanced down the letter only long enough to grasp the gist. He was not overly shocked by the contents. George Hanson had only done what Mori's father believed he had done in arranging Mori's marriage to Sumiko when they were nothing but infants.

He'd made an advantageous match.

The difference was, Sumiko had been perfectly aware of the point of the union. Helen, clearly, had not.

He wondered which was worse.

Refolding the letter, he lifted the lid of the wooden box himself to place it inside.

As he did so, he noticed a crisp dried leaf lying alongside a thin silver bracelet.

The leaf from their walk in the park?

A muscle was working in Helen's fine jaw, proof of her tension. He placed the letter inside the box and closed the lid, hiding the leaf and all the rest once more.

"It is difficult to have one's life manipulated," he told her. "There are things we can control, and things we cannot. I could not control Sumiko, and you could not control George. That does not mean you were wrong to love him."

Her long, lovely throat worked in a swallow.

"Nor does it mean you were foolish."

She turned her head slightly, but not quickly enough for him to miss the sheen of tears in those jade eyes. "I wasted ten years trying to be the woman he wanted, and it turns out he didn't care, anyway. Believe me, Mori. That feels *extremely* foolish."

"And now, you are still trying to be the woman he wanted, by ensuring Hanson Media Group does not fold?"

Her posture straightened. She leveled him a long look, shaking her hair back a little until it rippled over her shoulders like cool moonlight. "I'm doing *that* to prove to myself that I'm more than just George Hanson's trophy wife, and to make sure that my stepsons don't lose their entire heritage because of their father's poor judgment. Whether they like it or not, they *are* my family and I want them to have everything they deserve."

"They do not know of this." He tapped the top of the jewelry box.

She looked horrified. "Of course not. I don't want their pity. As far as that goes, I shouldn't have told *you*."

As far as Mori was concerned, he was not entirely convinced her stepsons merited her championship. But he recognized one thing.

Helen Hanson was more deeply honorable than he would ever have believed just a short while ago. She might not describe her actions as that, but the result was the same.

She was caring for her family in whatever manner she could.

And the reasons why he should leave, immediately, were becoming harder to obey when the reasons why he should stay were gaining a strength that he could not deny.

That he did not *want* to deny.

Chapter Ten

"It has been a day of revelation," Mori murmured, taking a step toward her and feeling a jolt of satisfaction when she made a nervous movement as a result.

Helen's hand tightened over the lapels of her robe, holding them together. But her green eyes were *not* afraid.

He realized he had never seen her truly afraid of anything and it, too, was a heady realization.

He closed his hands over her shoulders. She was slender, but he did not have a sense that she was fragile. "You need to sleep," he reminded.

Her chin lifted a little. "So do you."

When had he thought her voice was not musical? Her low words stroked over his nerves with a mellow tone.

He smoothed his hand down her hair. "You do not often wear your hair down."

Her eyes nearly closed, and her head pressed against his palm, like a cat unconsciously seeking petting.

"It's easier pulled back."

He slowly threaded his fingers through the strands. It was thick. Smooth and silky and infinitely pale against his hand. "I have dreamed of you."

Her lips parted and he saw another swallow work down her throat. "You…have?"

"That surprises you? It should not. You have been consuming my thoughts much longer than I wish to admit."

Her lips curved. "How long?"

"Always wanting to clarify the details."

"That would be me," she agreed. Her fingers slid inside his shirt collar. Rested against his pulse that beat heavily, only to move again, finding a button and toying with it.

"I have wanted you from the beginning," he admitted.

She made a soft sound. Of disagreement?

"I believed I could want and not touch, however, until the night Kimiko made her hair pink. At dinner."

"We did nothing but have dinner that evening."

"You asked when, not why."

She lifted her lashes, slanting a look up at him. "How is it that you can get me to want to laugh, after a day like this has been?"

"Laughing is good," he murmured, "but it is not my specific goal at the moment."

"And you are a goal-oriented man."

"Hai."

She continued toying with his button. He wondered how long she intended to torment him in such a manner.

"If I might ask, what *is* your specific goal?"

He flattened his hand over her tantalizing fingertips, stilling them against his chest. "You."

Her eyes darkened. "We have established that isn't a wise decision."

He traced the lapel of her robe from her neck, down the slope of her breast to the belt that was, even now, falling loose. "I am thinking right now that wisdom is rated too highly."

She moistened her lips. Swallowed. "Is that so?"

He slowly pulled the loop of her belt free. The thick white terry cloth began to part.

She caught his wrists in her hands. "Mori."

She was shaking. He frowned. "You do not wish this."

"No!" She shook her head, her cheeks turning pink. "I—I do. Really. It's just—I haven't—" She raked her fingers through her hair, holding it back from her face. "I'm sorry. I'm a grown woman, I should be better at this. But I told you. George and I didn't…hadn't…it…it's just been a while," she finished in a rush. "A really long while."

He slid his hands along her jaw, cupping her face. She was blushing and he wanted her more than ever. "Are you in need of a refresher course?"

She stared at him for a moment, seemingly speechless. Then a soft smile touched her lips. "Perhaps I am. *Sensei* is the word for teacher?"

"It has a wider reference, but yes."

"Sensei," she repeated. Her fingers returned to his shirt collar, sliding over it, then under it and his skin heated wherever her gliding grazed. "So…refresh me."

He tilted her chin up, lowering his head toward hers.

"First, there is the touch." He slipped his fingers beneath the thick skein of pale hair and touched the nape of her neck. Drew his fingertip down the line of her spinal cord. She trembled against him, her own fingers faltering unsteadily.

"Mori." His name sounded like a soft ache in her husky voice. "The…light?"

He had no desire to turn off the single lamp burning near the bed. "Second is the kiss," he continued and kissed the corner of her eye.

Her lashes fluttered like butterfly wings against his lips. "But—"

"Why do you wish to hide in the dark, Helen?" He kissed the high curve of her cheekbone.

"I don't hide," she defended, arching against him when his hand slid over the robe as he explored the long length of her back.

"You wish the darkness," he murmured against her ear before he caught her unadorned earlobe between his lips.

Her head twisted against his shoulder, her fingers knotting in his shirt. "I wish I were a decade or two younger," she muttered. "*Oh.*" She moaned softly when he pressed his mouth against the side of her neck.

He pulled at the sleeve of her robe and it slid unimpeded, over her shoulder, falling down to her bent elbow. He lifted his head to study his work. If she knew the way he had to work to form thoughts when he would rather just stare at the perfection before him, she would never make such a comment.

He drew her head up from where it was pressed against his shoulder. He caught a flash of vulnerability in her eyes before her lashes swept down, hiding it. "I have no desire to be with a girl twenty years younger than me. I wish a partner who matches me. I wish for you."

She caught her lip between her teeth. He tsked and rubbed his thumb over the tiny spot and felt her indrawn breath when she dragged in a breath.

"What is the third thing to remember?"

"The heart."

She drew one of her palms down the center of his chest to rest over his heart. "You are a romantic," she whispered. "Who would have thought it?"

"I am a man and I want a woman," he corrected huskily. He mimicked her actions, drawing his hand down the center of her chest until he felt her heartbeat racing against his palm. The robe fell off her other shoulder, fully baring her body to him.

She wasn't an ivory candle, slender and tall and unlit.

She was golden and warm and wherever, whenever he touched, she seemed to glow.

And he ached.

"I think it's coming back to me," she said huskily, and covered his hand with hers, sliding her fingers between his for a moment, then retreating to his wrist for a moment, only to return to his fingers. Her heart raced beneath their joined hands and she shifted slightly, her gaze on his face as she drew his hand over the swell of her breast. Her lips parted, her gaze flickering.

His hand tightened on her breast, circled the rigid peak that rose greedily to his touch, then his taste.

Her head fell forward again, her cool hair sliding over them both. "Take me to bed, Mori," she whispered.

He kicked aside her robe and pulled her tightly against him.

She inhaled sharply. "You know I like things to be fair." Her hands worked between them to tear at his shirt buttons.

He caught her lips with his, helping her and in moments, his clothes were a thing of the past.

Her arms clung around his shoulders as he backed her to the bed, following her down. Her hair streamed around them and her eyes glowed in the soft light.

"Let me see if I remember, now. Touch." She dragged her fingertips down the length of his spine and a faint smile touched her lips when he let out a low breath.

"Hai."

Her knee slowly slid along his thigh. She pressed her mouth against his chest, tasting him. "Kiss."

"Hai." He caught her head in his hands and kissed her deeply.

The green of her eyes turned glassy when he lifted his head and staring into them, he slid against her. She made a soft sound, her arms tightening against him. Her legs tangled with his. "Please. My heart can't take teasing."

"No teasing," he promised, and slowly, inexorably pressed into her.

She moaned his name and he exhaled roughly, curving over her. But she lifted herself against him, removing any protective distance he would have created between him and her slender body, which was already quaking against him.

She was welcoming and warm, and female to male, and if he'd held any notion of control, it was suddenly lost.

His hands found her hips and he sank deeply.

She cried out and held him even closer, twining herself around him. "Yes," she gasped. "Yes."

Then the lapping waves of her shuddering pleasure became a tidal wave that dragged him under.

And he was drowning with her, for nothing in life had ever prepared him for a woman like Helen.

Helen overslept the next morning.

It wasn't until she heard the heavy pounding on her hotel room door that she finally opened her eyes and stared at the empty pillow next to hers on the bed.

The tumbled covers helped assure her that she hadn't merely dreamed of Mori.

Not this time.

He hadn't stayed the rest of the night, which wasn't much of a night, given the dawn light that had been slipping around the window drapes when he left.

She'd wanted him to stay. But it was simply too foolhardy for him to do so.

Knowing it didn't make her miss him any less, however.

Another pounding rattled the door from the living area. She heard the muffled sound of her name being called.

Feeling lazy and not entirely rested, she glanced at the clock on the bedside table.

The time finally registered.

"Oh, *hell.*" She jumped out of the bed, grabbing up the robe that was lying on the floor. She was just tying the sash when she reached the door.

A glance through the peephole revealed Jack's face, his expression as thunderous as his pounding.

She opened the door, already turning away before he

could step inside. “Give me ten minutes, and I’ll be ready to go.”

“Jesus, Helen.” He entered the suite behind her, slamming the door. “I thought something was wrong!”

First Andrew’s concern and now Jack’s. Oh, they were such surprising men.

“I’m fine,” she assured. “I just overslept.” She raced into the bedroom, closing the door behind her. The shower water wasn’t even warm before she was jumping back out of it and toweling off. She flipped on the blow dryer, directing it through her hair long enough that she could pin it into a chignon without looking like a wet cat, and forced herself to slow down enough to apply some makeup without smearing mascara or lipstick over her face. She didn’t seem to need much color, anyway. Her lips were pinker than usual. Fuller than usual, too.

Thinking about the reason for that slowed her movements when she had no time to spare, so she just would not think about it.

But every movement she made as she stepped into an ivory-colored suit made a mockery of that particular vow.

There wasn’t a part of her that didn’t bear the memory of Mori’s touch.

She shoved her feet into her shoes and went back out to join Jack. “I’m sorry. I just need my briefcase.”

He picked it up off the table where she’d left it and handed it to her. “I thought you always left a wake-up call.”

“I do.” She took the case from him and headed for the door. The last thing she wanted was for Jack to begin speculating. “I didn’t sleep much last night.” That was true enough. “I guess I slept through the call this morning.”

"And Samantha's when I couldn't get you to answer the door?"

"Evidently. Oh. My room key." She glanced around. The small credit-card-size piece of plastic was on the coffee table.

Next to Mori's glass from the night before.

Worse, it was within a foot of Mori's jacket, laying on the end of the couch. Jack *had* to have noticed it.

She snatched up the key and turned back to the door. Her feet dragged to a halt, though, at Jack's low voice.

"Whose jacket is that?"

"Mine," she lied blatantly, and grabbed his arm, hustling him out the door, which she slammed behind her.

"Right. Looks like it'd *fit* you, too, Helen, if you grew about half a foot and gained about sixty pounds." He caught her arm, stopping her in her tracks. "Who was here?"

She gave him a long look. The elevator door slid open beside them. "Actually, Jack, that isn't your business."

"Dammit, Helen, Samantha and I were *concerned.*"

"And I appreciate it," she said sincerely. "But there is nothing to be concerned about. Now let's get to this meeting. Obviously, you got the message from TAKA."

"A courier brought by a schedule last night after we got back from Jenny and Richard's."

Mori hadn't mentioned a schedule. She punched the button for the lobby floor and the elevator began its dizzying descent.

"It was Mori Taka, wasn't it?"

She swallowed. "He came to tell me what happened at the board meeting."

"And *left* his jacket."

"Is that so unlikely?"

"Why did he take it off in the first place?"

"For pity's sake, Jack. This isn't the Inquisition. The man came to speak with me. I offered him a drink. Do you think it was *easy* for him to face that meeting yesterday? His own father was trying to undermine him." She shot him a look. "You of all people should have some sympathy over that."

His expression only tightened. "You never change, do you, Helen? One wealthy husband is out of the way, so you're looking for another? I really thought I might have been wrong about you before, but I wasn't, was I? I'll give you credit, though. At least this one isn't old enough to be your damned father, *and* he could buy and sell Hanson Media several times over. Nice work."

He might as well have slapped her.

She stared hard at the number display but his anger was a physical thing sucking all the oxygen out of the small space. She actually felt dizzy.

"I haven't given up everything I've worked for to see the deal go down the tubes because you and Mori can't keep your hands off each other. The man's not going to be interested in you forever, you know. You're an American, for God's sake, and he's about as Japanese as they come."

The elevator doors opened and Jack stepped off.

She followed him slowly, vaguely surprised that he'd bothered to keep the taxi waiting for her. Without a word, she climbed in beside him.

The drive to the TAKA building had never seemed to take so long.

Wasn't it the height of irony that in finding one night—not even an entire *night,* for that matter—of happiness with a man, she would end up losing what little progress she'd made with the family that had never wanted her, anyway?

She could feel Jack's sidelong look and deliberately pulled out her leather portfolio and flipped it open to her notes.

She didn't read a single word of them.

The meeting ran through lunch, which was brought in on several rolling carts and distributed around the conference table.

It was Italian food, and the sight of the lasagna, garlic bread and green salad made Helen want to laugh.

Hysterically.

Mori had not said one word personally to her since the moment he'd entered the room and taken his place at the head of the table.

He'd barely looked at her, for that matter.

Jack, however, seemed to be looking from Mori to her and back again. She didn't need a degree in rocket science to interpret the "I told you so" look in Jack's eyes when he happened to catch her gaze.

She jabbed her fork into a lettuce leaf and ignored *all* of the men surrounding her.

The lunch break was mercifully brief, and the meeting resumed.

About a hundred years later, it concluded.

Helen tucked her pen in her portfolio and closed it, pushing back from the table.

Mori cast her an inscrutable look.

Well, she'd known that their relationship would remain private, hadn't she?

It wasn't as if he could go around crowing that he'd slept with Helen Hanson, after all. Mori's father might have recanted his accusation, but that didn't mean that he couldn't put it forward yet again. Or that someone else within TAKA couldn't do it for him.

Still, the complete lack of acknowledgment in Mori's demeanor toward her *hurt.* He was even cooler to her than he had been at the very beginning.

As if such a thing were possible.

She squared her shoulders, though, and looked around the occupants of the room as they began pushing back from the table. "Have a good evening, gentlemen. I look forward to tomorrow."

She angled toward Mori, bowed and then strode out of the room, uncaring of the stunned silence that her abrupt departure caused.

Chapter Eleven

"Here." A glass of red wine appeared in Helen's line of sight. She followed the glass to the feminine hand that held it to the woman it belonged to. "You look like you need it," Samantha continued.

Helen slowly took the glass. It was nearly midnight and she was sitting at a small round table next to a window in the hotel's top floor cocktail lounge. She'd never been up there before, and it had seemed an admirable choice when she hadn't wanted to remain alone in her hotel room all evening.

Instead, she'd sat alone at this table, staring out at the lights and wondering what had become of her life. "Thanks." She silently toasted the other woman with the glass before taking a sip. She had half a dozen empty glasses on the table. None of them had contained a drop of alcohol. "Who would have thought, back when I was once your babysitter, that we'd be on the other side of the world like this?"

"I'll take that as an invitation," Samantha said, as she slid into the chair opposite Helen.

"Sorry." Helen shook herself. "Of course, join me."

"As long as I don't have Jack with me?" Samantha's gaze was sympathetic. "He told me you two had words this morning before the meeting."

"That's one way of putting it."

"He didn't mean it, Helen."

She lifted her eyebrows. "I never realized just *how* optimistic you were, Samantha." She tilted her glass again in the other woman's direction. "Here's to the hope that that trait always serves you well."

"He's stressed out over the merger. And he's somewhat unnerved over the fact that he's realizing you aren't the woman he's always made you out to be."

"Samantha, I love you. I'm glad you and Jack are together and making each other happy. But I do not want to talk about this."

"Well, maybe you get to call the shots a little too often, Helen," Samantha countered gently. "Come on. We're a family. Families say stuff all the time that they don't really mean."

Helen drank the wine down in only a few gulps. Family? She wanted badly to think so, but reality had a way of eroding such hopes. "Does Jack know you're up here?" She could tell by Samantha's expression that he did not. "Go back to your husband, sweetheart, and don't worry about me. I'm fine."

Samantha let out a long breath. She rose and came

around to Helen's side, dropping a kiss on her head. "You're not fine and *families* are allowed to worry, whether *you* like it or not."

"She is right."

Helen nearly toppled the wineglass at Mori's voice. She looked past Samantha at him. "Where did you come from?"

"Nesutotaka," he said calmly.

Her lips tightened. "Very funny."

"Join Jack and me for breakfast before tomorrow's session," Samantha whispered for Helen's ears, then she turned to Mori and bowed. "Good evening, Mr. Taka. If you'll excuse me?"

He returned the greeting. "Of course, Mrs. Hanson."

Samantha shot Helen another look as she hurried out of the bar.

Mori took the seat that Samantha had occupied so briefly. "I have been calling your room."

She focused her gaze somewhere around his temple. Anything to avoid looking in those black-brown eyes of his. "Really? Why?"

"To speak with you."

"I think our speaking together should be kept in the conference room, don't you?"

He reached across the table and caught her chin, moving it an inch until her gaze met his. "What has upset you? You were not yourself at our meeting today, either."

The glass of wine had been a mistake, just as it always was. "I guess I find it harder than I thought it would be to face the man I spent hours making love with across a negotiating table."

"Do you regret it?"

Her throat tightened. "The way you must?"

"I did not say that *I* did."

She leaned toward him, keeping her voice carefully low. "Well, what *do* you feel, Mori? Because I have realized that I do not have the first clue when it comes to reading you."

"Do you wish that I would sweep you into my arms like some foolish American movie regardless of the setting? It was a *meeting,* Helen."

"No, I don't wish you to act like some besotted idiot in a stupid movie! I expect…I expect…oh, damn!" She pushed back from the table. "I don't know what I expect, that's how badly you've got me twisted up. Look, I am a big girl. Last night was…a diversion for both of us. A one-time deal where we both got what we wanted out of it."

He stood also, his expression hardening. "That is what you believe?"

"What else can I believe, Mori? You looked right through me today." She hated the fact that her voice caught. She wasn't a teenager begging her boyfriend not to desert her when he left her pregnant. She was a forty-one-year-old adult who, for years and years, had been playing the cards her life had dealt.

So why did she feel as if she hadn't learned one thing in all that time? And why did everything seem to hurt more now?

"It's late. I'm going to bed. I'll see you tomorrow at TAKA." She turned away.

He caught her arm, preventing her from getting more than two inches.

She looked up at his face and was abruptly reminded

of the night he'd held the Samurai sword in his suite at the Anderson hotel.

Her mouth dried.

"I could not *look* at you without giving away my feelings," he said grimly. "Is that what you wish to hear, Helen? Do you *want* my brother and my associates to know from my expression or my actions that I am consorting with you?"

"Consorting with the enemy, you mean? We're not enemies, Mori. You and I both want the same thing—for Hanson Media to be part of TAKA Corporation. Why do you think I made sure you even *heard* of Hanson Media?"

The challenge seemed to linger in the air long after it should have.

"You sent a prospectus."

"A good six weeks after I knew you'd already been investigating the advantages of an acquisition," she said tiredly. "I made sure that Hanson Media was on the list of companies you routinely review for acquisition."

"How?"

"I was the wife of George Hanson. I worked with more committees for more social functions or philanthropic events than you can possibly imagine. I have contacts, Mori, from many corners of the world, quite honestly. And I used them."

"Why TAKA?"

"Because despite the fact that your company is so traditional that there are no women in senior management, TAKA is still the best in the industry. Your assets, your operating principles. And because I respected the leadership of TAKA's new CEO," she told him bluntly. Why not? What more damage could she do now? She'd already slept with the man, breaking all manner of ethical behavior. What was one more—one *last*—revelation between them?

"You investigated TAKA."

"I investigated *you.* And don't pretend to be shocked. We both know that you investigated me, as well."

"Had my people done a better job, the existence of Jenny Anderson would not have come as such a surprise."

She wasn't amused and couldn't pretend to be.

"You are cannier than I realized," he finally said.

"A trait I'm sure you will never be able to appreciate."

"You think, because of my culture, that I do not understand shrewd behavior?"

"Shrewd, yes. Secretly manipulative? Probably not."

"You did this to save your late husband's company."

"We've been over that point already. Now, if you'll excuse me." She started to bow, but he caught her shoulders.

"Do not patronize me, Helen."

Was he so oblivious that he couldn't recognize that she was dying by slow degrees? "*Sumimasen.* That was not my intention. I just want to get through the next few weeks, Mori. That's all."

"And us?"

"As you've made plain to me, there is no *us* to concern myself with."

"Because I do not acknowledge you in front of my associates."

"That's just it, Mori. I don't need you to tell them that something important has occurred between us. But I don't want you hiding the fact even from me! Don't treat me as if I don't exist in that conference room. I won't ever be involved again with a man who cannot bring himself to acknowledge my value in a business setting."

She looked around them, profoundly grateful for the fact that, at that hour, there were only a few patrons in the place, and they looked three sheets to the wind. "I won't do that to myself again. I *can't.* And I'm sorry if you can't understand why that is so important to me. So all I can say now is...good night." When she moved, he released her, which was a good thing because she wasn't sure what she'd have done had he not.

Bursting into tears wasn't an acceptable action, even if she felt like she'd earned having one darned good howl.

The elevator that opened directly into the lounge was waiting, doors wide and she stepped on, turning to face outward.

Mori hadn't moved.

He stood where she'd left him, his expression closed.

She pushed the button for her floor and the doors slid shut.

Only then did she blink.

A hot tear slid down her cheek.

"Messages and mail for you, Hanson-san."

Helen headed for the reception desk and the smiling young woman who'd called out for her. She took the stack. *"Domō arigatō."*

The girl smiled and nodded. "It is my pleasure, Missus. Please enjoy your morning."

If only.

Helen slid the items inside her portfolio and followed Jack out into the morning sunshine. David, Evan and

Andrew were there, waiting, also. On this, the last scheduled meeting for the merger, they would all also be attending the meeting.

By the end of the day, the merger would be complete. Signed, sealed and delivered.

And Mori hadn't spoken privately with her since the night nearly two weeks earlier when he'd tracked her down in the cocktail lounge.

She felt a cowardly urge to hang back, to join Samantha and the other women for their day of playing tourists while the men bellied up to the bargaining table.

A limo was already waiting at the curb. "What are the messages for?" Jack asked. If he was aware of her nerves, he gave no hint.

She didn't look at the slips clenched in her hand. "The voice mail on my phone isn't working properly. I'm sure it's just stuff from Sonia."

He didn't ask any further questions and she climbed into the vehicle. Since the day they'd argued, he hadn't brought up the subject again. She supposed his uncommon reticence was probably Samantha's influence. She didn't care where it came from as long as it came. She didn't have any more stamina to keep facing Mori without losing her composure *and* stay firm against Jack's open censure.

She found herself sitting next to Jack and David, facing Evan and Andrew.

"We only have three points left to cover." Jack was looking out his side window. His fingers drummed against his knee. "One of which is the corporate philanthropy issue."

"I suppose you think I should just let them cut the

corporate match to whatever they want." She looked at the other men, waiting for some response.

"No." Jack's voice held a wealth of impatience. "But the sixty that Mori has already put on the table isn't completely out of the question."

Andrew nodded. Evan just looked distracted.

"What do you think, David?"

"If they'll go to sixty, they'll go up."

"That's what I think, too. I want seventy-five," Helen said.

"You should have been a defense lawyer," Jack muttered.

"Given the circumstances, I'll take that as a compliment." Whether he'd meant it as one, or not.

He snorted softly.

Helen opened her portfolio and glanced through the messages and mail.

Judge Henry had finally sent the letter.

She glanced at Jack from the corner of her eye, but he was still looking out the window. She discreetly slipped open the envelope, reading through the Judge's brief handwritten note. It accompanied another, smaller sealed envelope for Jack.

Satisfied, she tucked the second envelope in a pocket in the portfolio to save for later and continued paging through the messages. "Jack, I know the whole family is having dinner together tonight, but I was hoping to grab a few minutes of time with you and Evan."

Her middle stepson looked across at her. "Why?"

"There're a few things I want to talk with you both about." She closed her portfolio just as the taxi stopped in front of the TAKA building.

Evan's eyes narrowed. "What things?"

Sometimes he was *so* much like Jack, a fact he would undoubtedly deny. Adamantly, since he considered himself far less rigid than his older brother.

"It'll wait," she dismissed smoothly. "Jack, remember, seventy-five percent. You can argue it, if you like. I know how you like to do that."

"Well, that's the truth," Andrew agreed drily.

The men all eyed each other, half smiles on their faces.

She took in a slow, deep breath and let it out.

Everything was going to be fine. Just fine.

After dozens of meetings, the security guards had become familiar faces. Helen smiled and greeted them by name as she passed them for the elevator.

"You do have a way with people," Andrew muttered as they climbed on the elevator.

As they rode up, Helen was too nervous to worry whether Andrew's comment was a compliment or a condemnation.

When they walked into the conference room, Mori, typically, had not yet arrived. But Richard was already there and they joined him by the tea tray.

Anticipation seemed to hover, thick and heady, in the air.

"There are going to be a few board members here for this," Richard warned under his breath. "I overheard Shiguro talking about it."

Helen looked over to where Mori's younger brother was holding court with half a dozen other men. "Board members haven't joined any of the previous meetings."

"We haven't had the entire Hanson contingent here

at once, either. We're in the homestretch, kiddo." Richard squeezed her elbow. "You done good."

She swallowed the knot of nervousness that continued rising in her throat despite her efforts otherwise. Who was she kidding? She had an MBA and a decent mind on her, with no real work history other than the internship where she'd met George. The fact that she'd gotten this far was a major miracle and she knew it.

Then Mori's father, Yukio, strode slowly into the room. He was immediately surrounded by bowing TAKA employees.

Her heart sunk to her toes. She turned slightly toward Richard so that only he would hear her whisper. "Yukio Taka is one of the board members coming today?"

"Kind of looks that way," he murmured, looking around her at the man in question. "Guy walks around like he's the emperor himself."

Helen turned again to face Yukio's direction and decided it was an apt description. He was not as tall as Mori, nor as broad in the shoulders, but his iron gray hair was as thick as Mori's clipped hair. More than his physical presence, though, it was Yukio's aging face that caught at Helen.

It gave new meaning to the word *stern.*

And the look he was giving her would have probably meant death in some previous century.

Even though she hated having to do it, she lowered her lashes respectfully, put her hands on her thighs and bowed deeply. When she raised up again, she liked to believe she caught a glint of surprise in the man's eyes.

But the moment was too brief to be certain, and then Mori entered the room.

He nodded at his father and went to the head of the table, his motions uncommonly brisk. "Shall we begin?"

Everyone quickly moved to the table and assumed their seats. Yukio sat directly across the table at the far end from his son. Moments later, two other elderly men shuffled into the room and took the two empty seats on either side of him. The other board members, she presumed.

Shiguro rose and introduced the TAKA visitors and then he sat down again, looking clearly rattled. While Richard stood and introduced Evan, Andrew and David, Helen looked past Jack to Mori.

He was watching her. She felt her cheeks warm and reminded herself just how easily the man had blocked out their personal relationship.

Then he spoke, seeming to direct his comment directly to her. "We will be brief today." A faint smile touched his lips and he finally looked around the table. "At least that is my hope."

A smattering of chuckles sounded. Helen glanced at the far end.

Yukio's expression had not changed.

She pulled out her gold pen, holding it tightly. The homestretch, she reminded herself. She could smell the barn.

Shiguro directed them to open their agreements to the suitable page. "The last remaining points, as we all remember, are the duration of the transitional management, the appointment of Hanson representatives to the TAKA board and setting policy for the philanthropic corporate match for Hanson North America."

There it was. No longer Hanson Media Group, but *Hanson North America.*

Helen stared hard at the pages in front of her and listened to Richard set forth their proposed timetable for the transitional management to ensure that all elements of the agreement actually took place. "While we realize TAKA would like to work through the transition as quickly as possible, we believe that a three-month period will be most feasible."

They'd begun requesting a five-month duration.

TAKA had wanted one month, but that was more noise than sense, and everyone was perfectly aware of it.

"Three months is acceptable," Mori agreed, cutting off any debate or discussion that might have occurred. He flipped open his leather-bound calendar. "January 30."

Everyone except Helen scribbled on their pages. She was busy watching Mori, wondering why he was suddenly being so agreeable.

"The appointment of board members has been reviewed." Shiguro moved to the next item. "Based on the list previously provided by Hanson."

They had only three seats, but those seats were permanent and as valuable as gold.

Helen had proffered the names herself, after some deep searching over what was best: Jack, Evan and David. She'd hoped to manage to get Andrew on the board, too, but TAKA had been inflexible about a fourth seat. Fortunately, Andrew hadn't taken the news too hard. He himself had seen the value of those chosen.

"The proposed board members are acceptable," Mori said, once again taking unilateral control.

"We are happy to hear that," Richard said.

Jack looked less satisfied. She knew he considered this just one more sign of his servitude to his father's company. But he'd had an opportunity to decline, and he hadn't. Which *she* considered one more sign of his true commitment to his family's heritage *despite* his father.

"As to the matter of the corporate match." Shiguro hesitated, looking from his brother to his father. "It is the position of TAKA that sixty percent remains the highest feasible amount."

Helen rolled her pen between her fingers. "With the consolidation of our scholastic divisions, as well as the additional seven percent cut in payroll, there is ample budget remaining for an eighty percent match. The additional twenty percent will remain under the control of Hanson Radio, which becomes a separate entity subsequent to the merger of the other divisions with TAKA Incorporated, and as such, is outside the bounds of this agreement."

"Silence!"

Helen nearly jumped out of her skin at the harsh command from Yukio. She looked toward him. "Excuse me?"

Both Jack and Richard touched their knees to hers beneath cover of the heavy conference table.

"*We* do not wish to hear from you, *gaijin.*"

Being ignored was one thing. Being chastised like an unwelcome child was another. "I am sorry for your displeasure, Taka-san," she said calmly, "but I *will* be part of this discussion."

Yukio stood. He folded his knuckles on the table and leaned forward. "Not while I have breath," he said flatly.

Helen looked toward Mori. His father may still hold a seat on the board, but Mori was the one in charge. His father had already tried to take control back from him.

Surely he would say *something* that would take the wind from Yukio's sails.

He was glaring at his father. "You do not have authority."

Yukio spoke sharply to his son in Japanese. By the reaction of the TAKA side of the table, he wasn't commenting on Mori's red tie. The two board members by his side looked uneasy, but they were nodding, clearly in agreement with whatever it was that Yukio said.

Mori's voice grew colder. "She *stays*."

"My son—" Yukio looked around the table, finally speaking in English "—has been unfortunately influenced by *that*—" he hesitated "—woman."

Helen could feel things spiraling out of control.

"Oh, come on." Andrew looked disgusted. "Suck it up, Mr. Taka. We have."

Helen went still.

Andrew grimaced. "That didn't come out right, Helen. I didn't mean it the way it sounded."

She twisted the pen between her fingers. The pen that had been the only thing she could think of to give the man that she was married to, because he certainly hadn't been interested by then in anything of a more personal nature from her.

"Then what *did* you mean, Andrew?" Her voice was careful.

"Helen, now is not the time for this," Jack warned.

She turned and looked at him. "I don't know. Maybe this is the perfect time."

Even David and Evan looked uncomfortable.

And Mori...well, Mori wasn't saying a word, now.

He was just watching her. Always watching her with those all-seeing eyes of his.

Jack tilted his head closer to her, lowering his voice. "None of this would be happening if you could have kept your fingers off of Mori."

She looked down her side of the table at Jack's brothers. "Is that what you all think? That I'm only here for my *own* gain?"

"Helen," Richard cautioned, putting a hand over hers. "Remember where we are."

"As if I can forget." She slowly pushed back her chair and stood.

She'd given ten years of her life—willingly given them—to the Hansons. Believing in George's sons even when their own father had neglected them.

But even now, after everything that had happened since George had died, they couldn't at least offer the *appearance* of family unity. Not with her.

She stepped back from the table. "Helen," David protested. "What are you doing?"

"It's all right, David."

It wasn't, but that was entirely beside the point. It was nobody's fault but her own for having believed that she could get Hanson Media to this point and somehow gain the family that they'd never before been.

She pulled out the letter from Judge Henry from her portfolio and set it in front of Jack. "This will give you hope," she told him quietly. "That there is life again beyond this."

"What the hell are you doing?"

She didn't answer his furious demand. "Remember what I said. Seventy-five percent. Finish it, now."

Then she turned to Mori and bowed. "*O-jama shima-shita.* I am sorry to have disturbed you." She directed herself toward the opposite side of the table and bowed again. Finally, she faced Yukio Taka.

And though it galled, she managed to bow a final time.

Then leaving George's sons and brother behind, she walked out of the meeting.

And nobody stopped her.

Not Jack or Evan. Not Andrew or David.

Most particularly, not Mori.

Chapter Twelve

Silence reigned, thick and heavy, after the door slowly closed behind Helen's back.

Mori looked down the table at his brother and attorneys. "You will excuse us." He included his father's sidekicks in his request.

Shiguro looked regretful. He rose and the men silently left the room.

Yukio continued standing there and Mori had to struggle against his own anger with his father. "I will be speaking with the Hansons privately," he said.

Yukio glared.

Mori stared back. There were a lot of things he disagreed with his father about—in business and in life. But now was not the time for an argument over things that would always exist between them. They were simply too different.

Yukio finally made a disgusted sound and stomped out of the room.

A collective sigh seemed to escape Helen's family.

Mori studied them all for a moment. He moved around the side of the table and picked up the gold pen that Helen had left behind.

It sat on her open portfolio. The pad of paper beneath the pen was covered with her handwriting. The notes that she had been forever making to herself during their meetings.

He slowly closed the portfolio and slid the pen in his pocket.

"Perhaps it would be best to reschedule this for tomorrow," Richard suggested sensibly. "Give everyone a chance to cool off a little. Clearly, the stress of all this has gotten to us all."

"You heard Helen," Evan said quietly. "Finish it now."

Mori could see the silent debate being waged in the looks the men exchanged among themselves. "There is nothing to finish," he said, his voice flat.

Jack stood up like a shot. "Nothing to finish?" He lifted the corner of the merger agreement and let it drop heavily on the table. "I beg to differ, Mr. Taka. You've come too far to pull out now."

Mori moved around the table again until he faced them. "The night of your wedding—" he nodded toward Richard "—I observed to Helen that I believed her sons lacked honor. That they treated her with disrespect."

"We're not her sons," Andrew pointed out, his voice stiff.

"You are her family, nonetheless."

"Damn straight, we are," Evan said. "And we don't need you lecturing us about *our* family."

Mori almost smiled. So. There was more to them than he'd observed. "Helen strongly disagreed with me," he continued. "She insisted that her husband's sons had done nothing to be ashamed of. She spoke of all the Hansons with pride."

Jack tapped the edge of the envelope Helen had left him on the table. "We're not going to discuss Helen with you, Mr. Taka. Now, if you'd like to discuss the corporate pledge percentage, we can get this over with."

There'd been a time when Mori had used the Hansons' propensity for scandal to put the brakes on the merger. He had no regrets about that, still.

It was business.

But eyeing the men across from him, he knew it was no longer *only* business.

"Without Helen here, negotiations will not proceed."

"That's not what she wanted," Richard protested. "You heard her. Finish it."

"Are you certain that you know what Helen wants?"

"I suppose you think that *you* do?" Jack challenged. "What's she going to get out of this, Taka? Another decade of life with another guy who doesn't have time for her?"

"This is not about Helen and me," Mori assured. "This is about *you* and Helen."

"What? Unless we start acting like the adoring sons, you're not going to continue the deal?" Andrew stood. "How we feel about Helen is none of your damn business."

"I am making it my business. Do any of you have the first idea of all that she has done for you?"

"Well, her latest act is evidently putting the skids on the merger," Andrew said tightly.

"What do you mean, all she has done?" David asked slowly. "It was her idea to approach TAKA. We know that."

"It was her idea to have TAKA approach *you,*" Mori corrected. "Had we not already become aware of Hanson Media's struggle and seen the value for ourselves of acquiring the company, we would not be here today."

"She manipulated it," Jack finished abruptly. He angrily tapped the envelope once more, then pushed away from the table and began pacing. "Just like she manipulates a lot of things."

"To what purpose does she do this?" Mori watched them all for a moment. When no answer was immediately forthcoming, he walked to the door and opened it. "When you can truthfully answer that and Helen is present for what she has every right to be present *for,* I will—perhaps—consider resuming our business relationship. Until then, we are finished." He barely inclined his head, he was so annoyed with the entire lot of them. "*Sayonara.*"

Helen heard the knocking on her hotel room door but ignored it and continued fitting her clothes in the two suitcases opened on her bed.

Eventually, the knocking ceased.

She closed the first suitcase, zipped it shut and placed it on the floor in the living area. Then she returned to her packing.

Simple, methodical actions.

It was all she could concentrate on. If she let herself

think of the debacle she'd created, she would simply cease functioning altogether.

She went into the bathroom to collect her toiletries and caught a glimpse of herself in the mirror. "Haggard, Helen," she murmured. "Don't much look like George's sexy trophy wife now, do you?"

Her small perfume bottle escaped her blind reach and clattered into the sink. It shattered.

She sighed and grabbed a thick hand towel to scoop up the mess. She dumped the entire bundle in the tiny trash can and went back to the sink to rinse the strong perfume away. A swirl of red made its way down the drain, too. She'd cut her finger. Not badly enough to cause real pain, but enough to let a few drops of blood run.

She stuck her hand under the faucet and George's diamond ring winked up at her as water flowed over it.

She'd only been a Hanson because she'd been George's wife. And George was gone.

She turned off the water.

The ring slid off easily.

She set it on the sink and slowly dried her hands.

Her finger had already stopped bleeding.

She left the ring and went back to finish her packing. She hoped she'd be able to catch a flight back to the States without too much delay.

Hanging around the airport waiting any longer than necessary held little appeal.

"What are you doing?"

She gasped and whirled around, startled out of her wits.

Mori stood in the bedroom doorway.

"How did you get in?"

He held up a key card. "You are packing."

"They just *gave* you a key to my room at the front desk?"

"So it appears. You are running away?"

Her jaw tightened. She turned back to her suitcase and dropped her toiletry bag inside. "I prefer to think of it as going *home*."

"To your husband's house."

Her vision blurred. She blinked hard and reached for the suit she'd exchanged for jeans and a sweater when she'd gotten back to her hotel after walking out of the meeting. "Where else?" she asked flippantly. "No reason to hang around here. You men can handle everything most admirably, after all. No need for me to keep getting in the way, making things awkward for everyone. Just assure me that my guys got at least seventy-two percent out of you."

"Your *guys,* as you say, got nothing. I stopped the meeting."

She dropped the skirt and turned to face him. "Why would you do that?"

"You should not have left as you did."

"What was the point of staying? To be the cause of more dissension between you and your father? To have everyone on my side of the room blame me for that, as well?"

"Is that the true reason you left?"

"Why else?"

He frowned and shook his head. "Some days I wish I had never heard of Hanson Media Group."

"Then you'd be missing out on the best opportunity to gain a market share in North America," she countered immediately.

His lips twisted. "You still defend your company like a mama tiger."

"It's not my company. It is my husband's sons' company."

"Choosing to think of it that way is your prerogative, but that does not make it a fact. There will be no merger unless you are there until the last, Helen. And that is why I stopped the meeting."

"Jack and the others were working on my authority. They could have—"

"No."

She pressed her hands together. "You cannot possibly call off the merger at this late stage. It would be a public relations nightmare for TAKA. You've invested too much time and too much money."

"I could, Helen." His voice wasn't grim. It was factual. "Yes. It would create some inconveniences for us to overcome when next I venture into the North American market. But we both know that Hanson Media stands to lose far much more than does TAKA."

Her stomach was tipping over. She badly wanted to sit. "What is it that you want, Mori?" The last time she'd asked him that, he'd admitted he'd wanted *her.*

"I want two days of your time."

She felt like shaking her head to jar loose whatever was stuck inside. "For what?"

"An…experiment."

She finally gave up on appearances and sank down on the foot of the bed before her wobbling knees gave way. "Experiment for what?"

"To see if we can exist for even that amount of time without TAKA and Hanson Media Group."

He was speaking English, but it might as well have been Japanese. "I don't understand."

"Two days. You, a woman. Me, a man. No business. Nothing but us."

As quickly as it had turned somersaults, now her stomach was tightening. "You can't be serious. We were ten minutes away from signing the deal."

"Until you walked out."

"I walked out because it was clear that my presence was a hindrance!"

"That is a matter of opinion that not everyone shares."

"Well, I know you're not referring to my stepsons. And *you* didn't offer a dissenting opinion when your father was giving me a look that could have killed. When he was saying whatever it was that had everyone in the room who understood him looking at me with *pity!*"

"You wanted me to defend your presence to my father."

She knew it sounded infantile. That it made her sound like her ego was ruling her, that her pride was having a temper tantrum.

But it wasn't any of that.

It was the very basic root of self-esteem that she'd let wither on the vine as George's wife. It was finally back in bloom again, and to let it die would be to doom herself to a life of knowing that she was exactly what everyone had been saying—a pretty little trophy, of no use other than to decorate the arm of a man.

"What will two days prove?"

"That remains to be seen."

Which told her exactly nothing. She didn't need two days with the man to know that she'd done the unforgivable. She'd let him get under her skin where she'd never get rid of him.

"I could agree to this and you would never know if I was doing it for the sake of the merger."

He stepped forward and caught her chin in his, lifting it until their gazes met. "I would know."

She swallowed. Yes. He probably *would* know.

She shifted, lifting her chin away from his touch, and stood, putting several feet of distance between them. She'd thought alcohol clouded her senses, but Mori clouded her entire ability to think straight. "What did you have in mind? A two-day cooling off period or something?"

"This is not about the merger."

"Everything is about the merger."

"Maybe in the next few days you will learn that is not true."

"Then what?"

"I wish to take you to Nesutotaka. We can be alone there."

She locked her knees. "That's your home."

"Hai."

"You…want to take me to your home."

"Do you need it in writing? Yes. My home. We will have privacy there. No interruptions."

"I think if you go home, you should take your daughter, not me."

"Would you prefer to have her with us? A twelve-year-old chaperone?"

"Maybe."

"You do not have to sleep in my bed, Helen, whether Kimiko joins us or not."

"For a man who often dances politely around a topic, that's pretty blunt."

"I *hope* that you will choose to sleep in my bed," he allowed. "But you have a choice. You always do."

"She probably has school classes."

"Hai."

"If I said I wanted her to go with us, you would take her out, anyway?"

"Hai."

She tilted her head, studying him. "Even though my dreaded American ways might rub off on her during that time."

"How many ways do I say *yes?*"

"All right," she said abruptly. "Two days. And then we come back and you sign on the dotted line."

"And Kimiko? Do I call her headmaster?" He moved toward the phone as he spoke.

Helen bit her lip. She was charmed by Mori's daughter and the idea of the young girl's company was more than appealing. But she knew a portion of that appeal was because of the barrier Kimiko would provide between her and Mori.

"No," she said huskily. "I'll go with you. Alone."

He nodded. "Do you have a smaller suitcase that you can use? You will not need all of that." He gestured toward the suitcase still on the bed.

"You want to leave right *now?*"

"We will stop by my hotel only briefly. We will be in Nesutotaka by lunchtime if we leave now."

"Jack and everyone else must be furious."

"I am not concerned with them right now."

"I…okay." Proving what a weak-willed soul she was, she couldn't even summon another protest. "I don't have a smaller suitcase, but I've got a purse that ought to work." She rummaged through what she'd already packed and pulled it out. "I can't just leave, though. I've got to let them know where I'm going."

"Then make your calls," he said. "But if you delay too long, I suspect you will soon have more visitors."

She thought about that for a long moment. Sooner or later she'd have to deal with them. But at the moment, *later* seemed the more appealing choice.

She opened the empty hobo-style purse and dropped her toiletry bag inside. "I'll hurry," she told Mori.

"Pack those tennis shoes. Or wear them. You will need them."

She didn't ask why. She already felt like she was doing what he'd accused—running away. What was more appropriate than wearing running shoes on her feet when she did it?

Three hours later, as they drove into the village of Nesutotaka, Helen knew Mori hadn't exaggerated in his description of it as a collection of houses spread along a dirt road at the base of a mountain. What it looked like to Helen, though, was an oasis of simpler life set in the jewel tones of miles and miles of lush, green farmland.

She turned to Mori. The uncertainty over what they were doing had abated somewhat during the drive. "It's beautiful."

He smiled faintly.

He'd chosen to drive them to Nesutotaka himself, rather than take the car and Akira, his driver. The sports car was exorbitantly expensive and very eye-catching. Not at all what Helen might have expected of the man.

It also had them sitting for the drive from Tokyo extremely close.

She didn't have the heart to fake a complaint about it when the truth was that his nearness was as much a pleasure as it was a consternation.

The moment his car made its slow way along the bumpy, rutted road, word clearly spread that he'd arrived in the village.

Children, men and women suddenly appeared out of their houses, walking directly toward the road, waving their hands and greeting him by name.

Finally, he simply stopped right there in the center of it all, and rolled down his window.

Helen watched, entranced despite herself, as he laughed and spoke to everyone who tucked their head low enough to peer into the window.

She could only smile and nod as they eyed her and chattered rapidly and grinned and nodded in return. "They say you look like a movie star," Mori told her when they finally started moving again.

"A movie star?" She made a face. "No, that would have been my *former* look."

"You are not allowed to think right now of the man who was your husband," Mori told her. He closed his hand around hers and set it on his thigh. "It is only you and I here, remember?"

She was excruciatingly aware of the physique beneath her hand. But if he would act casually about it, then so could she.

She turned and looked through the rear window. There was still a cluster of people standing in the road, watching their progress. "Yes, just you and I," she agreed. "And a village that clearly delights in your presence. I suppose you know most of them?"

"I know all of them. They are all cousins in one way or another. Either on my mother's side, or my father's."

She turned back around. "You're kidding."

"Unfortunately, no." His assurance was arid. "We will stop and greet my mother, and then go on to my home."

She nodded, still distracted by the notion of possessing so many relatives. He'd already warned her they would visit his mother. "I don't have even one cousin," she told him. "Both of my parents were only children, born to their parents who were only children."

"I'm certain that if you went far enough back, you would find cousins exist."

"Sure. Distant ones whom I've never met and wouldn't know if I tripped over."

He looked amused. "Would you like to be an honorary cousin of mine?"

She shook her head, eyeing his lips for a moment. "No, thanks."

His lips curved faintly. "I thought not."

The car was moving at the bracing speed of—perhaps—five miles an hour and she was suddenly impatient to be alone with him in his home.

The strength of that particular yearning was still vaguely shocking to her.

Yes, she'd loved George. But—

No thoughts of George.

"Thank you for bringing me here," she whispered softly to Mori.

"Thank you for coming with me." He leaned forward suddenly and brushed his lips over hers, and then, when the car bounced harder than usual, they pulled apart. "This road is almost needing to be graded again."

"Almost?" She shook her head and laughed.

His dimple appeared.

After passing another half dozen homes and other unidentifiable structures that she supposed were used as barns for the cattle and goats that grazed, he turned off the road onto an even more unbeaten track. But that path was short and in moments, he'd pulled to a stop in front of a house that had an ancient pickup truck and a luxury sedan parked on the grass, as well.

Mori eyed the sedan. "My father is here," he said, all of the humor now gone from his face.

Uncertainty came back with a nauseating vengeance. "Did you tell him you were coming here?"

"No."

There was no point suggesting that he not go in. She knew he wouldn't avoid seeing his father, even if he wanted to. "I'll wait in the car." It seemed the wisest choice.

The senior Mr. Taka loathed her on the business field; she could only imagine how he'd feel seeing her here now with his eldest son. Undoubtedly, he'd be on the phone immediately, calling for another board meeting.

"No. You will come inside with me."

"Mori, why give your father more ammunition?"

"My father has no need for ammunition and he will not dishonor a guest in his wife's home. Trust me. My mother is expecting us." He squeezed her hand and pushed open his car door. "She will not share my father's opinion."

Helen wasn't all that certain of that. Not when she

was far more accustomed to having the family of the man she was involved with barely tolerating her presence. "What do you mean that your father has no need for more ammunition?"

"He and I resolved matters before I came to your hotel. Now, please. Come inside with me."

Clearly, Mori had no intention of sharing with her just *how* he'd resolved matters with Yukio. And she wasn't going to argue with him over the issue.

She reached behind her seat for the gift she'd brought for Mori's mother in the spare minutes she'd had while Mori had packed his own belongings. "How can you be sure your mother won't share your father's assessment?" she asked when he came around the car to help her out onto the uneven grass.

He touched her cheek, then took her hand and led her to the house. "She will see that I am happy to be with you," he said simply.

Her heart squeezed.

Maybe she wasn't making the biggest mistake of her life, after all.

As was typical, Mori did not knock on the front door, but slid it open, calling a greeting as they stepped into the *genkan.*

"You can leave your shoes here." He stepped out of his own street shoes, and then stepped directly onto the gleaming wood floor that was about half a foot higher than the ground-level floor where they'd entered.

She followed suit, being careful not to touch her stockinged feet to the *genkan* floor, knowing that would be bad form, as it might track dirt into the house, thereby defeating the purpose of the entry in the first place.

Two pairs of soft ivory slippers were waiting on the house level and they pushed their feet into them before walking along a short hallway that opened into a surprisingly large living area.

Given the traditional nature of the house up to that moment, Helen had expected tradition to continue in the living room. But instead of reed-mat flooring, low tables and floor cushions, there were Western-style couches, chairs and an enormous grand piano in one corner. It was a very comfortable, lived-in room that Helen found appealing.

The sight of Mori's father sitting like some royal entity in a large chair in the far corner of the room was considerably less appealing.

Thank goodness they'd had warning of his presence by the sight of his car outside.

Helen bowed slightly, acknowledging his presence. He, however, pretty much ignored her.

That was fine. It was certainly better than his open animosity.

Mori's mother—she could be no other—entered the room from another doorway, her small face wreathed in smiles and a very direct contrast to her husband's countenance.

"Mori-chan," she cried, grabbing him practically by the ears as she tugged his head down to kiss his face. She spoke rapidly in between hugs and kisses.

"English, Mama," Mori told her when she took a breath. "This is my friend, Helen Hanson."

"Friend," a deep voice repeated the word caustically.

Mrs. Taka shot her husband a quick look, which seemed to make the man subside in his chair. Then she turned to Helen and bowed deeply. "It is a great pleasure to meet my son's friend," she said carefully. "Welcome to our home."

Helen bowed, too. "*Domō arigatō gozaimasu.* Thank you very much. I am very pleased to meet you, too." She extended the basket of fresh flowers and tissue-wrapped pastries that she'd selected from the kitchen at her hotel. In this case, it had definitely paid to be who she was. The manager of the hotel had been incredibly eager to assist her.

"I hope you'll enjoy these," Helen told the woman.

"So pretty," the older woman said, lifting the blooms to her nose. "Thank you." She turned suddenly toward her husband. "*O-jii-san.*" Her tone sharpened and the man frowned mightily at her. A frown over which Mrs. Taka seemed to take little offense and the man finally stood.

"Please to be seated," he told Helen and Mori, his English stiff and cold.

Helen wasn't sure *which* seat she was supposed to take, but Mori solved the problem by taking her hand—which earned another eagle-eyed look from Daddy—and leading her to the couch nearest them.

Mrs. Taka was nodding her pleasure and she excused herself after a moment, returning almost immediately with a beautiful wooden tray full of refreshments which she set on the low ebony table in front of them.

Instead of sitting on one of the chairs, however, she kneeled down, sitting on her folded legs next to the coffee table. "You had a good travel?"

"*Hai,*" Mori answered. "Traffic was light. We made good time. Arrived here earlier than I had anticipated."

He looked at his father. "Apparently, earlier than anyone had anticipated."

Helen kept her focus on the welcoming demeanor of Mori's mother. "Mrs. Taka, Nesutotaka is every bit as lovely as Mori described. You grew up here?"

"My family has been here for generations. I find the busyness of the cities—" she hesitated, searching for the word she wanted "—chaotic. My son has told me you live in Chicago."

"Yes. And it, too, can be chaotic."

"But your family is there?"

"My stepsons and their families. Well, Jack, the eldest, is in Tokyo now because of the merger."

Mr. Taka muttered something that Helen felt relieved not to hear clearly. Mori replied, his voice equally low.

"Do you speak Japanese?" Mrs. Taka asked.

"Regrettably, only a little." Helen lifted her hands slightly, palms turned up apologetically. "I am learning, but not as quickly as I'd like."

"You have intelligence," Mrs. Taka said. "My son has told me this. You will learn in time."

Helen flicked a glance at Mori, sitting beside her. His entire body was tense, and concern for that almost overrode her quiet pleasure that he'd told his own mother that she was intelligent.

"Mori-chan." Mrs. Taka turned her focus on her son. "When will you bring my granddaughter to see me?"

"In a few weeks, Mama. She'll have a break from school, then."

"I miss my granddaughter," Mrs. Taka told Helen. "I do not see her often enough. Each time, she has grown much between visits."

"She is a lovely girl." Helen smiled. "Her English, as yours is, was much better than my Japanese."

The woman laughed a little. "Kimiko is a challenge to her father, but I delight in everything she does."

"I think that's the right of grandparents."

"Your pretty Hanson-san is very correct," Mrs. Taka told Mori. "You will tell Kimi-chan that she can bring her favorite movies to share with me on my new television."

"Mama, you have a TV?"

"*Hai.* Your father made me a gift of one even though I told him I did not want it. He has a liking for the American football," she divulged.

Helen couldn't have been more surprised. She'd believed that Mr. Taka had a disliking for everything American. Maybe it *was* just her he detested.

"The satellite doesn't always work," Mrs. Taka was saying, "but he is content when he is here."

"Speaking of contentment—" Mori set down his cup and stood "—that is what I seek for the next few days. So, you will please excuse us. We will stop by again before returning to Tokyo."

Helen hid her relieved surprise at the abruptness of Mori's announcement, and stood as he kissed his mother's cheek and exchanged a few words with his father.

Mrs. Taka accompanied them out to the foyer where they exchanged their slippers for their street shoes and walked out into the cool afternoon. Helen felt as if she towered over the diminutive woman as she bowed and thanked her for her hospitality. The woman stood there, watching, until she and Mori drove away from the house.

Helen was silent until they turned back onto the main track. "Doesn't your father think he's won, given the fact that we didn't sign the papers this morning?"

"No." He cast Helen a sideways glance. "And now, we put all talk of TAKA and Hanson Media out of doors. We are just a man and a woman. Remember?"

She bit the inside of her lip. That had been a fantasy—one that would be nearly impossible to realize. But for these few days, she would give it her best effort and not think about the hell to pay when they returned to Tokyo and the people who were waiting in a holding pattern. "I remember."

He squeezed her hand then pointed through the windshield at the mountain. The closer they drew to it, the more she realized the car was climbing.

"We will watch the sunrise from the top of that peak," he told her.

She pressed her lips together, eyeing the peak in question. The mountain was not as imposing as it could have been, but it was *still* a mountain. "And how do we *get* to the top of that peak?"

His dimple appeared. "We climb, Mrs. Hanson. How did you think?"

"I don't know." She leaned forward, peering through the window. "Helicopter?" she said hopefully.

"What is the challenge in that?" he said, amused.

"Exactly." But as long as he had that sexy half smile on his face, she knew she'd agree to nearly any sort of mountain climbing.

"You realize—" she cast him a sidelong look "—that if I'm to get to the top of that peak by sunrise, that I'll have to have an early night tonight."

"That was my plan." He suddenly stopped the slow progress of the car, putting it into Park right there in the center of the path. "We're here."

Helen looked around them. All she could see was the village slightly below them and the side of the mountain. "Are we camping out?"

His grin widened and he pushed out of the car. She didn't wait for him to come around and open her door and climbed out, too. He'd popped the trunk and pulled out his small bag and her somewhat larger impromptu overnighter-purse. "Come with me." He walked ahead of the car several yards.

And then she saw the iron gate that opened right off the road. He pushed it open to reveal stone steps leading even farther up the hill.

"I feel like I'm entering a sanctuary," she told him as she preceded him up the steps.

"Now you understand why I come here."

"I understand why you're in great shape," she said, lifting her chin at the dozens of steps that lay before them. "This is all part of the hike to get to that peak, right?"

He laughed softly. "Keep going, Helen."

She groaned, but did as he bid. At least she was wearing her tennies. If she'd had to ascend these stairs wearing her typical high-heeled pumps, she'd be lame by the time she reached the top.

Her breath was short by the time the steps leveled out in a clearing that fronted the beautiful wood house. A very *modern*-looking house. "Well." She stopped, smoothing her hand down her ponytail. "I guess I don't have to ask if this house has been in your family for generations."

"I built it after my wife died."

So, his arranged wife had never been inside the walls. She didn't like the relief that she felt over that particular fact. It seemed petty and small.

But she still felt it.

"And you found some peace here?"

"I always find peace here." He took her hand and led her toward the house.

The front sliding door was unlocked and opened at his touch. "There is no need for security here. The only way here is through the village."

"Who would notice any strangers, I suppose. What about by air?"

"There is no place to land. An intruder would have to rappel or parachute from the craft, which takes at least a few minutes. They would still be noticed. Besides, nothing here is related to TAKA. A person who thinks otherwise will be very disappointed."

The exterior of the house was far more updated than that of his mother's, but it still possessed a similar vestibule where he toed off his shoes before stepping up onto the elevated main floor. "I will get you slippers," he told her, and disappeared beyond a short hall.

She removed her shoes and stepped up onto the wood floor, looking around her curiously as she followed the direction he'd taken. The first room she came to was everything that she'd expected his mother's living area to be. Reed-mat floors. One low, central table. Brilliant red cushions stacked against a wall.

Though there was a wealth of deep, gleaming wood, the sense of the place was still airy and light. Many tall, narrow windows closely placed together afforded an expansive view of the village below.

"It is not what you expected." He came up behind her and slid his arm around her waist.

She closed her eyes for a moment against the rush of desire that hit her. "You're never quite what I expect, Mori."

"That is good in business. Is it good in personal matters?"

She threaded her fingers through his where they rested on her hip. "In this personal matter, I'd have to admit I have no complaints." She pressed her head back against his shoulder, looking up at him.

She felt like Alice, having fallen down the rabbit hole, so odd did it seem to be there with him when just that morning they'd been at the bargaining table. "I...I haven't felt like this before, Mori."

"This?" His eyes were hooded, his voice low.

She didn't know how to answer. "This passion," she finally settled on. "I know it probably seems unlikely at my age, but—" She broke off when he touched his forefinger to the corner of her mouth.

"Turn your frown upside down," he murmured with a smile. "Does passion have an age limit?"

She turned in his arms, finally pushing out all other thoughts but of him. She looped her hands around his neck. "I certainly hope it doesn't."

"My grandfather was ninety-two when he died. He told me once that the secret to his long life was not his harmony with the world around him, but the warmth of the woman who lay beside him every night."

"Your grandfather really told you that?"

"My grandfather taught me what matters in life," he murmured. His mouth touched the point of her chin, then the spot directly below her ear.

She dropped the slippers he'd handed her. "Mori?"

He tugged on her ponytail, tilting her head back. "Yes?"

"We don't have to wait until nighttime, do we?"

"What do you think?" She felt the smile on his face when he closed his mouth over hers.

Then he lifted her right in his arms and carried her to his room.

Reality, Helen thought hazily, as he placed her on his low bed, was sometimes even better than the dream.

Chapter Thirteen

Mori hadn't been joking about watching the sun rise.

Helen shivered as she pulled on the thick ivory fisherman's sweater he tossed across the bed to her. A small table lamp was lit in the dark room. The only other illumination came from the glow of the spectacular fish tank built into one of the walls. Mori was already dressed in jeans and a dark blue sweater and the house smelled of coffee.

The scent had her salivating, and the sight of him had her fumbling with the sweater as she dragged it over her head. "I thought you didn't *drink* coffee," she said when her head poked through.

"You do."

Her hands tightened on the jeans she was pulling out of her overnight bag. He'd fixed coffee just for her?

"Smells wonderful," she told him huskily.

He smiled a little and headed back out of the room. "Hurry. We have only forty-five minutes before sunrise. Then we will return and cook breakfast."

Helen dragged on her jeans, looking somewhat longingly at the comfortable bed. She didn't doubt the beauty of the sunrise Mori was determined to share, but couldn't he find something interesting to occupy himself with if they remained in bed?

He'd certainly had no trouble in that regard throughout the night.

When she was finished dressing, she quickly cleaned her face and teeth and dragged her hair into a ponytail. Then she headed out to the kitchen that—contrary to the traditional nature of his living area—provided every convenience known to man.

He stuck a stainless steel travel cup in her hand and aimed her toward the *genkan* where he crouched at her feet. "Lift."

Pouring the coffee down her throat, she lifted her foot. He stuffed it into her tennis shoe and tied it and repeated the process.

She wanted to giggle, but squelched it in her coffee mug.

He pulled on his own shoes, much sturdier looking than her pristinely white court shoes, and then nudged her out the door.

The air was cold enough to make her suck in her breath, and wish she hadn't. "Mori, wouldn't you rather be in that wonderful, soft bed of yours, all warm and cozy?"

He closed his hand over her shoulder and flipped on a small flashlight, shining the beam over the ground in front of her. "It will be worth it."

She hugged her arms closer, hunching over the coffee mug. "Better be," she mumbled. "I don't get up at this hour for just anyone, you know."

"Then I am deeply honored." His tone, however, told her he was deeply amused. "You will be glad for the climb, Helen. Never will you have a better morning than after you have seen these mountains."

They walked beside each other for several minutes, then Mori took the cup from her hands and replaced it with the flashlight. "Go first."

She looked longingly at the gleam of stainless steel. It still had a healthy measure of steaming hot coffee inside. "How about if you let me carry my coffee and I follow you?"

"You do nothing without a debate, do you?"

"Well." She tilted her head and smiled slightly. "There are a few things with you I haven't debated."

He laughed softly. "True. I am most aware of that. Now, go before me."

"Why?" She swept the beam of the flashlight ahead of her, seeing what—to her—looked like a straight, upward shot. "So if I fall on my rear end, you can catch me?"

"Perhaps I will just be enjoying the view."

She choked back a surprised snort. "Morito Taka, you have a naughty mind."

"You have a delightful derriere that inspires me. Now, move. There is a path. You will see when you start heading upward."

Biting her tongue to keep from laughing, she went ahead of him. "I thought we'd been heading *upward,* all along." But the climb wasn't *quite* as difficult as she'd feared. The path was visible. Just. It took most of concentration not to stray.

Around them, she could smell the biting scent of vegetation and earth, and heard the occasional rustle of something she figured she was glad not to see.

Mori surely heard it, too, and he wasn't the least concerned so she took her cue from him.

The higher they went, the more her thighs felt the pull of the ascent, the more grateful she was for the cool air, since it wasn't long before she felt herself beginning to sweat. Clearly, her Pilates class wasn't going to cut the mustard if she were to make *this* climb very often.

The thought sneaked in.

Her foot dragged over the loose dirt. The beam of light bobbled in her hand.

Behind her, Mori's hand planted itself on the small of her back, steadying her. "Are you all right?"

Where did she get the nerve to begin thinking that this little diversion was likely to be repeated?

And why did she feel any sort of regret at the notion that it wouldn't be?

"Helen?"

"Just swell," she puffed.

"We are nearly there," he assured.

She gestured with the flashlight. It was still pitch dark beyond the glow of yellow light. "I'll have to take your word for that, too."

"Do you think I would send you into harm?"

"No, but I think you might be sending me along the garden path," she returned drily.

His hand on her back urged her gently forward. "The

sun will be up soon. The path will even out and widen a few yards ahead."

"Promises, promises." She forced her tired legs into motion. "I feel I must tell you that I am *quite* certain we have been climbing for more than forty-five minutes."

He chuckled. "Try about twenty-five minutes."

"You're slaughtering my ego here, Mori."

"My humble apologies." He stepped beside her, when the path widened, just as he'd promised. "I will trade you again." He took the flashlight and handed her the coffee mug.

When she took a sip, it was as piping hot as it had been before they'd set out. She let out an appreciative sigh. "How do you know how to make such good coffee when you don't even drink it?"

"I know how to operate a good coffee machine." He played the flashlight ahead of them. "We have one more little climb."

Just hearing the word *climb* made her thighs protest. "Seriously?"

"Come." He took her arm and led her forward. When he stopped, he let go of her and easily stepped up onto a high boulder. "Give me your hand."

The sky was just beginning to lighten. She looked up at the shadow of his outstretched hand and settled her palm on his.

The realization dawned on her as abruptly as a sliver of light began peaking over the horizon that she hadn't even realized she was facing.

She was in love with him.

"Helen?"

Shaking herself, telling herself not to be utterly ridiculous, she stepped up, feeling him nearly take her weight as he lifted her to the top of the boulder.

He led her forward again off the boulder and onto hard-packed earth, and then stopped. "We can sit here."

She nodded and sat down when he did, her numb attention focused on the darkening band of scarlet color stretching out in front of them for as far as she could see.

He shifted around until he sat directly behind her, pulling her back against his chest. "Warm enough?"

"Mmm-hmm." Was she out of her mind? George hadn't even been gone a year yet. She *couldn't* be in love with someone else.

Mori slid his arm around her waist, his hand flat against her belly through her thick sweater. "Now, you see why I brought you here?"

She made herself concentrate. The mountainside on which they sat faced away from the village. In the gradual lightening that bathed the view in cool, silvery light, she couldn't see a single mark of human hand. She pressed her lips together for a moment. "Yes, I see. I've never been anywhere like it." She balanced her mug on the ground beside them and folded her hands over his arm.

He closed his other arm around her, enclosing her in his warmth as the temperature seemed to drop. It was as if the energy of the emerging sun was sucking away at everything else.

His fingers threaded through hers. "You took off your wedding ring."

"Yesterday."

"I noticed at your hotel room."

"You didn't say anything."

"Nor did you."

Well, that was certainly true. She imagined the ring would still be sitting on the edge of the sink when they returned.

"Do you still think of yourself as married to him?"

"No. Yes." She rubbed her head against his chin. "Sometimes. When I'm with his boys, I tend to."

"When you are with me?"

That one was easy. "Not when I am with you." She relaxed even more against his chest. She could feel the even cadence of his breathing, and realized hers was slowing to match his.

It struck her suddenly as incredibly arousing.

She bit the inside of her lip, sternly redirecting her attention to the horizon. An undulating stripe of yellow had joined the gleam of scarlet. "Have you photographed this?"

"Hai." His voice was low, a soft rumble against her ear that sent heat coursing through her.

"Hai, indeed," she murmured.

They were entirely alone. They could do anything they wanted, there on the mountainside.

She lowered her hands onto his thighs and unfolded her crossed legs, stretching them out, as his were. The tips of her tennis shoes barely reached his ankles.

Her fingertips flexed against his unyielding thighs. "Who else have you brought here?"

He laughed softly and pressed his lips against the side of her neck. "Only Kimiko," he assured. "We take a slightly different path and watch the sun set. She does not wish to be roused from her bed at an hour such as this."

"Well." Her head tilted back, giving him better access

to her throat. "I am beginning to see the—" she let out her breath when he kissed her neck again "—the, um, the appeal of *rousing* this early."

"I thought you might." His breath was warm against her ear when he spoke. "Are you cold?"

"Not at the moment." She reached up and caught her hand behind his neck, finding his mouth with hers.

His hands tightened on her and the satisfied sound he made rumbled along her spine as he briefly deepened the kiss. Too briefly.

"Open your eyes and watch the sunrise, Helen."

She dragged her eyes open. The silver cast had turned golden. The mountains around them were no longer mere shadows, but cool, purple peaks. A curve of the sun was nudging its head above a horizon that writhed with fiery tendrils of orange and pink and red.

This was seduction of the headiest kind, she decided. And as steadily as the sun began its rise, the emotion inside Helen gathered together. She was in love with Mori.

"See the sun? That is what it feels like when I hold you."

"You don't have to say things like that, Mori." Her throat was tight.

"I think I do." Not until he wiped his thumb down her cheek did she realize that tears had been leaking from her eyes. "You are unhappy?"

The sun was up. The brilliant colors were fading away. She would never again look at a sunrise without thinking of Mori. She shook her head. "I'm very happy. You were right. It was a magnificent sight. Thank you for sharing it with me."

"Forcing you to share it with me, you mean."

She smiled slightly. "*Force* might be a bit strong. I was willing enough."

He grinned. "When the coffee beckoned. Come." He kissed her hard on the lips. "We will now go down and have breakfast. The finest you will ever taste."

She pressed her palm against his cheek, slowing him for just a moment. "The finest *you* will ever taste," she returned huskily. She wasn't speaking of food.

The appreciative gleam that entered his deep brown eyes told her he was well aware of that fact.

And she was suddenly in a tearing hurry to get off the mountain and she scrambled inelegantly to her feet. "Come on. You were in a hurry to get up here. I'm in a hurry to get down there."

He rose and there was nothing ungainly about his movement. "I do not hurry. I am a man of patience."

"When you want to be," she allowed, slipping her hands beneath his sweater and loving the way his hard abdomen jumped a little at her touch. "When it suits you. Other times, you're like a freight train, charging through life."

His eyebrows drew together, creating a fierce dark slash across his striking face. "I am more careful than a mindless train."

She smiled. Flickered her fingers against his belly. He caught her fingers and she knew she'd found at least one secret where he was concerned.

The man was ticklish.

"Nobody said you were mindless, Mori." She stepped close to him, until barely a breath separated them. "You are a man of action." Her voice dropped. "Aren't you?"

She felt the tension that filled his body and with a

woman's instinct, knew that he felt the heat streaking through her, as well.

His gaze focused on he lips. After a long moment—long enough that Helen considered the dwindling likelihood that they might even make it off the mountainside before her control deserted her—he took a step back.

Oddly enough, the heat inside her only increased.

"Lead the way."

She swallowed. Picked up the coffee mug and headed back down the mountain, increasingly aware of his deliberate, sure steps behind her.

When they finally reached his house, they toed off their shoes. Mori wrapped his fingers around her wrist, starting to lead her through the kitchen, but she dragged her feet. "Too far," she whispered at his look when she slipped off her sweater and shook out her hair.

A faint smile grew around the corners of Mori's lips. "Who wishes to turn out a light now?"

She dragged his sweater up and off his head next. He had the most extraordinarily well-defined body she'd ever seen. Probably earned from activities like climbing that very mountain. Looking at him was almost as mind-boggling as touching him, she'd realized. "You have only yourself to blame."

His smile widened. "I will accept the responsibility."

"Such honor." She pushed him back until they met the very rustic and very substantial table that sat in the middle of the room. The warmth of his knuckles brushing against the button at her waist maddened her.

"This is the honor," he murmured. His hand drifted upward, sliding against the tiny center clasp of her bra. She moistened her lips, anticipation making her want to squirm. But he didn't unfasten it as his unreasonably light touch grazed over her breast, circling her nipple, which tightened even more for him. "Touching you."

A knot grew in her throat again. She wanted to tear off the rest of his clothes, to ravage him as thoroughly as his gentle, skimming touch ravaged her. "Touch more." Her plea was husky but she was too filled with need to care that she'd begged.

"Anything in particular?"

Her head felt heavy. She pressed her forehead against the satiny skin that hugged his broad shoulder and slid her hands from his waist, down his hips. "Everything," she sighed. "Oh, Mori. Everything. And hurry."

His breath drew in on a chuckle that was as much hiss as humor. "Impatient American." He reached between them, and her bra separated. She wanted to cry with delight when her bare flesh finally met his hard chest.

"That would be me," she agreed, smiling against him.

But it wasn't long before smiles turned to sighs and laughter turned to longing that could no longer be denied. She dragged at his jeans. He dragged at hers. The tabletop was cool, but the table legs were sturdy and Helen didn't care if she was shocking Mori or not. Because he was inside her again, and pleasure blasted through them both.

And Helen knew, once again, that her life would never again be the same.

By the time they finally started the meal, it was well past breakfast time. So she sat at the table she felt increasingly fond of and watched him fix their lunch, instead.

He'd never bothered to shut the door they'd left open

and a cool breeze occasionally blew through. She propped her elbows on the table and rested her chin on her hands as she watched him.

Morito Taka.

Barefoot.

He had *very* sexy feet, she decided lazily.

Fact was, he was very sexy from those feet all the way up to the top of his closely cut black hair.

He glanced at her occasionally as he chopped fresh vegetables and deftly filleted a salmon, all of which, he'd told her, had been delivered from the village while they'd been communing with nature. "What are you smiling at? I told you once that I enjoy the kitchen, did I not?"

"Well—" her lips curved "—at the time you told me that, I thought you were referring to *cooking*."

His grin widened.

"You just look good, that's all," she finished. "So I'm smiling."

His gaze lingered on her face for a moment. "You look good, also."

She certainly felt good. Hadn't felt so good in weeks. Months.

Years.

"I'm happy," she said finally.

"I am glad." He turned back to his preparations.

"What would you be doing if you weren't running TAKA?"

He shrugged. "I would not be *not* running TAKA."

"Use your imagination."

He shot her an amused look over his shoulder.

"You've already proven you're quite adept at that," she reasoned.

He popped a slice of red pepper in his mouth and seemed to contemplate the question as he chewed. "I would garden," he finally said.

She could have fallen off her chair. "Garden?"

He pointed the tip of his deadly-looking knife at the plants that grew in profusion outside the kitchen windows. "Garden. You have seen the one in my suite at the Anderson hotel."

"*You're* the one who takes care of that jungle?"

"Who did you think?"

She shook her head. "I don't know. The hotel, I suppose."

"No. I do. It is…satisfying."

He'd surprised her, yet again.

"What would you be doing if not for Hanson Media?"

"Having my hair or nails done," she said immediately. Then, at his long look, she shrugged. "I don't honestly know. For so long, I wanted to be a part of that side of George's life and he refused. I can hardly remember *not* wanting to be doing something there, even if it meant filing press clippings."

"What is it you like most?"

"I don't know. I haven't been involved in Hanson until recently. And since then I've been working on the merger."

"You like the hunt?"

She wrinkled her nose. "I don't know that I'd put it that way."

He laughed softly and tossed his peppers into the wok he'd placed on the stove.

"I think I'm not too awful at negotiations," she finally said.

He shook his head. "No, you are not awful at all."

She decided that was pretty high praise, coming from him. "Mori? How did you convince your father to back off?"

"Why?"

She studied the lines of his strong back as he tended the vegetables. Already the kitchen was fragrant with them and her stomach was growling so loudly, she feared he would hear. "How do you know he won't try to stop the merger yet again? He doesn't really want you to step down from TAKA, does he?"

"I will see that my father is voted off the board if he does."

She pressed her lips together, swallowing her shock.

Mori sighed a little and continued. "He wishes that he were still the head of that household. But he also knows his time there has passed. He struggles with that. Some day, that will be my struggle."

Helen couldn't honestly see Mori behaving the way Yukio had. "I'm not sure I could be as understanding if I were in your position," she said faintly.

"You do not have understanding for your stepsons?" His voice was dry. "You defend them even when you wish to throttle them."

"They're my family," she murmured. "And I don't usually wish to throttle them. Andrew, oh, he'll make such a great father when Delia has the baby. He'll bend over backward being exactly what his own father was not. If ever there was a playboy happy to trade it in for a woman, it's Andrew with Delia. Not that he started out feeling quite that way. And Jack will make an incredibly fair judge one day. Samantha is just enough of a free spirit to keep him from becoming *too* set in his ways."

"And Evan? He is not married."

"Not yet. It's only a matter of time, though. He and Meredith have been *it* for each other since they were in high school together. They've just needed some time to adjust to that particular fact. Evan's had the hardest time since his father's death. George completely cut him out of the will." She shook her head. "He refused to see Evan's potential. It was so wrong of him. Yet I know he was really quite proud of the way Evan never asked him for *anything*."

"What about your brother-in-law? He was not close to your husband?"

"Remember that David is considerably younger than George was. They hardly knew each other, really. David was mostly raised by nannies. If it weren't for Hanson Media, they would have probably been complete strangers."

"And then there is you. Who brings their focus together for the company."

"David already worked there before I came along."

"Do not downplay what you have done, Helen. I know the other three had nothing to do with Hanson Media until they had to." He set a plate of vividly colored stir-fried vegetables and flaking salmon in front of her.

"Which they can all blame me for," Helen said, striving for matter-of-factness and falling short. "They'd have come together without me, though, Mori. I still believe that. They'd have done what was necessary to save their heritage."

"So, you believe that about them when their own father told you in that letter that he did not."

"George shouldn't have underestimated his family

the way he did. But even he wanted them to have the company in the end, or he wouldn't have bothered writing that letter and leaving it for me to find. He knew I was the one person who wouldn't be able to ignore his request. He played on my feelings for him. If he truly didn't care about any of his sons, he wouldn't have done that."

She forked a piece of fish to her mouth and nearly groaned in pleasure as she ate it. "You know, if this chancy TAKA thing doesn't work out for you," she finally told him, "and the gardener thing falls through, you could definitely get a gig as a chef."

His eyes crinkled as he settled himself on the chair next to her with his own plate. "A comforting thought, indeed."

Helen grinned and tucked into her meal.

After, they washed the dishes together and drove into the village to call on his mother.

She insisted they stay the afternoon and have dinner with her.

Mori's father had returned to the city, she told them.

Helen, for one, was relieved.

Before long, additional people began arriving at the house until the living area was fairly bulging with them.

Helen even managed to converse with some of them in Japanese, and by the time the women began setting out dishes of food on a long table that Mori and some of his cousins set up, she'd even lost her nervousness about making some faux pas.

She was laughing over her fumbling attempts to pick up a burstingly plump shrimp with her chopsticks when she looked toward Mori, across and several seats down from her.

He lifted his wineglass in a silent toast.

Helen's amusement didn't fade, but a deeply satisfying contentment filled her.

Yes. She was happy. And she was not going to worry about how long that happiness was going to last.

For now, for this moment there with Mori and his amazingly boisterous and generous family, she had everything she'd ever wanted.

Chapter Fourteen

"Back to the real world." Helen looked through the window of Mori's car up at the exterior of the sky-high hotel. She had no idea what sort of welcome—or *un*-welcome—she would receive.

And appealing as it was to think she could hide out with Mori, their escape had not been indefinite.

"I will go up to your room with you."

She turned to him and laid her hand along his jaw. She slowly kissed his lips. "Thanks, but no." She'd already told him she would face George's family on her own. "I don't need you distracting me," she added, not untruthfully.

"Pity. We distract each other well together."

She smiled and kissed him once more. Inside, however, she was nowhere near as calm as she let on. "I was thinking that I might stay in Tokyo for a while. You know. After the merger. I could take a leaf out of Samantha and Jack's book. They want to find an apartment or something a little more permanent than the hotel during the transition."

"Why would you want to remain in Tokyo?"

Everything inside her stopped cold at his question.

Why?

Why?

Perhaps because she'd stupidly set aside common sense, once again?

Because she'd allowed herself to think beyond the moment, to contemplate some sort of future with both of them in it?

Because she'd believed him when he'd told her that not *everything* was about the merger?

Mori was watching her curiously, a faint line showing between his eyebrows at her protracted silence.

She made herself shrug. "It was just a thought," she finally said smoothly and though she wanted to pound her head against the window, she simply pushed open the car door and stepped out, grabbing her purse that she'd used for Mori's interlude. "You'll let me know when the meeting will be rescheduled?"

"Hai."

She nodded, smiled smoothly and turned on her heel, heading straight into the hotel.

She did not allow herself to look back.

"She's back." Samantha hung up the telephone and faced the others. "That was the concierge. He said Helen went up to her room about twenty minutes ago."

"High time," Jack said.

Samantha gave him a look and he made a face. She knew he felt badly about the way things had turned out.

"I just don't like sitting here cooling our heels while she's out—"

"Living *her* life for a few days?" Meredith put in. Nina, David's wife, sat beside her on the settee and she was nodding her agreement.

"Every one of you has said you never understood what the deal was between your father and Helen," Delia reminded. She sat in a chair, her hands folded over her very pregnant stomach. "Andrew says he thought his father always put Helen last."

"She could have done something about it," Jack argued.

Samantha went to him and slipped her arm through his. "Regardless of the dynamics of their marriage, Helen loved your dad."

"She sure hasn't grieved very long," Andrew murmured. "Going off with Taka like that."

Delia eyed him. "And what *is* the acceptable time frame for falling in love, Andrew?"

He looked back at her. She was nearly a decade older than he was, and he'd never been happier in his life than he was with her.

And Helen had encouraged their relationship.

He went over and sat on the arm of the chair next to his wife and kissed the top of her head. "Point taken."

Meredith looked across the room at Evan, who'd been pacing like some sort of anxious jungle cat. Evan, who was the most laid-back person she'd ever met. "Someone should call her. Have her come up here. Or we should go to her suite."

"Doesn't much matter where we meet," Evan said.

"Either way, we've got a pretty big helping of crow to choke down."

"It's the right thing to do," Jack said. He looked at his brothers, who nodded in turn.

David had picked up the letter from Judge Henry that had been sitting on the coffee table for the past few days where Jack had left it. "She was pretty smart to try and put you and Judge Henry together. When he retires next year, there's going to be a temporary vacancy on the bench that you might well be perfect for."

"I'd have preferred not to have it come about through my stepmother's manipulation," Jack countered.

"How is that any different than the connections your old law firm worked on? All she is doing is introducing the two of you," Samantha defended. "It's entirely up to you what comes out of it. The judge can't give you his old job, after all. You'll have to be appointed and then win an election to *keep* it. And you know you want to get back to the law so badly you can taste it."

He couldn't deny it.

"I think, if I'd been in her shoes," David said, "I'd have told us all to take a flying leap. She could have sold off her shares in Hanson and still made a fortune, despite the state the company was in."

"Suffice it to say that we have all underestimated her," Andrew conceded.

"Well, I know Helen from way back," Samantha said. "So I'm not the least surprised that she didn't cut her losses and run. That's not her—" she hesitated when they all heard a knock on the door "—way," she finished.

Evan, closest, opened the door.

Helen wasn't expecting to see Evan's face when the door to Samantha and Jack's suite was pulled open.

His gaze drifted over her appearance with some surprise.

"Yes," she said evenly, "Even I own jeans. May I come in?"

He jerked a little. "Sorry. Of course. You just look—"

She lifted her eyebrows, waiting.

"Tired," he finally settled on. "Are you all right?"

"I'm fine." She stepped into the room, trying not to show her nervousness when she realized that not only was Evan there, but the rest of the Hansons were, as well.

She tugged the hem of her thin green sweater around her hips and walked to the center of the room. "I'm glad you're all here," she said smoothly. "It saves me from having to make a bunch of phone calls."

"Look, we know we owe you an apology, Helen." Jack spoke first. "Nothing like cooling our heels for a few days to put together some realizations."

"I'm not here for apologies," she assured. "Mori is going to let us know when the meeting will be rescheduled."

"He still wants to do the deal?" Evan rounded the couch and put his hands over Meredith's shoulders.

"Of course. Why wouldn't he?"

"He didn't exactly give us that impression," David told her. "Guy was pretty pissed."

"Made us feel like a bunch of bratty kids," Andrew added.

"Ones he had no interest in conducting any kind of business with," Evan finished.

Mori had said nothing of the kind to her. But she couldn't let herself think about Mori or she was going to completely lose any semblance of composure. "He would not have spoken of another meeting if that were the case. But before we *do* have the sit-down, I'd like you all to consider something. Before, I'd figured we could deal with the matter after the merger was final—since they are decisions that can be made without TAKA approval. But I realize now there is no time like the present."

"Helen." Samantha came to her side, touching her arm. "You look like you're ready to fall over. Sit down. Please."

"Sam's right. You look like hell. Just what did Taka do to you the last few days?" Andrew pulled a side chair out from the gilt-edged table and carried it over to Helen.

She found herself pushed down into the chair.

What had Mori done to her? He'd made her feel again and she supposed at some point, when she was feeling more…mature about it all, she would feel glad for that and accept all that had happened for what it was.

Right now, she couldn't think about him without her throat closing and her eyes stinging. "I just need a good night of sleep," she said, not even thinking about the impression that statement would make.

"Well, you go, girl," Samantha murmured under her breath, grinning.

All of the women were grinning, in fact. The guys, however, just looked distinctly uncomfortable.

At any other time, Helen might have found the entire matter incredibly amusing.

"That is *not* what I meant," she said evenly, which

unfortunately seemed to have no effect. She pushed at her hair. "What I wanted to discuss was the future. Your future."

Jack picked up the letter from the judge. "I suppose you mean this?"

She nodded. Jack didn't look quite fit to draw and quarter her for her interference. It was something, at least.

"Anyway, when Jack hopefully resumes his practice, I think Evan should assume the head of Hanson North America."

"What?" Evan looked stunned. "Oh hell, yeah. Great idea. That'd have the old man rolling over in his grave."

"George wanted Hanson to continue for *all* of you," Helen said. "I don't know why you can't believe that." She could prove it if she were willing to produce George's letter. Which she wasn't. The humiliation would be more than she could survive.

"That's why he gave you the majority shares," Jack said. "We get it, Helen. He trusted you to do what he figured we wouldn't. Keep Hanson in existence."

"That doesn't mean he'd want me sitting in his old chair," Evan said.

"Does it matter that much to you what George wanted? Think about it, Evan. This is not George's decision. This is yours. All of yours, for that matter."

"I think it's brilliant," Meredith commented.

Evan wasn't so quick to agree, but Helen could see the glint of interest in his eyes. "What about the radio division?" he asked.

"David can take it over." Helen looked toward her brother-in-law. "I know public relations is your thing, David, but I also think it's high time you have your own shop to run. Why not radio? It's either you, or we really will have to sell it off."

"We were prepared for that, anyway," Evan reminded.

"I couldn't keep a seat on the TAKA board and run radio." David looked toward Nina.

"You admitted that you were taking the seat because you felt you needed to, not because you really wanted to," she told him. "Actually, I think it's a marvelous idea, too."

Helen smiled at Nina, grateful for the support. "That just leaves Andrew." She looked up at George's youngest son. "You've proven yourself a powerhouse, Andrew, when it comes to getting new business. If David forfeits his board position, then that leaves you to take it. Are you willing?"

"Maybe *you* should take it," he said, eyeing her speculatively.

She shook her head. "I won't be involved in Hanson after this."

"What do you mean?" Delia sat forward. "You can't just walk away after all of this."

"I'm not walking away," Helen said huskily. "I'll find something to challenge my time. But I'm going to sign my shares equally over to Jack, Evan and Andrew."

"You mean sell them," Evan corrected.

She shook her head. "I meant exactly what I said."

"Don't you want to give some shares to Jenny?"

"I've thought about that, Jack. And the truth is, Jenny doesn't need Hanson shares from me. She needs what she's already realized—that giving her up didn't mean that she was unwanted or unloved by me. Now that I've found her, I have no intention of losing her again. She knows that."

"But what are you going to *do?*" Samantha looked shell-shocked.

Helen looked toward the window. The drapes were open and she could see the clear blue sky outside. "I'll figure something out," she said with much more assurance than she felt. "This is what I want. I just need to know what you all think."

"You don't need our approval," Andrew said.

"She *wants* it," Jack said. "Don't you, Helen." It wasn't a question, but an observation.

And Helen's throat tightened all over again. She hadn't expected anything from the men other than debate and—eventually—seeing the logic of her ways. "Yes."

"I only see one drawback," Evan said.

She should have known it wouldn't be so easy. "What?"

"If you're not involved at Hanson, then you've got nothing to keep you around." He glanced at his brothers. Leaned over and took Meredith's hand in his. "And Meredith and I kind of figured you'd be around for the wedding."

Silence settled on them all for a moment. Then delight struck Helen, giving a seriously hard nudge in reminding her to focus on what was important. "You're getting married! When? Why didn't you say something earlier?"

"We just decided," Meredith said. She looked up at Evan and happiness seemed to radiate from her. "And you *have* to be there, Helen."

"Plus, the baby is going to need a grandma who is way too young for the term," Andrew added, looking wry.

"We were wrong, Helen," Jack said. And his brothers

nodded. "*I* was wrong. No matter what is going on with you and Mori—" he lifted his hand when she opened her mouth to protest "—or not going on, you *are* a Hanson. You are family. *We* are a family, and more. Maybe for the first time. And we owe that to you."

Samantha crouched next to Helen, sliding her arm around her shoulder. "You see? I told you everything would work out."

It seemed that Helen had told Samantha that a time or two. She blinked, but the burning behind her eyes didn't abate. "Okay. Then I guess maybe I won't tell the broker to sell the house, after all. It's a pretty good place to have big old family dinners." Her voice broke a little.

Samantha looked teary, too.

"All right then," David suddenly stood up, clapping his hands together. "Before this gets too damn sappy, I'm starving. What say we get out and try to find some decent sushi?" He grinned.

And everyone laughed.

Even Helen. Which just went to prove, she supposed, that a person could have a broken heart and still find something to smile about.

Helen dressed with extraordinary care for the final meeting with TAKA the next afternoon. If there was one thing she'd learned as Mrs. George Hanson, it was that it was a lot easier to feel impervious when you looked like a million dollars.

The pristine white mandarin-style blouse and severely tailored black jacket and slim skirt fit that particular bill.

"Nervous?"

She was flanked by Jack, Evan, Andrew and David as they walked from the elevator down the corridor to the TAKA boardroom. "No," she lied.

Andrew snorted softly. "Right."

She wasn't nervous about their last bit of business. She *was* nervous about seeing Mori face-to-face. She'd rather kiss a toad than reveal that to anyone, however, most particularly Mori.

When they entered, and Mori was already there, standing near the windows with Shiguro by his side, Helen had to force herself not to turn tail and run.

This was *not* about her feelings for Mori.

This was about the merger.

Period.

She angled her head in a polite bow when his gaze didn't easily release hers and she caught the momentary frown that marred his handsome face before she turned and accepted the filled china teacup offered by a server.

Richard arrived and he joined them for a few minutes before he went over and exchanged pleasantries with the TAKA crew. Because of Jenny, he'd decided to make his stay in Japan permanent and his position had already been outlined during the negotiations. Helen watched him for a moment over the brim of her teacup.

He would do well, she knew. She was completely happy about how things had worked out for him and Jenny, but she knew she would still miss him—as well as Jenny—when she returned to Chicago. He'd been a friend as well as a business associate.

And now, married to Jenny, he was…family.

“You all right?” Evan stepped in front of Helen. “You’re looking pale.”

“I’m fine.” She squeezed his arm and smiled. “It’s just been a momentous few days.” He’d never know just *how* momentous.

“If we could all be seated,” Shiguro announced. “We will begin.”

Evan gave her a faint wink and she deposited her half-drunk tea on the tray alongside everyone else’s cups and headed toward her usual position next to Jack along the “Hanson” side of the table.

In all of the times since she’d sat at the table, not a single thing had ever been out of place. But Jack’s agreement was sitting at her spot. It didn’t bear his name, but she clearly recognized his distinctive handwriting on the front of it.

She glanced at his spot, saw her own bound document and casually reached for it, intending to switch the two without drawing undue attention when it was such a minor matter.

Shiguro saw, however. “Mrs. Hanson, you will please to sit where your agreement is located.”

She didn’t know why she hesitated. She’d spent the past several months working like a fiend to gain that measure of distinction from their opponents.

Shiguro lowered his head slightly. “Please.”

Jack moved behind her and nudged her over, pulling the chair out for her. “Go ahead,” he encouraged and sat in her typical seat—the “lesser” seat of importance.

Helen slipped into Jack’s former seat, keeping her eyes focused within the square of space she was to occupy. If she let her gaze drift even a fraction, she would encounter Mori. She pulled the agreement closer.

This really was it.

The end.

A commotion at the door drew her attention and the jolt of nervousness she suddenly felt barely had time to settle before a video crew—and *not* Yukio with more protests—entered.

She frowned and then did look toward Mori. "What is this?"

"We have much to mark on this occasion," he said. "Footage may be used for the press release announcing the completion of the merger."

She nodded, but she was still surprised. TAKA Corporation might have been a media monster, but when it came to its own internal workings, they were about as tightlipped as it came.

Mori seemed to give the three-person crew no mind, then. "I am certain that you all were expecting another protracted discussion about the guidelines for the Hanson North America's philanthropic interests." He flipped open the book that sat in front of him. "However, you will note that this item has been removed from the stipulations of the merger."

Helen's attention sharpened. Adrenaline surged through her veins. "You can't tell me that you're retracting the sixty percent you were previously willing to agree to?"

Mori's dark gaze locked with hers, but it was Shiguro who answered. "TAKA has determined that such a decision will remain within the local management of Hanson North America," he said.

Silence screamed from Hanson's side of the table.

A complete capitulation was so extraordinarily out of character that Helen didn't know *what* to say. She stared at Mori. Finally, one word emerged. "Why?"

"You may accept the decision as a sign of confidence in the new management."

"Sounds good to me," Andrew said wryly from farther down the table.

Cautious chuckles from the other side of the table followed.

"Speaking of management," Helen said, "there may be some shifting around. The only portion of that which needs to be addressed here, though, is the possibility of Andrew Hanson taking the TAKA board position in place of David Hanson."

"It's more than a possibility," Evan told her, leaning forward to look at her from his position next to Andrew. "We all talked last night, Helen. I'll be assuming Jack's position and David will resign from Hanson North America to assume control of the newly independent broadcasting company. Which means Andrew has to take the board position."

"I didn't expect such a quick decision from you all," Helen admitted faintly.

"You're not the only one who can move decisively," Andrew drawled, but he was smiling as he said it.

Helen folded her hands tightly together in her lap beneath cover of the table. She nodded, too full of emotion to speak just then.

"Andrew Hanson will assume the third board position, then," Mori said.

"Unless Helen wants it," Andrew interrupted.

"Helen cannot hold a position on the TAKA board of directors," Mori said smoothly.

Even though Helen knew a woman—particularly *her*—would never be allowed on the TAKA board, hearing it drop so easily from his lips still pained her.

"Not yet," Mori added.

She jerked and stared at him. Not *yet?* "What is that supposed to mean?"

"Patience." He looked down the table. "TAKA has added a condition of our own to the document. You will find the addendum inserted before the final page." He barely waited while pages rustled as people hurried to catch up with the unexpected.

Helen was no different. She flipped to the back of the hefty document and found the page. She was vaguely aware of the video crew moving discreetly closer to the table and its occupants.

"TAKA wishes to name Helen Hanson as Senior Vice President of TAKA mergers and acquisitions," Mori announced. "This means she will no longer be part of Hanson management, but part of TAKA." He was no longer looking at anyone else.

He was only looking at Helen.

"If she chooses to accept, of course," he finished.

The only sound in the room was the faint tick of someone's watch.

Helen swallowed. There was not a single female who held a senior management position within TAKA. "You're serious," she finally managed.

"It is in black and white for all the world to witness." He reached into his lapel pocket and pulled out a familiar pen.

Her gold pen.

He extended it to her. "Perhaps you have need for this, Mrs. Hanson." He smiled slightly.

Biting her lip, she looked at Jack. Then Richard, Evan, David. Andrew. All of these people who'd come to mean more to her in the past several months than she could have wished for.

Andrew's arms were crossed over his wide chest when she looked at him and his hand shifted slightly. His thumb popped up.

Could she work for TAKA? Could she function day in and day out within the confines of their strictly defined behaviors and ideologies?

Then she looked at Mori again.

What he was doing was already counterpoint to all of that, she realized. And if that wasn't proof that TAKA's internal practices were no longer set in stone, she couldn't fathom what would be.

"Some things are meant to be," he said quietly, still holding out the pen.

Even though they had a room full of witnesses, Helen couldn't simply leave it at that. Not when her *life* was finding paths she had never considered. "Which things? A career with TAKA? Or being with you? You didn't say a word about this when I suggested I might like to stay on in Tokyo."

"I asked why you wanted to do so," he reminded her. "You chose not to answer."

"I couldn't understand how you could ask the question in the first place, after we'd—" She broke off, flushing, suddenly painfully aware that not only were there witnesses, but there was a video crew taping the entire exchange. "Would it have mattered to you what reason I had?"

"Yes. But it would not change the offer on the table today. You are a worthy opponent, Mrs. Hanson. I prefer to make allies of such people and turn their abilities to my benefit. You will be breaking new ground for TAKA," Mori said. "I cannot assure you that it will always be easy. You are too intelligent a woman to believe otherwise. The question is, are you willing?"

She slowly took the pen from Mori and their fingers grazed. *"Hai."*

While the video camera moved closer, Helen turned to the last and final page of the merger agreement.

Mori had already signed it.

She stared at his signature, her hand tightly holding on to George's pen.

Maybe George's behavior hadn't been as selfishly calculated as she'd believed. Maybe, just maybe, he'd somehow been watching out for her, all along.

It was a good thought. A very good thought. One that she figured she'd just have to hold on to.

She let out a little breath.

And she signed her name.

Mori nodded, clearly satisfied. He took the document from her, closed it with great care and stood to look around the table. "Now, finally, we will adjourn to the lobby and celebrate. Mrs. Hanson and I will join you shortly."

Even the TAKA side looked relieved, clapping their hands together as spontaneously as the Hanson side as men pushed back from the table and rose, shaking hands and bowing and generally congratulating each other. Laughter and voices grew more enthusiastic and less restrained as people—no longer teams on opposing sides, but people who'd ultimately succeeded in a common effort—began filing out of the boardroom.

Helen rose, also, though she wasn't entirely certain her wobbling legs would serve the task. "Well." She moistened her lips. "I guess you are my boss now. I'll have to learn how not to debate every point with you."

"I do not wish you to change your methods, Helen. They are already admirable. You will need to learn to speak Japanese more fluently, of course, but you will have much assistance for that. The only other thing I wish you to change is your name."

She blinked. "My name? Whatever for? You don't want a *Hanson* on the TAKA staff roster?"

"Do you not understand yet?" He looked vaguely amused as he took the pen from her that she hadn't realized she still held and set it on the table.

Her frayed nerves were in danger of complete disintegration. She looked around, but everyone had deserted them.

"It is just you and me," he said, clearly reading her mind. He took her hands in his and whatever amusement he'd shown was now utterly absent. "I wish for you not to be Hanson-san, but Taka-san."

She swayed and his grip tightened, steadying. "I'm sorry. I don't think I heard you right."

"I think you did," he countered gently. "I want you to be my wife."

His words hovered between them like some tantalizing wish. "But you just gave me a job!"

"We cannot work together yet be married?"

"George certainly never thought so," she said faintly.

"I am not George Hanson."

No. He wasn't. He'd been proving it again and again and again.

How much more would she need to believe in that?

"I once thought you were just like him," she admitted. "I was wrong. But, Mori, you're not going to win points with some people. I don't know which will strike them as more inflammatory. Employing me, or marrying me."

"Who is *them?*"

She shook her head, feeling oddly panicked. "I don't know. Your father, for one."

"He is a traditional man but the world we inhabit is not so traditional any longer. In time, he will adjust."

"But…marriage? Why marriage? Couldn't we just… be together?"

His dimple appeared. "I do not wish a mistress, Helen. I want a wife. A puzzling, intriguing, challenging American wife named Helen Hanson. I want Kimiko to have a mother named Helen Hanson. She agrees."

Her vision blurred with sudden tears. "You've talked to Kimiko about us?"

"Yes."

"What did you tell her?"

He stepped closer. "I told her that I loved you."

She pressed her lips together to stop them from trembling. "You *do?*"

"Yes. I love you. Why else would I ask you to be my wife?"

"People marry for all sorts of reasons."

"You do not. You only marry for love, remember?"

"I remember." She dragged in a shaking breath. "Are

you *sure?* I couldn't survive it if you changed your mind along the way."

"Do you love me, Helen?"

The tears finally spilled from the corners of her eyes. "Yes. I love you. I never expected it, but I do."

"Will you be changing your mind along the way?"

She shook her head knowing down in her soul that what she felt for this man would never cease. "No."

"Then trust me as I will trust you. I will not change my mind." He skimmed his hand down her cheek, wiping away her tears. "Do I need to put *that* in writing for you, as well?"

She slipped her arms around his neck. "Maybe," she whispered.

He reared his head back. His eyebrows drew together, making him look dark and fierce. "What?"

She smiled softly. "I assume even in Japan there is a marriage license that will need to be signed."

His eyes narrowed. Then his expression eased. A smile slowly curved his mouth. "You are agreeing? Kimiko lectured me for an hour that I must do this most perfectly. That I had to take you somewhere romantic. Give you flowers and sweets and bend on my knees like they do in the movies."

"Kimiko is twelve," Helen said huskily. "We met here in this boardroom so I think your choice was quite perfect. And yes. I am agreeing." She pressed her lips softly to his, grasping with both hands for their future. "I love you, Morito Taka. And I wish for you to be my husband."

"I was not sure what you would say."

Her heart ached at his gruff admission. "I don't argue

the really good ideas," she whispered. "And I'll give it a little while before I tell you that I think Kimiko should be living with her father and not at school."

"Do you think my daughter has not already realized that?" He caught her face in his hands and kissed her thoroughly.

She slid her arms beneath his jacket, fitting herself even more closely against him.

He inhaled sharply. "I am grateful the video crew has gone and that there is not a security camera in this room."

Helen couldn't help herself. She looked at the wide, sturdy surface of the conference table. "Really."

"*That* would be a merger the likes of which the table has never seen."

She slid her hands slowly up his spine and back down again and looked up at him from beneath her lashes. *"Never?"*

"Well." His dark eyes glinted. "Not yet, Mrs. Hanson. Not…just…yet."

Epilogue

"She looks beautiful, doesn't she? I wasn't sure we would live to see the day."

"Aw, come on. They're meant to be."

"I hear they're living in Japan."

"Hope they like sushi."

Helen listened to the whispered conversations behind her and hid a smile.

"Oh, my God. Is Meredith *barefoot?*"

"I'm still surprised she and Evan didn't get married right out of high school."

Mori leaned his head close to Helen's as they watched Evan take Meredith's hand when she joined him in front of the minister. The music, courtesy of a trio of steel drums, had not yet ceased. "Do all American weddings necessitate incessant whispering from the guests?" he asked.

She slipped her hand into his. “I’m afraid Hanson weddings probably do,” she whispered back.

“Did they whisper like this at *our* wedding?”

“Probably. You didn’t notice?”

“I was busy watching my bride,” he murmured.

“Well, if it’s any help, I didn’t notice, either. I was too busy watching my groom. He was very handsome in his kimono.” She lowered her voice even more. “I was curious what all he wore beneath it. Turned out…not much.” The steel drums finally faded into silence.

The sun was just beginning to set and color filled the Caribbean sky, almost matching the vivid colors of the orchids that wreathed Meredith’s and her attendants’ heads. It was she, proving she had more “free spirit” inside her than people thought, who had chosen the little island destination for her and Evan’s wedding. Despite the location, however, there were close to a hundred people who’d flown in for the event.

Mori slipped his arm around Helen’s shoulders and she sighed, leaning against him contentedly as she watched the couple exchange vows and thought about *their* wedding in Nesutotaka two months earlier.

It had been a mix of traditional and Western, just as their life together was. She and Mori had worn traditional Japanese wedding garb. Jack, Evan and Andrew—all in black suits—had given her away. Kimiko, Helen’s flower girl, had worn a long pink dress with spaghetti straps that her father had groaned over. When the official teenager hadn’t been preening in her dress to Zach, Nina’s twelve-year-old son, she’d been chasing around with Izzy, Nina’s ten-year-old youngest. Samantha, Meredith and Nina had worn summery dresses of their own choosing, and Jenny had worn a pale green suit that had masked her new pregnancy.

Nesutotaka had bulged at the seams with the guests who'd traveled there for the ceremony, and of course, every person who lived in the village had been present. Even Yukio Taka, who'd finally stopped openly disapproving of Helen and had taken to sending her e-mails regarding troubled companies he figured TAKA needed to be looking at. Ideas which he seemed to delight in fiercely debating with her.

"Would you rather have had a wedding like this?" Mori asked as they watched Evan slide a narrow band on Meredith's finger.

"I loved our wedding," Helen assured. "But it wasn't the wedding that really mattered. It's the life spent together that does."

"Do you think they know that?" He nodded toward the new couple as they sealed their exchanges with a kiss that went on long enough to have Evan's brothers and uncle who stood on his side of the sand, and their wives who stood on Meredith's side, grinning wryly.

Kimiko, not officially part of the wedding party, but still wearing a matching wreath of orchids in her hair, tugged on Helen's wrist. "When do we get to go scuba diving?" she whispered when Helen looked at her.

"Tomorrow," Helen promised, whispering back. On the other side of Kimi, Jenny stood holding hands with Richard. She'd caught Kimi's question and was smiling.

A balmy breeze drifted over them and Helen closed her hand over Kimi's and leaned her head against her husband's shoulder. She looked at Evan and Meredith as they joined hands and smiled broadly as they walked away from the minister, their bare feet sinking into the soft white sand. Behind them, the rest of the Hanson men found their mates and followed.

"Yes," Helen answered. "I think they *all* know that is what's really important. They are living proof of it."

Mori angled his head and brushed his lips over hers. "You are crying."

She smiled at him, not even trying to hide the moisture that had filled her eyes. "Happy tears, Mori. I promise. Always happy tears."

* * * * *

0211/05a

We're thrilled to bring you four bestselling collections that we know you'll love...

featuring

THE MARCIANO LOVE-CHILD
by Melanie Milburne

THE ITALIAN BILLIONAIRE'S SECRET LOVE-CHILD
by Cathy Williams

THE RICH MAN'S LOVE-CHILD
by Maggie Cox

featuring

ALL NIGHT WITH THE BOSS
by Natalie Anderson

THE BOSS'S WIFE FOR A WEEK
by Anne McAllister

MY TALL DARK GREEK BOSS
by Anna Cleary

On sale from 18th February 2011

By Request

0211/06

Her Not-So-Secret Diary

by Anne Oliver

Sophie's fantasies stayed secret—until her saucy dream was accidentally e-mailed to her sexy boss! But as their steamy nights reach boiling point, Sophie knows she's in a whole heap of trouble...

The Wedding Date

by Ally Blake

Under no circumstances should Hannah's gorgeous boss, Bradley, be considered her wedding date! Now, if only her disobedient legs would do the *sensible* thing and walk away...

Molly Cooper's Dream Date

by Barbara Hannay

House-swapping with London-based Patrick has given Molly the chance to find a perfect English gentleman! Yet she's increasingly curious about Patrick himself—is the Englishman she wants on the other side of the world?

If the Red Slipper Fits...

by Shirley Jump

It's not *unknown* for Caleb Lewis to find a sexy stiletto in his convertible, but Caleb usually has some recollection of how it got there! He's intrigued to meet the woman it belongs to...

On sale from 4th March 2011
Don't miss out!

Available at WHSmith, Tesco, ASDA, Eason and all good bookshops

www.millsandboon.co.uk

0211_26_MB331

Nora Roberts' *The O'Hurleys*

4th March 2011

1st April 2011

6th May 2011

3rd June 2011

www.millsandboon.co.uk